PENGUIN CLASSICS DELUXE EDITION

RASHŌMON AND SEVENTEEN OTHER STORIES

RYŪNOSUKE AKUTAGAWA (or, in the Japanese order, Akutagawa Ryūnosuke) continues to be read and admired today by virtually all Japanese as one of the country's foremost stylists, a master of the modern idiom enriched by a deep knowledge of both the classics and the contemporary literature of Japan, China, and the West. Born in Tokyo in 1892, he was raised in a family steeped in traditional Japanese culture, learned English at an early age, and proved himself a brilliant student in Japan's foremost educational institutions. He began setting up and writing for student publications at the age of ten, and even before he graduated from Tokyo Imperial University (now University of Tokyo) in 1916 with a degree in English literature, his contributions to university magazines were recognized for their accomplished style. He supported himself as a teacher of English for a little over two years, but the great demand for his stories and essays enabled him to resign his post in 1919 and concentrate on his writing. Soon he began to have doubts about his reliance on Japanese and Chinese classical materials in his fiction, and he responded to requests for more autobiographical work by revealing his own anguish as the child of a madwoman, a frail youth torn between his adoptive and biological fathers, a compulsive reader frightened by real life, a conscientious family head oppressed by his responsibilities, a devoted husband and father wracked by guilt for his extramarital affairs, a relentless intellect unable to find peace in religion, and a paranoid personality afraid of being overwhelmed by the insanity he was sure he had inherited from his mother. When he ended his own life in 1927 at the age of thirty-five, he left behind a unique body of stories marked by imagistic brilliance, cynicism, horror, beauty, wild humor, and icy clarity.

JAY RUBIN has translated Sōseki Natsume's novels *Sanshirō* and *The Miner* and Haruki Murakami's *Norwegian Wood, The Wind-up Bird Chronicle*, and *after the quake*. He is the author of *Injurious to Public Morals: Writers and the Meiji State* and *Haruki Murakami and the Music of Words*, and the editor of *Modern Japanese Writers*. He began his study of Japanese at the University of Chicago, where he received his Ph.D. in 1970, and has been a professor of Japanese literature at the University of Washington and at Harvard University.

HARUKI MURAKAMI (in Western order) has written eleven novels, ten volumes of short stories, and more than thirty books of non-fiction while also translating well over thirty volumes of American fiction, poetry, and nonfiction since his prizewinning debut in 1979 at the age of thirty. Known in the English-speaking world primarily for his novels *A Wild Sheep Chase*, *Hard-boiled Wonderland and the End of the World*, *Norwegian Wood*, *Dance Dance Dance*, *The Wind-up Bird Chronicle*, and *Kafka on the Shore*, Murakami has also published commentary on the 1995 Tokyo subway sarin-gas attack in *Underground*, and edited a book of American, British, and Irish fiction, *Birthday Stories*. His works have been translated into thirty-four languages.

RYŪNOSUKE AKUTAGAWA

Rashōmon and Seventeen Other Stories

Selected and Translated with Notes by JAY RUBIN
With an Introduction by HARUKI MURAKAMI

PENGUIN BOOKS

PENGUIN BOOKS
Published by the Penguin Group
Penguin Group (USA) Inc., 375 Hudson Street, New York, New York 10014, U.S.A.
Penguin Group (Canada), 90 Eglinton Avenue East, Suite 700, Toronto, Ontario,
Canada M4P 2Y3 (a division of Pearson Penguin Canada Inc.)
Penguin Books Ltd, 80 Strand, London WC2R 0RL, England
Penguin Ireland, 25 St Stephen's Green, Dublin 2, Ireland
(a division of Penguin Books Ltd)
Penguin Group (Australia), 250 Camberwell Road, Camberwell, Victoria 3124,
Australia (a division of Pearson Australia Group Pty Ltd)
Penguin Books India Pvt Ltd, 11 Community Centre, Panchsheel Park,
New Delhi – 110 017, India
Penguin Group (NZ), 67 Apollo Drive, Rosedale, North Shore 0632, New Zealand
(a division of Pearson New Zealand Ltd)
Penguin Books (South Africa) (Pty) Ltd, 24 Sturdee Avenue,
Rosebank, Johannesburg 2196, South Africa

Penguin Books Ltd, Registered Offices: 80 Strand, London WC2R 0RL, England

First published in Penguin Books (U.K.) 2006
First published in Penguin Books (U.S.A.) 2006

9 10 8

Translation, notes and selection copyright © Jay Rubin, 2006
Introduction copyright © Haruki Murakami, 2006
All rights reserved

This book has been selected by the Japanese Literature Publishing Project (JLPP)
which is run by the Japanese Literature Publishing and Promotion Center
(J-Lit Center) on behalf of the Agency for Cultural Affairs of Japan.

ISBN 978-0-14-303984-6
CIP data available

Printed in the United States of America

Contents

Note on Japanese Name Order and Pronunciation

All Japanese names hereafter are written in the Japanese order, with family name first. The author is known in Japan as Akutagawa Ryūnosuke, and the writer of the Introduction as Murakami Haruki. These have been given in the Western order on the cover and title-page because of their greater familiarity in the West and as standard in library cataloging and book lists.

Some Japanese names and terms have become so familiar in recent years that an elaborate guide to pronunciation hardly seems necessary. Specific cases where there might be confusion have been annotated. Unfortunately, one specific—and especially convoluted—example is the name of the author himself, so here are some guidelines:

All a's are long as in "father," and u's tend to disappear between unvoiced consonants. Thus, "Akutagawa" sounds more like "Ak-ta-ga-wa" (four syllables) with a slight stress on the "Ak."

Japanese "r" is a light tongue flap, almost a "d" as in a British "very." "Ryū" is only one syllable long, which can be approximated by using that tongue flap to pronounce the middle part of "incre(du)lous." The "u" between unvoiced consonants ("suke") gets lost here, too, and e's are short as in "Kevin." So we have what sounds like three syllables: "Dyū-noss-ke," with equal stress on the "Dyū" and the "noss" but slightly less on the "ke."

Macrons have been included to indicate long syllables but have been eliminated from the place names Tōkyō, Kyōto, Ōsaka, and Kyūshū.

Acknowledgments

These translations have benefited greatly from the advice and/ or close reading of a wide variety of friends and colleagues.

My wife Rakuko, my adviser of first resort in all things, made it possible for me to continue the day-to-day wrestling with difficult texts, as she has since 1966, and it is to her that this book is dedicated.

Fortunately for me, Shibata Motoyuki, the renowned translator of American literature into Japanese, is just as fascinated by the process of translating from Japanese into English; he went over every line with unflagging enthusiasm and marvelous insight. He also introduced me to Mutō Yasushi and Ueki Tomoko, who generously shared their scholarly expertise in modern and pre-modern Japanese literature with me and guided me to the indispensable Akutagawa studies of Sekiguchi Yasuyoshi. Ichiba Shinji read everything line-by-line under the auspices of the Japanese Literature Publication Project (JLPP), sponsored by the Agency for Cultural Affairs of Japan. JLPP also made it possible for Linda Asher to apply her supernatural editorial skills to the manuscript. Hirose Keiko and Hoshino Kiyo kept the JLPP wheels turning efficiently, and at Penguin, Lindeth Vasey provoked a whole new set of thoughts about the text and notes.

Other friends and scholars whose help and interest added to the considerable pleasure I derived from this project are Ted Goossen, Ted Mack, Harold Bolitho, David Knechtges, Kathy Lu, Mark Woolsey, Ryuichi Abe, Paul Rouzer, Rachel DiNitto, Royall Tyler, Mikael Adolphson, Shigehisa Kuriyama, Howard

Hibbett, Davinder Bhowmik, Philip Kuhn, Carole Cavanaugh, Matthew Fraleigh, Kelly Flannery, and Julia Twarog.

I would like to add one final note of thanks to Penguin Editor Simon Winder and to Murakami Haruki: Simon for suggesting the project—including the introduction by Haruki—in the first place, and Haruki for agreeing immediately to participate and for writing such a fine introduction.

Chronology

1868 Two and a half centuries of "centralized feudal" rule under the Tokugawa government of warrior-bureaucrats comes to an end with the "restoration" of the emperor to a position of theoretical sovereignty; the country is opened to the West; and the modernizing Meiji Period[1] (1868–1912) begins. Born in the 25th year of Meiji, Akutagawa will become the quintessential writer of the liberal Taishō Period (1912–26), and his suicide in the 2nd year of the Shōwa Period (1926–89) will be widely seen as marking the defeat of "Taishō Democracy," as the forces of repression and imperialism move toward the Second World War.

1892 1 March: Akutagawa Ryūnosuke born in Tokyo, the third child and only son of father Niihara Toshizō (1850–1919), dairy owner, and mother Niihara (née Akutagawa) Fuku (1860–1902). According to East Asian astrology, born in the hour of the dragon (7–9 a.m.) of the day of the dragon of the month of the dragon of the year of the dragon, he is named Ryūnosuke ("dragon-son"). His sisters are Hatsu (1885–91) and Hisa (1888–1956).

Mother goes insane in October, and will be kept hidden upstairs in the Niihara house until her death. Ryūnosuke taken into the childless household of Fuku's brother, Akutagawa Dōshō (1849–1928), a minor official in the Tokyo government's internal affairs division, his wife Tomo (1857–1937), and Fuku's sister Akutagawa Fuki (1856–1938), in Tokyo's drab industrial Honjo ward, east of the Sumida River. Aunt Fuki is primary caregiver. Family uses Akutagawa surname for the boy, though legally he is Niihara. Of

minor samurai origins, the family is not wealthy but sur-
rounds him with books and traditional arts.

1894 Family begins regularly taking him to Kabuki and other
theatrical performances.

1894–5 Sino-Japanese War.

1898 Enters elementary school. Outstanding student, but frail,
and frequently bullied. Mother's sister Fuyu (1862–1920)
bears half-brother Tokuji (d. 1930) to his father. Over the
years much close contact between the Niihara and Akutagawa families. Adoptive father retires, and enjoys traditional
Itchūbushi singing, *go*, bonsai cultivation, and haiku.

1899 Begins receiving private tutoring in English, Chinese, and
calligraphy.

1901 Writes first haiku, and begins reading contemporary Japanese literature.

1902 With school friends, begins circulating literary magazine,
contributing both text and art. Similar activity continues into
university. Mother dies.

1904 Formal adoption into Akutagawa family becomes final.
Father and aunt Fuyu legalize their relationship.

1904–5 Russo-Japanese War.

1905 Enters middle school at usual age, although qualified a
year earlier, but delayed by health problems and adoption
difficulties. Outstanding in all subjects, especially Chinese.
Active in jūdō and other physical training, unlike future
fictional alter ego Daidōji Shinsuke. Japan wins Russo-
Japanese War (1904–5): first victory over Caucasian nation
raises widespread interest in translation of recent and contemporary Western literature.

1907 Begins reading English books beyond class requirements,
and English becomes his primary portal for world literature.

1910 Enters elite First Higher School without examination,
owing to superior record. Right-wing government crushes
leftist political and literary activity. "Winter years" of socialism continue for a decade.

1912 Meiji emperor dies; Taishō Period begins.

1913 Enters Tokyo Imperial University, the pinnacle of the
educational system; majors in English literature.

1914 With classmates, founds student literary magazine, publishes his first story in May, "Rōnen" ("Old Age"; no English translation). Akutagawa family moves to newly constructed house in north suburban Tabata, where he will spend most of his life. Neighborhood doctor, Shimojima Isaoshi (1870–1947), becomes his physician and friend.

1915 Fifth story, "Rashōmon," published in university faculty's intellectual journal, but is generally ignored. Pays first visit to the novelist Natsume Sōseki (1867–1916) at home, and becomes one of Sōseki's[2] "disciples."

1916 "The Nose" published in student magazine; lavishly praised by Sōseki and receives other attention. Graduates from Tokyo Imperial University with a thesis on William Morris. "Yam Gruel" is his first story in a commercial magazine; more invitations follow. Begins teaching at Naval Engineering School (see "The Writer's Craft"), living in Kamakura, a seaside town south of Tokyo. Sōseki dies.

1917 "Dr. Ogata Ryōsai: Memorandum" and "Loyalty" published. First anthology, *Rashōmon*, appears from small publisher. Commercial literary magazines eager to print his stories. Second anthology, *Tobacco and the Devil*, published by major company.

1918 Marries Tsukamoto Fumi (1900–1968), and they move to new lodgings in Kamakura with aunt Fuki; tranquil time after Fuki returns to Tokyo. "The Story of a Head That Fell Off" and "The Spider Thread" published. "Hell Screen" serialized in two newspapers simultaneously. Severely stricken in Spanish flu epidemic.

1919 Experiences second attack of Spanish flu, and father dies from it. Resigns teaching post and signs exclusive agreement with *Osaka Mainichi Shinbun* newspaper. Moves back with Fumi to live with adoptive parents and aunt Fuki, and never again establishes separate household. Extended family increasingly rely on his income. "Dragon: The Old Potter's Tale" published. Travels to Nagasaki, and steeps himself in exotic culture of seventeenth-century Japanese Christian martyrdom; meets chief psychiatrist of Nagasaki Prefectural Hospital, poet Saitō Mokichi (1882–1953), who will later supply him with barbiturates for insomnia. Meets popular poet Hide Shigeko (1890–1973), who is married with one son, and begins painful affair with this "crazy girl" ("The Life of a Stupid Man," Section 21).

1920 Five stories (including "Green Onions") and seven non-fiction pieces published simultaneously in various major New Year publications as editors clamor for his work. Birth of first son, Hiroshi.

1921 January: Hide Shigeko gives birth to son, and tells Akutagawa the child is his. March: Partly to escape her, he leaves for China for nearly four months as special correspondent for *Osaka Mainichi Shinbun*. Dry pleurisy and other ills leave him weakened thereafter.

1922 "In a Bamboo Grove" and three other stories appear in New Year issues of major magazines, but autobiographical writing increases as historical fiction is less well received. Second trip to Nagasaki; buys Edo Period "secret Christian" image of Maria-Kannon. First of the fictional alter ego Yasukichi stories and "O-Gin" published. Birth of second son, Takashi. Health dramatically worse; with desire to write fading, declines all invitations for New Year issue stories.

1923 June: Infant Takashi hospitalized for more than ten days. "The Baby's Sickness" published in August. 1 September: Great Kantō Earthquake strikes at 11:58 a.m., followed by fires; over 100,000 killed. Tabata house loses a few roof tiles and stone lantern, but houses of his half-brother and his sister burn down. No injuries to relatives, but caring for them a great financial burden. Observes death and devastation, writes scathing critiques of "upright citizens" of Tokyo who took the occasion to commit mob violence against local Koreans with Police Bureau encouragement. Much editing of English and contemporary Japanese literary collections.

1924 Few new stories this year; much editing, reading up on socialism, but his name is still big enough for a major publisher to begin a new series of contemporary literature with a volume of his works. Sixth Yasukichi story, "The Writer's Craft," published. Near-affair with Katayama Hiroko ("Life," Section 37).

1925 Physical ills, insomnia. "Daidōji Shinsuke: The Early Years" and "Horse Legs" published in New Year issues of major magazines. Birth of third son, Yasushi. Publication of five-volume collection of contemporary Japanese literature which he has devoted much energy to editing since 1923; sales are poor, he earns little and is widely criticized by other writers for copyright problems. Insomnia, nervous exhaustion, and heavy responsibilities as head of the household.

1926 Close reading of Bible, but unable to believe in divine miracles. To Kugenuma seashore, south of Tokyo, with Fumi and infant Yasushi, leaving older boys with his family. Marriage "renewed," but physical and mental ills worsen as use of barbiturates increases. October: "Death Register" published, containing his first public revelation of his mother's insanity; negative review by novelist Tokuda Shūsei (1871–1943) is a shock. Taishō emperor dies; Shōwa Period begins.

1927 4 January: Sister's house partially burns; two days later, her husband, who is suspected of arson, throws himself under a train. Despite illness, Akutagawa forces himself to deal with the complications.

January–April: Several extended writing sessions in Imperial Hotel; writes "Kappa."

April–August: Essay series "Literary, All Too Literary" published, containing his side of famous debate with Tanizaki Jun'ichirō (1886–1965) on the importance of plot in fiction, and repudiating the artificiality of own earlier work.

7 April: Proposes "Platonic double suicide" to Hiramatsu Masuko (1898–1953), the unmarried, lifelong friend of wife Fumi ("Life," Sections 47–8). She informs Fumi and artist friend Oana Ryūichi (1894–1966), who force him to give up the idea.

16 April: Writes first of several "last testaments," and begins meeting with friends, though only he knows these are final farewells.

June: Worried about mental illness of writer-friend Uno Kōji (1891–1961), arranges for his involuntary hospitalization through Saitō ("Life," Section 50).

23 July: Cheerful lunch with Fumi and three sons, and

socializes with visitors. At night, finishes aphoristic manuscript on Christ as a poet who had profound insight into all
human beings but himself.

2.4 July: At 1:00 a.m. gives aunt Fuki a poem for Dr.
Shimojima entitled "Self-Mockery" with reference to "The
Nose": "Oh dripping snot!/The nose-tip all that's still in
view/As darkness falls."

2:00 a.m. Comes down from study, crawls into futon in
room where Fumi and three sons are sleeping; has probably
already taken his fatal dose of Veronal. Falls asleep reading
the Bible; leaves testaments addressed to wife and old friends
by pillow.

6:00 a.m. Fumi realizes something is wrong, and notifies
Oana and Dr. Shimojima; Akutagawa is pronounced dead
shortly after 7:00 a.m. Poet and old friend Kume Masao
(1891–1952) releases Akutagawa's most famous last testa-
ment, "A Note to a Certain Old Friend," to the press that
day. The suicide becomes a sensation in the news, seen as a
symbol of the defeat of bourgeois modernism at the hands of
both socialism and rising state power.

"Spinning Gears" and "The Life of a Stupid Man" published posthumously.

Akutagawa's cremated remains are interred at Tokyo's Jigenji
Temple. The plot later receives ashes of adoptive parents, aunt
Fuki, son Takashi (d. 1945, student draftee killed in Burma),
wife, and actor and director son Hiroshi (d. 1981). Composer
son Yasushi (d. 1989) in his own separate family plot in the
cemetery.

Literary friend and publisher Kikuchi Kan (1888–1948)
establishes biannual Akutagawa Prize in 1935 to memorialize
Akutagawa and promote Kikuchi's magazine *Bungei Shunjū*.
The prize remains the most sought-after seal of approval for
upcoming writers in Japan.

NOTES

1. On Japanese era names, see the article "nengō" in *Japan: An Illustrated Encyclopedia*, 2 vols. (Tokyo: Kodansha Ltd., 1993), 2:1073.
2. Like the haiku poet Bashō, Natsume Sōseki is known by his literary sobriquet "Sōseki," rather than his family name.

Introduction

Akutagawa Ryūnosuke: Downfall of the Chosen

In Japan, Akutagawa Ryūnosuke is a writer of genuinely national stature. If a poll were taken to choose the ten most important "Japanese national writers" since the advent of the modern period in 1868, Akutagawa would undoubtedly be one of them. He might even squeeze in among the top five.[1]

But what, in the most concrete terms, is a "writer of national stature" in Japan?

Such a writer would necessarily have left us works of the first rank that vividly reflect the mentality of the Japanese people of his or her age. This is the most essential point. Of course the works themselves—or at least the writer's most representative works—must not only be exceptional, they must have the depth and power to survive at least a quarter century after the writer's death.

The second important point would be that the writer's character or life should have inspired widespread respect or strong sympathy. Not that the author would have to be a person of high moral character; some exceptional writers (I will not name them here) have had questions raised about aspects of their private lives. But to be of national stature, they would have garnered the approval and sense of identification of many people with regard to their principled devotion to literature and general world view. The important thing is whether each of them as an individual human being embraced an awareness of the great questions of the age, accepted his or her social responsibility as an artist on the front line, and made an honest effort to shape his or her life accordingly.

One more point—and this should be the last—is that a writer

of national stature should have given us not only solid classics but popular works that appeal to a broad audience—and to young people in particular: works easy enough to read that they appear in the nation's primary and middle-school textbooks and can be memorized whole by most children. Natsume Sōseki's *Botchan* (1906),[2] for example, is read by virtually everyone in Japan who receives a middle-school education. *Botchan* is hardly Sōseki's most representative work, but it is a uniquely enjoyable, easy-to-read short novel. Much the same can be said for Shiga Naoya's innocent allegorical story, "The Shopboy's God" (1920) and Kawabata Yasunari's refreshing novella of youth, "The Dancing Girl of Izu" (1926).[3] Shimazaki Tōson produced not only ponderous long novels but also spontaneous and moving lyrical poems in the traditional *tanka* form.[4] Mori Ōgai is most respected for his scholarly historical novels, but he also wrote the love story "The Dancing Girl" (1890) in remarkably beautiful language, and "Sanshō the Steward" (1915)[5] is his rewrite of a medieval tale for a modern young audience. The number of readers who have made it all the way through Tanizaki Jun'ichirō's long novel *The Makioka Sisters* (1946–8)[6] may not be very large, but the work has been filmed several times with some of the most beautiful actresses of their generations in the roles of the four lovely sisters, leaving vivid images in the memories of thousands of viewers. In other words, like spring rain, these works in easily accessible forms have seeped silently into the fertile soil of people's minds to form something like the foundation of the culture or sensibility of the Japanese.

Surely in all nations, in all cultures, there exists this kind of basic cultural realm that functions almost subliminally. England has Dickens and Shakespeare, and the United States Melville and Fitzgerald among others. The French have Balzac and Flaubert. The works of these "national writers" are imprinted in the hearts and minds of each individual citizen during youth in forms that take on a nearly absolute authority, and, before anyone is aware of it, they go on to comprise a common perception of literature and culture in the region—i.e. a common identity.

These works are handed down from teacher to pupil, from parent to child, almost without question, like DNA. They are memorized, recited, discussed in book reports, included in university entrance exams, and once the student is grown up, they become a source for quotation. They are made into movies again and again, they are parodied, and inevitably they become the object of ambitious young writers' revolt and contempt. Finally, each becomes an autonomous sign or symbol or metaphor that functions much like the national flag or the national anthem or one of the country's primary landscapes (say, in the case of Japan, Mt. Fuji or cherry blossoms). And of course, for better or worse, each becomes an indispensable part of our culture. For without the creation of such archetypes—without such subliminal imprinting—it is almost impossible for us to possess a common cultural awareness.

For reasons like these, I, like most other Japanese people, came to read several stories by Akutagawa Ryūnosuke when I was in elementary school. Some I read in textbooks, and some as summer homework assignments requiring book reports. I have no idea how much of Akutagawa today's school children read (or are required to read), but I imagine the situation is not much different from my own time. What I mainly read then were several of the excellent stories that he wrote especially for children—"The Spider Thread," "Tu Tze-chun," "The Art of the Occult"—and several more that children can read with pleasure—"The Nose," "Yam Gruel,"[7] etc. When I got a little older, probably when I was in middle school, I read some of his stories containing more violent or burlesque elements such as "Rashōmon," "In a Bamboo Grove," "Hell Screen," and "Kappa,"[8] and then in high school I recall advancing to more difficult, introspective, seemingly autobiographical works of "pure literature" as such writing is known in Japan—"Spinning Gears," "The Life of a Stupid Man," "Death Register." I suspect I followed the usual course through Akutagawa's fiction that any Japanese in the habit of reading would take, advancing from the assigned youth works to where one seeks out the more difficult works on one's own. One arrives at a general grasp of

Akutagawa's unique fictional world, absorbs it as part of one's cultural foundation, and then—if one is so inclined—one goes on to range through a broader literary world.

My own personal favorites among the "Japanese national writers" are Sōseki and Tanizaki, followed—at some distance, perhaps—by Akutagawa.[9]

What, then, makes Akutagawa Ryūnosuke special as a Japanese writer?

What I see as the foremost virtue of his literature is the excellence of his style: the sheer quality of his use of the Japanese language. One never tires of reading and re-reading his best works. Akutagawa was a born short-story writer who produced a great many works, some more successful than others. In fact, there are a good number that would seem to be of no particular interest to the modern reader—or at least to the modern general reader. This may be owing in part to Akutagawa's own mental instability and to a loss of directional focus in his literature, but when his focus is steady, the sharpness of his style is uniquely and inimitably his own.

The flow of his language is the best feature of Akutagawa's style. Never stagnant, it moves along like a living thing. His choice of words is intuitive, natural—and beautiful. Thoroughly schooled in his youth in both foreign languages and Chinese literature, he was able to summon up words of classic elegance seemingly out of thin air—expressions that modern-day writers can no longer use—manipulating them at will into arrangements of remarkable grace. This can be seen with special clarity in his early works, particularly the modern-language rewrites of stories he took from Japan's two large and varied collections of medieval folktales, the twelfth-century *Tales of Times Now Past* and the thirteenth-century *A Collection of Tales from Uji*: "The Nose," "In a Bamboo Grove," "Rashōmon," "Hell Screen," "Yam Gruel," "The Lady, Roku-no-Miya."[10] The ease with which he is able, through sheer force of style, to bring the classic, fantastic world of the medieval tale vividly into the sphere of modern life is truly breathtaking. Akutagawa published his maiden works, "Rashōmon" (1915) and "The Nose" (1916), in university magazines when he was still a 23-year-old student, but in them we can already see his finished, fluent, elegant, and spontaneous style. They read like the work of a seasoned writer, not an unformed student.

Natsume Sōseki, Akutagawa's senior as "national writer," was amazed when he read "The Nose," and he made a point of writing the youthful new author a letter of encouragement: "Put together another 20 or 30 stories like this," he said, "and there will be nobody to match you in the literary world."[11] As kind as he is known to have been to young writers in general, Sōseki never lavished such unstinting praise on anyone else. Surely, with his deep understanding of literature, Sōseki must have discovered the diamond glowing at its core. Akutagawa debuted, thus, as a fully-formed writer—at least where style and literary sense were concerned.

Style and literary sense: these were, to be sure, the keenest weapons in Akutagawa's authorial arsenal, but they also became his authorial Achilles' heel. Precisely because these weapons of his were so sharp and effective, they hindered him somewhat when it came to establishing a long-term scope and direction for his literature. This may resemble the situation of a pianist who has been born with a natural gift for superb technique. Because his fingers move so swiftly and with such clarity, the task of pausing occasionally to look long and hard at something—at the inner depths of the music—can be inhibited before he is even aware of it. His fingers move with natural speed and grace and his mind hurries to keep up. Or perhaps his mind forges ahead and the fingers hurry to keep up. In either case an unbridgeable gap begins to form between him and the movement of time in the world around him. Just such a gap almost certainly added to Akutagawa's psychological burdens and impelled him toward suicide.

Still, there is an undeniably breathtaking ferocity to the uninhibited, slashing style of the stories that he wrote in his first five or six years. To take an example from abroad, Akutagawa might well be said to resemble F. Scott Fitzgerald. Fitzgerald, too, was a born writer for whom the short story became the primary battlefield of his career. He made his professional debut at the tender age of twenty at the time of the First World War, and he instantly took the world by storm with his keen, flowing style and his brilliance. He left a good number of excellent works for later generations, but writing at the popular author's hectic pace, he left fully twice as many works that were not particularly wonderful. Not that this was any great discredit to him. The short-story form itself is marked by just such a history. If ten stories out of a hundred survive to be read by later generations, this has to be counted as a great success. No writer can make every work a masterpiece, nor should a writer be faulted for leaving behind failed or less than fully realized works. In life, it's the long haul that counts. Sometimes things work out well, and sometimes they don't. Sometimes you have to write things you're not too crazy about to make a living. What matters is just how great those ten surviving masterpieces are, which is why both Akutagawa and Fitzgerald still rate highly as authors and their works continue to be read.

More important than the proportion of first- to second-rate works is the form in which the author brings his youthful brilliance to maturity and transforms it into a literary world of greater depth and breadth. Fitzgerald was by nature incapable of learning from anything but his own personal experience, and that experience was mainly domestic tragedy. His wife Zelda succumbed to mental illness, their marriage fell apart, the Great Depression occurred, and all the while he was drowning in alcohol, as a result of which his popularity plummeted. These things contributed to the deepening of his literature. In his last years, he succeeded in creating works of great poignance that were distinctly different in tone from the acute and lyrical style of his youth (though they never achieved the same commercial success).

What about Akutagawa? When he ended his life at thirty-five, he had been active as a writer for a mere twelve years, but during that period he attempted a number of literary transformations.

At the beginning of his career, he wrote a large number of stories modeled after historical events or classical fiction, the stylistic genius of which won him high praise. These are the

ones that continue to be read today as classics. Akutagawa
was unrivaled for his fine-grained depiction of psychology and
for his aphoristic wit. For a time he even became the darling
of his age. Then, beginning around 1922, came his middle
period, in which we see a degree of stagnation and confusion.
Doubts began to plague him: was it all right for him to go on
writing transcriptions of historical pieces, supernatural tales
divorced from reality, and witty anecdotes one after another?
And in fact such critiques began to arise in literary circles. An
image began to take shape of Akutagawa's works as defined
by one fellow author: they "seemed to be toying with life
with a pair of silver tweezers." Another called him "a writer
who can't write without props."[12] Nor were these views entirely unwarranted. A certain lofty detachment clung to Akutagawa's writings as though they were looking at the world from
a set distance through a pane of glass, and such a posture
naturally invited negative criticisms from the literary world.
Akutagawa's early works had nothing whatever to do with
the task we see being performed in Sōseki's novels, which do
remain loftily detached even as they descend to earth and, with
great acumen, depict the hearts of the human beings who live
there.

Of course, Akutagawa might conceivably have reacted to
such self-doubt and external criticism with defiance, insisting
that these were the unique qualities of his writing, whether we
like them or not (indeed, no one before him or after him has
been able to write as he did). But where this might have been
the reaction of a mediocre talent, it was not an available option
for Akutagawa, who had been recognized as—and paid the
respect due—an author of the first rank. As a writer on the
very front line of literature, he was fully awake to the problems
of his age and reacted to them with a sense of responsibility
and of mission. For better or worse, then, he was a star, one of
the chosen. A gallant admission of defeat, a silent withdrawal,
a relinquishment of the place he had won: these were not among
the life choices he could make. He had to remain where he was:
on the front line. And to do so, he would have to clear a new,
more ambitious path. This was no easy task for him, however:

he never seemed to find that single thing that he absolutely had to write about.

A period of trial and error followed in the years to 1925 in which the gap between his successful and unsuccessful works loomed especially large. Now he wrote not only stories modeled on classical works but he worked long and hard and in varied forms to produce a more contemporary fictional world that was also more his own. Still, he could not seem to find that one type of story that was a perfect fit for his own inborn mentality and sensibility. The stories he wrote during this time lacked intensity: they were never more than "well made." They did not convey an aura of necessity to the reader; there was never a clear sense that the author had something he needed to communicate. He put each story together well enough, but the very dexterity with which he managed to do this seemed to be holding him back.

Akutagawa was always pointed toward modernism. When he was born in 1892, nearly twenty-five years—a full generation—had gone by since Japan had ended two and a half centuries of isolation under the rule of the Tokugawa government and performed that major surgery on itself known as "modernization." In other words, Akutagawa was born a child of the modern age. Western civilization and Western-style education were already things that could be taken for granted. He studied in the modern educational system, was well versed in foreign languages, progressed along the elite course and compiled an outstanding record in the institution that stood at the apex of the educational pyramid, Tokyo Imperial University. He read many of the foremost writers of the age—Tolstoy, Dostoevsky, Anatole France, Maupassant, Strindberg—in the original language or English translation, and he internalized Western sensibilities. He wore Western suits, smoked cigars, drank coffee, ate beef, conversed now and then with foreigners, and appreciated opera. Such a Westernized lifestyle was, for him, entirely natural and entirely comfortable.

During the years in which Akutagawa was actively writing, 1915–27, the First World War sent Japan's economy into boom conditions. These were also the years known as "Taishō Democracy" (in the Taishō Period, 1912–26), which perhaps might be called Japan's Weimar Age. After the bitterly-fought Sino-Japanese (1894–5) and Russo-Japanese (1904–5) Wars, Japan had solidified its position in the world order, as a result of which the suffocating tensions of the Meiji Period (1868–1912) relaxed, liberal tendencies arose in their place, and people sang the praises of modernism. The impact of the Russian Revolution aroused the socialist labor movement. Skirts grew short and the movement for the emancipation of women got started. This liberal climate was thoroughly crushed by the 1929 stock market crash, the ensuing worldwide Depression, and the rise of militarism and fascism, but that all happened after Akutagawa had left the world. With him, we are still in the midst of Taishō Democracy, liberalism, and modernism.

Take a step back from Tokyo, in which these revolutionary changes were taking place, however, and the most basic aspects of the life of the Japanese were still being governed by the old indigenous culture. In reality, a world in pre-modern dress still enveloped the ways of the modernized city to which Akutagawa gave representation. Not that this should be cause for surprise: a mere fifty years earlier, samurai had been walking around with swords, their hair done up in topknots. For 220 years, the Japanese had been locked in their little islands, virtually out of touch with other countries, preserving their unique culture in a system resembling feudalism. Only one generation had gone by since the end of that age, hardly enough time to reshape people's inner landscapes. Superficial aspects such as new systems could be adopted eagerly (or in some cases reluctantly, through compulsion), but certain basic things remained untouched: sensibility, values, archetypal mental images. In fact, the Meiji government openly promoted a policy supporting precisely such a bifurcation, as represented by the slogan "Japanese spirit, Western technology." They wanted to incorporate the technological progressiveness and efficiency of Western systems, but they also wanted the people to remain good, submissive Confucianists. That made it easier for them to run the country. In other words, to some degree the dregs of feudalism were left in place intentionally. Amid this nearly overwhelming sea of indigenous culture, urban culture became increasingly isolated, and Akutagawa was simply one member of a tiny elite. Before long, this began to prey on his nerves.

Akutagawa successfully imported his propensity for modernism into a fictional world in the borrowed container of the folktale. In other words, he succeeded in giving his modernism a "story" by skillfully adapting the pre-modern—the medieval tale form that had flourished almost a thousand years earlier. Instead of creating a purely modernistic literature, he first transposed his modernism into a different form. This was his literary starting point, and it was an extremely stylish, intellectual approach. By employing this strategy, he was able to capture the sympathies of a large readership. Had he chosen instead to write modernistic literature as a pure modernist, he would almost certainly have had only the success of a salon writer with a limited, intellectual readership, and his fiction would have quickly run up against its own limitations. Akutagawa had the instinctive (or perhaps strategic) literary sense to avoid such a dead end. In the first part of this collection, "A World in Decay," the reader can enjoy several examples of Akutagawa's works that adapt pre-modern materials to modern ends.

One thing I hope to make clear here is that Akutagawa was by no means simply a modernist with Western affectations. He grew up in the "low city" (Shitamachi), the old eastern side of Tokyo where the common people had lived since the capital city of the Tokugawa Shōgun was called Edo and where the roots of Edo Period (1600–1868) culture were still strong. (The new middle class, with its strong individualist tendencies, generally preferred to live in the hilly "high city" known as Yamanote.)[13] From childhood he was deeply immersed in Kabuki, the popular drama that had continued to flourish in the low city, and he enjoyed the witty writings of the Edo literati. He also had a rich knowledge of the Chinese language and literature that had been indispensable to any educated person in pre-modern times. (The visual beauty of the Chinese characters that Akutagawa used deserves special mention, though unfortunately this cannot be seen in translation.)

Thus, the fierce clash between the modern and the pre-modern was occurring not only in his relations with the world around him but deep inside him as well. The same can be said of the Meiji literary giants who had immediately preceded him—Natsume Sōseki and Mori Ōgai, for example. East vs. West: for Japan's budding cultural elite, whose stance was far from definitively settled, it could be fatal to lean too far in one direction or the other. As if taking out a kind of insurance policy, they had to strive to internalize both Eastern and Western high culture in equal doses so that they could be ready at a moment's notice to switch from one to the other. There is an expression used to characterize cultured Japanese of the first rank: *Ko-kon-tō-zai ni tsū-jiru* (to be conversant with old-new-east-west), which was, for them, the essence of political correctness. It was precisely because he had thoroughly absorbed this kind of "old-new-east-west" education that Akutagawa could so freely switch between the pre-modern and the modern in constructing his own unique fictional world. He could just as easily transpose Western literary forms intact into Japanese, and this technique was another powerful weapon of the early Akutagawa.

Sheer technique, however, though skillfully applied, does not necessarily translate into original literature. A fictional world that was not truly his own and that used borrowed containers would eventually reach an impasse and come to stand in his way like a high wall. Further pursuit of fictional method could only yield technical polish. And not surprisingly, the novelty would wear thin and readers would tire of seeing the same devices.

For Akutagawa, however, after 1925 it was not possible to advance in the direction of writing purely modernistic fiction. He was already too important—and too old—to escape into sophisticated intellectual play. The era had moved on as well since his debut. The giant tremors of the Russian Revolution had reached Japan, and the dense shadow of Marxism had begun to stretch across the earth. The spirit of the age was edging toward a demand for "literature of substance." People's attention was beginning to shift toward a literature that depicted the burdens of life with realistic precision. In Japan, this new writing was called "Marxist" and later "proletarian" literature.

There was also the "I-novel" (*watakushi-shōsetsu*) to think about, a form that had been gaining strength in Japan since the turn of the century and which garnered the greatest critical respect as it became the mainstream of modern Japanese fiction. In the I-novel (or perhaps "I-fiction," since the style was employed in both full-length novels and short, essay-like stories), the author provides a scrupulous depiction of the trivia of his surroundings, with an exhibitionistic emphasis on negative aspects of his own life and personality. This was the way Japan modified European Naturalism for domestic consumption.

In this way, modernist fiction became the object of a pincer attack from both the I-novel and Marxist literature, which shared an inflexible emphasis on the principle of realism. Akutagawa, with his inborn quality of lofty detachment, could not easily contribute to either side. He could never fully accept either kind of bare-bones realism. What Akutagawa chose to do was to cloak human shame in the artifice of storytelling and a sophisticated stylistic technique: this was how he lived and this was how he wrote. The literary method upon which both the I-novel and proletarian fiction were based was fundamentally opposed to his lifestyle. Cornered by the forces of the age, however, and finding it necessary to weigh the I-novel method against the Marxist method on his own personal scale, Akutagawa inevitably inclined toward the former. He was far too skeptical, far too individualistic, and far too intelligent ever to believe that he could become an effective intellectual spokesman for the working class.

Akutagawa's later strategy was to borrow the I-novel style but to use it with a "reverse grip," so to speak, in order to insert artificial confessions into this seemingly artless container. This was a sophisticated and highly risky strategy. But for Akutagawa, who needed "props," it was probably an unavoidable choice.

Works from his last two or three years are included here in the last part, "Akutagawa's Own Story." Together they comprise an introspective, neurotic, and remarkably depressive group of stories. Their somberness never degenerates into a mere blurting out of emotion, however, but stands firmly upon a foundation of Akutagawa-style artifice. Some works may have their moments of wheel-spinning, but each work as a whole retains its artistic autonomy. He may be writing something close to the facts of his own life, yet his stylistic control remains strong, and his writing reveals enough literary design to put the reader on guard: "You will never quite know," he seems to be warning us, "how much of this is true and how much is fiction."

Opinion is divided as to whether these experiments of Akutagawa's are successful as literature. Some say that these late works are his only masterpieces, while others say just the opposite. I don't see either group of works as superior or inferior: each was conceived quite differently, each constitutes a wheel of the carriage we call Akutagawa Ryūnosuke, and each deserves to be evaluated on its own merits. Where the degree of literary perfection is concerned, the early works have qualities to which the late works cannot hope to aspire. But in some of the late works—"Spinning Gears" in particular—the acuity of the protagonist's vision and the elegantly spare style have a truly spine-tingling brilliance, and their meticulously wrought mental images attain a powerful reality that will long remain deep in the reader's psyche.

I read "Spinning Gears" when I was fifteen—some forty years ago. Reading it again in order to write this introduction, I was amazed at how vividly I still recalled many of its images. There they were still, in my mind, not just as flat pictures but in all their three-dimensional reality, complete with the modulations of the light shining into the scene and tiny sounds in the background. Even taking into account the fifteen-year-old's special sensitivity to works of art, I believe we can declare such memories to be a product of the work's innate power. "Spinning Gears" leaves us with the impression that we have just read the story of a man who has pared his life down and then pared it down again until he was perilously close to the edge, and once he was sure he had reached the point where he could pare it down no farther, he turned the whole thing into fiction. It is a stunning performance. In Japanese there is the expression, "Let the enemy cut your flesh so that you can cut his bone." This is precisely what Akutagawa has accomplished in "Spinning Gears." There is no longer any sign here of technique for the sake of technique, and his tendency to flaunt his wit and erudition is also (in effect, at least) greatly reduced. Such are the reasons why, even as I retain some minor misgivings with regard to the degree of its maturity, I rank this posthumous work of Akutagawa's so highly.

For a psyche as vulnerable as Akutagawa's, writing such works was by no means healthy. He drove himself as far as he could possibly go despite a tendency to mental illness in the family. His mother had suddenly gone insane less than eight months after his birth, and he was raised by his mother's brother and sister and the brother's wife. He spent his life plagued by a fear that he himself might go mad at any moment, and the maintenance of his mental stability was complicated by his infrequent contacts with his birth parents. We will never know for certain whether the neuroses from which he suffered later in life were caused by hereditary factors, mental instability, or his latent fears, but sickness of mind casts a heavy shadow on the late stories and would end up taking his life. Surely it would be no exaggeration to say that writing these late works effectively shortened his life, but it is also true that he was unable to find a way to go on living as a writer without writing works of this nature—and once he could no longer live as a writer, his life would cease to have meaning.

It well could be that Akutagawa had to turn to the world of storytelling and technique in order to find refuge from his dark heredity. Rather than face the real world, so full of terror and pain, he might have transported himself mind and body into another world in hopes of finding a kind of salvation in its fictionality. Or perhaps in the dynamism of such a move he hoped to find that life possessed some radiance after all. In the end, however, he was compelled to return to his starting place—to a world ruled by pain and fear, a world that demanded his isolation. For, at a certain point, he came to a profound realization that he must fulfill his social responsibility as a writer and as a leading intellectual of his age. He determined that he could not simply park himself in one comfortable spot as a kind of cultural correspondent.

Perhaps the true reason that Akutagawa Ryūnosuke continues to be read and admired today as a "national writer" lies in this—in the realization and determination that effectively pushed him into a dead end. He started out as one of the chosen few: a Japanese intellectual with a consciousness torn between the West and Japan's traditional culture, in the border regions of which he succeeded in erecting a uniquely vigorous world of story. As he matured, he attempted to fuse the two different cultures inside himself at a higher level. He attempted structurally to combine the distinctively Japanese style of the I-novel with his own elegant fictional method. He hoped, in other words, to pioneer a newer, more uniquely Japanese form of serious literature. But this would have required a strenuous, long-term effort that his hypersensitive nerves and delicate constitution could not sustain. Pursued by the dark visions that crawled out of the gloom, he would finally despair and cut his life short. Akutagawa's terrible suicide administered a great shock to the minds of his contemporaries. It signaled both the defeat of a member of the intellectual elite and a major turning point in history.

Many Japanese would see in the death of this one writer the triumph, the aestheticism, the anguish, and the unavoidable downfall of the Taishō Period's cultivated elite. His individual declaration of defeat also became a signpost on the road of history leading to the tragedy of the Second World War. In the period just before and after his death, the flower of democracy that had bloomed with such promise in the Taishō Period simply shriveled and died. Soon the boots of the military would resound everywhere. The writer Akutagawa Ryūnosuke stands as an illuminating presence in the history of Japanese literature, a symbol of his age's brief glory and quiet defeat.

Has Akutagawa left behind a lesson for Japan's contemporary writers (including me)? Of course he has, both as a great pioneer and, in part, as a negative example. One thing he has to teach us is that we may flee into a world of technique and storytelling artifice but will eventually collide with a solid wall. It is possible to borrow the containers for our first stories, but sooner or later we have to transform the borrowed container into our own. Unfortunately for Akutagawa (and it really was unfortunate), he took too long to make his move, and that may well have ended up costing him his life. Perhaps, though, for a life so short, there was no other choice.

The other lesson he has for us concerns the way we overlay the two cultures of the West and Japan. With great pain and suffering, the self-consciously "modern" Akutagawa groped for his identity as a writer and as an individual in the clash of the two cultures, and just at the point where he had begun to find what was, for him, a hint of a way to fuse the two, he unexpectedly ended his life. For us now, this is by no means someone else's problem. Long after Akutagawa's time, we are still (with some differences) living amid the clash of things Western and Japanese, only now we may call them "global" and "domestic."

We can say for sure, however, whether with regard to Akutagawa's day or our own, that a half-baked eclecticism of the "Japanese spirit, Western technology" variety is not only fairly useless in the long run, it is downright dangerous. Joining the two cultural systems through a clever technique is never more than a temporary solution to the problem. Eventually, the bond just falls apart. Akutagawa was fully cognizant of the danger, and as an advanced intellectual of his time, he strove to discover the point of union that was right for him. He adopted the correct stance in this regard, and when we catch glimpses of it in his stories, it reverberates for us even now.

What we must aim for today, of course, is not a superficial accommodation with an alien culture but a more positive, essential, and interactive engagement. Having been born in Japan, a country with its own particular cultural environment, we have inherited its language and history, and we live here. Obviously, we need not—and cannot—become completely Westernized or globalized. On the other hand, we must never allow ourselves to descend into narrow nationalism. This is the one great lesson, the inflexible rule, that history has taught us.

Today, when the world is growing ever smaller through the spectacular development of the Internet and the increasingly rapid flow of economic interchange, we find ourselves in a pressing situation whereby, like it or not, our very survival depends on our ability to exchange cultural methodologies on an equivalent basis. To turn toward a stance of national exclusivity, regionalism, or fundamentalism in which nations become isolated politically, economically, culturally, or religiously could bring about unimaginable dangers on a worldwide scale. If only in that sense, we novelists and other creative individuals must simultaneously broadcast our cultural messages outward and be flexible receptors of what comes to us from abroad. Even as we unwaveringly preserve our own identity, we must exchange that which can be exchanged and understand that which can be mutually understood. Our role is perfectly clear.

Upon reflection, it seems to me that my departure point as a novelist may be rather close to the position adopted by Akutagawa. Like him, I leaned heavily in the direction of modernism at first, and I half-intentionally wrote from a standpoint of direct confrontation with the mainstream I-novel style. I, too, sought to create my own fictional world with a style that provisionally rejected realism. (In contrast to Akutagawa's day, though, we now have the handy concept of post-modernism.) I also learned most of my technique from foreign literature. Unlike him, however, I am basically a novelist rather than a short-story writer, and after a certain point I went on to actively construct my own original storytelling system. I also live an entirely different kind of life. Emotionally, though, I continue to be drawn to several of the best works that Akutagawa left us.

To be sure, I have not modeled my fictional world on his. This is not to say that one approach is right and the other wrong. Such simplistic comparisons are both impossible and meaningless. We live in different eras, our personalities are different, we grew up in different circumstances, and our aims are (as far as I can tell) different. All I want to say is that I— and probably most of Akutagawa's readers—learn a great deal from his works and from the vivid traces of his life, and we continue to draw from them as we move on through our own lives. In other words, Akutagawa Ryūnosuke still lives and functions in actuality as a "national writer" of ours. He lives on as an immovable fixed point in Japanese literature, as a part of our shared intellectual foundation.

Finally, I would like to commend the translator for his efforts in producing this book. From among Akutagawa's numerous short stories he has chosen several of the undisputed master-pieces and several highly interesting lesser works (most of which have not been translated into English before), assembled them into four apposite categories, and translated them with great accuracy while conveying the spirit of the originals. This has been done with a level of attention to detail that bespeaks a warm enthusiasm for Akutagawa's works and assured literary judgment. I can only hope that this book inspires a new appreci-ation for Akutagawa abroad.

Murakami Haruki

NOTES

1. On the list with Akutagawa would be such figures as Natsume Sōseki (1867–1916), Mori Ōgai (1862–1922), Shimazaki Tōson (1872–1943), Shiga Naoya (1883–1971), Tanizaki Jun'ichirō (1886–1965), and the 1968 Nobel Prizewinner Kawabata Yasu-nari (1899–1972). Less certain of a place might be Dazai Osamu (1909–48) and Mishima Yukio (1925–70). Sōseki would unquestionably come out at the top. This totals only nine; I can't think of a good candidate for tenth place.
2. Natsume Sōseki, *Botchan*, tr. J. Cohn (Tokyo: Kodansha Inter-national, 2005). On his name, see Chronology, note 2.
3. Shiga Naoya, "The Shopboy's God" ("Kozō no kamisama"), tr. Lane Dunlop, in *The Paper Door and Other Stories by Shiga Naoya* (San Francisco: North Point Press, 1987), and Kawabata Yasunari, "The Dancing Girl of Izu" ("Izu no odoriko"), tr. J. Martin Holman, in *The Dancing Girl of Izu and Other Stories* (Washington, D.C.: Counterpoint, 1998).
4. *Tanka* is the dominant verse form through most of Japanese

literary history, written in five lines of 5-7-5-7-7 syllabic structure.

5. Mori Ōgai, "The Dancing Girl" ("Maihime"), tr. Richard Bowring, in *Mori Ōgai: Youth and Other Stories*, ed. J. Thomas Rimer (Honolulu: University of Hawaii Press, 1994), and "Sanshō the Steward" ("Sanshō Dayū"), tr. J. Thomas Rimer, in *The Historical Fiction of Mori Ōgai* (Honolulu: University of Hawaii Press, 1991).

6. Tanizaki Jun'ichirō, *The Makioka Sisters* (*Sasameyuki*), tr. Edward Seidensticker (New York: Knopf, 1957).

7. "Tu Tze-chun" ("Toshishun"), in *The Essential Akutagawa, The Three Treasures*, and *The Spider's Thread and Other Stories*; "The Art of the Occult" ("Majutsu"), in *The Three Treasures* and *The Spider's Thread and Other Stories*; and "Yam Gruel" ("Imogayu"), in *Rashomon and Other Stories*, tr. Takashi Kojima. For bibliographical details here and below, see Further Reading.

8. "Kappa," in *Exotic Japanese Stories* and *Kappa*.

9. Mori Ōgai is fine, too, but to the eye of the modern reader the style of his language is a little too static and classical. Kawabata's works, to be quite honest, have always been a problem for me. I do, of course, recognize both their literary value and his considerable abilities as a novelist, but I have never been able to identify very closely with his fictional world. With regard to Shimazaki and Shiga, I can only say I have no particular interest in them. I have hardly read a thing of theirs aside from what I found in the school textbooks, and what I have read has left little trace in my memory.

10. "The Lady, Roku-no-Miya" ("Roku-no-miya no himegimi"), in *Exotic Japanese Stories*. For English translations of the classical collections, see Translator's Note, notes 2 and 3.

11. ARSJ, p. 176. (For publication information, see list of abbreviations, p. 237.)

12. Kikuchi Kan, "Inshōteki na kuchibiru to hidarite no hon," in *Shinchō* (October 1917), p. 30.

13. See Edward Seidensticker, *Low City, High City* (New York: Alfred A. Knopf, 1983).

Further Reading

AKUTAGAWA STORIES IN ENGLISH TRANSLATION

Most earlier anthologies tend to be out of print or difficult to find except in libraries. All those listed here contain stories not included in the present volume. Individual stories mentioned in the Introduction are noted along with other titles of particular interest.

The Essential Akutagawa, ed. Seiji M. Lippitt (New York: Marsilio, 1999). Contains "Tu Tze-chun" ("Toshishun"), "Kesa and Morito" ("Kesa to Moritō"), "The Faint Smiles of the Gods" ("Kamigami no bishō"), "A Note to a Certain Old Friend" ("Aru kyūyū e okuru shuki"), "Autumn Mountain" ("Shūsanzu")

Exotic Japanese Stories, tr. Takashi Kojima and John McVittie (New York: Liveright, 1964). Contains "Kappa" ("Kappa"), "The Lady, Roku-no-Miya" ("Roku-no-miya no himegimi"), "The Badger" ("Mujina"), "Heresy" ("Jashūmon", the unfinished sequel to "Hell Screen"), "The Handkerchief" ("Hankechi"), "The Dolls" ("Hina"), "A Woman's Body" ("Nyotai")

The Heart is Alone, ed. Richard McKinnon (Tokyo: Hokuseido, 1957). Contains "Flatcar" ("Torokko"), "A Clod of Soil" ("Ikkai no tsuchi")

Hell Screen and Other Stories, tr. W. H. H. Norman (Tokyo:

Hokuseido, 1948). Contains "Heresy" ("Jashūmon", the unfinished sequel to "Hell Screen")

Japanese Short Stories, tr. Takashi Kojima (New York: Liveright, 1961). Contains "A Clod of Soil" ("Ikkai no tsuchi"), "The Tangerines" ("Mikan")

Kappa, tr. Geoffrey Bownas (Tokyo: Tuttle, 1971, 2000). Contains "Kappa" and a lengthy introduction

Rashomon and Other Stories, tr. Takashi Kojima (New York: Liveright, 1952, 1999). Contains "Yam Gruel" ("Imogayu"), complete translation of "Dragon" ("Ryū"), "The Martyr" ("Hōkyōnin no shi")

Rashomon and Other Stories, tr. Glenn W. Shaw (Tokyo: Hara Shobo, 1964). Essentially a reissue of *Tales Grotesque and Curious*

The Spider's Thread and Other Stories, tr. Dorothy Britton (Tokyo: Kodansha International, 1987). Contains "Tu Tze-chun" ("Toshishun"), "The Art of the Occult" ("Majutsu"), "Flatcar" ("Torokko"), "The Dolls" ("Hina"), "The Tangerines" ("Mikan")

Tales Grotesque and Curious, tr. Glenn W. Shaw (Tokyo: Hokuseido, 1930). Contains "Tobacco and the Devil" ("Tabako to akuma"), "Lice" ("Shirami"), "The Handkerchief" ("Hankechi"), "The Wine Worm" ("Shuchū")

The Three Treasures, tr. Takamasa Sasaki (Tokyo: Hokuseido, 1951). Contains "Tu Tze-chun" ("Toshishun"), "The Art of the Occult" ("Majutsu")

STUDIES OF AKUTAGAWA

Cavanaugh, Carole, *Akutagawa Ryūnosuke: An Abbreviated Life* (Cambridge: Council on East Asian Studies, Harvard University, forthcoming)

Hibbett, Howard S., "Akutagawa Ryūnosuke and the Negative Ideal," in *Personality in Japanese History*, ed. Albert M. Craig and Donald H. Shively (Berkeley: University of California Press, 1970), pp. 425–51

——, "Akutagawa Ryūnosuke," in *Modern Japanese Writers*, ed. Jay Rubin (New York: Scribner's, 2001), pp. 19–30

Keene, Donald, *Dawn to the West: Japanese Literature of the Modern Era* (New York: Holt Rinehart and Winston, 1984), pp. 556–93

Lippitt, Seiji M., "The Disintegrating Machinery of the Modern: Akutagawa Ryūnosuke's Late Writings," *Journal of Asian Studies* 58, no. 1 (1999), pp. 27–50

Yu, Beongcheon, *Akutagawa: An Introduction* (Detroit: Wayne State University Press, 1972)

Translator's Note

*(New readers are advised that this section discusses
details of the plots.)*

The stories in this volume have been arranged in chronological
order according to the time of their setting rather than the order
of their publication, and the part titles are my own. Except as
noted below, the translations are based on texts in IARZ and
compared with those in CARZ and NKBT.[1] The completion
dates with which Akutagawa closed his manuscripts (usually
month and year) are preserved here in accordance with customary publishing practice. So, too, are the various text separators
he used in each story, such as the solid lines in "Loyalty" and
the asterisks in "The Writer's Craft." The choice of stories is
intended to reflect the great range of Akutagawa's fictional
world, based on my reevaluation of the complete works. Many
of the acknowledged masterpieces are here, including the two
on which the Kurosawa film *Rashōmon* is based, but the important late novella "Kappa," which is readily available in translation, has been excluded primarily because of its length. My
reasons for including several less well-known pieces appear in
the following remarks on the individual stories. I like to think
that the Akutagawa presented in this book is funnier, more
shocking, and more imaginative than he has been perceived to
be until now in the English-speaking world.

A WORLD IN DECAY

The Heian Period (794–1185) was Japan's classical era, a time
of peace and opulence, when the imperial court in Heian-kyō
("Capital of Peace and Tranquility": later Kyoto) was the foun-

tainhead of culture, and the arts flourished. Toward the end, however, political power slipped from the aristocracy to the warrior class, the decline of the imperial court led to the decay of the capital, and peace gave way to unrest. This was the part of the Heian Period that interested Akutagawa, who identified it with *fin-de-siècle* Europe, and he symbolized the decay with the image of the crumbling Rashōmon gate that dominates his story. Director Kurosawa Akira borrowed Akutagawa's gate and went him one better, picturing it as a truly disintegrating structure, entirely bereft of its Heian lacquer finish, and suggestive of the moral decay against which his characters struggle. His film *Rashōmon* (1950) was based on two of Akutagawa's stories, "Rashōmon" and "In a Bamboo Grove." Both—themselves based on tales from the twelfth century—reach far more skeptical conclusions than the film regarding the dependability of human nature and its potential for good.[2]

"Rashōmon" was one of Akutagawa's earliest stories, and in it he showed himself to be a master of setting and texture. He went on to become a master of voice. (He would learn not to throw French vocabulary—*sentimentalisme*—into narratives about ancient Japan for one thing.) The teller of the tale is usually a major character in his stories: a piece set in the late Heian Period could be narrated by an imagined member of the society ("Hell Screen"), by a quasi-scholarly modern observer who refers to "old records" ("Rashōmon"), by a disembodied editor who somehow manages to assemble several spoken eyewitness accounts of a single incident ("In a Bamboo Grove"), or by an objective-seeming writer who hardly acknowledges that he exists at all ("The Nose").

Two of these stories use the Heian setting to focus on the comical foibles of human nature. "The Nose" and "Dragon: The Old Potter's Tale" depict men of religion who are more concerned with their physical appearance than with nobler matters of the spirit, and both suggest that crass reality is far more important to people than the otherworldly questions of religion.[3] "Dragon" toys with the likelihood that religion is nothing more than mass hysteria, a force so powerful that even the fabricator of an object of veneration can be taken in by it.

"The Spider Thread" is included here despite its being time-less rather than set in any specific period. Given the "peep-box" mentioned near the beginning, the *telling* of the story might be said to have occurred in the eighteenth or nineteenth centuries when such mechanical contraptions were an important form of entertainment. The story's sinful robber/protagonist, Kandata, is meant to be Indian, and the tale has been traced to sources as diverse as Fyodor Dostoevsky's "The Onion" (from *The Brothers Karamazov* (1880)) and an 1894 story in *The Open Court*, an American journal "Devoted to the Work of Establishing Ethics and Religion Upon a Scientific Basis."[4] Its despairing view of human nature, however, fits the tone of the other stories of "a world in decay," and its traditional images of Hell reflect medieval Japanese religious conceptions and provide an ideal introduction to "Hell Screen." My translation of "The Spider Thread" follows Akutagawa's manuscript (as in CARZ) rather than the edited version that appeared in the children's magazine for which it was written (as in IARZ).

"Hell Screen," the story of an artist, can be seen as Akutagawa's examination of his devotion to his own art, but it works on a more universal level by pitting animal instinct against human intellect and questioning their place in human relationships. Based on a far simpler thirteenth-century classic,[5] the work is almost operatic in its bravura presentation of the doomed events, but it stops short of shrillness thanks to the measured tones of the narrator's voice. The elderly retainer of the Great Lord of Horikawa is not only a restrained commentator, but in denying what we all know to be true, he allows us to maintain the tension between denial and dread right up to the climactic fire. Akutagawa's detailed visualization of his late-Heian world—the clothing, the architecture, the construction of the oxcart, the balance of light and shadow, and, of course, the amazing conflagration that brings Hell into this world—shows him at his stylistic best. If only one work of his were going to survive, this should be it.

UNDER THE SWORD

Warfare dominated Japan's history between the end of the Heian Period and the imposition of peace under the Tokugawa Shōguns, the warrior-bureaucrats who ruled from 1600 to 1868. Once they had established their power base in Edo (modern Tokyo), the Tokugawas were afraid of change and did everything they could to remain at the pinnacle of a frozen social order. (They left the emperor in place as a figurehead and source of legitimacy for their own position.) Tokugawa "centralized feudalism" was remarkable for the way it imposed the principle of joint responsibility on all parts of society, punishing whole families, entire villages, or professional guilds for the infractions of individual members. This fostered a culture based on mutual spying, which promoted a mentality of constant vigilance and self-censorship.

One threat the Tokugawas dealt with early on was Christianity, which had been introduced by Portuguese missionaries in the sixteenth century, largely through Nagasaki, in the west of Japan. The foreign religion was perceived as a precursor of foreign invasion, partly because it threatened to undermine the absolute loyalty that the Tokugawas demanded of their retainers.

"Dr. Ogata Ryōsai: Memorandum" and "O-Gin" depict ordinary people trapped between an uncompromising faith and an intractable government. As in "Dragon," Akutagawa straddles the line between miracle and hysteria. By using the vocabulary of Edo Christianity, with its error-filled Portuguese and Latin and its mixing of Christian and Buddhist terms, Akutagawa suggests again that human beings create their own objects of veneration. No direct source has been determined for either story.

Based on two nineteenth-century fictionalized narratives about an actual eighteenth-century event, the psychological drama "Loyalty" depicts the pressure of Tokugawa rule on members of the samurai class. The startling parallels between the madness of the protagonist depicted in this early story, however, and the more openly autobiographical "Spinning Gears," written ten years later, reveal how thoroughly modern Akutagawa remained even as he maintained meticulous fidelity to his source materials.

MODERN TRAGICOMEDY

Akutagawa wrote many wholly fictitious stories set in his own time, though even here he tended to favor exotic materials, as seen in the Chinese settings of "The Story of a Head That Fell Off" and "Horse Legs." The former, set during the Sino-Japanese War, is more of a modern-historical piece than a contemporary work for Akutagawa, who was still a toddler at the time. Its intense cry against the horror and absurdity of war remains, unfortunately, as relevant in our barbaric twenty-first century as it was in his day.

"Horse Legs" is one of the funniest and wildest (and least well-known) pieces Akutagawa ever wrote. Reminiscent in its surrealistic twists of Gogol or Kafka, it is a nearly perfect—and perfectly hilarious—fictional portrayal of the universal human fear of having one's true nature revealed to others. Akutagawa performs a comic reversal of the commonly-used Sino-Japanese expression for an embarrassing self-betrayal, "Bakyaku o arawasu"—literally, "to reveal the horse's legs," as when the human legs of a stage horse are inadvertently exposed. The theme is pursued relentlessly (though with rich comic surprises at every turn), down to the final ironic two-line illustration of a moralist whose death leads to the revelation of his hypocrisy. No one is safe. My text incorporates the revisions that Akutagawa made after the story first appeared in a literary journal.[6]

"Green Onions" shows Akutagawa at his most technically playful. It is an unabashedly self-referential piece, a comic tour de force, a simultaneous send-up of romanticism and skepticism, and an unsparing look at the art and business of writing fiction. Akutagawa performs an amazing balancing act here by creating a heroine about whom we can truly care while reminding us repeatedly that she is an entirely artificial creation made to satisfy a magazine deadline. At one point, the author curses himself for becoming emotionally involved in her romanticized world, and at the end he bemoans the inevitable loss of her virginity while suggesting that she is going to be vanquished not only by her lover but by the critics.

AKUTAGAWA'S OWN STORY

The word "story" is used here advisedly. Throughout most of his career, Akutagawa refused to join the autobiographical mainstream of Japanese fiction, and he challenged his critics to see beneath the surface of his writings. He eventually succumbed to critical pressure, however, and began to examine his own life without the period costuming. The late pieces in this part all contain a strong autobiographical element, and they have been ordered so as to suggest the life story of a persona created by Akutagawa to resemble himself. Murakami's Introduction sensibly locates much of their fascination in the tension between their seeming confessionality and their perceptible manipulation of their materials.

The protagonists of these stories may be very much like Akutagawa, but fidelity to the facts of the author's life is less important than the consistency and intensity of the portrait of a hypersensitive individual trapped by the demands of family and profession and society. Like Akutagawa, this persona was adopted as an infant when his birth mother lost her mind, felt torn between his biological and adoptive fathers, and had a strong-willed aunt on the scene trying to control his life and the life of his wife. He yearned for liberation from family responsibilities but continued to live in the household of his adoptive parents with his wife and children. He was ambivalent about fatherhood, and he suffered the pangs of guilt when he strayed from his marriage. He became a writer, but writing at a time in Japan when only unadorned confession was deemed worthwhile, he became obsessed with the idea that the "man-made wings" ("The Life of a Stupid Man," "Spinning Gears") of his highly wrought art would lead him to disaster. He suffered, too, with the irrepressible fear that he had inherited from his mother a tendency to madness that would eventually reach out to claim him.

Ever since Akutagawa's suicide, it has been impossible to read this character's story in retrospect without knowing that Akutagawa could endure the strain of being himself no longer than thirty-five years. "His own works were unlikely to appeal to people who were not like him and had not lived a life like his," writes the narrator in Section 49 of "The Life of a Stupid Man." Had he lived longer, Akutagawa might have come to realize that he was far from alone.

"Daidōji Shinsuke: The Early Years" gives us the fullest account of Akutagawa's childhood and student years. He originally intended to extend the narrative with sequels, but when he subsequently wrote about his later life, he used other forms and other names for his protagonist. Even at his most autobiographical, Akutagawa is always consciously shaping his material for effect. He may well have believed, like the young Shinsuke, that his personality owed much to his having been raised on cow's milk; he may have been ashamed of his parents' petty-bourgeois behavior; and he certainly was a ferocious bookworm. But behind the startling images he relates to us we see a young man haunted by the virtually universal question, "Why am I different from everybody else?"

After graduating from the prestigious Tokyo Imperial University, Akutagawa taught at the Naval Engineering School from 1916 to 1919. Between 1922 and 1925, he wrote ten stories based on this phase of his life using a protagonist named Horikawa Yasukichi. "The Writer's Craft" is the most fully realized story of the series.

"The Baby's Sickness," which shows Akutagawa as a family man, has been included as an example of the kind of thing he most often chose *not* to write—an "I-novel" peek at the private life of an author—but which he could imbue with an intensity and focus not often seen in the form. The story opens with the dream of a dead man, which is never a good omen, and it resolves into a struggle between intellect and superstition, but for the most part it is set firmly in the world of reality. The writer's workaday world, described by Akutagawa with the kind of high-strung precision he brought to the world of the painter in "Hell Screen," offers the writer only interruptions, outrageous demands, and a sense of guilt for exploiting his family in the service of his art—yet another echo of "Hell Screen." "The Baby's Sickness," it might be noted, is the next-to-last story Akutagawa wrote before the deadly Kantō earthquake of 1 September 1923. Though he wrote some factual descriptions of the death and destruction wrought by the earthquake, surprisingly little of this horrific experience is directly reflected in the fiction (Section 31 of "The Life of a Stupid Man" is the one vivid exception). Thus we can only speculate as to what influence it might have had on the dark later works.

"Death Register," "The Life of a Stupid Man," and "Spinning Gears" all show Akutagawa probing the meaning of the life he has led to that point, and moving ever closer to the voluntary end of it. "Death Register" is the most lyrical and the most simply touching of the three, a sad look back at his estranged, insane mother, the elder sister he never knew, and the father who gave him up as an infant and tried unsuccessfully to win him back. The piece is more a contemplative essay than a story, and it reveals its traditional poetic roots by ending with a haiku. The ostensible subject of "Death Register" is three dead members of his family, but the haiku suggests that the difference between the living and the dead is something barely perceptible—a mere shimmer of heat in the summer air.

"The Life of a Stupid Man" reduces the entire life of the protagonist to a series of poetic moments of intense self-awareness, and it contains some of Akutagawa's most unforgettable imagery. Here more concrete treatment is given to his involvement with several women, an important factor in "Spinning Gears." The story opens in a bookstore and at many points shows the gradually aging protagonist experiencing life more through books than directly, always aware of his literary "master," the novelist Natsume Sōseki. Akutagawa's protagonist, like one of Sōseki's, sees his only options as faith, madness, or death.

If "Hell Screen" is Akutagawa's early masterpiece, "Spinning Gears" is undoubtedly the late one. Instead of the fragmented story of the entire "Life of a Stupid Man," here the whole life is boiled down to a few intense days of suffering. Like "Hell Screen," "Spinning Gears" conveys a sense of doom, but it replaces melodrama with inexhaustible paranoia in a phantasmagoric "night town" sequence. The narrator knows that the world is out to destroy him, but his ragged nerves do not permit him the luxury of creating the perfectly researched and recreated world of "Hell Screen." This is Hell itself.[7]

There could easily have been more categories than the above four to represent Akutagawa's broad interests, including Meiji Period settings, Chinese settings, and children's stories.

Nine of the stories in this volume are published in English for the first time: "Dr. Ogata Ryōsai: Memorandum," "O-Gin," "Loyalty," "Green Onions," "Horse Legs," "Daidōji Shinsuke: The Early Years," "The Writer's Craft," "The Baby's Sickness," and "Death Register."

All have been translated in their entirety except "Dragon: The Old Potter's Tale," which omits a ponderous framing device, and "The Baby's Sickness," which omits a brief dedication to Akutagawa's good friend Oana Ryūichi.[8]

A word about the annotations. As mentioned in the Introduction, Akutagawa's language is rich, which means it is full of vocabulary that requires annotation for modern Japanese readers. This is especially true when Akutagawa draws heavily from medieval or Chinese sources or mines his broad knowledge of European literature. Correspondences between the life and the autobiographical works call for annotation as well. Many of the notes contain information so widely shared among modern Akutagawa annotated texts that individual attribution would be nearly meaningless. Where no source is cited, IARZ, CARZ, and/or NKBT can be assumed. Some of the information also comes from useful Akutagawa Japanese "dictionaries."[9] In one or two cases I managed to identify items that had remained obscure in Japanese annotated texts, and I hope this will be a small repayment for the enormous benefit I gained from the extensive Japanese scholarship on Akutagawa. For some stories a headnote gives background information, and the reader may want to consult these before reading the story, especially "Loyalty."

NOTES

1. For publication information, see list of abbreviations, p. 237.

2. For English translations of the original "Rashōmon" story from *Konjaku monogatari*, see Marian Ury, *Tales of Times Now Past* (Ann Arbor, Center for Japanese Studies, University of Michigan, 1979/1993), pp. 183–4, Royall Tyler, *Japanese Tales* (New York: Pantheon Books, 1987), p. 88, or Yoshiko K. Dykstra, *The Konjaku Tales*, 3 vols. (Osaka: Intercultural Research Institute, Kansai Gaidai University, 1998–2003), 3:245–6, and of the original "In a Bamboo Grove" story from *Konjaku monogatari*, see Ury, *Tales*, pp. 184–6, or Dykstra, *Konjaku Tales*, 3:250–53. See also Ambrose Bierce's "The Moonlit Road" for a possible source of "In a Bamboo Grove" (*The Complete Short Stories of Ambrose Bierce*, compiled by Ernest Jerome Hopkins (Lincoln: University of Nebraska Press, 1984)). Akutagawa enthusiastically introduced Bierce to the Japanese reading public in 1921.

3. For an English translation of the early thirteenth-century sources for "The Nose" and "Dragon: The Old Potter's Tale", see D. E. Mills, *A Collection of Tales from Uji: A Study and Translation of Uji shūi monogatari* (Cambridge: Cambridge University Press, 1970), pp. 172–5 and 344–5.

4. The story, "Karma: A Tale with a Moral," was written by Paul Carus (1852–1919), a German-born scholar of Eastern philosophy and editor and publisher of *The Open Court*. Leo Tolstoy translated the piece into Russian. Akutagawa's immediate source was D. T. Suzuki's 1898 Japanese translation of the 1895 revised version of the Carus story. See Yamaguchi Seiichi, "Akutagawa Ryūnosuke to Pōru Kērasu: 'Kumo no ito' to sono zaigen ni kansuru oboegaki saihen," in Miyasaka Satoru (ed.), *Akutagawa Ryūnosuke sakuhinron shūsei*, 5 vols. (Kanrin shobō, 1999), 5:7–25.

5. For an English translation of the original see Mills, *Collection of Tales from Uji*, pp. 196–7.

6. As noted in IARZ 12:390–91.

7. On correspondences between "Spinning Gears" and Strindberg's *Inferno*, see Mats Arne Karlsson, "Boku wa kono angō o bukimi ni omoi . . . Akutagawa Ryūnosuke 'Haguruma,' Sutorindoberi, soshite kyōki," in *Nichibunken Fōramu*, No. 177 (Kyoto: Kokusai Nihon bunka kenkyū sentā, 2005). See August Strindberg, *Inferno and From an Occult Diary*, tr. and with an introduction by Mary Sandbach (Harmondsworth: Penguin Classics, 1979).

8. For a complete translation of the first under the original title, "Dragon," see *Rashomon and Other Stories*, tr. Takashi Kojima (New York: Liveright, 1952), pp. 102–19. On Oana Ryūichi, see Chronology (1927).

9. Kikuchi Hiroshi et al. (eds.), *Akutagawa Ryūnosuke jiten* (Meiji shoin, 1985); Sekiguchi Yasuyoshi and Shōji Tatsuya (eds.), *Akutagawa Ryūnosuke zensakuhin jiten* (Bensei shuppan, 2000); Sekiguchi Yasuyoshi (ed.), *Akutagawa Ryūnosuke shin-jiten* (Kanrin shobō, 2003).

A WORLD IN DECAY

RASHŌMON

Evening, and a lowly servant sat beneath the Rashōmon, waiting for the rain to end.*

Under the broad gate there was no one else, just a single cricket clinging to a huge red pillar from which the lacquer was peeling here and there. Situated on a thoroughfare as important as Suzaku Avenue, the Rashōmon could have been sheltering at least a few others from the rain—perhaps a woman in a lacquered reed hat, or a courtier with a soft black cap. Yet there was no one besides the man.

This was because Kyoto had been struck by one calamity after another in recent years—earthquakes, whirlwinds, fires, famine—leading to the capital's extraordinary decline. Old records tell us that people would smash Buddhist statues and other devotional gear, pile the pieces by the roadside with flecks of paint and gold and silver foil still clinging to them, and sell them as firewood. With the whole city in such turmoil, no one bothered to maintain the Rashōmon. Foxes and badgers came to live in the dilapidated structure, and they were soon joined by thieves. Finally, it became the custom to abandon unclaimed corpses in the upper story of the gate, which made the neighborhood an eerie place everyone avoided after the sun went down.

Crows, on the other hand, flocked here in great numbers. During the day they would always be cawing and circling the roof's high fish-tail ornaments. And when the sky above the gate turned red after sunset, the crows stood out against it like

---

*For this and other stories with historical backgrounds, see the headnote to each story in the Notes.

a scattering of sesame seeds. They came to the upper chamber of the gate to peck the flesh of the dead. Today, however, with the late hour, there were no crows to be seen. The only sign of them was their white droppings on the gate's crumbling steps, where long weeds sprouted from cracks between the stones. In his faded blue robe, the man had settled on the topmost of the seven steps and, worrying a large pimple that had formed on his right cheek, fixed his vacant stare on the falling rain.

We noted earlier that the servant was "waiting for the rain to end," but in fact the man had no idea what he was going to do once that happened. Ordinarily, of course, he would have returned to his master's house, but he had been dismissed from service some days before, and (as also noted earlier), Kyoto was in an unusual state of decline. His dismissal by a master he had served for many years was one small consequence of that decline. Rather than say that the servant was "waiting for the rain to end," it would have been more appropriate to write that "a lowly servant trapped by the rain had no place to go and no idea what to do." The weather, too, contributed to the *sentimentalisme* of this Heian Period menial. The rain had been falling since late afternoon and showed no sign of ending. He went on half-listening to the rain as it poured down on Suzaku Avenue. He was determined to find a way to keep himself alive for one more day—that is, a way to do something about a situation for which there was nothing to be done.

The rain carried a host of roaring sounds from afar as it came to envelop the Rashōmon. The evening darkness brought the sky ever lower until the roof of the gate was supporting dark, heavy clouds on the ridge of its jutting tiles.

To do something when there was nothing to be done, he would have to be prepared to do anything at all. If he hesitated, he would end up starving to death against an earthen wall or in the roadside dirt. Then he would simply be carried back to this gate and discarded upstairs like a dog. But if he was ready to do anything at all—

His thoughts wandered the same path again and again, always arriving at the same destination. But no matter how much time passed, the "if" remained an "if." Even as he told himself he was prepared to do anything at all, he could not find the courage for the obvious conclusion of that "if": *All I can do is become a thief.*

The man gave a great sneeze and dragged himself to his feet. The Kyoto evening chill was harsh enough to make him yearn for a brazier full of warm coals. Darkness fell, and the wind blew unmercifully through the pillars of the gate. Now even the cricket was gone from its perch on the red-lacquered pillar.

Beneath his blue robe and yellow undershirt, the man hunched his shoulders and drew his head down as he scanned the area around the gate. *If only there were some place out of the wind and rain, with no fear of prying eyes, where I could have an untroubled sleep, I would stay there until dawn,* he thought. Just then he caught sight of a broad stairway—also lacquered red—leading to the upper story of the gate. *Anybody up there is dead.* Taking care lest his sword, with its bare wooden handle, slip from its scabbard, the man set one straw-sandaled foot on the bottom step.

A few minutes later, halfway up the broad stairway, he crouched, cat-like, holding his breath as he took stock of the gate's upper chamber. Firelight from above cast a dim glow on the man's right cheek—a cheek inflamed with a pus-filled pimple amid the hairs of a short beard. The servant had not considered the possibility that anyone but dead people could be up here, but climbing two or three more steps, he realized that someone was not only burning a light but moving it from place to place. He saw the dull, yellow glow flickering against the underside of the roof, where spider webs hung in the corners. No ordinary person could be burning a light up here in the Rashōmon on a rainy night like this.

With all the stealth of a lizard, the servant crept to the top tread of the steep stairway. Then, hunching down and stretching out his neck as much as possible, he peered fearfully into the upper chamber.

There he saw a number of carelessly discarded corpses, as the rumors had said, but he could not tell how many because the lighted area was far smaller than he had thought it would be. All he could see in the dim light was that some of the corpses were naked while others were clothed. Women and men seemed to be tangled together. It was hard to believe that all of them had once been living human beings, so much did they look like clay dolls, lying there with arms flung out and mouths wide open, eternally mute. Shoulders and chests and other such prominent parts caught the dim light, casting still deeper shadows on the parts lower down.

The stink of the rotting corpses reached him, and his hand flew up to cover his nose. But a moment later the hand seemed to forget its task when a powerful emotion all but obliterated the man's sense of smell.

For now the servant's eyes caught sight of a living person crouched among the corpses. There, dressed in a rusty-black robe, was a scrawny old woman, white-haired and monkey-like. She held a burning pine stick in her right hand as she stared into the face of a corpse. Judging from the long hair, the body was probably a woman's.

Moved by six parts terror and four parts curiosity, the servant forgot to breathe for a moment. To borrow a phrase from a writer of old,[1] he felt as if "the hairs on his head were growing thick." Then the crone thrust her pine torch between two floorboards and placed both hands on the head of the corpse she had been examining. Like a monkey searching for fleas on its child, she began plucking out the corpse's long hairs, one strand at a time. A hair seemed to slip easily from the scalp with every movement of her hand.

Each time a hair gave way, a little of the man's fear disappeared, to be replaced by an increasingly violent loathing for the old woman. No, this could be misleading: he felt not so much a loathing for the old woman as a revulsion for all things evil—an emotion that grew in strength with every passing minute. If now someone were to present this lowly fellow again with the choice he had just been mulling beneath the gate—whether to starve to death or turn to thievery—he would probably have chosen starvation without the least regret, so powerfully had the man's hatred for evil blazed up, like the pine torch the old woman had stood between the floorboards.

The servant had no idea why the crone was pulling out the

dead person's hair, and thus could not rationally call the deed either good or evil. But for him, the very act of plucking hair from a corpse on this rainy night up here in the Rashōmon was itself an unpardonable evil. Naturally he no longer recalled that, only moments before, he himself had been planning to become a thief.

So now the servant, with a mighty thrust, leaped from the stairway and, grasping his sword by the bare hilt, he strode forcefully to where the old woman crouched. Terrified at the sight of him, the crone leaped up as if launched by a catapult.

"Where do you think you're going?" he shouted, blocking her way. Panic-stricken, she stumbled over corpses in an effort to flee. She struggled to break past him, but he pushed her back. For a time, the two grappled in silence among the corpses, but the outcome of the struggle was never in doubt. The servant grasped the old woman's arm—sheer skin and bone like the foot of a chicken—and finally twisted her to the floor.

"What were you doing there?" he demanded. "Tell me now, or I'll give you a piece of this."

Shoving her away, he swept his sword from its scabbard and thrust the white steel before her eyes. The old woman said nothing. Arms trembling, shoulders heaving, wide eyes straining from their sockets, she kept her stubborn silence and struggled to catch her breath. Seeing this, the servant realized that this old woman's life or death was governed entirely by his own will. The new awareness instantly cooled the hatred that had been burning so violently inside him. All he felt now was the quiet pride and satisfaction of a job well done. He looked down at her and spoke with a new tone of gentleness.

"Don't worry, I'm not with the Magistrate's Office. I'm just a traveler who happened to be passing beneath the gate. I won't be tying you up or taking you away. I just want you to tell me what you've been doing up here at a time like this."

The old woman stretched her wide eyes still wider and stared hard at the servant. Her red-lidded eyes had the sharpness of a predator-bird's. Then, as if chewing on something, she began to move her lips, which seemed joined with her nose by all her deep wrinkles. He could see the point of her Adam's apple

moving on her scrawny neck, and between her gasps the voice
that issued from her throat reached the servant's ears like the
cawing of a crow.

"I—I was pulling—I was pulling out hair to make a wig."

The servant was startled, and disappointed at how ordinary
the woman's answer turned out to be. But along with his disappointment, the earlier hatred and a cold contempt came back
to fill his heart. The woman seemed to sense what he was
feeling. Still holding in one hand the long hairs she had stolen
from the corpse, she mumbled and croaked like a toad as she
offered this explanation:

"I know, I know, it may be wrong to pull out dead people's
hair. But these people here deserve what they get. Take this
woman, the one I was pulling the hair from: she used to cut
snakes into four-inch pieces and dry them and sell them as dried
fish at the palace guardhouse. If she hadn't died in the epidemic,
she'd still be out there selling her wares. The guards loved her
'fish' and they bought it for every meal. I don't think she was
wrong to do it. She did it to keep from starving to death. She
couldn't help it. And I don't think what I'm doing is wrong,
either. It's the same thing: I can't help it. If I don't do it, I'll
starve to death. This woman knew what it was to do what you
have to do. I think she'd understand what I'm doing to her."

The servant returned his sword to its sheath and, resting his
left hand on the hilt, listened coolly to her story. Meanwhile,
his right hand played with the festering pimple on his cheek.
As he listened, a new kind of courage began to germinate in his
heart—a courage he had lacked earlier beneath the gate: one
that was moving in a direction opposite to the courage that had
impelled him to seize the old woman. He was no longer torn
between starving to death or becoming a thief. In his current
state of mind, the very thought of starving to death was so
nearly banished from his consciousness that it became all but
unthinkable for him.

"You're sure she would, eh?" the servant pressed her, with
mockery in his voice. Then, stepping toward her, he suddenly
shot his right hand from his pimple to the scruff of her neck.
As he grasped her, his words all but bit into her flesh: "You

won't blame me, then, for taking your clothes. That's what *I* have to do to keep from starving to death."

He stripped the old woman of her robe, and when she tried to clutch at his ankles he gave her a kick that sent her sprawling onto the corpses. Five swift steps brought him to the opening at the top of the stairs. Tucking her robe under his arm, he plunged down the steep stairway into the depth of the night.

It did not take long for the crone, who had been lying there as if dead, to raise her naked body from among the corpses. Muttering and groaning, she crawled to the top of the stairway in the still-burning torchlight. Her short white hair hung forward from her head as she peered down toward the bottom of the gate. She saw only the cavernous blackness of the night.

What happened to the lowly servant, no one knows.

(September 1915)

IN A BAMBOO GROVE

The Testimony of a Woodcutter under Questioning by the Magistrate

That is true, Your Honor. I am the one who found the body. I went out as usual this morning to cut cedar in the hills behind my place. The body was in a bamboo grove on the other side of the mountain. Its exact location? A few hundred yards off the Yamashina post road. A deserted place where a few scrub cedar trees are mixed in with the bamboo.

The man was lying on his back in his pale blue robe with the sleeves tied up and one of those fancy Kyoto-style black hats with the sharp creases. He had only one stab wound, but it was right in the middle of his chest; the bamboo leaves around the body were soaked with dark red blood. No, the bleeding had stopped. The wound looked dry, and I remember it had a big horsefly sucking on it so hard the thing didn't even notice my footsteps.

Did I see a sword or anything? No, Sir, not a thing. Just a length of rope by the cedar tree next to the body. And—oh yes, there was a comb there, too. Just the rope and the comb is all. But the weeds and the bamboo leaves on the ground were pretty trampled down: he must have put up a tremendous fight before they killed him. How's that, Sir—a horse? No, a horse could never have gotten into that place. It's all bamboo thicket between there and the road.

The Testimony of a Traveling Priest under Questioning by the Magistrate

I'm sure I passed the man yesterday, Your Honor. Yesterday at—about noon, I'd say. Near Checkpoint Hill on the way to Yamashina. He was walking toward the checkpoint with a woman on horseback. She wore a stiff, round straw hat with a long veil hanging down around the brim; I couldn't see her face, just her robe. I think it had a kind of dark-red outer layer with a blue-green lining. The horse was a dappled gray with a tinge of red, and I'm fairly sure it had a clipped mane. Was it a big horse? I'd say it was a few inches taller than most, but I'm a priest after all. I don't know much about horses. The man? No, Sir, he had a good-sized sword, and he was equipped with a bow and arrows. I can still see that black-lacquered quiver of his: he must have had twenty arrows in it, maybe more. I would never have dreamt that a thing like this could happen to such a man. Ah, what is the life of a human being—a drop of dew, a flash of lightning? This is so sad, so sad. What can I say?

The Testimony of a Policeman under Questioning by the Magistrate

The man I captured, Your Honor? I am certain he is the famous bandit, Tajōmaru. True, when I caught him he had fallen off his horse, and he was moaning and groaning on the stone bridge at Awataguchi. The time, Sir? It was last night at the first watch.[1] He was wearing the same dark blue robe and carrying the same long sword he used the time I almost captured him before. You can see he also has a bow and arrows now. Oh, is that so, Sir? The dead man, too? That settles it, then: I'm sure this Tajōmaru fellow is the murderer. A leather-wrapped bow, a quiver in black lacquer, seventeen hawk-feather arrows— they must have belonged to the victim. And yes, as you say, Sir, the horse is a dappled gray with a touch of red, and it has a clipped mane. It's only a dumb animal, but it gave that bandit just what he deserved, throwing him like that. It was a short way beyond the bridge, trailing its reins on the ground and eating plume grass by the road.

Of all the bandits prowling around Kyoto, this Tajōmaru is known as a fellow who likes the women. Last fall, people at Toribe Temple found a pair of worshippers murdered—a woman and a child—on the hill behind the statue of Binzuru.[2] Everybody said Tajōmaru must have done it. If it turns out he killed the man, there's no telling what he might have done to the woman who was on the horse. I don't mean to meddle, Sir, but I do think you ought to question him about that.

The Testimony of an Old Woman under Questioning by the Magistrate

Yes, Your Honor, my daughter was married to the dead man. He is not from the capital, though. He was a samurai serving in the Wakasa provincial office. His name was Kanazawa no Takehiro, and he was twenty-six years old. No, Sir, he was a very kind man. I can't believe anyone would have hated him enough to do this.

My daughter, Sir? Her name is Masago, and she is nineteen years old. She's as bold as any man, but the only man she has ever known is Takehiro. Her complexion is a little on the dark side, and she has a mole by the outside corner of her left eye, but her face is a tiny, perfect oval.

Takehiro left for Wakasa yesterday with my daughter, but what turn of fate could have led to this? There's nothing I can do for my son-in-law anymore, but what could have happened to my daughter? I'm worried sick about her. Oh please, Sir, do everything you can to find her, leave no stone unturned: I have lived a long time, but I have never wanted anything so badly in my life. Oh how I hate that bandit—that, that Tajōmaru! Not only my son-in-law, but my daughter . . . (Here the old woman broke down and was unable to go on speaking.)

     *   *   *   *   *

Tajōmaru's Confession

Sure, I killed the man. But I didn't kill the woman. So, where did she go? I don't know any better than you do. Now, wait just a minute—you can torture me all you want, but I can't tell you what I don't know. And besides, now that you've got me, I'm not going to hide anything. I'm no coward.

I met that couple yesterday, a little after noon. The second I saw them, a puff of wind lifted her veil and I caught a peek at her. Just a peek: that's maybe why she looked so perfect to me—an absolute bodhisattva of a woman.[3] I made up my mind right then to take her even if I had to kill the man.

Oh come on, killing a man is not as big a thing as people like you seem to think. If you're going to take somebody's woman, a man has to die. When *I* kill a man, I do it with my sword, but people like you don't use swords. You gentlemen kill with your power, with your money, and sometimes just with your words: you tell people you're doing them a favor. True, no blood flows, the man is still alive, but you've killed him all the same. I don't know whose sin is greater—yours or mine. (A sarcastic smile.)

Of course, if you can take the woman without killing the man, all the better. Which is exactly what I was hoping to do yesterday. It would have been impossible on the Yamashina post road, of course, so I thought of a way to lure them into the hills.

It was easy. I fell in with them on the road and made up a story. I told them I had found an old burial mound[4] in the hills, and when I opened it it was full of swords and mirrors and things. I said I had buried the stuff in a bamboo grove on the other side of the mountain to keep anyone from finding out about it, and I'd sell it cheap to the right buyer. He started getting interested soon enough. It's scary what greed can do to people, don't you think? In less than an hour, I was leading that couple and their horse up a mountain trail.

When we reached the grove, I told them the treasure was buried in there and they should come inside with me and look at it. The man was so hungry for the stuff by then, he couldn't refuse, but the woman said she'd wait there on the horse. I

figured that would happen—the woods are so thick. They fell
right into my trap. We left the woman alone and went into the
grove.

It was all bamboo at first. Fifty yards or so inside, there was
a sort of open clump of cedars—the perfect place for what I
was going to do. I pushed through the thicket and made up
some nonsense about how the treasure was buried under one
of them. When he heard that, the man charged toward some
scrawny cedars visible up ahead. The bamboo thinned out, and
the trees were standing there in a row. As soon as we got to
them, I grabbed him and pinned him down. I could see he was
a strong man—he carried a sword—but I took him by surprise,
and he couldn't do a thing. I had him tied to the base of a tree
in no time. Where did I get the rope? Well, I'm a thief, you
know—I might have to scale a wall at any time—so I've always
got a piece of rope in my belt. I stuffed his mouth full of bamboo
leaves to keep him quiet. That's all there was to it.

Once I finished with the man, I went and told the woman
that her husband had suddenly been taken ill and she should
come and have a look at him. This was another bull's-eye, of
course. She took off her hat and let me lead her by the hand
into the grove. As soon as she saw the man tied to the tree,
though, she whipped a dagger out of her breast. I never saw a
woman with such fire! If I'd been off my guard, she'd have
stuck that thing in my gut. And the way she kept coming, she
would have done me some damage eventually no matter how
much I dodged. Still, I *am* Tajōmaru. One way or another, I
managed to knock the knife out of her hand without drawing
my sword. Even the most spirited woman is going to be helpless
if she hasn't got a weapon. And so I was able to make the
woman mine without taking her husband's life.

Yes, you heard me: without taking her husband's life. I wasn't
planning to kill him on top of everything else. The woman was
on the ground, crying, and I was getting ready to run out of the
grove and leave her there when all of a sudden she grabbed my
arm like some kind of crazy person. And then I heard what she
was shouting between sobs. She could hardly catch her breath:
"Either you die or my husband dies. It has to be one of you.

It's worse than death for me to have two men see my shame. I want to stay with the one left alive, whether it's you or him." That gave me a wild desire to kill her husband. (Sullen excitement.)

When I say this, you probably think I'm crueler than you are. But that's because you didn't see the look on her face—and especially, you never saw the way her eyes were burning at that moment. When those eyes met mine, I knew I wanted to make her my wife. Let the thunder god kill me, I'd make her my wife—that was the only thought in my head. And no, not just from lust. I know that's what you gentlemen are thinking. If lust was all I felt for her, I'd already taken care of that. I could've just kicked her down and gotten out of there. And the man wouldn't have stained my sword with his blood. But the moment my eyes locked onto hers in that dark grove, I knew I couldn't leave there until I had killed him.

Still, I didn't want to kill him in a cowardly way. I untied him and challenged him to a sword fight. (That piece of rope they found was the one I threw aside then.) The man looked furious as he drew his big sword, and without a word he sprang at me in a rage. I don't have to tell you the outcome of the fight. My sword pierced his breast on the twenty-third thrust. Not till the twenty-third: I want you to keep that in mind. I still admire him for that. He's the only man who ever lasted even twenty thrusts with me. (Cheerful grin.)

As he went down, I lowered my bloody sword and turned toward the woman. But she was gone! I looked for her among the cedars, but the bamboo leaves on the ground showed no sign she'd ever been there. I cocked my ear for any sound of her, but all I could hear was the man's death rattle.

Maybe she had run through the underbrush to call for help when the sword fight started. The thought made me fear for my life. I grabbed the man's sword and his bow and arrows and headed straight for the mountain road. The woman's horse was still there, just chewing on grass. Anything else I could tell you after that would be a waste of breath. I got rid of his sword before coming to Kyoto, though.

So that's my confession. I always knew my head would end

up hanging in the tree outside the prison some day, so let me
have the ultimate punishment. (Defiant attitude.)

Penitent Confession of a Woman in the Kiyomizu Temple

After the man in the dark blue robe had his way with me, he
looked at my husband, all tied up, and taunted him with laughter. How humiliated my husband must have felt! He squirmed
and twisted in the ropes that covered his body, but the knots
ate all the deeper into his flesh. Stumbling, I ran to his side.
No—I *tried* to run to him, but instantly the man kicked me
down. And that was when it happened: that was when I saw
the indescribable glint in my husband's eyes. Truly, it was
indescribable. It makes me shudder to recall it even now. My
husband was unable to speak a word, and yet, in that moment,
his eyes conveyed his whole heart to me. What I saw shining
there was neither anger nor sorrow. It was the cold flash of
contempt—contempt for *me*. This struck me more painfully
than the bandit's kick. I let out a cry and collapsed on the spot.

When I regained consciousness, the man in blue was gone.
The only one there in the grove was my husband, still tied to
the cedar tree. I just barely managed to raise myself on the
carpet of dead bamboo leaves, and look into my husband's
face. His eyes were exactly as they had been before, with that
same cold look of contempt and hatred. How can I describe
the emotion that filled my heart then? Shame . . . sorrow . . .
anger . . . I staggered over to him.

"Oh, my husband! Now that this has happened, I cannot go
on living with you. I am prepared to die here and now. But
you—yes, I want you to die as well. You witnessed my shame.
I cannot leave you behind with that knowledge."

I struggled to say everything I needed to say, but my husband
simply went on staring at me in disgust. I felt as if my breast
would burst open at any moment, but holding my feelings in
check, I began to search the bamboo thicket for his sword. The
bandit must have taken it—I couldn't find it anywhere—and
my husband's bow and arrows were gone as well. But then I

had the good luck to find the dagger at my feet. I brandished it before my husband and spoke to him once again.

"This is the end, then. Please be so good as to allow me to take your life. I will quickly follow you in death."

When he heard this, my husband finally began moving his lips. Of course his mouth was stuffed with bamboo leaves, so he couldn't make a sound, but I knew immediately what he was saying. With total contempt for me, he said only, "Do it." Drifting somewhere between dream and reality, I thrust the dagger through the chest of his pale blue robe.

Then I lost consciousness again. When I was able to look around me at last, my husband, still tied to the tree, was no longer breathing. Across his ashen face shone a streak of light from the setting sun, filtered through the bamboo and cedar. Gulping back my tears, I untied him and cast the rope aside. And then—and then what happened to me? I no longer have the strength to tell it. That I failed to kill myself is obvious. I tried to stab myself in the throat. I threw myself in a pond at the foot of the mountain. Nothing worked. I am still here, by no means proud of my inability to die. (Forlorn smile.) Perhaps even Kanzeon,[5] bodhisattva of compassion, has turned away from me for being so weak. But now—now that I have killed my husband, now that I have been violated by a bandit—what am I to do? Tell me, what am I to . . . (Sudden violent sobbing.)

The Testimony of the Dead Man's Spirit Told through a Medium

After the bandit had his way with my wife, he sat there on the ground, trying to comfort her. I could say nothing, of course, and I was bound to the cedar tree. But I kept trying to signal her with my eyes: *Don't believe anything he tells you. He's lying, no matter what he says.* I tried to convey my meaning to her, but she just went on cringing there on the fallen bamboo leaves, staring at her knees. And, you know, I could see she was listening to him. I writhed with jealousy, but the bandit kept his smooth talk going from one point to the next. "Now that your flesh has been sullied, things will never be the same with your husband. Don't stay with him—come and be my wife! It's because I love you so much that I was so wild with you." The bandit had the gall to speak to her like that!

When my wife raised her face in response to him, she seemed almost spellbound. I had never seen her look so beautiful as she did at that moment. And what do you think this beautiful wife of mine said to the bandit, in my presence—in the presence of her husband bound hand and foot? My spirit may be wandering now between one life and the next, but every time I recall her answer, I burn with indignation. "All right," she told him, "take me anywhere you like." (Long silence.)

And that was not her only crime against me. If that were all she did, I would not be suffering so here in the darkness. With him leading her by the hand, she was stepping out of the bamboo grove as if in a dream, when suddenly the color drained from her face and she pointed back to me. "Kill him!" she screamed. "Kill him! I can't be with you as long as he is alive!" Again and again she screamed, as if she had lost her mind, "Kill him!" Even now her words like a windstorm threaten to blow me headlong into the darkest depths. Have such hateful words ever come from the mouth of a human being before? Have such damnable words ever reached the ears of a human being before? Have such— (An explosion of derisive laughter.) Even the bandit went pale when he heard her. She clung to his arm and screamed again, "Kill him!" The bandit stared at her, saying neither that he would kill me nor that he would not. The next thing I knew, however, he sent my wife sprawling on the bamboo leaves with a single kick. (Another explosion of derisive laughter.) The bandit calmly folded his arms and turned to look at me.

"What do you want me to do with her?" he asked. "Kill her or let her go? Just nod to answer. Kill her?" For this if for nothing else, I am ready to forgive the bandit his crimes. (Second long silence.)

When I hesitated with my answer, my wife let out a scream and darted into the depths of the bamboo thicket. He sprang after her, but I don't think he even managed to lay a hand on her sleeve. I watched the spectacle as if it were some kind of vision.

After my wife ran off, the bandit picked up my sword and bow and arrows, and he cut my ropes at one place. "Now it's my turn to run," I remember hearing him mutter as he disappeared from the thicket. Then the whole area was quiet. No—I could hear someone weeping. While I was untying myself, I listened to the sound, until I realized—I realized that I was the one crying. (Another long silence.)

I finally raised myself, exhausted, from the foot of the tree. Lying there before me was the dagger that my wife had dropped. I picked it up and shoved it into my chest. Some kind of bloody mass rose to my mouth, but I felt no pain at all. My chest grew cold, and then everything sank into stillness. What perfect silence! In the skies above that grove on the hidden side of the mountain, not a single bird came to sing. The lonely glow of the sun lingered among the high branches of cedar and bamboo. The sun—but gradually, even that began to fade, and with it the cedars and bamboo. I lay there wrapped in a deep silence.

Then stealthy footsteps came up to me. I tried to see who it was, but the darkness had closed in all around me. Someone— that someone gently pulled the dagger from my chest with an invisible hand. Again a rush of blood filled my mouth, but then I sank once and for all into the darkness between lives.

(December 1921)

THE NOSE

You just had to mention "Zenchi Naigu's nose," and everyone in Ike-no-o knew what you were talking about. Never mind that his name ascribed to him the "wisdom of Zen" (Zenchi) or that he was one of only ten priests honored to "minister within" (Naigu) the imperial palace in Kyoto: all that mattered was that nose of his. Uniform in thickness from base to tip, it hung a full six inches from above his upper lip to below his chin, like a sausage dangling down from the middle of his face.

The nose had been a constant source of torment for the Naigu from his earliest days as a young acolyte until now, past the age of fifty, when he had reached his present lofty post. On the surface, of course, he pretended it did not bother him—and not only because he felt it wrong for a priest to worry over his nose when he should be thirsting exclusively for the Pure Land to come. What he hated most of all was for other people to become aware of his concern over his nose. And what he feared most of all was that the word "nose" would come up in conversation.

There were two reasons why his nose was more than the Naigu could manage. One was that it actually got in his way much of the time. He could not eat by himself; whenever he tried to, the tip of his nose would touch the rice in his metal bowl. To deal with this problem, he had a disciple sit across from him at mealtime and hold his nose up with a long, narrow wooden slat, an inch wide and two feet long. This was not an easy thing to do—either for the slat-wielding disciple or for the Naigu himself. A temple page who stood in for the disciple at one meal sneezed and let the nose drop into the rice gruel. The story immediately spread across the river to Kyoto. Still, this was not the main reason the Naigu was troubled by his nose. He suffered most because of the harm it was doing to his self-esteem.

The people of Ike-no-o used to say that Zenchi Naigu was lucky to be a priest: no woman would ever want to marry a man with a nose like that. Some even claimed it was because of his nose that he had entered the priesthood to begin with. The Naigu himself, however, never felt that he suffered any less over his nose for being a priest. Indeed, his self-esteem was already far too fragile to be affected by such a secondary fact as whether or not he had a wife. And so, by means both active and passive, he sought to repair the damage to his self-esteem.

He tried first of all to find ways to make his nose look shorter. When there was no one around, he would hold up his mirror and, with feverish intensity, examine his reflection from every angle. Sometimes it took more than simply changing the position of his face to comfort him, and he would try one pose after another—resting his cheek on his hand or stroking his chin with his fingertips. Never once, though, was he satisfied that his nose looked any shorter. In fact, he sometimes felt that the harder he tried, the longer it looked. Then, heaving fresh sighs of despair, he would put the mirror away in its box and drag himself back to the scripture stand to resume chanting the Kannon Sutra.[1]

The second way he dealt with his problem was to keep a vigilant eye out for other people's noses. Many public events took place at the Ike-no-o temple—banquets to benefit the priests, lectures on the sutras, and so forth. Row upon row of monks' cells filled the temple grounds, and each day the monks would heat up bath water for the temple's many residents and lay visitors, all of whom the Naigu would study closely. He hoped to gain peace from discovering even one face with a nose like his. And so his eyes took in neither blue robes nor white; orange caps, skirts of gray: the priestly garb he knew so well hardly existed for him. The Naigu saw not people but noses. While a great hooked beak might come into his view now and then, never did he discover a nose like his own. And with each failure to find what he was looking for, the Naigu's resentment would increase. It was entirely due to this feeling that often, while speaking to a person, he would unconsciously grasp the dangling end of his nose and blush like a youngster.

And finally, the Naigu would comb the Buddhist scriptures and other classic texts, searching for a character with a nose like his own in the hope that it would provide him some measure of comfort. Nowhere, however, was it written that the nose of either Mokuren or Sharihotsu was long. And Ryūju and Memyō, of course, were Bodhisattvas with normal human noses. Listening to a Chinese story once, he heard that Liu Bei, the Shu Han emperor,[2] had long ears. "Oh, if only it had been his nose," he thought, "how much better I would feel!"

We need hardly mention here that, even as he pursued these passive efforts, the Naigu also took more active steps to shorten his nose. He tried everything: he drank a decoction of boiled snake gourd; he rubbed his nose with rat urine. Nothing did any good, however: the nose continued to dangle six inches down over his lips.

One autumn, however, a disciple of his who had gone to Kyoto—in part on an errand for the Naigu himself—came back to Ike-no-o with a new method for shortening noses that he had learned from a doctor friend. This doctor was a man from China who had become a high-ranking priest at a major Kyoto temple, the Chōrakuji.

Pretending, as usual, that he was unconcerned about his nose, the Naigu would not at first agree to submit to the new treatment. Instead, at mealtimes he would offer a casual expression of regret that the disciple had gone to so much trouble. Inwardly, of course, he was hoping that the disciple would press him to try the treatment. And the disciple must have been aware of the Naigu's tactics. But his master's very willingness to employ such tactics seemed to rouse the aide to sympathy more than resentment. Just as the Naigu had hoped, the disciple used every argument he could think of to persuade his master to adopt the treatment. And, as he knew he would, the Naigu finally submitted to the disciple's fervent exhortations.

The treatment itself was actually quite simple: boil the nose and have someone tread on it.

Boiling water could be had any day at the temple bathhouse. The disciple immediately brought a bucket full of water that was too hot for him to touch. If the Naigu simply dipped his nose straight into the bucket, however, his face might be scalded by the rising steam. So they bored a hole in a tray, set the tray on the bucket, and lowered the nose through the hole into the boiling water. The nose itself felt no heat at all.

After the nose had been soaking for a short while, the disciple said, "I believe it has cooked long enough, Your Reverence."

The Naigu gave him a contorted smile. At least, he thought with some satisfaction, no one overhearing this one remark would imagine that the subject was a nose. The boiled nose itself, however, was itching now as if it had been bitten by fleas.

The Naigu withdrew his nose from the hole in the tray, and the disciple began to tread on the still-steaming thing with all his might. The Naigu lay with his nose stretched out on the floorboards, watching the disciple's feet moving up and down before his eyes. Every now and then, the disciple would cast a pitying glance down toward the Naigu's bald head and say, "Does it hurt, Your Reverence? The doctor told me to stamp on it as hard as I could, but . . . does it hurt?"

The Naigu tried to shake his head to signal that it did not hurt, but with the disciple's feet pressing down on his nose, he was unable to do so. Instead, he turned his eyes upward until he could see the raw cracks in the disciple's chapped feet and gave an angry-sounding shout: "No, it doesn't hurt!"

Far from hurting, his itchy nose almost felt good to have the young man treading on it.

After this had been going on for some time, little bumps like millet grains began to form on the nose until it looked like a bird that had been plucked clean and roasted whole. When he saw this, the disciple stopped his treading and muttered as if to himself, "Now I'm supposed to pull those out with tweezers."

The Naigu puffed out his cheeks in apparent exasperation as he silently watched the disciple proceed with the treatment.

Not that he was ungrateful for the efforts. But as much as he appreciated the young man's kindness, he did not like having his nose handled like some kind of *thing*. The Naigu watched in apprehension, like a patient being operated on by a doctor he mistrusts, as the disciple plucked beads of fat from the pores of his nose with the tweezers. The beads protruded half an inch from each pore like stumps of feathers.

Once he was through, the disciple said with a look of relief, "Now we just have to cook it again."

Brows knit in apparent disapproval, the Naigu did as he was told.

After the second boiling, the nose looked far shorter than it ever had before. Indeed, it was not much different from an ordinary hooked nose. Stroking his newly shortened nose, the Naigu darted a few timid glances into the mirror the young man held out to him.

The nose—which once had dangled down below his chin—now had shrunk to such an unbelievable degree that it seemed only to be hanging on above his upper lip by a feeble last breath. The red blotches that marked it were probably left from the trampling. No one would laugh at *this* nose anymore! The face of the Naigu inside the mirror looked at the face of the Naigu outside the mirror, eyelids fluttering in satisfaction.

Still, he felt uneasy for the rest of that day lest his nose grow long again. Whether intoning scriptures or taking his meals, he would unobtrusively reach up at every opportunity and touch his nose. Each time, he would find it exactly where it belonged, above his upper lip, with no sign that it intended to let itself down any lower. Then came a night of sleep, and the first thing he did upon waking the next day was to feel his nose again. It was still short. Only then did the Naigu begin to enjoy the kind of relief he had experienced once before, years ago, when he had accumulated religious merit for having copied out the entire Lotus Sutra by hand.

Not three full days had passed, however, before the Naigu made a surprising discovery. First, a certain samurai with business at the Ike-no-o temple seemed even more amused than before when, barely speaking to the Naigu, he stared hard at the nose. Then the page who had dropped his nose into the gruel passed him outside the lecture hall; the boy first looked down as he tried to keep his laughter in check, but finally, unable to control himself, he let it burst out. And finally, on more than one occasion, a subordinate priest who remained perfectly respectful while taking orders from the Naigu face-to-face would start giggling as soon as the Naigu had turned away.

At first the Naigu ascribed this behavior to the change in his appearance. But that alone did not seem to explain it sufficiently. True, this may have been what caused the laughter of the page and the subordinate. But the way they were laughing now was somehow different from the way they had laughed before, when his nose was long. Perhaps it was simply that they found the unfamiliar short nose funnier than the familiar long one. But there seemed to be more to it than that.

They never laughed so openly before. Our dear Naigu would sometimes break off intoning the scriptures and mutter this sort of thing to himself, tilting his bald head to one side. His eyes would wander up to the portrait of the Bodhisattva Fugen[3] hanging beside him. And he would sink into gloom, thinking about how it had been for him a few days earlier, when he still had his long nose, "just as he who can now sink no lower fondly recalls his days of glory." The Naigu, unfortunately, lacked the wisdom to find a solution to this problem.

The human heart harbors two conflicting sentiments. Everyone of course sympathizes with people who suffer misfortunes. Yet when those people manage to overcome their misfortunes, we feel a certain disappointment. We may even feel (to overstate the case somewhat) a desire to plunge them back into those misfortunes. And before we know it, we come (if only passively) to harbor some degree of hostility toward them. It was precisely because he sensed this kind of spectator's egoism in both the lay and the priestly communities of Ike-no-o that the Naigu, while unaware of the reason, felt an indefinable malaise.

And so the Naigu's mood worsened with each passing day. He could hardly say a word to people without snapping at them—until finally, even the disciple who had performed the treatment on his nose began to whisper behind his back: "The

Naigu will be punished for treating us so harshly instead of teaching us Buddha's Law." The one who made the Naigu especially angry was that mischievous page. One day the Naigu heard some loud barking, and without giving it much thought, he stepped outside to see what was going on. There, he found the page waving a long stick in pursuit of a scrawny long-haired dog. The boy was not simply chasing after the dog, however. He was also shouting as if for the dog, " 'Can't hit my nose! Ha ha! Can't hit my nose!' " The Naigu ripped the stick from the boy's hand and smacked him in the face with it. Then he realized this "stick" was the slat they had used to hold his nose up at mealtimes.

His nose had been shortened all right, thought the Naigu, but he hated what it was doing to him.

And then one night something happened. The wind must have risen quite suddenly after the sun went down, to judge by the annoying jangle of the pagoda wind chimes that reached him at his pillow. The air was much colder as well, and the aging Naigu was finding it impossible to sleep. Eyes wide open in the darkness, he became aware of a new itching sensation in his nose. He reached up and found the nose slightly swollen to the touch. It (and only it) seemed to be feverish as well.

"We took such drastic steps to shorten it: maybe that gave me some kind of illness," the Naigu muttered to himself, cupping the nose in hands he held as if reverentially offering flowers or incense before the Buddha.

When he woke early as usual the next morning, the Naigu found that the temple's gingko and horse-chestnut trees had dropped their leaves overnight, spreading a bright, golden carpet over the temple grounds. And perhaps because of the frost on the roof of the pagoda, the nine-ring spire atop it flashed in the still-faint glimmer of the rising sun. Standing on the veranda where the latticed shutters had been raised, Zenchi Naigu took a deep breath of morning air.

It was at this moment that an all-but-forgotten sensation returned to him.

The Naigu shot his hand up to his nose, but what he felt there was not the short nose he had touched in the night. It was the same old long nose he had always had, dangling down a good six inches from above his upper lip to below his chin. In the space of a single night, his nose had grown as long as ever. When he realized this, the Naigu felt that same bright sense of relief he had experienced when his nose became short.

Now no one will laugh at me anymore, the Naigu whispered silently in his heart, letting his long nose sway in the dawn's autumn wind.

(January 1916)

DRAGON: THE OLD POTTER'S TALE

When I was still a youngster, there was a Buddhist monk named
E'in living in Nara. Now, E'in had a gigantic nose that was
almost as big as his official title: Former Keeper of His Majesty's
Storehouse and Master of the Profound Dialogue. To make
matters worse, the tip of his huge nose was bright red all year
round, as if it had just been stung by a bee. The people of Nara
called him "Storenose." They had first called him "Bignosed
Former Keeper of His Majesty's Storehouse," but this was too
long a nickname for some, who soon shortened it to "Keeper
of the Storehouse-nose." Even that began to seem too long,
and the next thing you knew everybody was calling him
"Storenose." I myself caught a glimpse of the man once or twice
in the Kōfukuji Temple grounds, and I can tell you he had a
magnificent red monster of a snout that really did look as big
as a storehouse. No wonder people made fun of him!

Well, anyway, one night E'in slipped out of the temple
alone—without his usual band of disciples. He stepped across
the road to Sarusawa Pond, and there, on the embankment by
the Court Maiden's Willow, he erected a signboard proclaiming
in bold calligraphy, "On the third day of the third month, the
dragon of this pond will ascend to heaven." In fact, E'in had
no idea whether a dragon even lived in Sarusawa Pond, and his
announcement that it would ascend to heaven on the third day
of the third month was a total fabrication. He might have been
safer to announce that it would *not* ascend to heaven. Why,
then, would he even bother pulling such a prank? The answer
is that the people of Nara—his priestly brothers and laity
alike—had upset E'in with their constant jokes about his nose.

He was determined to put one over on them and have a good laugh at their expense. This probably sounds ridiculous to you, but it happened a long time ago, and back in those days there were pranksters like this everywhere.

So anyway, the first one to notice the signboard was an old lady who came every morning to worship the Kōfukuji's Buddha. She was holding her prayer beads and trudging along the bank of the pond, leaning on her bamboo stick, when out of the morning mist, beneath the Court Maiden's Willow, emerged a sign that she had not seen the day before. This was a very strange place to put up a sign announcing a service at the temple, she thought, and besides, she didn't know how to read, so she was going to pass on by when, as luck would have it, a monk happened along from the opposite direction and she asked him to tell her what it said.

"On the third day of the third month, the dragon of this pond will ascend to heaven," he read.

This would have come as a surprise to anyone, of course, but the stooped old woman was so stunned she straightened right up and asked the monk, "Could there be a dragon in this pond?"

He, on the other hand, with complete equanimity delivered her a lecture on the spot: "Long ago, in distant Cathay, there was a scholar who had a swelling that formed over one eyebrow. It itched so badly he couldn't stand it. Then suddenly one day the heavens grew overcast and with a clap of thunder the clouds released torrents of rain. No sooner did the scholar see the downpour than his lump burst open and from it a black dragon rose straight up to heaven in a swirl of clouds—or so the story goes. If a dragon could live in a face lump, how much more likely that dozens of dragons or poisonous snakes could be slithering around in a big pond like this just waiting for a chance to soar up to the sky."

Long convinced that a priest would never tell a lie, the old woman could hardly fail to be shocked at his story. "Now that you mention it, the color of the water over there looks a little strange to me," she said, and though it was still far from the third day of the third month, she left the priest and rushed off,

panting the holy name of Amida,[1] too impatient to bother
leaning on her bamboo stick. If no one else had been looking,
the priest would have doubled over with laughter. Because yes,
it was he, the one who had started it all, Master of the Profound
Dialogue, E'in—nickname, Storenose—out walking around the
pond just to see if any unsuspecting pigeons would be taken in
by the signboard he had put up the night before. And no sooner
had the old woman run off than he saw someone else reading
the sign—a woman with a servant carrying her baggage (probably a traveler getting an early start). She was peering up from
under her round straw hat through the veil hanging around the
brim. So then E'in, trying hard as he could not to laugh, walked
up to the signboard and pretended to read it. He snorted in
feigned amazement with that big red nose of his, and then he
strolled back to the Kōfukuji.

At the Great South Gate, E'in ran into Emon, a priest who
lived in the same cell. For eyebrows, this Emon had two cur-
mudgeonly caterpillars, which he screwed up on seeing E'in,
and said, "Well, my brother monk is up unusually early, I see.
I suppose it means the weather's going to change."

Seizing his chance, E'in gave him a triumphant, big-nosed
grin and said, "The weather's not all that's going to change, I
hear. Did you know a dragon's supposed to ascend to heaven
from Sarusawa Pond on the third day of the third month?"

Emon glared at him suspiciously, but then he sniffed and said
with a mocking smile, "Sounds as if my brother monk has had
a pleasant dream. They say a dream about a dragon ascending
to heaven is a good omen."

Holding high his bowl-shaped, flat-topped head, he started
past E'in, but then he seemed to hear E'in muttering to himself,
". . . no salvation for sentient beings without ties to the
Buddha . . ."

Emon dug his hemp-thonged clog into the earth and spun
around angrily as if challenging E'in to a doctrinal debate: "I
don't suppose you've got any proof about that dragon . . . ?"

With a deliberately casual wave in the direction of the pond,
which was now beginning to glitter in the rays of the morning
sun, E'in said dismissively, "If you doubt your brother monk,

I suggest you have a look at the signboard at the Court Maiden's Willow."

This seemed to put at least a crack in the lance of even the stubborn Emon, who squinted and blinked once. "Oh? There's a signboard?" he said feebly and started walking again. This time, instead of holding his head high, he tipped it to one side as if emptying the bowl, a sure sign that E'in had given him something to think about. You can well imagine how amused the Former Keeper of the Storehouse-nose was as he watched Emon walking away. E'in's red nose got a ticklish feeling inside, and even as he solemnly climbed the stone steps of the Great South Gate, he couldn't help exploding with laughter.

The public notice that "On the third day of the third month, the dragon of this pond will ascend to heaven" began working its effect so well on the very first morning that within a day or two people everywhere in Nara were talking about the dragon of Sarusawa Pond. To be sure, there were those who asserted that the signboard was only a prank, but word happened to circulate just then about a dragon ascending from the Shinsen'en Imperial Garden in Kyoto, so even the skeptics began to half-believe and wonder if there were at least *some* possibility that such an awe-inspiring event might occur.

Ten days later, much to everyone's surprise, a truly mysterious event did occur in Nara. The only daughter of a Shintō priest at the Kasuga Shrine—nearly nine years old—was half-dozing on her mother's knee one night when a black dragon came down like a cloud from the sky and spoke to her in human words: "I will soon be ascending to heaven on the third day of the third month, but rest assured I will cause you townspeople no hardship." She woke up and told her mother every detail, and before you knew it everyone in town was talking about how the dragon from Sarusawa Pond had made a dream visitation.

So then the story really started to grow a tail and fins: the dragon took possession of a child from over here and made him write a poem, the dragon appeared to a shrine maiden over there and gave her a divine revelation. There was such a fuss that you expected the dragon of Sarusawa Pond to stick his head up out of the water any minute. One man even swore he

saw the dragon with his own two eyes: maybe not the head
sticking up, but it was the real thing, he was sure. This was an
old man who came to the market every morning to sell river
fish. That particular morning, when he got to Sarusawa Pond,
it was still dark, but right near where the branches of the
Court Maiden's Willow hung down, below the bank where the
signboard stood, he could see that one patch in the predawn
water had a faint glow. Of course, this was just when they were
making all the fuss about the dragon, so his first thought was
that this must be a visitation by the Dragon God himself. He
started shaking all over—either out of joy or fear—set down
his pack of river fish, tiptoed over to the bank, and, hanging
onto the willow branches, peered down into the water. There,
at the bottom of the glowing area, some kind of weird, eerie
thing was sitting stock still, coiled up like an iron chain—but
the sudden sound of a human being may have frightened it: it
started slithering and uncoiling itself, and as it moved away he
watched the trail it stirred up on the surface of the pond until
the eerie thing simply vanished somewhere. Sweating now from
head to toe, the old man came back to where he had left his pack,
but his merchandise—twenty carp and crucian—was gone!
"Some crafty old otter probably tricked him," said those who
laughed at the old man, but a surprisingly large number of people
agreed with this assessment: "No otter could be living in that
pond where His Majesty the Dragon King deigns to rule in peace.
It must be that His Majesty took pity on the fish and to save their
lives he summoned them down to where He Himself resides."

Meanwhile, the more people talked about the proclamation
that "On the third day of the third month, the dragon of this
pond will ascend to heaven," the more the Reverend Storenose
E'in smiled to himself and twitched that big nose of his in
exultation. But then, with only four or five days to go until the
third day of the third month, he was shocked by the sudden
arrival of his aunt, a nun from Sakurai in Settsu Province, who
had made the long trip to see the ascent of the dragon. E'in felt
terrible about this, and he did everything he could—threatening, cajoling—to make her go back to Sakurai, but his aunt
refused to budge.

"I've lived this long," she said, "and if I can do reverence just once at the sight of His Majesty the Dragon King, I can die happy."

In the face of such determined resistance, it was impossible for E'in to confess that he had erected the signboard as a joke. He could only give in and promise not only to see to his aunt's needs until the third day of the third month, but also to escort her on the big day to witness the Dragon God's ascent. Now that he thought about it, if news of the dragon had reached his aunt the nun, then the rumor must have spread not only to the immediate Yamato area and to Settsu, but to Izumi and Kawachi, and maybe even as far as Harima, Yamashiro, Ōmi, and Tamba. The trick he had hoped to play on the people of Nara had ended up fooling tens of thousands of others in the surrounding provinces. He found the thought more frightening than amusing, and the whole time he was showing his aunt the nun around the many temples of Nara from morning to night, he was feeling as guilty as a criminal hiding out from the police. On the other hand, when he heard people on the street saying that flowers and incense were being offered up before the signboard, it not only made him feel strange, it gave him a delicious sense of having accomplished something really big.

The remaining days passed quickly enough, and the third day of the third month arrived, when the dragon was supposed to ascend to heaven. E'in now had no choice but to keep his promise and reluctantly to accompany his aunt the nun to the top of the stone steps of the Kōfukuji's Great South Gate, where they had a panoramic view of Sarusawa Pond. The sky was perfectly clear that day, and it seemed as though there wouldn't be enough of a breeze even to sound the gate's wind chime. The eager spectators poured in—from the town of Nara, of course, but in such numbers that they must also have come from the provinces of Kawachi, Izumi, Settsu, Harima, Yamashiro, Ōmi, and Tamba as well. From his vantage point on the stone steps, E'in took in a sea of people that stretched east and west as far as the eye could see, a milling throng of black caps of all shapes and sizes that filled Nara's main thoroughfare to its far, far end, where it dissolved in the mist. Here and there, the sea of

black was parted by an aristocrat's ox-drawn carriage pushing
its way through, its high canopy done in stylish green or red
with a white sandalwood visor, the gold and silver fittings
mercilessly reflecting the springtime sun into the eyes of the
crowd. Some spectators thrust parasols aloft, others strung up
cloth canopies, and some even went so far as to set up a row of
viewing stands in the middle of the road. From high above, the
scene around the pond was enough to make you think that one
of the great annual Kyoto processions—the Hollyhock Festival,
say—was about to pass by out of season.[2] Never in his wildest
dreams had the Reverend E'in imagined that putting up a simple
signboard would provoke such a commotion as he saw before
him now. Overwhelmed by it all, he could only turn to his aunt
the nun and bleat pitifully, "I can't believe this crowd!" He
didn't even seem to have the energy today for one of his big-
nosed snorts. Instead, he sank down in a pathetic crouch below
a pillar of the Great South Gate.

His aunt the nun had no idea what was going on inside E'in,
of course. She stretched so hard to see everything around her
that she almost lost her hood, and she pelted him with a steady
stream of comments: "You can see there's something special
about this pond: after all, it's where the Dragon God lives,"
she said. Or: "I'm sure the Dragon God will reveal himself
today: just *look* at all these people!" E'in could hardly go on
squatting at the base of the pillar. He dragged himself up to
find a mountain of soft caps and angular samurai hats around
him, but in their midst the Reverend Emon was holding his
bowl-shaped head aloft as usual, his eyes locked on the pond.
E'in immediately forgot his qualms, tickled to think that he had
succeeded in hoodwinking this particular man.

"Brother monk!" he called out to him playfully, "Are *you*
here too to watch the dragon ascend to heaven?"

Emon tossed him a contemptuous glance and, without
moving his bushy caterpillar eyebrows, said with a surprisingly
serious look on his face, "Yes indeed. And I'm finding this wait
just as long as you are."

E'in thought he might have been a bit too hard on his fellow
priest, which put an end to his jovial remarks. Reverting to his

earlier anxious expression, he let his gaze drift over the sea of humans and down to Sarusawa Pond. On its softly glowing, now warmer-looking surface, however, the pond just went on reflecting the still, vivid images of the cherry trees and willows on the surrounding embankment. It gave absolutely no sign that it was ever going to send a dragon aloft. And today especially, rimmed as it was for miles around by an unbroken carpet of spectators, the pond looked a size smaller than usual. The very idea that there could be a dragon in it seemed like a bald-faced lie.

The crowd, however, barely swallowing, continued to wait patiently for the dragon to ascend, as if unconscious of the passing of the hours. The sea of people below the gate kept spreading, and the number of aristocrats' carriages kept growing so that in some places their axle hubs were scraping against one another. You can probably imagine from what I said before how miserable this sight made E'in feel. But then something odd began to happen. Somehow or other, E'in too began to feel that the dragon would actually ascend—though at first, it was more a feeling that he could not be certain it would *not*. Since he was the one who had put the signboard up, you wouldn't think he could possibly entertain such idiotic thoughts, but as he watched the waves of black hats beneath him surging and ebbing, he came to be convinced that some awe-inspiring event was going to take place. Could it be that the feeling shared by the many spectators came at some point to possess Storenose himself? Or might it be that he felt so guilty about the uproar he had caused by simply putting up his signboard that, before he knew it, he had begun wishing with all his might that a dragon really *would* ascend for him? In any case, though he knew perfectly well that he himself had written the words on the signboard, his misgivings began to fade little by little, and he joined his aunt the nun in staring tirelessly at the surface of the pond. In fact, if *not* for some such change in feeling, it would have been impossible for him to spend the better part of a day—even grudgingly—standing beneath the Great South Gate, waiting for a dragon that could not possibly come.

Meanwhile, Sarusawa Pond just kept on reflecting the spring

sunlight without raising a ripple on its surface. The sky
remained so perfectly clear you couldn't have found a cloud
the size of your fist in it. And the spectators, beneath their
parasols or their canopies or behind the railings of their viewing
stands, stayed piled one upon another, seemingly unconscious
that the sunlight was shifting from morning to noon, from noon
to evening, as they waited for the Dragon King to reveal himself
at any moment.

E'in had been there more than half the day when a long, thin
cloud like a trail of incense smoke formed in the air overhead
and began to grow. All at once the clear, tranquil sky turned
dark and a gust of wind blew down to the pond, stirring waves
on its heretofore mirror-like surface. As patient as the spectators
had been, the sudden change sent a flurry through the crowd,
and before they knew it the heavens seemed to tip and pour a
gushing, white shower of rain over them. Horrific thunder
began to peal, and streaks of lightning flashed back and forth
like shuttles weaving a great cloth in the sky. They tore apart a
bank of clouds that had formed an angular mass, and with their
remaining force they seemed to swirl the pond water up into a
mighty pillar. In that instant, between the spray and the clouds,
E'in's eyes caught the faint image of a hundred-foot-long black
dragon rising straight up into the sky, its golden talons flashing.
That lasted but a split-second, and then, I'm told, all you could
see was the storm whipping cherry blossoms from the trees
around the pond up into the pitch-dark sky. The panicked
spectators scattered in all directions under the lightning, in
waves as violent as the pond's—but there's no point in going
into all that now.

Well, then, the torrential downpour soon ended, and blue
sky began to appear between the clouds. E'in looked around
him, wide-eyed, wearing an expression that suggested he had
forgotten all about his big nose. Had his eyes been playing
tricks on him when he saw the image of the dragon? The
thought made him feel—especially since he was the one who
had put up the signboard—that the ascent of the dragon could
not have happened. Still, though, he'd seen what he had seen.
Yet the more he thought about it, the less he could be sure of

anything. His aunt the nun was sitting on the ground next to him at the base of a gate pillar, looking more dead than alive. He helped her up and, unable to hide the strange embarrassment he felt, he asked her timidly, "Did you see the dragon?"

She took a deep breath and, as though terrified and maybe even unable to speak, she just nodded several times. Eventually, though, her voice trembling, she answered, "I did see it. I did. Black all over except for its golden talons flashing: it must have been a Dragon God."

So, then, it wasn't just a trick of the eyes of Storehouse-nose, Master of the Profound Dialogue, E'in. No, when he heard later what people were saying to each other, it turned out that almost everyone gathered there that day—old and young, men and women—had seen the image in the clouds of a black dragon ascending to heaven.

Sometime after that, I hear, on a sudden impulse E'in confessed that he had been the one who erected the signboard, but none of his fellow priests—including Emon—would believe him. So, then, had his prank with the signboard hit the bull's-eye? Or had it missed the target completely? You might try asking that question of Storenose/Storehouse-nose/Big-nosed Former Keeper of His Majesty's Storehouse and Master of the Profound Dialogue, the Reverend E'in, but even he won't be able to give you an answer.

(May 1919)

THE SPIDER THREAD

And now, children, let me tell you a story about Lord Buddha Shakyamuni.[1]

It begins one day as He was strolling alone in Paradise by the banks of the Lotus Pond. The blossoms on the pond were like perfect white pearls, and from their golden centers wafted forth a never-ending fragrance wonderful beyond description. I think it must have been morning in Paradise.

Soon Lord Shakyamuni stepped to the edge of the pond, where He glanced down through the spreading lotus leaves to the spectacle below. Directly beneath the Lotus Pond of Paradise lay the lower depths of Hell, and as He peered through the crystalline waters, He could see the River of Three Crossings and the Mountain of Needles as clearly as if He were viewing pictures in a peep-box.[2]

Down there His eye came to rest upon a man named Kandata, who was writhing in Hell with all the other sinners. This great robber had done many evil deeds: he had even killed people, and burned down houses. But it seems that Kandata had performed one single act of goodness. Passing through a deep wood one day, he had noticed a tiny spider creeping along the wayside. His first thought was to stamp it to death, but as he raised his foot, he told himself, "No, no. Even this puny creature is a living thing. To take its life for no reason would be too cruel." And so he had let it pass unharmed.

Now, as He looked down at the nether world, Lord Shakyamuni recalled how Kandata had saved the spider, and He decided to reward him for it by delivering him from Hell if possible. By happy chance, He turned to see a heavenly spider spinning a beautiful silver thread atop a lotus leaf the color of shimmering jade. Gently lifting the spider thread, He lowered it straight down through the pearl-like blossoms to the depths far below.

2

Here, with the other sinners at the low-point of the lowest Hell, Kandata was endlessly floating up and sinking down again in the Pond of Blood. Wherever he looked there was only pitch darkness, and when a faint shape did pierce the shadows, it was the glint of a needle on the horrible Mountain of Needles, which only heightened his sense of doom. All was silent as the grave, and when a faint sound did break the stillness, it was the feeble sigh of a sinner. As you can imagine, those who had fallen this far had been so worn down by their tortures in the seven other hells that they no longer had the strength to cry out. Great robber though he was, Kandata could only thrash about like a dying frog as he choked on the blood of the pond.

And then, children, what do you think happened next? Yes, indeed: raising his head, Kandata chanced to look up toward the sky above the Pond of Blood and saw the gleaming silver spider thread, so slender and delicate, slipping stealthily down through the silent darkness from the high, high heavens, coming straight for *him*! Kandata clapped his hands in joy. If only he could take hold of this thread and climb up and up, he could probably escape from Hell. And maybe, with luck, he could even enter Paradise. Then he would never again be driven up the Mountain of Needles or plunged down into the Pond of Blood.

No sooner had the thought crossed his mind than Kandata grasped the spider thread and started climbing with all his might, higher and higher. As a great robber, Kandata had had plenty of practice at this kind of hand-over-hand rope climbing.

Hell and Heaven, though, are untold thousands of leagues apart, so it was not easy even for a man like Kandata to escape, no matter how hard he tried. He soon began to tire, until he couldn't raise his arm for even one more pull. He had no choice but to stop for a rest, and as he clung to the spider thread, he looked down far below.

Then he realized that all his climbing had been worth the effort: the Pond of Blood was hidden now in the depths of the darkness. And even the dull glint of the terrifying Mountain of Needles was far down beneath his feet. At this rate, it might be easier than he had imagined to climb his way out of Hell. Twining his hands in the spider thread, Kandata laughed aloud as he had not in all the years since he had come to this place: "I've done it! I've done it!"

And then what do you think he saw? Far down on the spider thread, countless sinners had followed after him, and they were clambering up the thread with all their might like a column of ants! The sight struck him with such shock and fear that for a time his mouth gaped open like an idiot's; only his eyes moved. This slim thread seemed likely to snap from his weight alone: how could it possibly hold so many people? If it were to break midway, then Kandata himself would plummet back down into the Hell he had struggled so mightily to escape. How terrible that would be! Still, from the pitch-dark Pond of Blood, an unbroken column of sinners came squirming up the fragile, gleaming thread by the hundreds—by the thousands. He knew he would have to do something now or the thread would break in two.

Kandata screamed at them, "Listen to me, you sinners! This spider thread is *mine*! Who said *you* could climb it? Get off! Get off!"

At that very instant the spider thread, which until then had been perfectly fine, broke with a "snap!" just where Kandata was hanging from it. Before he could even cry out, Kandata fell, slicing through the air, spinning like a top, down head-first into the darkest depths.

Behind him all that remained was the dangling short end of the spider thread from Paradise, delicately gleaming in the moonless, starless sky.

3

Standing at the edge of the Lotus Pond in Paradise, Lord Shakyamuni watched everything that happened. And when, in the end, Kandata sank like a stone into the Pond of Blood, the Holy One resumed His stroll, His face now tinged with sorrow. Kandata had thought to save himself alone, and as just punishment for this lack of compassion, he had fallen back into Hell. How shameful it must have seemed in the eyes of Lord Shakyamuni!

The lotuses of the Lotus Pond, however, were unperturbed. They swayed their perfect pearl-white blossoms near the feet of Lord Shakyamuni, and from their golden centers wafted forth each time a never-ending fragrance wonderful beyond description. I think it must have been close to noon in Paradise.

(April 1918)

HELL SCREEN

I

I am certain there has never been anyone like our great Lord of Horikawa, and I doubt there ever will be another. In a dream before His Lordship was born, Her Maternal Ladyship saw the awesomely armed Guardian Deity of the West—or so people say. In any case, His Lordship seemed to have innate qualities that distinguished him from ordinary human beings. And because of this, his accomplishments never ceased to amaze us. You need only glance at his mansion in the Capital's Horikawa district to sense the boldness of its conception. Its—how shall I put it?—its grandeur, its heroic scale are beyond the reach of our mediocre minds. Some have questioned the wisdom of His Lordship's undertaking such a project, comparing him to China's First Emperor, whose subjects were forced to build the Great Wall, or to the Sui emperor Yang,[1] who made his people erect lofty palaces; but such critics might be likened to the proverbial blind men who described the elephant according only to the parts they could feel. It was never His Lordship's intention to seek splendor and glory for himself alone. He was always a man of great magnanimity who shared his joys with the wider world, so to speak, and kept in mind even the lowliest of his subjects.

Surely this is why he was left unscathed by his encounter with that midnight procession of goblins so often seen at the lonely intersection of Nijō-Ōmiya in the Capital;[2] it is also why, when rumor had it that the ghost of Tōru, Minister of the Left, was appearing night after night at the site of his ruined mansion by the river at Higashi-Sanjō (you must know it: where the minister had recreated the famous seascape of Shiogama in his garden), it took only a simple rebuke from His Lordship to make the spirit vanish.[3] In the face of such resplendent majesty, no wonder all residents of the Capital—old and young, men and women—revered His Lordship as a reincarnation of the Buddha. One time, it is said, His Lordship was returning from a plum-blossom banquet at the Palace when the ox pulling his carriage got loose and injured an old man who happened to be passing by. The old fellow knelt and clasped his hands in prayerful thanks for having been caught on the horns of His Lordship's own ox!

So many, many stories about His Lordship have been handed down. His Imperial Majesty himself once presented His Lordship with thirty pure white horses on the occasion of a New Year's banquet. Another time, when construction of the Nagara Bridge seemed to be running counter to the will of the local deity, His Lordship offered up a favorite boy attendant as a human sacrifice to be buried at the foot of a pillar.[4] And then there was the time when, to have a growth cut from his thigh, he summoned the Chinese monk who had brought the art of surgery to our country. Oh, there's no end to the tales! For sheer horror, though, none of them measures up to the story of the screen depicting scenes of hell which is now a prized family heirloom. Even His Lordship, normally so imperturbable, was horrified by what happened, and those of us who waited upon him—well, it goes without saying that we were shocked out of our minds. I myself had served as one of His Lordship's men for a full twenty years, but what I witnessed then was more terrible than anything I had ever—or *have* ever—experienced.

In order to tell you the story of the hell screen, however, I must first tell you about the painter who created it. His name was Yoshihide.

2

I suspect that even now there are ladies and gentlemen who would recognize the name "Yoshihide." He was famous back then as the greatest painter in the land, but he had reached the age of perhaps fifty, and he looked like nothing more than a thoroughly unpleasant little old man, all skin and bones. He dressed normally enough for his appearances at His Lordship's mansion—in a reddish-brown, broad-sleeved silk robe and a tall black hat with a soft bend to the right—but as a person he was anything but normal. You could see he had a mean streak, and his lips, unnaturally red for such an old man, gave a disturbing, bestial impression. Some people said the redness came from his moistening his paint brush with his lips, but I wonder about that. Crueler tongues used to say that he looked and moved like a monkey, and they went so far as to give Yoshihide the nickname "Monkeyhide."

Ah, that nickname reminds me of an episode. Yoshihide had a daughter, his only child—a sweet, lovely girl utterly unlike her father. She had been taken into the Horikawa mansion as a junior lady-in-waiting for His Lordship's own daughter, the Young Mistress. Perhaps because she lost her mother at a tender age, she had an unusually mature and deeply sympathetic nature and a cleverness beyond her years, and everyone from Her Ladyship on down loved the girl for her quickness to notice others' every need.

Around that time someone from the Tamba Province presented His Lordship with a tame monkey, and the Young Master, who was then at the height of his boyish naughtiness, decided to name it "Yoshihide." The monkey was a funny-looking little creature as it was, but capping it with that name gave everyone in the household a hearty laugh. Oh, if only they had been satisfied just to laugh! But whatever the monkey did—whether climbing to the top of the garden pine, or soiling the mats of a staff member's room—people would find a reason to torment it, and always with a shout of "Yoshihide!"

Then one day, as Yoshihide's daughter was gliding down a long outdoor corridor to deliver a note gaily knotted on a branch of red winter plum, the monkey Yoshihide darted in through the sliding door at the far end, in full flight from something. The animal was running with a limp and seemed unable to climb a post as it often did when frightened. Then who should appear chasing after it but the Young Master, brandishing a switch and shouting, "Come back here, you tangerine thief! Come back here!" Yoshihide's daughter drew up short at the sight, and the monkey clung to her skirts with a pitiful cry. This must have aroused her compassion, for, still holding the plum branch in one hand, she swept the monkey up in the soft folds of her lavender sleeve. Then, giving a little bow to the Young Master, she said with cool clarity, "Forgive me for interfering, my young lord, but he is just an animal. Please pardon him."

Temper still up from the chase, the Young Master scowled and stamped his foot several times. "Why are you protecting him?" he demanded. "He stole my tangerine!"

"He is just an animal," she repeated. "He doesn't know any better." And then, smiling sadly, she added, "His name is Yoshihide, after all. I can't just stand by and watch 'my father' being punished." This was apparently enough to break the Young Master's will.

"All right, then," he said with obvious reluctance. "If you're pleading for your father's life, I'll let him off this time."

The Young Master flung his switch into the garden and stalked back out through the sliding door.

3

After this incident, Yoshihide's daughter and the little monkey grew close. The girl had a golden bell that her young mistress had given her, which she hung from the monkey's neck on a pretty crimson cord. And he, for his part, would almost never leave her side. Once, when she was in bed with a cold, the monkey spent hours by her pillow, biting its nails, and I swear it had a worried look on its face.

Then, strangely enough, people stopped teasing the monkey. In fact, they began treating it with special kindness, until even the Young Master would occasionally throw it a persimmon or a chestnut, and I heard he once flew into a rage when one of the samurai kicked the animal. Soon after that, His Lordship himself ordered the girl to appear before him with the monkey in her arms—all because, in hearing about the Young Master's tantrum, I am told, he naturally also heard about how the girl had come to care for the monkey.

"I admire your filial behavior," His Lordship said. "Here, take this." And he presented her with a fine scarlet underrobe. They tell me that his Lordship was especially pleased when the monkey, imitating the girl's expression of gratitude, bowed low before him, holding the robe aloft. And so His Lordship's partiality for the girl was born entirely from his wish to commend her filial devotion to her father and not, as rumor had it, from any physical attraction he might have felt for her. Not that such suspicions were entirely groundless, but there will be time for me to tell you about that later. For now, suffice it to say that His Lordship was not the sort of person to lavish his affections on the daughter of a mere painter, however beautiful she might be.

Well, then, having been singled out for praise this way, Yoshihide's daughter withdrew from His Lordship's presence, but she knew how to avoid provoking the envy of the household's other, less modest, ladies-in-waiting. Indeed, people grew fonder than ever of her and the monkey, and the Young Mistress almost never let them leave her side, even bringing them with her in her ox-drawn carriage when she went to observe shrine rituals and the like.

But enough about the girl for now. Let me continue with my story of her father, Yoshihide. As I have said, the monkey Yoshihide quickly became everyone's little darling, but Yoshihide himself remained an object of universal scorn, reviled as "Monkeyhide" by everyone behind his back. And not only in the Horikawa mansion. Even such an eminent Buddhist prelate as the Abbot of Yokawa hated Yoshihide so much that the very mention of his name was enough to make him turn purple as if he had seen a devil. (Some said this was because Yoshihide had drawn a caricature ridiculing certain aspects of the Abbot's behavior, but this was merely a rumor that circulated among the lower classes and as such can hardly be credited.) In any case, Yoshihide's reputation was so bad that anyone you asked would have told you the same thing. If there were those who spoke kindly of Yoshihide, they were either a handful of the brotherhood of painters or else people who knew his work but not the man himself.

His appearance was not the only thing that people hated about Yoshihide. In fact, he had many evil traits that repelled them even more, and for which he had only himself to blame.

4

For one thing, Yoshihide was a terrible miser; he was harsh in his dealings with people; he had no shame; he was lazy and greedy. But worst of all, he was insolent and arrogant. He never let you forget that he was "the greatest painter in the land." Nor was his arrogance limited to painting. He could not be satisfied till he displayed his contempt for every custom and convention that ordinary people practiced. A man who was his apprentice for many years once told me this story: Yoshihide was present one day in the mansion of a certain gentleman when the celebrated Shamaness of the Cypress Enclosure was there, undergoing spirit possession. The woman delivered a horrifying message from the spirit, but Yoshihide was unimpressed. He took up a handy ink brush and did a detailed sketch of her wild expression as if he viewed spirit possession as mere trickery.

No wonder, then, that such a man would commit acts of sacrilege in his work: in painting the lovely goddess Kisshōten, he used the face of a common harlot, and to portray the mighty flame-draped Fudō, his model was a criminal released to do chores in the Magistrate's office. If you tried to warn him that he was flirting with danger, he would respond with feigned innocence. "*I'm* the one who painted them, after all," he would say. "Are you trying to tell me that my own Buddhas and gods are going to punish me?" Even his apprentices were shocked by this. I myself knew several of them who, fearing for their own punishment in the afterlife, wasted no time in leaving his employ. The man's arrogance simply knew no bounds. He was convinced that he was the greatest human being under heaven.

It goes without saying that Yoshihide lorded it over the other painters of his time. True, his brushwork and colors were utterly

different from theirs, and so the many painters with whom he
was on bad terms tended to speak of him as a charlatan. They
rhapsodized over the work of old masters such as Kawanari or
Kanaoka[5] ("On moonlit nights you could actually *smell* the
plum blossoms painted on that wooden door," or "You could
actually *hear* the courtier on that screen playing his flute"), but
all they had to say about Yoshihide's work was how eerie and
unsettling they found it. Take his *Five Levels of Rebirth* on the
Ryūgaiji temple gate,[6] for example. "When I passed the gate
late at night," one said, "I could hear the dying celestials sighing
and sobbing." "That's nothing," another claimed. "I could
smell the flesh of the dead rotting." "And how about the
portraits of the household's ladies-in-waiting that His Lordship
ordered from Yoshihide? Every single woman he painted fell ill
and died within three years. It was as if he had snatched their
very souls from them." According to one of his harshest critics,
this was the final proof that Yoshihide practiced the Devil's Art.

But Yoshihide was so perverse, as I've said, that remarks like
this only filled him with pride. When His Lordship joked to
him one time, "For you, it seems, the uglier the better," old
Yoshihide's far-too-red lips spread in an eerie grin and he
replied imperiously, "Yes, My Lord, it's true. Other painters
are such mediocrities, they cannot appreciate the beauty of
ugliness." I must say, "Greatest Painter in the Land" or not, it
was incredible that he could spout such self-congratulatory
nonsense in His Lordship's presence! No wonder his apprentices called him Chira Eiju behind his back! You know: Chira
Eiju, the long-nosed goblin who crossed over from China long
ago to spread the sin of arrogance.

But still, even Yoshihide, in all his incredible perversity—yes,
even Yoshihide displayed human tenderness when it came to
one thing.

5

By this I mean that Yoshihide was truly mad about his only
daughter, the young lady-in-waiting. The girl was, as I said
before, a wonderfully kind-hearted young creature deeply

devoted to her father, and his love for her was no less strong than hers for him. I gather that he provided for her every need—every robe, every hair ornament—without the slightest objection. Don't you find this incredible for a man who had never made a single contribution to a temple?

Yoshihide's love for his daughter, however, remained just that: love. It never occurred to him that he should be trying to find her a good husband someday. Far from it: he was not above hiring street thugs to beat up anyone who might make improper advances to her. So even when His Lordship honored her with the position of junior lady-in-waiting in his own household, Yoshihide was far from happy about it, and for a while he always wore a sour expression whenever he was in His Lordship's presence. I have no doubt that people who witnessed this display were the ones who began speculating that His Lordship had been attracted to the girl's beauty when he ordered her into service despite her father's objections.

Such rumors were entirely false, of course. It was nothing but Yoshihide's obsessive love for his daughter that kept him wishing to have her step down from service, that is certain. I remember the time His Lordship ordered Yoshihide to do a painting of Monju[7] as a child, and Yoshihide pleased him greatly with a marvelous work that used one of His Lordship's own boy favorites as a model. "You can have anything you want as your reward," said His Lordship. "Anything at all."

Yoshihide should have been awestruck to hear such praise from His Lordship's own lips, and he did in fact prostrate himself in thanks before him, but can you imagine what he asked? "If it please Your Lordship, I beg you to return my daughter to her former lowly state." The impudence of the man! This was no ordinary household, after all. No matter how much he loved his daughter, to beg for her release from service in privileged proximity to the great Lord of Horikawa himself—where in the world does one find such audacity? Not even a man as grandly magnanimous as His Lordship could help feeling some small annoyance at such a request, as was evident from the way he stared at Yoshihide for a while in silence.

Presently he spoke: "That will not happen," he said, all but spitting out the words, and he abruptly withdrew.

This was not the first nor the last such incident: I think there might have been four or five in all. And with each repetition, it seemed to me, His Lordship gazed on Yoshihide with increasing coldness. The girl, for her part, seemed to fear for her father's welfare. Often she could be seen sobbing quietly to herself in her room, teeth clamped on her sleeve. All this only reinforced the rumor that His Lordship was enamored of the girl. People also said that the command to paint the screen had something to do with her rejection of His Lordship's advances, but that, of course, could not be so.

As I see it, it was entirely out of pity for the girl's situation that His Lordship refused to let her go. I am certain he believed, with great generosity, that she would be far better off if he were to keep her in his mansion and enable her to live in comfort than if he sent her back to her hardheaded old father. That he was partial to her, of course, there could be no doubt: she was such a sweet-tempered young thing. But to assert that he took his lustful pleasure with her is a view that springs from twisted reasoning. No, I would have to call it a groundless falsehood.

At any rate, owing to these matters regarding his daughter, this was a period when Yoshihide was in great disfavor with His Lordship. Suddenly one day, for whatever reason, His Lordship summoned Yoshihide and ordered him to paint a folding screen portraying scenes from the eight Buddhist hells.

6

Oh, that screen! I can almost see its terrifying images of hell before me now!

Other artists painted what they called images of hell, but their compositions were nothing like Yoshihide's. He had the Ten Kings of Hell and their minions over in one small corner, and everything else—the entire screen—was enveloped in a firestorm so terrible you thought the swirling flames were going to melt the Mountain of Sabers and the Forest of Swords. Aside from the vaguely Chinese costumes of the Judges of the Dark, with their swatches of yellow and indigo, all you saw was the searing color of flames and, dancing wildly among them, black smoke clouds of hurled India ink and flying sparks of blown-on gold dust.

These alone were enough to shock and amaze any viewer, but the sinners writhing in the hellfire of Yoshihide's powerful brush had nothing in common with those to be seen in ordinary pictures of hell. For Yoshihide had included sinners from all stations in life, from the most brilliant luminary of His Majesty's exalted circle to the basest beggar and outcast. A courtier in magnificent ceremonial vestments, a nubile lady-in-waiting in five-layered robes, a rosary-clutching priest intoning the holy name of Amida, a samurai student on high wooden clogs, an aristocratic little girl in a simple shift, a Yin-Yang diviner swishing his paper wand through the air: I could never name them all. But there they were, human beings of every kind, inundated by smoke and flame, tormented by wardens of hell with their heads of bulls and horses, and driven in all directions like autumn leaves scattering before a great wind. "Oh, look at that one," you would say, "the one with her hair all tangled up in a forked lance and her arms and legs drawn in tighter than a spider's: could she be one of those shrine maidens who perform for the gods? And, oh, *that* fellow there, hanging upside-down like a bat, his breast pierced by a short lance: surely he is supposed to be a greenhorn provincial governor." And the kinds of torture were as numberless as the sinners themselves—flogging with an iron scourge, crushing under a gigantic rock, pecking by a monstrous bird, grinding in the jaws of a poisonous serpent . . .

But surely the single most horrifying image of all was that of a carriage plummeting through space. As it fell, it grazed the upper boughs of a sword tree, where clumps of corpses were skewered on fang-like branches. Blasts of hell wind swept up the carriage curtains to reveal a court lady so gorgeously appareled she might have been one of His Imperial Majesty's own Consorts or Intimates, her straight black hip-length hair flying upward in the flames, the full whiteness of her throat laid bare as she writhed in agony. Every detail of the woman's form and the blazing carriage filled the viewer with an agonizing sense of the hideous torments to be found in the Hell of Searing Heat. The sheer horror of the entire screen—might I say?— seemed to be concentrated in this one figure. It had been executed with such inspired workmanship, you'd think that all who saw it could hear the woman's dreadful screams.

Oh yes, this was it: for the sake of painting this one image, the terrible event occurred. Otherwise, how could even the great Yoshihide have painted hell's torments so vividly? It was his cruel fate to lose his life in exchange for completing the screen. In a sense, the hell in his painting was the hell into which Yoshihide himself, the greatest painter in the realm, was doomed one day to fall.

I am afraid that, in my haste to speak of the screen with its unusual images of hell, I may have reversed the order of my story. Now let me continue with the part about Yoshihide when he received His Lordship's command to do a painting of hell.

7

For nearly six months after the commission, Yoshihide poured all his energy into the screen, never once calling at His Lordship's residence. Don't you find it strange that such a doting father should abandon all thought of seeing his daughter once he had started on a painting? According to the apprentice I mentioned earlier, Yoshihide always approached his work like a man possessed by a fox spirit.[8] In fact, people used to say that the only reason Yoshihide was able to make such a name for himself in art was that he had pledged his soul to one of the great gods of fortune; what proved it was that if you peeked in on him when he was painting, you could always see shadowy fox spirits swarming all around him. What this means, I suspect, is that, once he picked up his brush, Yoshihide thought of nothing else but completing the painting before him. He would spend all day and night shut up in his studio out of sight. His concentration seems to have been especially intense when he was working on this particular screen with its images of hell.

This is not merely to say that he would keep the latticed

shutters pulled down and spend all day by the tripod oil lamp, mixing secret combinations of paint or posing his apprentices in various costumes for him to sketch. No, that was normal behavior for the working Yoshihide, even before this screen. Remember, this was the man who, when he was painting his *Five Levels of Rebirth* on the Ryūgaiji temple gate, went out specially to inspect a corpse lying on the roadside—the kind of sight from which any ordinary person would recoil—and spent hours sitting before it, sketching its rotting face and limbs without missing a hair. I don't blame you, then, if you are among those who cannot imagine what I mean when I say that his concentration during his work on the hell screen was especially intense. I haven't time now to explain this in detail, but I can at least tell you the most important things.

One day an apprentice of Yoshihide's (the one I've mentioned a few times already) was busy dissolving pigments when the master suddenly said to him, "I'm planning to take a nap but, I don't know, I've been having bad dreams lately."

There was nothing strange about this, so the apprentice merely answered, "I see, Sir," and continued with his work.

Yoshihide, however, was not his usual self. Somewhat hesitantly, and with a doleful look on his face, he made a surprising request: "I want you to sit and work beside me while I sleep."

The apprentice thought it rather odd that his master should be worrying about dreams, but it was a simple enough request and he promptly agreed to it.

"All right, then," Yoshihide said, still looking worried, "come inside right away." He hesitated. "And when the other apprentices arrive," he added, "don't let any of them in where I am sleeping."

"Inside" meant the room where the master actually did his painting, and as usual on this day, the apprentice told me, its doors and windows were shut as tightly as at night. In the dull glow of an oil lamp stood the large folding screen, its panels arranged in a semi-circle and still only sketched out in charcoal. Yoshihide lay down with his head pillowed on his forearm and slipped into the deep sleep of an utterly exhausted man. Hardly any time had gone by, however, when the apprentice began to hear a sound that he had no way of describing. It was a voice, he told me, but a strange and eerie one.

8

At first, it was just a sound, but soon, in snatches, the voice began to form words that came to him as if from under water, like the muffled cries of a drowning man. "Wha-a-a-t?" the voice said, "You want me to come with you? . . . Where? Where are you taking me? To hell, you say. To the Hell of Searing Heat, you say. Who . . . who are you, damn you? Who can you be but—"

The apprentice, dissolving pigments, felt his hands stop of their own accord. He peered fearfully through the gloom at his master's face. Not only had the furrowed skin gone stark white, but fat beads of sweat oozed from it, and the dry-lipped, snaggle-toothed mouth strained wide open as if gasping for breath. The youth saw something moving in his master's mouth with dizzying speed, like an object being yanked by a cord, but then—imagine!—he realized the thing was Yoshihide's tongue. The fragmented speech had been coming from that tongue of his.

"Who could it be but—*you*, damn you. It *is* you! I thought so! What's that? You've come to show me the way there? You want me to follow you. To hell! My daughter is waiting for me in hell!"

The apprentice told me that an uncanny feeling overcame him at that point—his eyes seemed to make out vague, misshapen shadows that slid over the surface of the screen and flooded down upon the two of them. Naturally, he immediately reached over and shook Yoshihide as hard as he could; but rather than waking, the master, in a dreamlike state, went on talking to himself and showed no sign of regaining consciousness. Desperate now, the apprentice grabbed the jar for washing brushes and splashed all the water into Yoshihide's face.

"I'm waiting for you," Yoshihide was saying, "so hurry and get into the cart. Come along to hell!" but the moment the water hit him his words turned to a strangled moan. At last he opened his eyes, and he sprang up more wildly than if he had been jabbed with a needle. But the misshapen creatures must have been with him still, for he stared into space, with mouth agape and with terrified eyes. At length he returned to himself and, without a hint of gratitude, barked at the poor apprentice, "I'm all right now. Get out of here."

The apprentice knew he would be scolded if he resisted his master at a time like this, so he hurried out of the room, but he told me that when he saw the sunlight again he felt as relieved as if he were waking from his own nightmare.

This was by no means Yoshihide at his worst, however. A month later he called yet another apprentice into the inner room. The young man found Yoshihide standing in the gloom of the oil lamps biting the end of his paintbrush. Without a moment's hesitation, Yoshihide turned to him and said, "Sorry, but I need you naked again." The master had ordered such things in the past, so the apprentice quickly stripped off his clothes, but now Yoshihide said with a strange scowl, "I want to see a person in chains, so do what I tell you. Sorry about this, but it will just take a little while." Yoshihide could mouth apologetic phrases, but he issued his cold commands without the least show of sympathy. This particular apprentice was a well-built lad who looked more suited to wielding a sword than a paintbrush, but even he must have been shocked by what happened. "I figured the Master had gone crazy and was going to kill me," he told people again and again long afterward. Yoshihide was apparently annoyed by the young man's slow preparations. Instead of waiting, he dragged out a narrow iron chain from heaven knows where and all but pounced on the apprentice's back, wrenching the man's arms behind him and winding him in the chain. Then he gave the end of the chain a cruel yank and sent the young man crashing down on the floor.

9

The apprentice lay there like—what?—like a keg of saké that someone had knocked over. Legs and arms mercilessly contorted, he could move only his head. And with the chain cutting off the circulation of his blood, you know, his skin swelled red—face, torso, everywhere. Yoshihide, though, was apparently not the least bit concerned to see him like this; he circled this saké-keg of a body, observing it from every angle and drawing sketch after sketch. I am certain that, without my spelling it out, you can imagine what torture this must have been for the poor apprentice.

If nothing had interrupted it, the young man's ordeal would almost surely have lasted even longer, but fortunately (or perhaps unfortunately) a narrow, winding streak like black oil began to flow from behind a large jar in the corner of the room. At first it moved slowly, like a thick liquid, but then it began to slide along the floor more smoothly, glinting in the darkness until it was almost touching the apprentice's nose. He took a good look at it, gasped and screamed, "A snake! A snake!" The way he described the moment to me, he felt as if every drop of blood in his body would freeze, which I can well understand, for in fact the snake's cold tongue was just about to touch the flesh of his neck where the chain was biting. Even Yoshihide, for all his perversity, must have felt a rush of horror at this unforeseeable occurrence. Flinging his brush down, he bent and gripped the snake by the tail, dangling it upside-down. The snake raised its head and began to coil upward around its own body, but it could not reach Yoshihide's hand.

"You cost me a good brush stroke, damn you," he growled at the snake, flinging it into the jar in the corner. Then, with obvious reluctance, he loosened the chains that bound the apprentice's body. In fact, loosening the chains was as far as he was willing to go: for the youth himself he spared not a word of sympathy. I suspect he was more enraged at having botched a single brush stroke than concerned that his apprentice might have been bitten by a snake. I heard afterward that he had been keeping the snake to sketch from.

I imagine that what little you have heard is enough for you to grasp the fanatic intensity with which Yoshihide approached his work. But let me give you one last terrible example concerning a young apprentice—no more than thirteen or fourteen—who could have lost his life for the hell screen. It happened one night when the boy, whose skin was fair as a girl's, was called into the master's studio. There he found Yoshihide by the tripod lamp balancing a piece of raw meat on his palm and feeding it to a bird the likes of which he had never seen before. The bird was the size of a cat, and in fact, with its two feather tufts sticking out from its head like ears and its big, round amber-colored eyes, it did look very much like a cat.

10

Yoshihide was a man who simply hated to have anyone pry into his business, and—the snake I told you about was one such case—he would never let his apprentices know what kinds of things he had in his studio. Depending on the subject he happened to be painting at the time, he might have a human skull perched on his table, or rows of silver bowls and gold-lacquered stands—you never knew. And his helpers told me they had no idea where he kept such things when he was not using them. This was surely one reason for the rumor that Yoshihide was the beneficiary of miraculous aid from a god of fortune.

Well then, the young apprentice, assuming for himself that the strange bird on the table was a model Yoshihide needed for the hell screen, knelt before the painter and asked in all humility, "How can I help you, Master?"

Almost as if he had not heard the boy speak, Yoshihide licked his red lips and jerked his chin toward the bird. "Not bad, eh? Look how tame it is."

"Please tell me, Master, what is it? I have never seen anything like it before," the boy said, keeping his wary gaze fixed on the cat-like bird with ears.

"What? Never seen anything like it?" Yoshihide responded with his familiar scornful laugh. "That's what you get for growing up in the Capital! It's a bird. A horned owl. A hunter brought it to me a few days ago from Mount Kurama. Only, you don't usually find them so tame."

As he spoke, Yoshihide slowly raised his hand and gave a soft upward stroke to the feathers of the owl's back just as the bird finished swallowing the chunk of meat. Instantly the bird emitted a shriek and leaped from the table top, aiming its outstretched talons at the apprentice's face. Had the boy not shot his arm out to protect himself, I have no doubt that he would have ended up with more than a gash or two on his face. He cried out and shook his sleeve in an attempt to sweep the bird away, which only added to the fury of the attack. Beak clattering, the owl lunged at him again. Disregarding Yoshihide's presence, the apprentice ran wildly around the cramped room, now standing to defend himself, now crouching to drive the bird away. The monster, of course, stuck with him, flying up when he stood up and down when he crouched down, and using any opening to go straight for his eyes. With each lunge came a tremendous flapping of wings that filled the boy with dread. He felt so lost, he said later, that the familiar studio felt like a haunted valley deep in the mountains, with the smell of rotting leaves, the spray of a waterfall, the sour fumes of fruit stashed away by a monkey; even the dim glow of the master's oil lamp on its tripod looked to him like misty moonlight in the hills.

Being attacked by the owl, however, was not what most frightened the lad. What really made his flesh crawl was the way the master Yoshihide followed the commotion with his cold stare, taking his time to spread out a piece of paper, lick his brush, and then set about capturing the terrible image of a delicate boy being tormented by a hideous bird. At the sight, the apprentice was overcome by an inexpressible terror. For a time, he says, he even thought his master might kill him.

I I

And you actually couldn't say that such a thing was out of the question. For it did seem that Yoshihide's sole purpose in calling the apprentice to his studio that night had been to set the owl on him and draw him trying to escape. Thus, when the apprentice caught that glimpse of his master at work, he felt his arms come up to protect his head and heard an incoherent scream escape his throat as he slumped down against the sliding door in the corner of the room. In that same instant Yoshihide himself cried out and jumped to his feet, whereupon the beating of the owl's wings grew faster and louder and there came the clatter of something falling over and a tearing sound. Having covered his head in terror, the apprentice now raised it again to find that the room had gone pitch dark, and he heard Yoshihide's angry voice calling to the other apprentices.

Eventually there was a far-off cry in response, and soon an apprentice rushed in with a lantern held high. In its sooty-smelling glow, the boy saw the tripod collapsed on the floor and the mats and planking soaked in the oil of the overturned lamp. He saw the owl, too, beating one wing in apparent pain as it flopped around the room. On the far side of the table, looking stunned, Yoshihide was raising himself from the floor and muttering something incomprehensible. And no wonder! That black snake was tightly coiled around the owl from neck to tail and over one wing. The apprentice had probably knocked the jar over as he slumped to the floor, and when the snake crawled out, the owl must have made the mistake of trying to grab it in its talons, only to give rise to this struggle. The two apprentices gaped at the bizarre scene and at each other until, with a silent bow to the master, they slipped out of the room. What happened to the owl and snake after that, no one knows.

This was by no means the only such incident. I forgot to mention that it was the beginning of autumn when His Lordship commanded Yoshihide to paint the hell screen; from then until the end of winter the apprentices were continually subjected to their master's frightening behavior. At that point, however, something seemed to interfere with Yoshihide's work on the screen. An even deeper layer of gloom came to settle over him, and he spoke to his assistants in markedly harsher tones. The screen was perhaps eight-tenths finished, but it showed no further signs of progress. Indeed, Yoshihide occasionally seemed to be on the verge of painting over those parts that he had already completed.

No one knew what he was finding so difficult about the screen, and what's more, no one tried to find out. Stung by those earlier incidents, his apprentices felt as if they were locked

in a cage with a tiger or a wolf, and they found ways to keep
their distance from the master.

12

For that reason, I have little to tell you about that period. The
only unusual thing I can think of is that the hardheaded old
codger suddenly turned weepy; people would often see him
shedding tears when he was alone. An apprentice told me that
one day he walked into the garden and saw the master standing
on the veranda, gazing blankly at the sky with its promise of
spring, his eyes full of tears. Embarrassed for the old man, the
apprentice says, he silently withdrew. Don't you find it odd
that this arrogant man, who went so far as to sketch a corpse
on the roadside for his *Five Levels of Rebirth*, would cry like
an infant just because the painting of the screen wasn't going
as well as he wanted it to?

In any case, while Yoshihide was madly absorbed in his work
on the screen, his daughter began to show increasing signs of
melancholy, until the rest of us could see that she was often
fighting back her tears. A pale, reserved, sad-faced girl to begin
with, she took on a genuinely mournful aspect as her lashes
grew heavy and shadows began to form around her eyes. This
gave rise to all sorts of speculation—that she was worried
about her father, or that she was suffering the pangs of love—
but soon people were saying that it was all because His Lordship was trying to bend her to his will. Then the gossiping
ground to a halt, as though everyone had suddenly forgotten
about her.

A certain event occurred at that time. Well after the first
watch of the night, I was walking down an outdoor corridor
when the monkey Yoshihide came flying at me from out of
nowhere and started tugging at my trouser skirts. As I recall it,
this was one of those warm early spring nights when you expect
at any time now to be catching the romantic fragrance of plum
blossoms in the pale moonlight. But what did I see in the moon's
faint glow? It was the monkey baring its white fangs, wrinkling
up its nose, and shrieking with almost manic intensity. An eerie

chill was only three parts of what I felt: the other seven parts were anger at having my new trousers yanked at like that, and I considered kicking the beast aside and continuing on my way. I quickly changed my mind, however, recalling the case of the samurai who had earned the Young Master's displeasure by tormenting the monkey. And besides, the way the monkey was behaving, there was obviously something wrong. I therefore gave up trying to resist and allowed myself to be pulled several paces farther.

Where the corridor turned a corner, the pale surface of His Lordship's pond could be seen stretching off through the darkness beyond a gently drooping pine. When the animal led me to that point, my ears were assaulted by the frantic yet strangely muffled sounds of what I took to be a struggle in a nearby room. All else was hushed. I heard no voices, no sounds but the splash of a fish leaping in the mingled moonlight and fog. The sound of the struggle brought me up short. If this was an intruder, I resolved, I would teach him a lesson, and, holding my breath, I edged closer to the sliding door.

13

My approach, however, was obviously too slow and cautious for the monkey. Yoshihide scampered around me in circles—once, twice, three times—then bounded up to my shoulder with a strangled cry. Instinctively, I jerked my head aside to avoid being scratched. The monkey dug its claws into my sleeve to keep from slipping down. This sent me staggering, and I stumbled backward, slamming against the door. Now I could no longer hesitate. I shot the door open and crouched to spring in beyond the moonlight's edge. At that very moment something rose up to block my view. With a start I realized it was a woman. She flew toward me as if someone had flung her out of the room. She nearly hit me but instead she tumbled forward and—why, I could not tell—went down on one knee before me, trembling and breathless, and staring up at me as if at some terrifying sight.

I am sure I need not tell you it was Yoshihide's daughter.

That night, however, my eyes beheld her with a new vividness, as though she were an utterly different person. Her eyes were huge and shining. And her cheeks seemed to be burning red. Her disheveled clothes gave her an erotic allure that contrasted sharply with her usual childish innocence. Could this actually be the daughter of Yoshihide? I wondered—that frail-looking girl so modest and self-effacing in all things? Leaning against the sliding wooden door, I stared at this beautiful girl in the moonlight and then, as if they were capable of pointing, I flicked my eyes toward the hurried footsteps receding into the distance to ask her soundlessly, *Who was that?*

The girl bit her lip and shook her head in silence. I could see she felt deeply mortified.

I bent over her and, speaking softly next to her ear, now put my question into words: "Who was that?" But again she refused to answer and would only shake her head. Indeed, she bit her lip harder than ever as tears gathered on her long lashes.

Born stupid, I can never understand anything that isn't perfectly obvious, and so I had no idea what to say to her. I could do nothing but stand there, feeling as if my only purpose was to listen to the wild beating of her heart. Of course, one thing that kept me silent was the conviction that it would be wrong of me to question her any further.

How long this went on, I do not know, but eventually I slid shut the door and gently told the girl, "Go to your room now." Her agitation seemed to have subsided somewhat. Assailed by an uneasy feeling that I had seen something I was not meant to see, and a sense of shame toward anyone and no one in particular, I began to pad my way back up the corridor. I had hardly walked ten paces, however, when again I felt a tug—a timid one—at the skirt of my trousers. I whirled around, startled, but what do you think it was?

I looked down to find the monkey Yoshihide prostrating himself at my feet, hands on the floor like a human being, bowing over and over in thanks, his golden bell ringing.

14

Perhaps two weeks went by after that. All of a sudden, Yoshihide arrived at the mansion to beg a personal audience with
His Lordship. He probably dared do such a thing despite his
humble station because he had long been in His Lordship's
special favor. His Lordship rarely allowed anyone to come into
his presence, but that day, as so often before, he assented
readily to Yoshihide's request and had him shown in without a
moment's delay. The man wore his usual reddish-brown robe
and tall black soft hat. His face revealed a new level of sullen-
ness, but he went down on all fours before His Lordship and
at length, eyes down, he began to speak in husky tones:

"I come into your honored presence this day, My Lord,
regarding the screen bearing images of hell which His Lordship
ordered me to paint. I have applied myself to it day and night—
outdone myself—such that my efforts have begun to bear fruit,
and it is largely finished."

"This is excellent news. I am very pleased."

Even as His Lordship spoke these words, however, his voice
seemed oddly lacking in power and vitality.

"No, My Lord, I am afraid the news is anything but excellent," said Yoshihide, his eyes still fastened on the floor in a
way that hinted at anger. "The work may be largely finished,
but there is still a part that I am unable to paint."

"What? Unable to paint?"

"Indeed, sir. As a rule, I can only paint what I have seen. Or
even if I succeed in painting something unknown to me, I myself
cannot be satisfied with it. This is the same as not being able to
paint it, does His Lordship not agree?"

As His Lordship listened to Yoshihide's words, his face
gradually took on a mocking smile.

"Which would mean that if you wanted to paint a screen
depicting hell, you would have to have seen hell itself."

"Exactly, My Lord. In the great fire some years ago, though,
I saw flames with my own eyes that I could use for those of the
Hell of Searing Heat. In fact, I succeeded with my *Fudō of*

Twisting Flames only because I experienced that fire. I believe
My Lord is familiar with the painting."

"What about sinners, though? And hell wardens—you have
never seen those, have you?" His Lordship challenged Yoshihide with one question after another as though he had not
heard Yoshihide's words.

"I have seen a person bound in iron chains," said Yoshihide.
"And I have done a detailed sketch of someone being tormented
by a monstrous bird. No, I think it cannot be said that I have
never seen sinners being tortured. And as for hell wardens,"
said Yoshihide, breaking into an eerie smile, "my eyes have
beheld them any number of times as I drift between sleeping
and waking. The bull-headed ones, the horse-headed ones, the
three-faced, six-armed devils: almost every night they come to
torture me with their soundless clapping hands, their voiceless
gaping mouths. No, they are not the ones I am having so much
difficulty painting."

I suspect this shocked even His Lordship. For a long while
he only glared at Yoshihide until, with an angry twitch of the
brow, he spat out, "All right, then. What is it that you say you
are unable to paint?"

15

"In the center of the screen, falling from the sky, I want to paint
an aristocrat's carriage, its cabin woven of the finest split palm
leaf." As he spoke, Yoshihide raised himself to look directly at
His Lordship for the first time—and with a penetrating gaze. I
had heard that Yoshihide could be like a madman where painting was concerned; to me the look in his eyes at that moment
was terrifying in that very way.

"In the carriage, a voluptuous noblewoman writhes in agony,
her long black hair tossing in the ferocious flames. Her face . . .
well, perhaps she contorts her brows and casts her gaze skyward
toward the ceiling of the cabin as she chokes on the rising
clouds of smoke. Her hands might tear at the cloth streamers
of the carriage blinds as she struggles to ward off the shower
of sparks raining down upon her. Around her swarm fierce,

carnivorous birds, perhaps a dozen or more, snapping their beaks in anticipation—oh, My Lord, it is this, this image of the noblewoman in the carriage, that I am unable to paint."

"And therefore . . . ?"

His Lordship seemed to be deriving an odd sort of pleasure from this as he urged Yoshihide to continue, but Yoshihide himself, red lips trembling as with a fever, could only repeat, as if in a dream, "This is what I am unable to paint."

Then suddenly, all but biting into his own words, he cried, "I beg you, My Lord: have your men set a carriage on fire. Let me watch the flames devour its frame and its woven cabin. And, if possible—"

A dark cloud crossed His Lordship's face, but no sooner had it passed than he broke into a loud cackle. He was still choking with laughter when he spoke: " 'Possible'? I'll do whatever you want. Don't waste time worrying about what is 'possible.' "

His Lordship's words filled me with a terrible foreboding. And in fact his appearance at that moment was anything but ordinary. White foam gathered at the corners of his mouth. His eyebrows convulsed into jagged bolts of lightning. It was as if His Lordship himself had become infused with Yoshihide's madness. And no sooner had he finished speaking than laughter—endless laughter—exploded from his throat once again.

"I'll burn a carriage for you," he said. "And I'll have a voluptuous woman inside it, dressed in a noblewoman's robes. She will die writhing with agony in flames and black smoke.— I have to salute you, Yoshihide. Who could have thought of such a thing but the greatest painter in the land?"

Yoshihide went pale when he heard this, and for a time the only part of him that moved was his lips: he seemed to be gasping for breath. Then, as though all the muscles of his body had gone limp at once, he crumpled forward with his hands on the matted floor again.

"A thousand thanks to you, My Lord," Yoshihide said with rare humility, his voice barely audible. Perhaps the full horror of his own plan had come all too clear to him as he heard it spelled out in His Lordship's words. Only this one time in my life did I ever think of Yoshihide as a man to be pitied.

16

Two or three nights later, His Lordship summoned Yoshihide as promised to witness the burning of the carriage. He held the event not at the Horikawa mansion, but outside the Capital, at his late younger sister's mountain retreat, widely known as the "Palace of the Melting Snows."

No one had lived at this "palace" for a very long time. Its spacious gardens had gone wild, and the desolate sight must have given rise to all sorts of rumors, many about His Lordship's sister, who had actually died there. People used to say that on moonless nights Her Ladyship's broad-skirted scarlet trousers would glide eerily along the outdoor corridor, never touching the floor. And no wonder there were such stories! The palace was lonely enough in the daytime, but once the sun set it became downright unnerving. The garden stream would murmur ominously in the darkness, and herons would swoop in the starlight like monstrous creatures.

As it happened, the carriage burning took place on one of those pitch-dark, moonless nights. Oil lamps revealed His Lordship seated in cross-legged ease on the veranda. Beneath a turquoise robe he wore deep-lavender patterned trousers. On a thick round mat edged in white brocade, his position was of course elevated above the half-dozen or so attendants who surrounded him. One among them appeared most eager to be of service to His Lordship, a burly samurai who had distinguished himself in the campaign against the northern barbarians some years earlier. He was said to have survived starvation by eating human flesh, after which he had the strength to tear out the antlers of a living stag with his bare hands. On this night he knelt in stern readiness below the veranda, in the scabbard at his armored waist a sword tipped up and back like a gull's tail, ready to be drawn at a moment's notice. These men presented a strangely terrifying, almost dreamlike spectacle. The lamplight flickering in the night wind turned them all dark one moment, bright the next.

And then there was the carriage itself. Even without an ox attached to its long black shafts, their ends resting on the usual

low bench that tilted the whole slightly forward, it stood out
against the night, its tall cabin woven of the finest split palm
leaf, exactly as Yoshihide had requested: truly, a conveyance
worthy of His Imperial Majesty or the most powerful ministers
of state. When I saw its gold fittings gleaming like stars in the
sky, and considered what was soon to happen to this lavishly
appointed vehicle, a shiver went through me in spite of the
warm spring night. As for what might be inside the carriage,
there was no way to tell: its lovely blinds, woven of still-green
bamboo and edged in patterned cloth, had been rolled down
tight, and around it alert-looking conscripts stood guard, holding flaming torches and showing their concern that too much
smoke might be drifting toward His Lordship on the veranda.

Yoshihide himself was situated at some remove, kneeling on
the ground directly opposite the veranda. He wore what seemed
to be his usual reddish-brown robe and tall black soft hat, and
he looked especially small and shabby, as though the star-filled
sky were a weight pressing down upon him. Behind him knelt
another person in an outfit like his—probably an apprentice he
had brought along. With them crouching down low in the
darkness like that, I could not make out the color of their robes
from my place below the veranda.

17

Midnight was approaching, I believe. I felt as if the darkness
enveloping the garden were silently watching us all breathing,
the only sound an occasional rush of night wind, each gust
wafting toward us the resinous smell from the pine smoke of
the torches. His Lordship remained silent for some moments,
observing the mysterious scene, but then, edging forward where
he sat, he cried sharply:

"Yoshihide!"

Yoshihide may have said some word in response, but to my
ears it sounded like nothing so much as a moan.

"Tonight, Yoshihide, I am going to burn a carriage for you,
as you requested."

When he said this, His Lordship glanced at the men around

him. I thought I saw a meaningful smile pass between him and certain of them. Of course, it could have been my imagination. Now Yoshihide seemed to be timidly raising his head and looking up toward the veranda, but still he waited, saying nothing.

"I want you to look at this," His Lordship said. "This is *my* carriage, the one I use every day. You know it well, I'm sure. I will now have it set afire in order that you may see the Hell of Searing Heat here on earth before your eyes."

His Lordship reverted to silence and his eyes flashed another signal to his men. Then, with sudden vehemence, he cried, "Chained inside the carriage is a sinful woman. When we set the carriage afire, her flesh will be roasted, her bones will be charred: she will die an agonizing death. Never again will you have such a perfect model for the screen. Do not fail to watch as her snow-white flesh erupts in flames. See and remember her long black hair dancing in a whirl of sparks!"

His Lordship sank into silence for yet a third time, but— whatever could have been in his mind?—now all he did was laugh soundlessly, his shoulders quaking.

"Never again will there be a sight like this, Yoshihide! I shall join you in observing it. All right, men, raise the blind. Let Yoshihide see the woman inside!"

On hearing this command, one of the conscripts, torch held high, strode up to the carriage, stretched out his free hand, and whipped the blind up. The torch crackled and flickered and cast its red gleam inside. On the carriage's matted floor, cruelly chained, sat a woman—and oh, who could have failed to recognize her? Her long black hair flowed in a voluptuous band across a gorgeous robe embroidered in cherry blossoms, and the golden hairpins on top of her downcast head sparkled beautifully in the firelight. For all the differences in costuming, there was no mistaking that girlish frame, that graceful neck (where now a gag was fastened), that touchingly modest profile: they belonged to none other than Yoshihide's daughter. I could hardly keep from crying out.

Just then the samurai kneeling across from me sprang to his feet and, pressing threateningly on his sword hilt, glared at

Yoshihide. Startled by this sudden movement, I turned my gaze toward Yoshihide. He looked as if this spectacle were driving him half mad. Where he had been crouching until then, he was on his feet now and poised—arms outstretched—to run toward the carriage. Unfortunately, though, as I said before, he was in the shadows far away from me, and so I did not have a clear view of his face. My frustration lasted but a moment, however. Now, drained of color though it was, Yoshihide's face—or, should I say, Yoshihide's entire form, raised aloft by some invisible power—appeared before me with such clarity it seemed to have cut its way through the surrounding darkness. For suddenly His Lordship had cried "Burn it!", the conscripts flung their torches, and the carriage, with Yoshihide's daughter inside, burst into flame.

18

The fire engulfed the entire carriage. The purple roof tassels blew aside, then clouds of smoke swirled aloft, stark white against the blackness of the night, and finally a shower of sparks spurted upward with such terrifying force that in a single instant the blinds, the side panels, and the roof's metal fittings were ripped off in the blast and sent flying. Still more horrible was the color of the flames that licked the latticed cabin vents before shooting skyward, as though—might I say?—the sun itself had crashed to earth, spewing its heavenly fire in all directions. As close as I had come to crying out before, now I could only gape in mute awe at the horrifying spectacle.

But what of the girl's father?

I will never forget the look on Yoshihide's face at that moment. He had started toward the carriage on impulse but halted when the flames flared up. He then stood there with arms outstretched, eyes devouring the smoke and flames that enveloped the carriage. In the firelight that bathed him from head to toe, I could see every feature of his ugly, wrinkled face. His wide-staring eyes, his contorted lips, the twitching flesh of his cheeks: all drew a vivid picture of the shock, the terror, and the sorrow that traversed Yoshihide's heart by turns. Such anguish, I suspect, would not be seen even on the face of a convicted thief about to have his head cut off or the guiltiest sinner about to face the judgment of the Ten Kings of Hell. Even the powerful samurai went pale at the sight and stole a fearful glance at His Lordship above him.

But what of His Lordship himself? Biting his lip and smiling strangely now and then, he stared straight ahead, never taking his eyes off the carriage. And the girl in the carriage—ah, I don't think I have the courage to describe in detail what she looked like then. The pale whiteness of her upturned face as she choked on the smoke; the tangled length of her hair as she tried to shake the flames from it; the beauty of her cherry blossom robe as it burst into flame: it was all so cruel, so terrible! Especially at one point when the night wind rushed down from the mountain to sweep away the smoke: the sight of her against a flaming background of red flecked with gold dust, gnawing at her gag, writhing as if to snap the chains that bound her: it was enough to make our flesh creep, not only mine but the powerful samurai's as well—as if the tortures of hell were being pictured right there before our eyes.

Just then the night wind gusted once more, rustling the branches of the garden's trees—or so it seemed to me and, I am sure, to everyone else. Such a sound seemed to race through the dark sky, and in that instant some black thing shot from the palace roof into the blazing carriage. It traveled in a perfectly straight line like a ball that has been kicked, neither touching the earth nor arcing through space. And as the carriage's burning side lattices collapsed inward, glowing as if coated in crimson lacquer, the thing grasped the girl's straining shoulders and hurled a long, piercing, and inexpressibly anguished scream out beyond the billowing smoke. Another scream followed, and then a third, until we all found ourselves crying out with it. For though it had been left tethered back at the Horikawa mansion, what we saw now clinging to the girl's shoulders against a flaming backdrop was the monkey Yoshihide.

19

We could see the monkey for only the briefest moment, though. A fountain of sparks shot up to the sky like gold dust in black lacquer, and then not only the monkey but the girl, too, was shrouded in black smoke. Now in the middle of the garden there was only a carriage of fire seething in flames with a terrible roar. No—"pillar of fire" might better describe this horrific conflagration boiling up to the starry heavens.

But oh, how strange it was to see the painter now, standing absolutely rigid before the pillar of fire! Yoshihide—who only a few moments earlier had seemed to be suffering the torments of hell—stood there with his arms locked across his chest as if he had forgotten even the presence of His Lordship, his whole wrinkled face suffused now with an inexpressible radiance—the radiance of religious ecstasy. I could have sworn that the man's eyes were no longer watching his daughter dying in agony, that instead the gorgeous colors of flames and the sight of a woman suffering in them were giving him joy beyond measure.

The most wondrous thing was not that he watched his only daughter's death throes with apparent joy, but rather that Yoshihide at that moment possessed a strange, inhuman majesty that resembled the rage of the King of Beasts himself as you might see him in a dream. For this reason—although I might have been imagining it—the countless night birds that flew around us squawking in alarm at each new eruption of flames seemed to keep their distance from Yoshihide's tall black hat. Perhaps even these insentient birds could see the mysterious grandeur that hung above Yoshihide like a radiant aura.

If the birds could see it, how much more so the rest of us, down to the lowly conscripts. Trembling inwardly, scarcely breathing, and filled with a bizarre sense of adoration, we kept our eyes fastened on Yoshihide as if we were present at the decisive moment when a lump of stone or wood becomes a holy image of the Buddha. The carriage flames that filled the heavens with a roar; Yoshihide under the spell of the flames, transfixed: what sublimity! what rapture! But among us only one, His Lordship, looked on as if transformed into another person, his noble countenance drained of color, the corners of his mouth flecked with foam, hands clutching his knees through his lavender trousers as he panted like a beast in need of water . . .

20

Word soon spread that His Lordship had burned the carriage that night in the Palace of the Melting Snows, and there seem to have been many who were highly critical of the event. First of all came the question of Yoshihide's daughter: why had His Lordship chosen to burn her alive? The rumor most often heard was that he had done it out of spite for her rejection of his love. I am certain, however, that he did it to punish the twisted personality of an artist who would go so far as to burn a carriage and kill a human being to complete the painting of a screen. In fact, I overheard His Lordship saying as much himself.

And then there was Yoshihide, whose stony heart was also apparently the topic of much negative commentary. How, after seeing his own daughter burned alive, could he want to finish the screen painting? Some cursed him as a beast in human guise who had forgotten a father's love for the sake of a picture. One who allied himself with this opinion was His Reverence the Abbot of Yokawa, who always used to say, "Excel in his art though he might, if a man does not know the Five Virtues,[9] he can only end up in hell."

A month went by, and the screen with its images of hell was finished at last. Yoshihide brought it to the mansion that very day and humbly presented it for His Lordship's inspection. His Reverence happened to be visiting at the time, and I am certain that he was shocked at the sight of the horrible firestorm blasting through it. Until he actually saw the screen, he was glowering at Yoshihide, but then he slapped his knee and exclaimed, "What magnificent work!" I can still see the bitter smile on His Lordship's face when he heard those words.

Almost no one spoke ill of Yoshihide after that—at least not in the mansion. Could it be because all who saw the screen—even those who had always hated him—were struck by strangely solemn feelings when they witnessed the tortures of the Hell of Searing Heat in all their reality?

By then, however, Yoshihide numbered among those who are no longer of this world. The night after he finished the screen, he tied a rope to a beam in his room and hanged himself. I suspect that, having sent his daughter on ahead to the other world, he could not bear to go on living here as if nothing had happened. His body lies buried in the ruins of his home. The little stone marker is probably so cloaked in moss now, after decades of exposure to the wind and rain, that no one can tell whose grave it is anymore.

(1918)

UNDER THE SWORD

DR. OGATA RYŌSAI:
MEMORANDUM

The following memorandum is intended to comply with the order that I provide the government with a detailed report of my observations regarding adherents of the Kirishitan sect who have been misleading people of this village through the practice of their heretical doctrines.

To wit: On the seventh day of the third month of this year, a woman named Shino, widow of the farmer Yosaku, late of this village, visited my residence and pleaded with me to perform a pulse diagnosis on her daughter, Sato (age 9), who, she said, was gravely ill.

This Shino was born the third daughter of the farmer Sōbē. She married Yosaku ten years ago and gave birth to Sato, but she was soon preceded in death by her husband. She did not remarry, but instead survived one day at a time through weaving and other piecework. At the time of Yosaku's illness and death, however, owing to some error in judgment, she professed an exclusive devotion to the Kirishitan sect and began frequenting the home of one Bateren[1] Rodrigue in the neighboring village. Some in this village said that she had become the bateren's mistress, and she was widely condemned. Her entire family, including her father Sōbē and all her sisters and brothers, tried to reason with her, but she insisted that the most auspicious of all gods was her Deus Come Thus.[2] She and daughter Sato worshiped each day before a tutelary image called a *"kurusu"* shaped like one of our impalement racks. She even failed to tend her husband Yosaku's grave. Soon she was disowned by her relatives, and the village officials were

said to be meeting frequently to discuss formally banishing her
from the village.

Given the woman's history, I had to tell her, despite her
bitter pleas, that I could not perform a pulse diagnosis on her
daughter. She went home in tears but returned the next day,
the eighth. "I shall remain forever in your debt," she begged,
"if only you will examine her pulse." She would not accept my
repeated refusals and finally threw herself down, sobbing, in
my entryway. Then, angrily, she said, "I thought it was the duty
of doctors to cure people's illnesses. I tell you that my daughter
is gravely ill, and yet you ignore me. This, I cannot understand."

"What you say is entirely reasonable," I replied, "but my
refusal to perform a pulse examination is not devoid of reason
either. Your behavior of late is truly offensive. In particular, I
have heard that you often vilify the people of our village[3]—
including me; you say that our worship of the gods and Buddhas
is an act of heresy, that we are possessed by the devil. If you
are such a pure follower of the path of righteousness, how can
you now ask someone like me, possessed by evil spirits, to cure
your daughter of her grave illness? Instead, you should ask for
help from your own 'Deus Come Thus' in whom you believe
so deeply. If you want me to perform a pulse diagnosis, you
must first renounce your faith in the Kirishitan sect and never
go back to it. Unless you agree to do so, I absolutely refuse to
perform the pulse diagnosis. Medicine may be, as they say, a
compassionate art, but I also fear the dark punishments of the
gods and Buddhas."

There was nothing Shino could say in response to such an
argument. Recognizing that it would be futile for her to persist,
she went home looking utterly dejected.

On the next day, the ninth, a heavy rain began to fall at dawn
and for a time the entire village seemed deserted. It was still the
hour of the hare[4] when Shino arrived at my doorstep without
an umbrella, drenched to the skin. Again she begged me to
perform the pulse diagnosis, to which I replied, "I may not be
a samurai, but I am no less true to my word. I must ask you to
choose between your daughter's life and Deus Come Thus."

This time, Shino turned into a madwoman. She prostrated

herself before me, pressing her forehead to the ground again and again, and clasping her hands together as if in prayer. "What you say makes perfect sense," she sobbed, "but in the teachings of the Kirishitan sect, if I fall but once, then both my soul and my body will perish for all the future lives to come. Please try to understand and take pity on me; please show me mercy on this one matter alone." All but strangled with emotion, she implored me again and again.

Follower of the evil faith though she was, she seemed to be as devoted a parent as any, and so I did feel some degree of pity for her, but one cannot simply abandon the proper path because of personal feelings. I continued to insist, therefore, that unless she "fell," I could not perform the pulse examination. Shino stared at me for a time with an indescribable expression on her face, but then, with a sudden gush of tears, she cringed at my feet and muttered something that I could not hear clearly over the sound of the rain then pouring down. Finally, after I had urged her several times to repeat herself, it became clear that she was saying she had given up and would indeed allow herself to fall.

I told Shino that she would have to prove to me that she had "fallen," whereupon, without a word, she took one of those *kurusu* things out of the breast of her kimono, laid it on the entryway step, and silently trod upon it three times. She gave no sign of being agitated, and her tears seemed to have dried up by then, but all my servants said that there was an eerie gleam in her eyes, like that of a person in fever, as she looked down at the *kurusu* underfoot.

Now that Shino had honored my request, I immediately set out through the downpour with her, my servant carrying my medicine case. At Shino's house, I found Sato lying alone in a cramped little room, her pillow to the south.[5] Her body was extremely hot to the touch and she seemed barely conscious. Her little hand traced a cross shape in the air again and again, and she kept deliriously uttering the word *haluleya*, a joyous smile forming on her lips each time. This "*haluleya*" is the Kirishitan version of the "All hail," which they say in praise of the Buddha of that sect. Shino told me this, crying, as she knelt by her daughter's pillow. I immediately examined the girl's pulse and determined both that she was suffering from cold damage disorder[6] and that it was too late to treat her: she would probably not survive the day. I had no choice but to tell this to Shino, who once again seemed to lose her mind.

"The one and only reason that I fell was to save my daughter's life. If you let her die now, it will have all been in vain. Please try to understand my anguish at having turned my back on Deus Come Thus. You *must* save my daughter's life!" She prostrated herself not only before me but before my servant as well, pleading with us to do something, but I tried to convince her that she must realize there was no longer anything that any human power could do. The rain happened to let up just then and so I placed three packets of infusion medicine on the floor next to her and started to leave. Shino, however, clung to my sleeve and would not let go. She seemed to be attempting to speak, but no words emerged from her trembling lips. I watched as the blood drained from her face, and suddenly she began writhing in agony. I was greatly startled by this, and my servant and I immediately set about treating her. Eventually she came to her senses, but she no longer had the strength to stand up.

"Unworthy woman that I am, all I have done is lose both my daughter's life and Deus Come Thus," she sobbed. I tried my best to comfort her, but nothing I said seemed to make an impression on her, and since, furthermore, her daughter's condition appeared to be hopeless, there was nothing more for me to do but take my servant and hurry home again.

That afternoon, however, when the village headman Tsukagoshi Yazaemon brought his mother for a pulse examination, I learned from him that Shino's daughter had died and that Shino had finally lost her mind out of grief. Sato had apparently died about an hour after I took her pulse, and by mid-morning Shino was already deranged and clutching at the corpse, loudly intoning one of her barbarian-language sutras. Yazaemon told me that he saw this himself. Also present were the village officials Kaemon, Tōgo, and Jihē, and so there is no doubting its factual accuracy.

On the next day, the tenth, a light rain fell starting at dawn, followed by a spring thunder shower late in the hour of the dragon.[7] During a brief clear spell, the village samurai Yanase Kinjūrō sent a horse for me and requested that I visit him to perform a pulse examination. I set out immediately, but when I came as far as Shino's house, I encountered a crowd of villagers gathered out front angrily shouting to each other about the "Kirishitan" and the "bateren" such that I could not make the horse pass by. The house door was wide open, and from where I sat on the horse, I could see one of the red-hairs[8] and three Japanese wearing some kind of long black garments like the Buddhist priests' clerical robes. Each of them was holding up a *kurusu* or a thing that looked like a censer and they were chanting "*haluleya*" over and over again. In addition, crouching at the feet of the red-hair in an apparent swoon, her hair in disarray, was Shino, clutching her daughter Sato. What utterly amazed me, however, was that Sato had her arms wrapped around Shino's neck and was alternately intoning her mother's name and "*haluleya*" in a sweet little voice. Of course, at that distance I could not make everything out with perfect clarity, but Sato's color appeared to be quite good, and every now and then she would release one hand from her mother's neck and make as if to grasp the smoke rising from the censer-like object. I dismounted and asked the villagers to give me the details of Sato's revival.

They told me that the red-hair Bateren Rodrigue had come to Shino's house from the neighboring village that morning, bringing with him a number of his iruman. After he had heard Shino's *kohisan*,[9] the group performed incantations to their Buddha, they sent up clouds of their alien incense, they scattered their sacred water, and did other such things, whereupon Shino's derangement quieted down, and soon afterward—the men told me fearfully—Sato came back to life. Since ancient times, there have been not a few examples of people dying and coming back to life, but most of these have been cases of alcohol poisoning or of contact with natural miasmas. I have never heard of a case like Sato's, in which a person who has died from cold damage disorder regains his soul.

This account, then, should serve to illustrate the heterodox practices of the Kirishitan sect. In addition, let me note that the spring shower produced intense thunder just as the bateren was entering this village. I take this to mean that Heaven was showing its abhorrence for him.

Because the village headman, Tsukagoshi Yazaemon, has already tendered his report concerning the fact that Shino and daughter Sato have moved to the neighboring village with Bateren Rodrigue, and also that Shino's house was burnt to the ground at the behest of Nikkan, the chief priest of the Jigenji Temple, I will limit my account to this rough outline of what I myself have observed. If, however, I have omitted anything, I will tender additional written reports as called for at a later date. The above, then, constitutes my provisional memorandum.

Signed this 26th day of the third month of the year of the Monkey, —— Village, Uwa County, Iyo Province.

Ogata Ryōsai, Doctor of Medicine

(7 December 1916)

O-GIN

This happened sometime during Genna or Kan'ei—in any case, a long time ago.

Back then, as soon as a person was discovered to be following the teachings of the Heavenly Lord, he was either burned at the stake or impaled on the rack. "The Lord for whom all things are possible" seemed to provide especially miraculous protection to believers here in proportion to the severity of the persecutions they had to endure. Angels and saints often came with the light of the setting sun to visit the villages around Nagasaki, and tradition has it that San Jo-an Batista himself once appeared to the believer Miguel–Yahei[1] in his Urakami mill. Satan also frequently appeared in the villages then to disrupt the devotions of believers. He would take the form of a strange black man, say, or an imported flowering plant, or a wickerwork carriage. Even the rat that tormented Miguel–Yahei in his underground dungeon, where he could not distinguish night from day, was said to be an incarnation of Satan. Yahei was burned at the stake with eleven other believers in the autumn of the eighth year of Genna.

This, then, was the situation in Urakami during Genna and Kan'ei—a long time ago.

In the village of Yamazato in Urakami there lived a girl named O-Gin. Her father and mother had wandered to Nagasaki from far-off Osaka, but before they could establish a life there, they died, leaving O-Gin alone. Because they came from another part of the country, they could not have known anything about the teachings of the Heavenly Lord. What they believed in was Buddhism—Zen, perhaps, or Tendai, or Pure

Land Buddhism—in any case, the teachings of Shakyamuni Buddha. Jean Crasset, a French Jesuit, tells us that Shakyamuni was a man of innate cunning who roamed across the length and breadth of China, preaching the Way of a Buddha called Amida.[2] From China, Shakyamuni came to the Land of Japan to teach the same Way. His doctrine claimed that at death a human being's *anima* would become a bird or an ox or a tree depending on the degree of the person's sinfulness. According to Crasset, Shakyamuni killed his own mother at the time of his birth; his teachings were obviously a pack of lies, and just as obvious was the enormous evil of Shakyamuni himself.

As suggested earlier, however, O-Gin's parents would not have had the opportunity to learn these truths. Even after death, they continued to believe in the teachings of Shakyamuni, dreaming their fragile dreams of a Buddhist Paradise there beneath the graveyard pines, never knowing that, in the end, they would fall into Inherno.

Fortunately, however, O-Gin was not tainted by her parents' ignorance, for the farmer Jo-an–Magoshichi, a longtime resident of Yamazato and a man of deep compassion, poured the holy water of baptismo upon the girl's forehead and gave her the name Mariya. O-Gin did not believe that Shakyamuni was born pointing to the sky and the ground and proclaiming, "Throughout heaven and earth, I alone am the honored one." Instead, she believed that "Santa Maria, a maiden profoundly gentle, profoundly compassionate, and sweet above all others," had come spontaneously to be with child. She believed that Zesus, who had "died upon the cross and been laid in a stone sarcophagus deep in the earth," came back to life three days later. She believed that when the trumpet sounds on Judgment Day, "Our Lord will descend from Heaven in great power and glory, and reunite people's material bodies, which have turned to dust, with their original *anima*. Then the good people will enjoy the pleasures of heaven above, and the bad people will fall down into hell with the devil." And she especially believed in the holy sagramento in which "the bread and wine, though unchanged in shape and color, became the actual flesh and blood of Our Lord through the divine power of the Word."

O-Gin's heart was not, like those of her parents, a desert swept by searing winds. It was an abundant field of ripened wheat mingled with simple wild roses.

After she lost her parents, O-Gin was adopted by Jo-an–Magoshichi. His wife, Joanna–O-Sumi, was as tender-hearted as her husband. O-Gin spent day after happy day with them, tending the cattle and mowing the wheat. Nor did the three of them fail, as they went about their chores, to observe fasting and prayer as often as they could without attracting the attention of the other villagers. Many times O-Gin would stand in the shade of the fig tree by the well, looking up at the large crescent moon and praying with her whole heart. So young that her hair still hung loose to her shoulders, this sweet girl would offer up prayers of great simplicity:

"All hail to you, O compassionate Mother. This wanderer, this child of Ewa, cries out to you alone. Please turn your gentle gaze upon this vale of tears. Ammei."

But then one Natala (Christmas) eve, Satan burst into Mago-shichi's house along with several officials. In the great sunken hearth of Magoshichi's house blazed the Yule log, and on this special night alone, the holy crucifix was ceremonially displayed upon the soot-smeared wall. And finally, in the stable out back, the officials found the manger full of water for the infant Zesus' first bath. They nodded to each other and bound Magoshichi and his wife with ropes. O-Gin, too, they tied up. None of the captives, however, showed anything but the most complete composure. They were prepared to endure any torment for the salvation of their *anima*. They shared the same deep, unspoken faith: *Our Lord will surely favor us with His divine protection. Is not the very fact that we were arrested on Natala eve proof of the depth of His love for us?*

The officials led their bound prisoners to the residence of the local magistrate. But along the way, even as the night wind struck them, the three continued to intone their nativity prayers. "O Young Lord of Ours, born in the Land of Belem, where art thou now? Honored and praised be thy Name!"

As he watched them being captured, Satan laughed and clapped his hands with joy. But he was obviously more than a little angered by their courageous demeanor. Later, alone again, he spat in disgust and, transforming himself into a great millstone, he rolled into the darkness and disappeared.

Jo-an–Magoshichi, Joanna–O-Sumi, and Mariya–O-Gin were not only thrown into an underground dungeon: they were subjected to many tortures to make them abandon the teachings of the Heavenly Lord. Despite torture by water and torture by fire, however, their resolve remained firm. Even as their torn flesh began to fester, they knew the gates of Haraiso would open to them with but another moment's endurance. Indeed, at the thought of the Heavenly Lord's great benevolence, even this dark underground dungeon had all the sublimity of Haraiso. And often at times when they drifted between dream and waking, august angels and saints would come to comfort them. O-Gin in particular was favored with such moments of bliss. Once, she saw San Jo-an Batista scooping up many locusts upon his broad palms and saying to her, "Eat!" Another time she saw the great angel Gabriel, his white wings folded, giving her water in a golden cup.

The local magistrate, meanwhile, ignorant of the teachings of the Heavenly Lord (and of the teachings of Shakyamuni, for that matter), had no idea why his prisoners were being so obstinate. He sometimes wondered if all three of them were crazy. When he finally realized that they were by no means crazy, he began to feel they might be serpents or unicorns—or at least some kind of animal unrelated to humanity. To allow such animals to go on living would not only be a violation of present-day law, it could compromise the security of the country. And so, after he held them for a month in the earthen prison, the magistrate decided that he would burn all three of them. (In fact, like most people, this magistrate hardly ever thought about the security of the country. He had both the law and popular custom to rely on. That was quite enough for him without the extra effort of thinking about such things.)

The believers showed no sign of fear as they were led to the execution ground on the village outskirts, an empty, rock-strewn patch of earth next to the cemetery. Upon arrival, they were read the indictments against them and tied to stout square posts. The posts were then set in the center of the execution ground, with Joanna–O-Sumi on the right, Jo-an–Magoshichi in the middle, and Mariya–O-Gin on the left. O-Sumi looked suddenly much older now after days of torture. Magoshichi's bewhiskered cheeks seemed drained of blood. And O-Gin . . . O-Gin, by comparison, looked more like her usual self. Standing on top of piles of firewood, all three wore the same calm expression.

A large crowd had been gathering all day along the edges of the execution ground. Against the sky above the spectators, a half-dozen pines stretched out their branches like a sacred canopy above a Buddhist altar.

When all preparations were complete, one of the officials stepped out grandly before the three convicts and announced that he would offer them a reprieve: they could take a few more minutes to think about giving up their faith in the teachings of the Heavenly Lord. All they need do was say they renounced the holy teachings, and he would immediately loosen their bonds. None of the three responded to him. All kept their gazes fixed on the distant heavens, and all had smiles on their lips.

The next few minutes were a time of utter silence—for the officials, of course, but for the crowd as well. Countless eyes were locked, unblinking, on the faces of the convicts. This is not to say that all the spectators were holding their breath out of pity for the victims. Rather, most were waiting in suspense for the moment when the fires would be lit. And the execution was taking so long that the officials, for their part, were too bored to talk to each other.

Then suddenly the ears of the assembled throng caught a wholly unexpected declaration:

"I have decided to abandon the holy teachings."

The voice was that of O-Gin. A stir went through the crowd, but no sooner had the muttering begun than the spectators fell silent again, for Magoshichi had turned sadly toward O-Gin with a feeble cry:

"O-Gin! Have you been blinded by Satan? Just hold on a little longer, and you will be able to see Our Lord's holy face!"

Even before his words had ended, O-Sumi strained to make

herself heard from her distant perch: "O-Gin! O-Gin! Satan is
taking possession of you! Pray hard, now! Pray hard!"

But O-Gin answered neither Magoshichi nor O-Sumi. Her
eyes stayed trained on the canopy of the graveyard pines above
the heads of the spectators. Before long, an official gave the
order for O-Gin to be untied.

As soon as he saw this, Jo-an–Magoshichi closed his eyes in
apparent resignation. "O Lord, to whom all things are possible,
I humbly submit to Your Divine Plan."

Once her ropes were off, O-Gin merely stood where she was,
a blank expression on her face. But then, catching sight of
Magoshichi and O-Sumi, she went down on her knees in front
of them and wept. Magoshichi's eyes were still closed, and
O-Sumi averted her face.

"Father! Mother! Please forgive me!" O-Gin cried at last. "I
have abandoned the holy teachings, and it is because I noticed
the canopy of pines over there. Asleep under those pines in
the graveyard, my parents do not know the teachings of Our
Heavenly Lord, and by now they must have fallen down into
Inherno. It would be unforgivable of me to enter the gates of
Haraiso without them. And so I will follow them down to the
bottom of Hell. Please go now, Mother and Father, to be
with Lord Zesus and the holy Maria. And I—now that I have
abandoned the holy teachings—I cannot go on living . . ."

O-Gin said this in broken snatches, and then she gave way
to weeping. Now Joanna–O-Sumi, too, rained down tears on
the firewood beneath her feet. To indulge in useless lamentation
was by no means proper behavior for a believer about to enter
Haraiso. Jo-an–Magoshichi turned a look of loathing on his
wife next to him, and screamed at her, "Have you been possessed by Satan, too? Go ahead if you want to: abandon the
teachings of Our Heavenly Lord. I'll burn to death alone. Just
watch!"

"No no," said O-Sumi. "I will go with you. But not . . . but
not . . ."

Swallowing her tears, O-Sumi, half-shouting, flung out her
words: "Not because I want to go to Haraiso, but because I
want to be with you."

Magoshichi remained silent for a long time, but his face changed from ghastly pale to blood red and back, and broke out in beads of sweat. Now, in his mind's eye, Magoshichi was watching his *anima*. He watched as an angel and Satan struggled to gain possession of it. If O-Gin, collapsed in tears at his feet, had not at that moment raised her face to him—but it was too late now, for that is exactly what she did. She fixed her overflowing eyes on his with a strange gleam. The light that flashed in those eyes revealed not merely the heart of an innocent girl. It was the heart of all human beings, all the "wandering children of Ewa."

"Father! Let's go to Inherno together! And Mother, and I, and my father and mother who are already there—let's let Satan take us all together!"

And in the end Magoshichi, too, fell from grace.

Among the many stories of Christian martyrdom in this country of ours, this one has been handed down to posterity as the single most embarrassing failure. When all three of them abandoned the holy teachings together, the entire crowd of spectators—men and women of all ages, not one of whom had any grasp of what the Heavenly Lord even was—conceived a tremendous hatred for them. It may well be that the crowd felt cheated out of the promised burning at the stake.

Another tradition has it that Satan, overjoyed at the way things turned out, changed himself into a huge book and flew around the execution ground all night. The author of the present tale is highly skeptical: was it so great a victory for Satan as to prompt such excessive celebrating?

(August 1922)

LOYALTY

1. Maejima Rin'emon

No sooner had he begun to recover from his fatigue after a period of illness than young Itakura Shuri suffered a terrible attack of nervous exhaustion.

His shoulders felt painfully stiff. His head ached. He could not even apply himself to his reading, normally one of his favorite activities. The mere sound of footsteps in the corridor or of voices in the house was enough to break his concentration. As the symptoms grew more severe, the tiniest stimuli kept preying on his nerves.

If, for example, a black-lacquer tobacco tray bore a decoration of creeping vines in gold, the delicate stalks and leaves would upset him. The sight of sharp, pointed objects such as ivory chopsticks or bronze fire tongs would make him anxious. His condition finally deteriorated to the point where the intersecting borders of tatami mats or the four corners of a ceiling would fill him with the same nervous tension he might experience in staring at a sharp blade.

Shuri could do nothing but cower in his room all day, scowling. Anything and everything he did was painful. He often wished that he could end his awareness of his own existence, but his splintered nerves did not permit that. He felt like an ant in a pit, struggling to crawl out of the sand flowing hellishly in on him. Meanwhile, he was surrounded by the family's "hereditary retainers," men with no comprehension of what was going on inside him, who wasted their time and energy dreading the worst.

None of them can understand my suffering. Such thoughts

seemed to intensify Shuri's nervous condition. Every little thing sent him into a frenzy. His shouts could frequently be heard in the next estate. Often he would reach for a sword on the rack. To everyone who witnessed these outbursts, he seemed almost to have become a different person. Spasms would run through his sunken yellow cheeks, and his eyes would take on a strange, murderous glint. During his worst attacks, his trembling hands would tear at the hair of his temples. His attendants saw that he was having one of his fits, and would warn each other to keep away from him.

Shuri feared that he was losing his mind, as of course did those around him. Just as naturally, he resented their fear, but he could not quell his own. When a fit subsided and a greater melancholy weighed down upon him, he would sometimes feel the fear shoot through him like a bolt of lightning, along with an ominous suspicion that the fear was itself a sign of impending madness. *What if I go crazy?* Everything turned dark at the thought.

Eventually the irritation caused by the endless stream of stimuli from the outside world would expunge the fear of madness. The irritation could also, conversely, awaken him to his fear. His mind ran in endless circles from one anxiety to the next, like a cat chasing its own tail.

Shuri's fits became a source of dread for his entire retinue. The one most seriously troubled by them was the House Elder, Maejima Rin'emon.

Although officially titled "House Elder," as if he were the hereditary chief retainer in Shuri's branch of the Itakura family, Rin'emon had in fact been dispatched by Itakura Shikibu,[1] lord of the main house, to be "attached" to Shuri's household. He was, in effect, a spy for the main house keeping watch over the branch house. Thus even Shuri, the master here, always treated him with deference. Rin'emon was a big, ruddy man who had almost no experience of illness, and among the household's many samurai, there were few with superior accomplishments in both the civil and martial arts. Thus, Rin'emon acted as

Shuri's advisor in all matters. His custom of freely offering "loyal remonstrance" to his master won him the nickname "the Itakura Family's Ōkubo Hikoza."[2]

Once it became obvious to him that Shuri's fits were growing worse, Rin'emon began to agonize over the fate of the household, to the point of being unable to sleep at night. Shuri would soon be visiting Edo Castle, where he would formally announce to the Shōgun that he had recovered from his illness. If he suffered a fit while in the Castle, there was no telling how he might offend one of the Great Lords in attendance or one of the other bannermen with whom he would be seated. If an insult led to bloodshed in the Castle, Shuri's entire 7,000-*koku* estate could well be confiscated. Nor were cautionary precedents difficult to find: was there not the Hotta–Inaba clash[3] to consider?

Such thoughts kept Rin'emon in a continual state of agitation. As far as he was concerned, moreover, Shuri's fits were due not to an illness of the body but to an illness of the spirit. And so, just as he used to remonstrate with Shuri against willfulness and extravagance, now he boldly sought to remonstrate with him about his nervous exhaustion.

Rin'emon would offer Shuri his unpalatable counsel whenever the occasion arose, but there was no sign this did anything to moderate the fits. Quite the opposite: the more Rin'emon found fault and fretted over Shuri's behavior, the worse the condition became. One time the young lord came dangerously close to slashing Rin'emon with his sword. "How dare you speak to me that way?" he shouted. "You forget that I am your lord! I'd cut you down if I didn't have the Main House to think about." What Rin'emon saw in Shuri's eyes was no longer simple anger. It had become an unquenchable hatred.

As Rin'emon continued to demonstrate his loyalty by feeding Shuri one bitter pill after another, the convoluted feelings between master and retainer grew increasingly turbulent. No longer was it merely a matter of Shuri's coming to hate Rin'emon: a feeling of hatred had begun to germinate in Rin'emon's heart as well. Rin'emon was not aware of this, of course. He believed that his loyalty toward Shuri would remain forever unchanged—except in one eventuality.

"If the master does not behave like a master, the retainer need not behave like a retainer": this was not only the Way taught by the philosopher Mencius[4] but the natural Way of humanity that lay behind Mencius. Not that Rin'emon agreed with such a view; he was determined to give his all as a loyal retainer. But bitter experience had shown him that his unpalatable counsel had no effect. He therefore resigned himself to resorting to the final measure that he had, until now, kept locked in his breast: he would have to force Shuri into retirement and arrange for the adoption of an heir from another branch of the Itakura lineage.

The House came before anything else, Rin'emon believed. The incumbent must be sacrificed before the House was sacrificed. This was especially true for the eminent House of Itakura, which had maintained an unblemished reputation ever since the time of its founding progenitor, Itakura Shirōzaemon Katsushige. His son Matazaemon Shigemune won fame as the Shōgun's Military Governor[5] in Kyoto, a post he inherited from his father. Matazaemon's younger brother, Mondo Shigemasa, was honored by the great Tokugawa founder, Ieyasu, himself, who assigned him the crucial role of supervising the signing of the peace treaty after the Winter Siege of Osaka Castle in the nineteenth year of Keichō.[6] This was the beginning of an illustrious career for Mondo: as commander of the Western Army when the Tokugawa forces suppressed the Shimabara Rebellion in the fourteenth year of Kan'ei, he was honored to fly the Shōgun's family banner at the siege of Amakusa.[7] Rin'emon knew that he could never face the Itakura ancestors in the other world if he allowed a stain upon the honor of such a distinguished lineage.

With such thoughts in mind, Rin'emon conducted a private search for other likely members of the Itakura family, and he was happy to find that Itakura Sado-no-kami Katsukiyo, who was serving the Shōgun as a Junior Councilor[8] at the time, still had three sons living at home. If Rin'emon were to apply to the

Shōgun for permission to adopt one of those sons as the heir to the house in place of Shuri, the plan would almost surely be approved. Such negotiations would, of course, have to be kept absolutely secret from both Shuri and his consort. Only when his desperate ruminations had reached this point did Rin'emon feel he had emerged into the light. The feeling was clouded, though, by an undeniable tinge of sorrow such as he had never known before. "This is all for the sake of the House," he told himself, but behind his resolve he sensed, indistinctly, a certain effort at self-vindication, and the awareness hovered there like a barely perceptible halo around the moon.

What Shuri, with his delicate health, hated most about Rin'emon was his robust constitution. Next he hated the quiet power that Rin'emon possessed over him as an "attached" House Elder. And finally he hated the way Rin'emon's loyalty was centered entirely upon the House. "You forget that I am your lord!" he had shouted at Rin'emon, his words smoldering with the dark flames of his complex hatred.

And now, suddenly, from his own lady's mouth, came word of this plot against him! Rin'emon was planning to force him into retirement and adopt the son of Itakura Sado-no-kami to take his place. She had heard of it by chance, and when Shuri heard it from her in turn, he was, understandably, wide-eyed with rage.

Yes, it well could be that Rin'emon was deeply concerned for the House of Itakura. But did "loyalty" mean serving the House to the point of casting one's present master aside? Moreover, Rin'emon's fears for the House could well be groundless. *And for these groundless fears he is willing to force me into retirement*, thought Shuri. Perhaps behind Rin'emon's great show of "loyalty" lay an ambition to seize control of the House for himself. For such an outright act of disloyalty, no punishment could be too cruel.

As soon as he heard about Rin'emon's plot from his consort, Shuri summoned old Tanaka Usaemon,[9] who had been his primary mentor and guardian in childhood.

"I want you to strangle that Rin'emon bastard!"

Usaemon cocked his graying head to one side. Aged beyond his years, his face had added still more wrinkles owing to the recent anxieties. Usaemon was not happy about Rin'emon's plan either, but after all, Rin'emon had been "attached" here by the Main House.

"Strangulation would be too harsh a punishment," he said. "Ordering him to slit his belly open like a true samurai would be another matter, however."

Shuri looked at Usaemon with mocking eyes. Then he gave two or three hard shakes of his head.

"No, that animal doesn't deserve *seppuku*. Strangle him! Strangle him!"

Inexplicably, though, even as he spoke these cruel words, tears gushed down his pale cheeks, and he once again began tearing at the hair of his temples.

Almost immediately, word of the order for his strangulation reached Rin'emon from a good friend who was one of Shuri's close retainers.

"Fine," he declared. "That does it. I have my own pride. I have no intention of letting them strangle me just like that."

The moment he heard the news, he felt the indefinable anxiety that had been dogging him melt away without a trace. Now his heart was filled with outright hatred for Shuri. Shuri was no longer a lord to him. He could hate the man without reserve. Such was the instantaneous—though unconscious—reasoning behind the sudden brightening in Rin'emon's heart.

Rin'emon thereupon took his wife and children and retainers with him and vacated Shuri's compound in broad daylight. Following proper procedure, he left his new address posted on an inside wall. Rin'emon himself led the way, carrying his lance under his arm. The entire retinue, including young samurai and servants helping the infirm and carrying military gear and footwear, amounted to no more than ten people. With total composure, they walked out through the front gate together.

This occurred on the last day of the third month of the fourth year of Enkyō. Outside the gate, a tepid wind hurled clouds of

mingled sand and cherry blossoms against the compound's
fortified latticed windows. Rin'emon stood in the wind, surveying the thoroughfare that stretched away to either side. And
then, with his lance, he signaled to the group, "Go left."

2. Tanaka Usaemon

After Rin'emon's departure, Tanaka Usaemon served as House
Elder in his place. Having helped to raise the young Shuri,
Usaemon naturally viewed him with different eyes from the
other retainers. He nursed Shuri through his fits with the emotions of a parent. Shuri, for his part, seemed more pliant with
Usaemon. And so the relationship between master and retainer
worked far more smoothly than it had in Rin'emon's time.

Usaemon was delighted to find that Shuri's attacks began to
diminish somewhat with the arrival of summer. He did worry
that Shuri might offend someone in the Castle of the Shōgun,
but where Rin'emon had feared such an event for the danger it
might pose to the House of Itakura, Usaemon feared it for the
danger it might pose to his master.

To be sure, the House was of concern to Usaemon as well.
But if an untoward event were to occur, it would be a disaster
not simply because it would destroy the House but because, in
causing his lord to destroy the House, it would cause his lord
to be branded as unfilial. What, then, should he do to prevent
such a disaster? On this point, Usaemon did not seem to have
Rin'emon's clarity. Perhaps there was nothing he could do but
trust in the protection of the gods and in his own purity of
spirit, and pray for Shuri's fits to subside.

On the first day of the eighth month that year, then, when
the Tokugawa government held the so-called Ceremony of the
First Fruits, Shuri attended an event at the Castle for the first
time since his illness. Like the other lords, both greater and
lesser, he dressed entirely in white and joined the solemn procession marking the initial entry, one hundred and fifty-seven
years earlier, of the great Tokugawa founder, Ieyasu, into Edo
Castle on this day celebrating the year's harvest. On his way
home, Shuri also visited Junior Councilor Itakura Sado-no-

kami, who was living in the Castle's Western Enclosure at the time. When Shuri reached home, apparently without having given offense to anyone in the Castle, Usaemon felt he could breathe freely once again.

But his joy did not survive the day. Soon after night fell, like a terrible omen, a messenger arrived from Itakura Sado-no-kami demanding that Usaemon come to the Castle immediately. Usaemon had never heard of any such occurrence—a sudden summons to the Castle after dark—in all the years that Rin'emon had been House Elder before him. He hurried to Sado-no-kami's mansion with a deep sense of foreboding.

And, just as he had feared, Sado-no-kami told Usaemon that Shuri had indeed committed an offense. After attending the ceremony, and still dressed from head to toe in white, Shuri came to visit Sado-no-kami in the Western Enclosure. Noting that Shuri's color was bad, Sado-no-kami had supposed that he was still not fully recovered from his illness, but once they started conversing, Shuri evidenced no sign of infirmity. Relieved, Sado-no-kami had gone on chatting with Shuri about one thing or another until he happened to ask after Maejima Rin'emon as he always did. Shuri's brow suddenly darkened and he said, "That Rin'emon bastard ran off from my house." Sado-no-kami knew quite well what sort of person Rin'emon was: he was certainly not a man who would desert his master's house without a good reason. Sado-no-kami asked Shuri for an explanation and, at the same time, admonished him: if a retainer "attached" by the Main House committed a blunder of any kind, it was a serious violation for Shuri not to have informed the relatives and sought their advice. Shuri's eyes flashed with rage when he heard this and, grasping his sword hilt, he declared, "Rin'emon may be one of your special favorites, Sado-no-kami, but let me tell you this: whatever my shortcomings, I will punish my own retainers as I see fit. You may be the 'Junior Councilor' of the moment, but I will thank you to keep your advice to yourself." Even Sado-no-kami, with all his experience, was stunned by this outburst, and, using the press of his official duties as a convenient excuse, he hurried out of the room.

Having recounted the day's events thus far, Sado-no-kami scowled at Usaemon and said, "Now listen to this." First of all, Usaemon was seriously at fault in having failed to notify the relatives of Rin'emon's departure. Secondly, Usaemon was also wrong to allow Shuri to enter the Castle while he was still apt to have fits. Fortunately, today's offense had only been against Sado-no-kami, himself another Itakura; but if Shuri had uttered such abusive remarks in the presence of the assembled Great Lords, his 7,000-*koku* estate would have been confiscated then and there.

"From now on, Usaemon, you must adopt a strict policy of keeping Shuri at home. It is especially important that you never allow him to attend any functions at the Castle." Sado-no-kami glared at Usaemon as he spoke. "I am worried that you may begin taking after your master and having fits yourself. Remember, now, I have given you strict orders."

Usaemon knit his brow and declared, "I understand completely, Your Lordship. From now on, I will exercise the utmost caution."

"Good. Make sure that nothing like this ever happens again," said Sado-no-kami, all but spitting out his words.

"I will stake my life on it, Your Lordship." Usaemon looked at Sado-no-kami with pleading tear-filled eyes. These were eyes that begged for pity and, at the same time, displayed Usaemon's unshakable determination—not that he would succeed in preventing Shuri from leaving the house but that, if he failed to prevent such an occurrence, his way was clear.

Sado-no-kami saw this, scowled again, and looked away as if utterly weary of the whole business.

If I follow the will of my master, the House will be placed in danger. If I act to support the House, I will have to contravene the will of my master. Rin'emon, too, was caught in this dilemma. But Rin'emon had the courage to cast his master aside for the sake of the House. Or rather, he placed far less importance on his master to begin with. And so it was easy for him to sacrifice his master for the House.

For me, however, that is impossible. I am far too close to my master to think only of what is best for the House. How could I possibly force this master of mine into retirement for the sake of the "House"—a mere name? Shuri may no longer have the toy "devil-quelling bow" I gave him at New Year's long ago, but in my eyes he is still that same little boy. I still have vivid memories of explaining picture books to him, of holding his hand in writing practice, of putting the tail on his kite . . .

And yet, if I simply let my master have his way, the House is not the only thing that will perish. Terrible things may happen to my master himself as well. In calculating what is best for everyone, the policy adopted by Rin'emon was undoubtedly the wisest—indeed, the only course to take. I see that perfectly well. And yet, for me it is an impossibility.

Mind running over the same ground again and again, Usaemon walked back to Shuri's residence, arms folded in dejection, as lightning flashed in the distant sky above.

The next day Shuri heard in detail from Usaemon about everything that Sado-no-kami had ordered. His face clouded over, but that was all. He gave no sign of flying into one of his rages. Usaemon, though still concerned, felt some relief as he withdrew that day from his master's presence.

For some ten days thereafter, Shuri remained shut up in his room, staring into space, lost in thought. Not even the appearance of Usaemon would prompt him to speak.

There was one exception, however. On a day when a light rain was falling, he heard a cuckoo cry, and he muttered, "They say cuckoos rob nightingales' nests."

Usaemon leaped on the opportunity to make conversation with him, but Shuri fell silent again and cast his eyes toward the murky sky. At other times he kept his mouth clamped shut like a mute, staring at the paintings on the room's sliding doors or at the white paper shoji in the window. His face revealed no emotion whatever.

One night, though, two or three days before the assembly of the 15th, at which all the greater and lesser lords residing in

Edo were due to participate in a joint audience before the
Shōgun, without warning Shuri summoned Usaemon. He
ordered his attendants out of the room, and, alone, the two
men took up formal positions on the matted floor, sitting opposite each other on their heels and looking into each other's eyes.
With a gloomy expression, Shuri began to speak:

"Sado-no-kami was right: my physical condition makes it
impossible for me to perform my duties properly. I, too, believe
that I should retire as head of this household."

Usaemon hesitated to respond. He could only hope that Shuri
was expressing his true feelings. But how could he have so easily
come to accept the idea of ceding his inheritance to another?

"I agree with you entirely, My Lord. I am sorry to say this,
but if His Lordship Sado-no-kami says so, there really is nothing
else we can do. But first ... it might be a good idea ... to
inform the close relatives —"

"No, not at all. My retirement is quite another matter from
my punishing Rin'emon. My relatives need not be consulted.
They will assent readily enough." Shuri said this with a bitter
smile.

"Oh no, surely not, My Lord."

Usaemon's expression made it clear that his heart was breaking for Shuri, but Shuri did not respond to his remark.

"So, in any case, once I retire, I will not be able to present
myself at the Castle even if I want to. Therefore ..." Shuri
looked hard at Usaemon and continued as if weighing each and
every word. "Before I retire, I wish to present myself at the
Castle one more time and be granted an audience with His
Sequestered Lordship of the Western Enclosure.[10] Tell me now:
will you let me go to the Castle on the 15th?"

Usaemon fell silent and knit his brows.

"Just this one time," Shuri said.

"Forgive me, Your Lordship, but going to the Castle is the
one thing ..."

"... you won't let me do, eh?"

They sat looking at each other, saying nothing. In the silent
room, the only sound was that of the lamp wick sucking up oil.
To Usaemon, this short interval felt like a year. Having sworn

as he did to Sado-no-kami, he could not give Shuri permission without forfeiting his honor as a samurai.

"I ask this of you knowing full well what Sado-no-kami told you," Shuri said. "I also know that you will earn the displeasure of the family if you allow me to enter the Castle. But think about it from my point of view: I am deranged, a madman who has been abandoned not only by his entire family but by his own retainers."

As Shuri spoke, his voice began to tremble with emotion. Usaemon saw his eyes filling with tears.

"The whole world mocks me. I must yield my inheritance to the hands of a stranger. The sun may never shine on me again. This is what has become of me! I can't believe that you, Usaemon—that you of all people would deny me the one desire I have left in this life: merely to present myself at the Castle one last time. You might pity me, Usaemon, but I know you do not hate me. I think of you as a father, Usaemon. As a brother. No, I feel even closer to you than to a father or a brother. You are the one person in the whole wide world that I can depend upon. And it is precisely because I feel so close to you that I dare to ask you this one impossible favor. But it is something I will never ask of you again in this life. This one time is all I ask for. Please, Usaemon, try to understand what I feel in my heart. Please grant me this one impossible wish. I beg you, like this . . ."

Shuri leaned forward, dropping his hands to the floor before his House Elder. With tears streaming from his eyes, he began to lower his forehead to the mat. This was more than Usaemon could bear.

"Please, Your Lordship, raise your hands from the mat, raise your hands. Please don't humble yourself to me this way. I don't deserve . . ."

He grasped Shuri's hands, forcing them up from the mat. And then he cried. And the more he cried, the more his heart seemed to fill—and then to flood—with a calm confidence. In the midst of his tears, he vividly recalled the declaration he had made in the presence of Sado-no-kami.

"All right, then, My Lord," he said to Shuri. "Whatever

Sado-no-kami might say, I can settle any eventuality by slitting open this wrinkled old belly of mine. I *will* let you go up to the Castle, and the fault will be mine alone."

Shuri's face shone with joy when he heard this: he looked like a different person. The sudden change reflected the skill of an actor, but it had a naturalness that no actor could summon. He let out a wild burst of laughter.

"Then you *will* let me go? Oh, thank you, Usaemon! Thank you so much!"

Beaming, Shuri looked to his left and right.

"Did you hear that, everyone? Usaemon is going to let me go to the Castle!"

Everyone? Shuri had cleared his attendants from the room beforehand; there was no one present but him and Usaemon. Still on his knees, Usaemon inched anxiously closer to Shuri, and, in the light filtering through the lantern's paper shade, he peered fearfully into the young man's eyes.

3. Bloodshed

Shortly after the fifth hour of the morning on the fifteenth day of the eighth month of the fourth year of Enkyō, in the Castle of the Tokugawa Shōgun, Shuri murdered Hosokawa Etchū-no-kami Munenori,[11] Lord of Kumamoto Castle in Higo Province, a man he neither loved nor hated. The particulars of the event are as follows:

Among the Great Lords of the realm, those of the Hosokawa family were outstanding for their military attributes. Even Her Ladyship, Munenori's consort, known as "the Princess," was talented in the martial arts. It was inconceivable, therefore, that there might be anything lacking in the martial skills of Munenori himself. That such a man from such a distinguished lineage should have met such a miserable end at the hands of a relative amateur could only have been due to sheer bad luck.

In retrospect, however, it became clear that there had been any number of omens in the Hosokawa house foretelling the

occurrence of this calamity. First, the Hosokawas' villa in suburban Shinagawa-Isarago had burned to the ground earlier that
year. What made this all the more ominous was that the house
contained a shrine to the god of the North Star with a miraculous stone that spurted water before any fire could spread, and
so the villa had never burned down before. Then, early in the
fifth month, someone noticed that a protective amulet from
the Aizen'in Temple had been miswritten. Hanging on the
front gate, where it should have said "MAY THIS HOUSE
KNOW CONTINUED LUCK IN BATTLE AND FREE-
DOM FROM CALAMITIES," the word "CALAMITIES"
had been omitted. They consulted with a priest from a family
temple and decided to have the plaque rewritten immediately
at Aizen'in. The third omen came early in the eighth month,
when mysterious big lights appeared night after night from
the area of the mansion's great hall and flew off toward the
neighborhood of Shiba.

In addition to these signs, at noon on the 14th a retainer well
versed in astrology—a man named Saiki Moemon—came to
see the Tokugawa censor stationed in Munenori's Tokyo residence and said, "Something terrible might happen to His Lordship tomorrow, the fifteenth. When I was studying the skies last
night, the General's Star[12] looked as though it was ready to fall.
Better to err on the side of caution. Please make certain that
His Lordship does not leave the house." The censor himself
had little faith in astrology, but he knew that Lord Munenori
had great respect for this man's prognostications. He decided
at least to tell one of Munenori's close attendants, and from
him it reached the ear of Etchū-no-kami himself. As a result,
they decided that on the fifteenth he would forgo both a performance of Nō and Kyōgen[13] and a courtesy call that he had
planned to make on his way home from the Castle. Attendance
at the Castle itself, however, he would not put off.

Then, on the very day, the 15th, there was one more evil
omen in addition to all the others. It was Etchū-no-kami's
custom on the 15th of every month to dress in linen ceremonial
robes and, with his own hand, to offer sacred saké before the
war god, Hachiman Daibosatsu. On that particular morning,

however, after he had received the tray holding two round earthenware bottles of sacred saké from the hands of a page and turned to offer it up before the god, both bottles inexplicably toppled over, spilling their sacred contents. As might be expected, everyone in the room went pale.

When Etchū-no-kami proceeded to the Castle later that day accompanied by the Buddhist attendant Tashiro Yūetsu,[14] he first entered the Great Hall. Soon afterward, however, he felt the need to move his bowels and, accompanied this time by another Buddhist attendant, Kuroki Kansai, he entered the privy beside the anteroom and relieved himself. He then emerged from the privy and was washing his hands in the dark lavatory when suddenly, from behind, some unknown person cried out and slashed at him with a sword. Taken off guard, he spun around and in that instant the sword flashed again, cutting him down the forehead. Blinded by his own blood, Etchū-no-kami could not see the face of his attacker, who used this advantage to rain blow after blow on him. Etchū-no-kami stumbled out of the lavatory and collapsed on the veranda of Chamber Four, just off the hall. The attacker threw down his weapon—a short sword—and disappeared.

Meanwhile, the attendant who had accompanied Etchū-no-kami to the privy, Kuroki Kansai, reacted to this unanticipated catastrophe with panic. He fled back to the Great Hall, and then went into hiding, as a result of which no one knew that Etchū-no-kami's blood had been shed. The victim was finally found some time later by an officer of the Shōgunal guard named Homma Sadagorō, who was on his way from the guard-room to the servants' quarters. Homma immediately informed the Castle foot patrol, and from that office rushed the chief patrolman, Kuge Zenbē, with such other foot patrolmen as Tsuchida Han'emon and Komoda Niemon. Then the entire castle erupted as if someone had broken open a hornet's nest.

They lifted the wounded man from where he lay, but his face and body were so covered with blood that no one recognized him. Someone bent toward him and spoke into his ear until, at last, he replied in a feeble voice, "Hosokawa Etchū."

"Who did this to you?"

His only reply was, "A man in formal dress," which could have been any man allowed into the Castle. No further questions seemed to reach him. His wounds were recorded as, "Nape of the neck, 7 inches; left shoulder, 6–7 inches; right shoulder, 5 inches; 4–5 cuts on each hand; 2–3 cuts around the head: above the nose, beside the ear, top of the head; diagonal cut down the back to right flank, 1 foot 6 inches." Attended not only by the duty inspectors, Tsuchiya Chōtarō and Hashimoto Awa-no-kami, but also the Chief Inspector, Kōno Buzen-no-kami, the wounded man was carried to the Hearth Room. They set low screens around him and assigned five Buddhist attendants to watch over him, after which one Great Lord after another came from the Great Hall to tend to his needs. Matsudaira Hyōbushōyū treated him most tenderly of all as they were still carrying him in, such that all who witnessed this, it was said, could see the depth of his devotion.

The Senior and Junior Councilors having meanwhile been notified of the emergency, orders went out to lock every gate in the Castle to forestall any eventuality. The crowd of retainers who had accompanied their masters as far as the Great Main Gate saw the huge gate being closed and immediately assumed there was a crisis in the Castle. This set off a tremendous commotion, and though several inspectors came out to try to quiet the men down, time and again the crowd would surge toward the gate like a tsunami. The confusion inside the Castle continued to grow as well. Inspector Tsuchiya Chōtarō took a number of men with him from among the foot patrol and the fire watch. They searched everywhere, including all guard stations and even the kitchen, in a determined effort to find the attacker. They were, however, unable to discover the "man in formal dress."

Rather than these men, the culprit was found by a Buddhist attendant named Takarai Sōga, much to everyone's surprise. Sōga was a bold young fellow, and he went around searching in places that the group had ignored. When he peeked into the privy near the Hearth Room, he found there, crouching like a shadow, a man whose hair had come loose at the temples. Because it was dark inside, he could not be sure what he was seeing, but it looked as though the man had pulled a scissors from his leather pouch and was cutting the disordered locks. Sōga leaned into the privy and called out to the man:

"Sir . . . may I ask who you are?"

The man replied hoarsely, "I am a man who is cutting his hair[15] because he has just killed someone."

This left no room for doubt. Sōga immediately called for help and they pulled the man from the privy, entrusting him for the moment to the foot patrol.

The foot patrol in turn brought him to the Sago Palm Room, where the Chief Inspector and the other inspectors gathered and interrogated him about the bloody attack. All he did, however, was stare blankly at the Castle's great commotion, offering no coherent reply. And when he did open his mouth, it was to say something about a cuckoo. Now and then his blood-stained hands would tear at the hair of his temples. Shuri had lost his mind.

Hosokawa Etchū-no-kami drew his last breath in the Hearth Room. By secret order of His Sequestered Lordship Yoshimune, he was removed from the Castle as having been "wounded," his palanquin carried through the Middle Gate to the Hirakawa Gate. Formal announcement of his death did not come until the 21st of the month.

On the actual day of the murder, Shuri was put in the custody of Lord Mizuno Kenmotsu of Okazaki and removed from the Castle, also through the Middle Gate to the Hirakawa Gate, but in a palanquin covered with green netting and surrounded by fifty Mizuno foot soldiers. The men were uniformly dressed in brand-new dark-orange jackets and brand-new white breeches, and they carried brand-new poles, the ends of which they set on the ground with each step. The display was said to have won Kenmotsu praise as evidence that he was always well prepared for any eventuality.

Seven days later, on the 22nd of the month, acting as the envoy of the Shōgun, Chief Censor Ishikawa Tosa-no-kami read the official verdict to Shuri: "Although you are judged to have become mentally deranged, whereas Hosokawa Etchū-no-kami died from the untreatable wounds you inflicted upon him, you are hereby ordered to commit *seppuku* in the residence of Mizuno Kenmotsu."

Shuri sat formally on his heels in the presence of the envoy, but though he was presented with a short sword in the customary manner, his limp hands remained on his knees. When he made no move to lift the sword from its tray and slash himself across the belly, the Mizuno retainer assigned to second him, Yoshida Yasōzaemon, did what he had to do, lopping off Shuri's head from behind. The cut could not have been more perfect, leaving a flap of skin at the throat so that the head did not drop to the ground. Yasōzaemon lifted the head and displayed it to the Shōgun's official witness. With its high cheekbones and yellowed skin, the head was almost painful to look at. The eyes, of course, were not closed.

The witness examined the head and, smelling the blood, expressed his satisfaction to the swordsman: "An excellent cut."

That same day, at the residence of Itakura Shikibu, Tanaka Usaemon was punished with strangulation. The bill of indictment against him read as follows: "Although Itakura Sado-no-kami had expressly ordered Usaemon to enforce the domiciliary confinement of Shuri due to the latter's illness, Usaemon, at his own discretion, allowed Shuri to enter the Castle, thus bringing about the present calamity, leading to the confiscation of Shuri's 7,000-*koku* estate. This is an inexcusable offense."

Needless to say, other Itakura relatives such as Itakura Suō-no-kami, Itakura Shikibu, Itakura Sado-no-kami, Sakai Saemon-no-jō, and Matsudaira Ukon Shōgen were ordered to undergo a period of house arrest. In addition, Kuroki Kansai, the Buddhist attendant who had abandoned Etchū-no-kami at the time of the attack, was deprived of his stipend and banished from the capital.

Itakura Shuri might have killed Hosokawa Etchū-no-kami by mistake. The nine-circle crest on formal clothing of the Hosokawa family so closely resembled the nine-circle crest worn by members of the Itakura family that Shuri may have meant to kill Itakura Sado-no-kami. Precisely this kind of mistaken identity had occurred in the slashing of Mōri Mondo-no-shō by Mizuno Hayato-no-shō.[16] Such an error would have been particularly easy to commit in the dark lavatory—or so went the most widely-held opinion at the time.

Only Itakura Sado-no-kami objected to this view. Whenever the subject came up, he would fume, "Shuri had absolutely no reason to kill me. He was a madman. He killed Etchū-no-kami for nothing at all. This wild speculation about a mistaken identity I find deeply offensive. How much more proof do you need that he was mad? What did he talk about when he appeared before the Chief Inspector? Cuckoos! Maybe he thought he was killing a cuckoo!"

(February 1917)

MODERN TRAGICOMEDY

THE STORY OF A
HEAD THAT FELL OFF

I

Xiao-er threw his sword down and clutched at his horse's mane, thinking *I'm sure my neck's been cut.* No, perhaps the thought crossed his mind only *after* he started hanging on. He knew that something had slammed deep into his neck, and at that very moment he grabbed hold of the mane. The horse must have been wounded, too. As Xiao-er flopped over the front of his saddle, the horse let out a high whinny, tossed its muzzle toward the sky, and, tearing through the great stew of allies and enemies, started galloping straight across the corn field that stretched as far as the eye could see. A few shots might have rung out from behind, but to Xiao-er they were like sounds in a dream.

Trampled by the furiously galloping horse, the man-tall corn stalks bent and swayed like a wave, snapping back to sweep the length of Xiao-er's pigtail or slap against his uniform or wipe away the black blood gushing from his neck. Not that he had the presence of mind to notice. Seared into his brain with painful clarity was nothing but the simple fact that he had been cut. *I'm cut. I'm cut.* His mind repeated the words over and over while his heels kicked mechanically into the horse's lathered flanks.

Ten minutes earlier, Xiao-er and his fellow cavalrymen had crossed the river from camp to reconnoiter a small village when, in the yellowing field of corn, they suddenly encountered a mounted party of Japanese cavalry. It happened so quickly that neither side had time to fire a shot. The moment the Chinese troops caught sight of the enemy's red-striped caps and the red ribbing of their uniforms, they drew their swords and headed their horses directly into them. At that moment, of course, no one was thinking that he might be killed. The only thing in their minds was the enemy: killing the enemy. As they turned their horses' heads, they bared their teeth like dogs and charged ferociously toward the Japanese troops. Those enemy troops must have been governed by the same impulse, though, for in a moment the Chinese found themselves surrounded by faces that could have been mirror images of their own, with teeth similarly bared. Along with the faces came the sound of swords swishing through the air all around them.

From then on, Xiao-er had no clear sense of time. He did have a weirdly vivid memory of the tall corn swaying as if in a violent storm, and of a copper sun hanging above the swaying tassels. How long the commotion lasted, what happened during that interval and in what order—none of that was clear. All the while, Xiao-er went on swinging his sword wildly and screaming like a madman, making sounds that not even he could understand. His sword turned red at one point, he seemed to recall, but he felt no impact. The more he swung his sword, the slicker the hilt grew from his own greasy sweat. His mouth felt strangely dry. All at once the frenzied face of a Japanese cavalryman, eyeballs ready to pop from his head, mouth straining open, flew into the path of Xiao-er's horse. The man's burred scalp shone through a split in his red-striped cap. At the sight, Xiao-er raised his sword and brought it down full force on the cap. What his sword hit was not the cap, though, nor the head beneath it, but rather the other man's steel slashing upward. Amid the surrounding pandemonium, the clash of swords resounded with a terrifying transparency, driving the cold smell of filed iron sharply into his nostrils. Just then, reflecting the glare of the sun, a broad sword rose directly above Xiao-er's head and plunged downward in a great arc. In that instant, a thing of indescribable coldness slammed into the base of his neck.

The horse went on charging through the corn field with Xiao-er on its back, groaning from the pain of his wound. The densely planted corn would never give out, it seemed, no matter how long the horse kept running. The cries of men and horses, the clash of swords had faded long before. The autumn sun shone down on Liaodong just as it does in Japan.

Again, Xiao-er, swaying on horseback, was groaning from the pain of his wound. The noise that escaped his firmly gritted teeth, however, was more than a groan: it carried a somewhat more complex meaning. Which is to say that he was not simply moaning over his physical pain. He was wailing because of his psychological pain, because of the dizzying ebb and flow of his emotions, centering on the fear of death.

He felt unbearable sorrow to be leaving this world forever. He also felt deep resentment toward the men and events that were hastening his departure. He was angry, too, at himself for having allowed this to happen. And then—each one calling forth the next—a multitude of emotions came to torment him. As one gave way to another, he would shout, "I'm dying! I'm dying!", or call out for his father or mother, or curse the Japanese cavalryman who did this to him. As each cry left his lips, however, it was transformed into a meaningless, rasping groan, so weak had he become.

I'm the unluckiest man alive, coming to a place like this to fight and die so young, killed like a dog, for nothing. I hate the Japanese who wounded me. I hate my own officer who sent me out on this reconnaissance mission. I hate the countries that started this war—Japan and China. And that's not all I hate. Anyone who had anything to do with making me a soldier is my enemy. Because of all those people, I now have to leave this world where there is so much I want to do. Oh, what a fool I was to let them do this to me!

Investing his moans with such meaning, Xiao-er clutched at the horse as it bounded on through the corn. Every now and then a flock of quail would flutter up from the undergrowth, startled by the powerful animal, but the horse paid them no heed. It was unconcerned, too, that its rider often seemed ready to slide off its back, and it charged ahead, foaming at the mouth.

Had fate permitted it, Xiao-er would have gone on tossing back and forth atop the horse all day, bemoaning his misfortune to the heavens until that copper sun sank in the western sky. But when a narrow, muddy stream flowing between the corn stalks opened in a bright band ahead of him where the plain began to slope gently upward, fate took the shape of two or three river willows standing majestically on the bank, their low branches still dense with leaves just beginning to fall. As Xiao-er's horse passed between them, the trees suddenly scooped him up into their leafy branches and tossed him upside-down onto the soft mud of the bank.

At that very instant, through some associative connection, Xiao-er saw bright yellow flames burning in the sky. They were the same bright yellow flames he used to see burning under the huge stove in the kitchen of his childhood home. *Oh, the fire is burning*, he thought, but in the next instant he was already unconscious.

2

Was Xiao-er entirely unconscious after he fell from his horse? True, the pain of his wound was almost gone, but he knew he was lying on the deserted river bank, smeared in mud and blood, and looking up through the willow leaves caressing the deep blue dome of the sky. This sky was deeper and bluer than any he had ever seen before. Lying on his back, he felt as if he were looking up into a gigantic inverted indigo vase. In the bottom of the vase, clouds like massed foam would appear out of nowhere and then slowly fade as if scattered by the ever-moving willow leaves.

Was Xiao-er, then, not entirely unconscious? Between his eyes and the blue sky passed a great many shadow-like things that were not actually there. First he saw his mother's slightly grimy apron. How often had he clung to that apron in childhood, in both happy times and sad? His hand now reached out for it, but in that instant it disappeared from view. First it grew thin as gossamer, and beyond it, as through a layer of mica, he could see a mass of white cloud.

Next there came gliding across the sky the sprawling sesame field behind the house he was born in—the sesame field in midsummer, when sad little flowers bloom as if waiting for the sun to set. Xiao-er searched for an image of himself or his brothers standing in the sesame plants, but there was no sign of anything human, just a quiet blend of pale flowers and leaves bathed in pale sunlight. It cut diagonally across the space above him and vanished as if lifted up and away.

Then something strange came slithering across the sky—one of those long dragon lanterns they carry through the streets on the night of the lantern festival. Made of thin paper glued to a bamboo frame a good thirty feet long, it was painted in garish greens and reds, and it looked just like a dragon you might see in a picture. It stood out clearly against the daytime sky, lighted from within by candles. Stranger still, it seemed to be alive, its long whiskers waving freely. Xiao-er was still taking this in when it swam out of his view and quickly vanished.

As soon as the dragon was gone, the slender foot of a woman came to take its place. A bound foot, it was no more than three inches long. At the tip of its gracefully curved toe, a whitish nail softly parted the color of the flesh. In Xiao-er's heart, memories of the time he saw that foot brought with them a vague, far-off sadness, like a fleabite in a dream. If only he could touch that foot again—but no, that would never happen. Hundreds of miles separated this place from the place where he had seen that foot. As he dwelt on the impossibility of ever touching it again, the foot grew transparent until it was drawn into the clouds.

At that point Xiao-er was overcome by a mysterious loneliness such as he had never experienced before. The vast blue sky hung above him in silence. People had no choice but to go on living their pitiful lives beneath that sky, buffeted by the winds that blow down from above. What loneliness! And how strange, he thought, that he had never known this loneliness until now. Xiao-er released a lengthy sigh.

All at once the Japanese cavalry troops with their red-striped caps charged in between his eyes and the sky, moving with far greater speed than any of the earlier images, and disappearing just as quickly. *Ah yes, those cavalrymen must be feeling a loneliness as great as mine.* Had they not been mere apparitions, he would have wanted to comfort them and be comforted by them, to forget this loneliness if only for a moment. But it was too late now.

Xiao-er's eyes overflowed with tears. And when, with those tear-moistened eyes, he looked back on his life, he recognized all too well the ugliness that had filled it. He wanted to apologize to everyone, and he also wanted to forgive everyone for what they had done to him.

If I escape death today, I swear that I will do whatever it takes to make up for my past.

Xiao-er wept as he formed these words deep in his heart. But, as if unwilling to listen, the sky, in all its infinite depth, in all its infinite blueness, slowly began to press down upon him where he lay, foot by foot, inch by inch. Faintly sparkling points in the vast blue expanse were surely stars visible in daylight. No longer did he see shadowy images passing before him. Xiao-er sighed once more, felt a sudden trembling of the lips, and, in the end, let his eyelids slowly close.

3

A year had gone by since the signing of the peace treaty between China and Japan. One morning in early spring, Major Kimura, military attaché to the Japanese legation in Beijing, and Dr. Yamakawa, a technician on official tour of inspection from the Ministry of Agriculture and Commerce in Tokyo, were seated at a table in the legation office. They were enjoying a quiet conversation over coffee and cigars in a momentary diversion from the press of their duties. Despite the season, a fire was burning in the wood stove and the room was warm enough to bring out perspiration. Every now and then, the potted red plum on the table wafted a distinctively Chinese fragrance into the air.

Their conversation centered on the Empress Dowager[1] for a while but eventually turned to recollections of the Sino-Japanese War, at which point Major Kimura suddenly stood up and brought over a bound copy of a Chinese newspaper from a rack in the corner. Spreading it open on the table before Dr. Yamakawa, he pointed to the page with a look in his eyes that said, "Read this!" Dr. Yamakawa was startled by this sudden gesture, but he had long known that Major Kimura was a good deal more sophisticated and witty than the typical military man, and he expected to find a bizarre anecdote relating to the war. He was not disappointed. In impressive rows of square Chinese characters, the article said:

A man named He Xiao-er, owner of a barber shop on —— Street, served with great distinction in the Sino-Japanese War and was cited for numerous acts of valor. Following his triumphant home-coming, however, he tended to indulge in dissolute behavior, debauching himself with drink and women. At the X Bar last ——day, he was arguing with his drinking companions and a scuffle broke out, at the conclusion of which he suffered a severe neck wound and died instantaneously. The strangest thing was the wound to the neck, which was not inflicted by a weapon during the incident. It was, rather, the reopening of a wound that Xiao-er had suffered on the battlefield. According to one eyewitness, a table fell over and the victim fell with it. The moment he hit the floor, his head fell off, remaining attached by only one strip of skin and spilling blood everywhere. The authorities are said to have serious doubts about the truth of this account and to be engaged in a determined search for the perpetrator, but since *Strange Tales of Liaozhai*[2] contains the account of a man's head falling off, can we say for certain that such a thing could not have happened to someone such as He Xiao-er?

Dr. Yamakawa had a shocked expression on his face when he finished reading the article. "What *is* this?" he asked.

Major Kimura released a long, slow stream of cigar smoke and, with a mellow smile, said, "Fascinating, don't you think? A thing like this could only happen in China."

"True," Doctor Yamakawa answered with a grin, knocking the long ash on his cigar into an ashtray. "It's simply unthink-able any place else."

"There's more to the story, though," Major Kimura said, pausing with a somber expression on his face. "I know the fellow, Xiao-er."

"You know him? Oh, come on, don't tell me a military attaché is going to start lying on a par with a newspaper reporter."

"No, of course I wouldn't do anything so ridiculous. When I was wounded back then in the battle of —— Village, Xiao-er was being treated in our field hospital. I talked to him a few times to practice my Chinese. He had a neck wound, so chances are eight or nine out of ten it's the same man. He told me he was on some kind of reconnaissance mission when he ran into some of our cavalrymen and got slashed in the neck."

"What a strange coincidence! The paper says he was a real trouble-maker, though. We would have all been better off if a fellow like that had died on the spot."

"Yes, but at the time he was a good, honest man, one of the best-behaved prisoners of war. The army doctors all seemed to have a soft spot for him and gave him extra-good treatment. I enjoyed the stories he told me about himself, too. I especially remember the way he described his feelings when he was badly wounded in the neck and fell off his horse. He was lying in the mud on a river bank, looking up at the sky through some willows, when he saw his mother's apron and a woman's bare foot and a sesame field in bloom—all right there in the sky."

Major Kimura threw his cigar away, brought his coffee cup to his lips, glanced at the red plum on the table, and went on as if talking to himself, "When he saw those things in the sky, he began to feel deeply ashamed of the way he had lived his life until then."

"So he turned into a trouble-maker as soon as the war ended? It just goes to show, you can't trust anybody." Dr. Yamakawa rested his head against the chair back, stretched his legs out, and, with an ironic air, blew his cigar smoke toward the ceiling.

"Can't trust anybody? You mean, you think he was faking it?"

"Of course he was."

"No, I don't think so. I think he was serious about the way

he felt—at the time, at least. And I'll bet he felt the same way again the moment 'his head fell off' (to use the paper's phrase). Here's how I imagine it: he was drunk when he was fighting, so the other man had no trouble throwing him down. When he landed, the wound opened up, and his head rolled onto the floor with its long pigtail hanging down. This time again, the same things passed in front of his eyes: his mother's apron, the woman's bare foot, the sesame field in bloom. And even though there was a roof in the way, maybe he even saw a deep blue sky far overhead. Again, he felt deeply ashamed of his life until then. This time, though, it was too late. The first time, a Japanese medical-corps man found him unconscious and took care of him. This time, the other man kept punching him and kicking him. He died full of regrets."

Dr. Yamakawa's shoulders shook with his laughter. "What a dreamer you are! If what you say is true, though, why did he let himself become a trouble-maker after the first time?"

"That's because, in a way different from what you meant by it, you can't trust anybody." Major Kimura lit a new cigar and, smiling, continued in tones that were almost exultantly cheerful. "It is important—even necessary—for us to become acutely aware of the fact that we can't trust ourselves. The only ones you can trust to some extent are people who really know that. We had better get this straight. Otherwise, our own characters' heads could fall off like Xiao-er's at any time. This is the way you have to read all Chinese newspapers."

(December 1917)

GREEN ONIONS

I plan to write this story in a single sitting tonight in time for the deadline I'm facing tomorrow. No, I don't "plan" to write it: I absolutely *have to* write it. So, then, what am I going to write about? All I can do is ask you to read what follows.

In a café in Jinbōchō, the used-bookstore neighborhood of Tokyo, there is a waitress named O-Kimi. They say she is only sixteen, but she looks more mature than that. And although the tip of her nose tilts up a little, her light complexion and limpid gaze definitely qualify her as a beauty. To see her standing in front of the player piano in her white apron, her hair parted in the middle and done up with forget-me-not hairpins, you would think she had stepped out of one of Takehisa Yumeji's illustrations[1] for a novel. Which seems to be one reason the café's regulars long ago decided to nickname her "Potboiler." She has other nicknames, too: "Forget-Me-Not" from her hairpins; "Miss Mary Pickford"[2] because she looks like the American movie star; "Sugar Cube" because the café can't do without her. Etc. etc.

There is another, older waitress who works at the café. Her name is O-Matsu, and her looks don't begin to match O-Kimi's. The two girls are as different as white bread and black bread, and the difference in what they earn in tips is also huge. O-Matsu is, of course, not happy about that, and as her dissatisfaction has mounted, it has led her to harbor some unkind thoughts.

One summer afternoon, a customer at O-Matsu's table—

apparently a student at the foreign language school—was trying hard to move the flame from his match to the tip of his cigarette. Unfortunately, the flame kept getting blown out by the powerful fan on the table next to his. O-Kimi happened by just then and stopped for a moment between the customer and the fan to block the breeze. It became clear that the student appreciated her thoughtfulness when, after managing to light his cigarette, he turned his suntanned face to her with a smile and said, "Thanks." This happened just as O-Matsu, standing by the counter, picked up the dish of ice cream that she was supposed to carry to that table. She glared at O-Kimi and said, "*You* take this to him," in a voice fuming with jealousy.

Complications like this happen several times a week, as a result of which O-Kimi rarely speaks to O-Matsu. She stations herself in front of the player piano, offering her silent affability to all the customers, who—because of the café's location among the bookstores—tend to be students. To the furious O-Matsu, however, O-Kimi offers only her wordless triumph over the hearts of all these young men.

O-Matsu's jealousy is not the only cause of their strained relationship, however. O-Kimi is also quietly contemptuous of O-Matsu's lowbrow taste. She is convinced that O-Matsu has done nothing since graduating from elementary school but listen to *naniwa-bushi*, eat *mitsu-mame*,[3] and chase after boys. But what of O-Kimi herself? What kind of taste does she have? To discover the answer to that, we should depart this bustling café scene for a moment and peek into a room over a beauty parlor at the far end of a nearby alley. O-Kimi rents this room, and this is where she spends most of her time when she is not waiting on tables at the café.

It is a low-ceilinged six-mat room. The western sun shines through its only window, from which there is nothing to be seen but tile roofs. A desk draped in printed cotton is set against the wall beneath the window. I call this piece of furniture a "desk" for convenience's sake: in fact, it is just a worn old table with stubby legs. Atop this "desk" sits a row of books in hard Western bindings, which are also old-looking: *The Cuckoo, Collected Poems of Tōson, The Life of Matsui Sumako, The*

New Asagao Diary, Carmen, and *High on the Mountain Looking Down in the Valley.*[4] Next to these are some women's magazines. Unfortunately, there is not a single volume of *my* stories to be seen. Next to the desk is a tea cabinet from which the varnish is peeling, and on top of that is a slender-necked glass vase in which is gracefully displayed an artificial lily that is missing a single petal. I'd guess that if the petal were still attached, the lily would still be decorating a table in the café. Finally, on the wall over the tea cabinet are tacked up a few pictures that seem to come from magazines. The one in the middle is *Genroku Woman* by our dear Kaburagi Kiyokata.[5] The little one below and overshadowed by it is probably a Raphael Madonna or some such thing. Meanwhile, above the Genroku beauty, a woman sculpted by Kitamura Shikai[6] is making lascivious eyes at her neighbor, Beethoven. This particular Beethoven, however, is just someone whom O-Kimi takes to be Beethoven. In fact, he is the American President, Woodrow Wilson, which is really too bad for old Kitamura Shikai.

This, then, should tell you more than you ever wanted to know about the artistically rich coloration of O-Kimi's cultural life. And in fact, when O-Kimi comes home from the café late at night, she invariably sits beneath the portrait of Woodrow Wilson *alias* Beethoven, reads more of *The Cuckoo*, gazes at her artificial lily, and indulges in an artistic ecstasy far more steeped in *sentimentalisme* than even the famous moonlit-shore scene in the movie version of the Shinpa tragedy based on *The Cuckoo.*[7]

One spring night when the cherry trees were in bloom, O-Kimi was alone at her desk almost till the cock's first crow, writing on page after page of pink letter paper. She did not seem to notice when one finished page fell under the desk. It remained there after the sun came up and she left for the café. The spring breeze then blew in through the window, lifted the sheet of paper, and carried it down the stairs, where the hairdresser's two mirrors stood in their saffron cotton slip-covers.[8] The beautician downstairs knew well that O-Kimi often received love letters, and she assumed that this sheet belonged to one of those. Out of curiosity, she decided to read it, but she was surprised to find that the handwriting seemed to be that of O-Kimi herself and that it was addressed to a woman: "My heart feels ready to burst with tears when I think of the time you parted from your dear Takeo." Takeo was the hero of *The Cuckoo*! So O-Kimi had stayed up practically the whole night writing a letter of condolence to Namiko, the heroine of the novel!

I have to admit that as I write this episode I can't help smiling at O-Kimi's *sentimentalisme*, but my smile contains not the slightest hint of meanness.

In addition to the artificial lily, the *Collected Poems of Tōson*, and the photo of Raphael's Madonna, O-Kimi's second-floor room contains all the kitchen tools she needs to survive without eating out. In other words, these kitchen tools symbolize the harsh reality of her life in Tokyo. Yet even a desolate life can reveal a world of beauty when viewed through a mist of tears. O-Kimi would take refuge in the tears of artistic ecstasy to escape the persecutions of everyday life. In such tears she need not think about her 6-yen monthly rent or the 70 sen it cost for a measure of rice.[9] Carmen has no electric bill to worry her; she only has to keep her castanets clicking. Namiko does suffer as she lies dying of tuberculosis, deprived of her beloved husband by her cruel mother-in-law, but she never has to scrape up money for her medicine. In a word, tears like this light a modest lamp of human love amid the gathering dusk of human suffering. Ah yes, I imagine O-Kimi all alone at night when the sounds of Tokyo have faded away, raising her tear-moistened eyes toward the dim electric lamp, dreaming dreams of the oleanders of Córdoba and the sea breeze of Namiko's Zushi, and then— damn it, "meanness" is the least of my sins! If I'm not careful, I could just as easily be swept away by *sentimentalisme* as O-Kimi! And this is *me* talking, the fellow the critics are always blaming for having too little heart and too much intellect.

O-Kimi comes home from the café late one winter night, and at first she sits at her desk as usual, reading *The Life of Matsui Sumako* or some such thing, but before she has completed a page, she slams the book down on the tatami-matted floor as if it has suddenly come to disgust her. She then turns sideways and leans against the desk, chin on hand, staring indifferently toward the portrait of Wils—uh, Beethoven—on the wall. Something is clearly bothering her. Has she been fired from the café? Has O-Matsu turned nastier? Has a decayed tooth begun to ache? No, the trouble now gripping O-Kimi's heart is nothing so mundane. Like Namiko, like Matsui Sumako, O-Kimi is suffering from love. Who, then, is the object of her affections? Fortunately for us, O-Kimi is apparently going to remain quite still, staring at Beethoven on the wall, and so, in the interval, let me give you a quick introduction to the lucky man.

The object of O-Kimi's affections is a young fellow named Tanaka, an unknown—let's say—artist. I call him that because he writes poetry, plays the violin, paints in oils, acts on the stage, knows the Hundred Poets card game inside out, and has mastered the lute for the martial music of Satsuma.[10] With so many talents, it's impossible to say which is his profession and which are mere hobbies. As for the man himself, he has the smooth features of an actor, his hair glows like the surface of an oil painting, his voice is as gentle as a violin, the words he speaks are as well chosen as a poem's, he can woo a woman as nimbly as he can snatch the right card in the Hundred Poets game, and he can skip out on a loan with the same heroic energy he brings to singing with his Satsuma lute. He wears a broad-brimmed black hat, inexpensive tweeds, a deep purple ascot—you get the picture. Come to think of it, Tanaka is a well-established type, two or three of whom are always scowling at the masses in any bar or café in the university district, in any concert at the YMCA or the Music Academy (though only in the cheapest seats), and at any of the more stylish art galleries. So if you would like a clearer portrait of young Mr. Tanaka, go to one of those places and have a look for yourself. I refuse to write another line about him. Besides, while I've been sweating over this introduction to Tanaka, O-Kimi has gotten up from her desk, has opened the shoji, and is now looking out at the cold moonlit night.

The light of the moon over the tile roofs shines down upon the

artificial lily in its slender-necked glass vase, the little Raphael
Madonna, and O-Kimi's upturned nose. It does not, however,
register upon the girl's limpid gaze. Neither do the frosty tile
roofs exist for her. Young Tanaka walked her home from the
café tonight, and the two have agreed to spend tomorrow
evening in each other's pleasant company. Tomorrow is the
one day that O-Kimi has off this month. They are to meet at
the Ogawamachi streetcar stop and go to see the Italian circus
that is presently set up in Shibaura. O-Kimi has never gone out
alone with a man before, so when she thinks about stepping
out with Tanaka like a pair of sweethearts going to the circus at
night, the sudden realization sets her heart aflutter. To O-Kimi,
Tanaka is like Ali Baba after he has learned the magic spell that
will open the treasure cave—what kind of unknown pleasure
garden will appear before her when the spell is uttered? For
some time now, O-Kimi has been gazing at the moon without
seeing it, for what she has been picturing in her throbbing
breast—throbbing like a wind-swept sea, or like the engine of
an accelerating bus—is a vision of this mysterious world-to-
come. There, on avenues buried in blooming roses, lie numberless cultured-pearl rings and imitation-jade obi clasps scattered
in profusion. Like dripping honey, the gentle voice of the night-
ingale has begun to sound from above the Mitsukoshi Department Store banner. And in a marble-floored palace, amid the
fragrance of olive blossoms, the dance of Douglas Fairbanks
and the lovely Mori Ritsuko[11] seems to be entering its most
wonderful passage . . .

Let me add something here in defense of O-Kimi's honor.
Across the vision that O-Kimi was picturing for herself just
now, ominous dark clouds would pass from time to time as if
to jeopardize her entire happiness. True, O-Kimi loves young
Tanaka. But the Tanaka she loves is a Tanaka on whose head
her artistic ecstasy has placed a halo—a Sir Lancelot who writes
poetry, plays the violin, paints in oils, acts on the stage, and is
skilled at both the Hundred Poets card game and the Satsuma
lute. Nevertheless O-Kimi's fresh, virginal instincts are not
entirely unaware that her Lancelot has something highly dubious at his core. Those dark clouds of anxiety cross O-Kimi's

vision whenever such doubts come to mind. Unfortunately, no sooner do the clouds form than they melt away. Mature though she may appear, O-Kimi is but a girl of sixteen or seventeen— a girl flushed with artistic ecstasy. No wonder she rarely takes note of clouds except when she is worried about having her kimono rained on, or is exclaiming in admiration for a picture postcard of a Rhine River sunset. How much less does she do so when on avenues buried in blooming roses, numberless cultured-pearl rings, and imitation-jade obi clasps . . . the rest of this is the same as in the passage above, so please just reread that.

Like Puvis de Chavannes' St. Geneviève,[12] O-Kimi stood there for a long time, gazing at the tile roofs in the moonlight until she sneezed once, banged the window's shoji closed, and went back to sitting sideways at her desk. What did she do until 6:00 p.m. the following day? Unfortunately, not even I know the answer to that. How can the author of the story not know, you ask? Well (tell them the truth now!), I don't know because I have to finish this thing tonight.

At 6:00 p.m. the next day, an unusually nervous O-Kimi made her way toward the Ogawamachi streetcar stop, which was already enveloped in the gloom of evening. She wore a deep purple silk crepe coat of dubious quality and a cream-color shawl. Tanaka was there as promised, waiting beneath a red light and wearing his usual broad-brimmed black hat low over his eyes. Under his arm he carried a slim walking stick with a nickel-silver cap, and the collar of his wide-striped short over- coat was turned up. His pale face glowed more handsomely than ever. That and the light smell of his cologne told her that he had taken special pains with his grooming tonight.

"Have I kept you waiting long?" O-Kimi asked, a little breathless as she looked up at him.

"No, forget it," he replied with a magnanimous flourish, fixing his gaze on her, his eyes hinting at a somewhat inscrutable smile. Then, with a quick shiver, he added, "Let's walk a little."

But he did more than say the words: he was already walking down the crowded avenue beneath the arc lights toward Suda- chō. Strange—the circus was in Shibaura. Even if they were going to walk there from here, they should be heading toward Kandabashi. Still standing in place, O-Kimi held down her cream-colored shawl, which was flapping in the dust-laden wind.

"That way?" she asked, looking puzzled.

"Uh-huh," he called out over his shoulder, continuing on toward Sudachō. O-Kimi had no choice but to hurry and catch up with him. They stepped gaily along beneath a row of leafless willows. At that point Tanaka got that inscrutable smile in his eyes and peered sidelong at O-Kimi saying, "I'm sorry to have to give you the bad news, but the circus in Shibaura ended last night. So let's go to this house I know and have dinner or something. What do you say?"

"That's fine with me," O-Kimi said in a tiny voice that trembled with hope and fear as she felt the soft touch of Tanaka's hand taking hers. Tears of deep emotion came to her eyes just as they did when she read *The Cuckoo*. Viewed through such tears, of course, each neighborhood they passed— Ogawamachi, Awajichō, Sudachō—took on a special beauty of its own. The music of a band luring shoppers to a big year-end sale, the dazzling lights of an electric billboard for Jintan breath freshener, Christmas wreaths, a fanned-out display of national flags of the world, Santa Claus in a show window, postcards and calendars laid out on street stands—to O-Kimi's eyes, everything seemed to sing of the magnificent joys of love and to stretch off in splendor to the ends of the earth. Not even the gleam of the stars in heaven looked cold on this special night, and the dusty wind lapping now and then at the skirts of her coat would suddenly change into a warm spring breeze. Happiness, happiness, happiness . . .

Soon O-Kimi saw that they must have turned a corner and now were walking down a narrow back street. On the right-hand side there was a small grocery store open to the street, its wares displayed in piles beneath a bright gas lamp: daikon radishes, carrots, pickling vegetables, green onions, small turnips, water chestnuts, burdock roots, yams, mustard greens, udo, lotus root, taro, apples, mandarin oranges. As they passed the grocery, O-Kimi happened to glance at a thin wooden card held aloft by a bamboo tube standing in the pile of green onions: "1 bunch 4 sen," it said in clumsy, dense black characters. With prices for everything surging upward these days, green onions at 4 sen a bunch were hard to find. In O-Kimi's happy heart, which until that moment had been intoxicated with love and art, the sight of this bargain instantaneously—literally, in that very instant—awoke latent real life from its torpid slumber. Her eyes were swept suddenly clean of images of roses and pearl rings and nightingales and the Mitsukoshi banner. Crowding in from all directions to take their place in O-Kimi's little breast, like moths to a flame, came rent payments, rice bills, electricity bills, charcoal bills, food bills, soy sauce bills, newspaper bills, make-up bills, streetcar fares—and all the other living expenses, along with painful past experience. O-Kimi's feet came to a halt in front of the grocery store. Leaving the flabbergasted Tanaka behind, she forged in among the green mounds beneath the brilliant gaslight. And then, extending a slender finger toward the pile of green onions among which stood that "1 bunch 4 sen" card, she said in a voice that might well have been singing "The Wanderer's Lament,"[13]

"Two bunches, please."

Meanwhile young Tanaka in his broad-brimmed hat, the collar of his wide-striped short overcoat turned up, slim walking stick with nickel-silver cap under his arm, stood alone on the dust-blown street like an abandoned shadow. In his imagination he had been seeing a lattice-doored house at the end of this street—a cheaply built two-story structure with a freshly washed stone platform for shoe removal in the entranceway and an electric sign on the eaves. Standing out in the street like this, however, he had a strange feeling that the image of that cozy little house was beginning to fade, to be replaced by a mound of green onions with a "1 bunch 4 sen" price card. Then suddenly, all such images were shattered as, with the next puff of wind, the very real stink of green onions—as penetrating and eye-stinging as real life itself—punched Tanaka in the nose.

"Sorry to keep you waiting."

Poor sad-eyed Tanaka stared at O-Kimi as if he were seeing a wholly different person. Hair neatly parted in the middle and fastened with forget-me-not hairpins, nose tilted slightly upward, O-Kimi lightly pressed her chin down on her cream-colored shawl as she stood there holding her 2-bunches-for-8-sen green onions in one hand, a happy smile dancing in her limpid gaze.

I did it! I finished the story! The sun should be coming up any minute now. I hear the chill-sounding crow of the rooster outside, but why do I feel depressed even though I've managed to finish writing this? O-Kimi made it back unscathed to her room over the beauty parlor that night, but unless she stops waiting on tables at the café, there's no saying she won't go out with Tanaka alone again. And when I think of what might happen then—no, what happens then will happen then. No amount of worrying on my part now is going to change anything. All right, that's it, I'm going to stop writing. Goodbye, O-Kimi. Step out again tonight as you did last night—gaily, bravely—to be vanquished by the critics!

(December 1919)

HORSE LEGS

The hero of this story is a man named Oshino Hanzaburō. He was nobody special, I am sorry to say—just a thirtyish employee in the Beijing office of the Mitsubishi Conglomerate. Hanzaburō moved to Beijing two months after his graduation from a Tokyo commercial college. His reputation among his colleagues and superiors was not especially good, but neither was it bad. Hanzaburō was just as ordinary as the way he dressed—or, I might add, as his home life.

Two years earlier, Hanzaburō had married a respectable young lady. Her name was Tsuneko. Theirs was not—I am also sorry to say—a love match. It had been arranged for their families by an old couple related to Hanzaburō. Tsuneko was no beauty. Neither, however, was she ugly. Her plump cheeks always wore a smile—always, that is, except when she was bitten by bedbugs in the sleeper coach from Mukden to Beijing. After that, however, she had no need to concern herself with bedbugs, for their company-owned house in XX Lane was always equipped with two cans of Bat Brand Insecticide.

I said before that Hanzaburō's family life was ordinary to the extreme. Indeed, it was no different from that of all the other Japanese company employees stationed in Beijing. He and Tsuneko would eat their meals, listen to their gramophone, and go to the moving pictures. Their ordinary life, however, was no more immune to the workings of destiny than anyone else's. With a single blow one mid-afternoon, destiny shattered the monotony of their supremely ordinary life. Mitsubishi Conglomerate employee Oshino Hanzaburō suffered a stroke and died on the spot.

He had been shuffling through papers at his desk as usual that afternoon in the company office at Dongdan Gate. The colleague at the facing desk had noted nothing unusual. Hanzaburō apparently reached a point in his work when he could take a break. He put a cigarette in his mouth and was striking a match when he collapsed face-down on his desk and died. It was a truly disappointing way to die. Fortunately, however, society rarely offers critical comment regarding the way a person dies. The way a person lives is what evokes criticism. Thus it was that Hanzaburō managed to avoid disparaging commentary. Far from it: without exception, his superiors and colleagues expressed their deepest sympathies to the widowed Tsuneko.

According to the diagnosis of Dr. Yamai, director of the Universalist Hospital, Hanzaburō died of a cerebral hemorrhage. Hanzaburō himself, however, did not believe that he had suffered a cerebral hemorrhage. Neither did he believe that he was dead. It did come as a surprise to him, though, to find himself standing in a strange office.

A breeze gently stirred the curtains in the sunlit window. Beyond the window, he could see nothing. On either side of a large desk at the center of the office two Chinese men, dressed in white ceremonial robes of the recently overthrown Qing dynasty,[1] were examining ledgers. One of the men seemed to be about twenty years old. The other had a long moustache that was beginning to yellow.

Without looking up, the younger man ran his pen across his ledger as he spoke to Hanzaburō.

"You are Mr. Henry Barrett, are you not?"

This came as a shock to Hanzaburō, but he answered as calmly as possible in his best Mandarin, "I am Oshino Hanzaburō, an employee of the Mitsubishi Conglomerate of Japan."

"What? You're Japanese?"

Finally raising his eyes, the young Chinese man seemed to be just as shocked as Hanzaburō was. The older man, still writing in his ledger, looked at Hanzaburō with an equal show of amazement.

"What are we going to do, Sir? We've got the wrong man!"

"Impossible! I don't believe it. Nothing like this has happened since the First Revolution." The old man's pen hand trembled with visible anger as he spoke. "Anyhow, send him back right away."

The young man turned to Hanzaburō. "Please wait a minute, Mr. ... uh ... Oshino, was it?" He spread his thick ledger open again and began to read, muttering the words to himself. And when he closed the book, he spoke to the old Chinese man with still greater amazement. "We can't do it," he said. "Oshino Hanzaburō died three days ago."

"Three days ago?!"

"And his legs are rotting. Right up to the thighs."

Hanzaburō was shocked again. First of all, according to what these two Chinese men were saying to each other, he was dead. Secondly, three days had gone by since his death. And thirdly, his legs were rotting. He knew this was ridiculous, though, because here his legs were perfectly—

He looked down and screamed. And no wonder: in his sharply-creased white trousers and white shoes, both his legs were swaying diagonally in the breeze from the window. He could hardly believe his eyes. But when he reached down and touched his legs, everything up to the thighs felt like air. Now, at last, he came down hard on his backside. At the same time, his legs—or, rather, his trousers—crumpled to the floor like a shriveling balloon.

"Don't worry. Don't worry. We're going to take care of you," the old Chinese man said, but when he spoke to his young assistant, his anger had by no means cooled. "This is your responsibility, do you hear me? Your responsibility. You'll have to send up a report right away. But what I would like to know is this: where is Henry Barrett now?"

"According to my information, he seems to have made a sudden departure for Hankou."

"All right, then, telegraph Hankou and get Henry Barrett's legs here immediately."

"But it's too late for that. By the time the legs arrive from Hankou, Mr. Oshino will be rotten to the torso."

"Impossible! I don't believe it." The old Chinese man heaved

a sigh. Even his moustache seemed suddenly to be drooping
more than before.

"This is your responsibility. Send up a report right away. I
don't suppose any passengers are still here . . . ?"

"No, they left an hour ago. There *is* a horse, though."

"Oh? Where from?"

"Beijing. The horse market in Desheng Menwai. It died a
little while ago."

"All right. Put a couple of the horse's legs on him. They'll be
better than nothing. Bring them now. Just the legs."

The young Chinese man turned from the desk and glided
away somewhere. Now Hanzaburō was experiencing his third
shock. They were going to put horse legs on him! Horse legs!
Down on the floor, he pleaded with the old Chinese man.

"I'm begging you, please don't put horse legs on me! Anything but that! I hate horses. Oh, please, give me human legs.
I'll even take Henry what's-his-name's legs. The shins might be
a little hairy, but I can stand it as long as they're human."

The old Chinese man looked down at Hanzaburō with an
expression of pity, and he nodded several times.

"I would be glad to give you human legs if we had any, but
we don't. You'll have to resign yourself. Call it an unfortunate
accident. And besides, horse legs are strong, you know. Change
horseshoes once in a while and any mountain path's a breeze."

The young subordinate glided in from somewhere carrying
two horse legs, like a hotel valet delivering a pair of boots.
Hanzaburō tried to escape, but sadly, without legs, he could
not lift himself. The subordinate approached him and started
to take off his white shoes and socks.

"Stop! Stop! Anything but horse legs! You have no right to
fix my legs without my permission!"

Hanzaburō kept up his shouting as the subordinate slipped
a horse leg into the opening of his right trouser leg. Its top end
bit into his right thigh as if it had teeth. Next, the young man
slipped the other horse leg into the left opening. This, too, bit
into his flesh.

"There. That'll do fine."

The young Chinese man rubbed his two long-nailed hands

together with a satisfied smile. Hanzaburō stared down at his lower extremities. Now, protruding from the ends of his white trousers were two thick chestnut horse legs, their hooves in proper alignment.

This was all Hanzaburō remembered—or at least, all he remembered with the same clarity as the events to that point. He seemed to recall arguing with the two Chinese men. Then he seemed to recall falling down a steep stairway. He could not be sure about either of those memories. In any case, when he regained consciousness after wandering through some kind of strange vision, he was lying in a coffin in his company-owned house in XX Lane. This occurred just at the moment that a young Honganji Buddhist missionary from Japan was reciting something like the last rites in front of the coffin.

Hanzaburō's sudden resurrection caused a sensation, of course. The *Shuntian Times*[2] ran a three-column article with a big photo of him. Tsuneko in her mourning outfit was smiling even more than usual, said the report. And, instead of "wasting" the traditional monetary offerings that had been donated for the funeral, a company executive and colleague of Hanzaburō's used the substantial sum to hold a "Resurrection Celebration" for the would-be mourners. Dr. Yamai's credibility came dangerously close to collapsing, to be sure, but he resuscitated it with great skill, blowing cigar smoke rings in a lordly manner. Hanzaburō's resurrection, he insisted, was a mystery of nature that transcended the powers of medicine. Which is to say, he restored his own personal credibility by sacrificing that of the medical profession.

The only person without a smile at Hanzaburō's "Resurrection Celebration" was Hanzaburō himself. And no wonder: with his resurrection his legs had changed to horse legs—chestnut horse legs with hooves instead of toes. Every time he saw them, he felt an indescribable wave of self-pity. For he knew that the day his legs were discovered, the company would let him go, his colleagues would turn their backs on him, and Tsuneko—oh, "Frailty, thy name is woman!"—Tsuneko would almost certainly refuse to stay married to a man who had suddenly grown two horse legs. Whenever such thoughts crossed his mind, he resolved anew to keep his legs hidden. He gave up wearing Japanese clothing. He started wearing boots. He always locked the bathroom window and door. Yet despite such precautions, he was continually anxious. And not without reason:

Hanzaburō had to remain on guard, first of all, against arousing the suspicions of his colleagues. This was perhaps among the less taxing of his efforts, but if we examine his diary, we find that he was continually struggling with some threat.

> July –. Damn that young Chinese guy for sticking me with these damn legs. I'm walking around on two fleas' nests! The itching drove me crazy today at work. I can see all my energy going into this for a while: I have to rig up something to get rid of these fleas.
>
> August –. Went to the manager's office to talk about sales today. Manager sniffing the whole time. I guess the smell is seeping out of my boots.
>
> September –. Controlling horse legs is a lot harder than horseback riding itself. Had a rush job before noon today, trotted down the stairway. Like anyone at a time like this, I was only thinking about the job, forgot about my horse legs. Next thing I know, my hoof goes straight through the seventh step.
>
> October –. I'm finally getting my horse legs to behave the way I want them to. It's all in the balance of the hips. I botched things today, though. Not that it was entirely my fault. I caught a rickshaw to work around nine o'clock this morning. The fare should have been 12 sen, but the rickshaw man insisted on 20. Then he grabbed me and wouldn't let me go in through the company gate. I got furious and gave him a quick kick. He flew through the air like a football. I was sorry about that, of course, but at the same time I couldn't help laughing. I really have to be more careful when I use my legs. . . .

Avoiding Tsuneko's suspicions, however, provided far greater sources of hardship than deceiving his colleagues, as Hanzaburō continually lamented in his diary:

July –. My greatest enemy is Tsuneko. I finally managed to convince her that we should be living a "modern, cultured" life, so we turned our only Japanese matted room into a wood-floored Western room. That way, I can get by without taking my shoes off in front of her. She's upset at the loss of the tatami, but there is no way I can walk on a matted floor with these legs—even with socks on.

September –. Sold our double bed to a used-furniture dealer today. I remember the day I bought it at an American's auction. On the way home, I walked under the row of pagoda trees in the foreign settlement. The trees were in full bloom. The soft glow of the canal was beautiful. But— No, this is no time for me to be clinging to such memories. I almost kicked Tsuneko in the side last night. . . .

November –. Took the washing to the laundry myself today. Not our usual laundry: the one over by Dongan Market. This is a chore I will have to take care of from now on. There's always horse hair stuck to my long johns, underpants, and socks.

December –. I'm constantly wearing holes in my socks. It's not easy putting together the money to buy new socks without Tsuneko finding out.

February –. I never take off my socks or underclothes, even in bed. Plus it's always a risky venture to keep my legs hidden from Tsuneko with a blanket. Before we got in bed last night, Tsuneko said, "I never realized how sensitive you are to cold! Have you got a pelt wound all the way up to your hips?" Maybe the time has come for the secret of my horse legs to come out.

Hanzaburō encountered many other threats besides these. Recounting each of them would be more than I can manage. Here, though, I will record the one event in his diary that shocked me the most:

February –. Went to have a look at the used-bookstore near Longfu Temple today on my lunch break. A horse-drawn cart was parked in a sunny spot in front of the shop. This was not a Western-type horse cart, but a Chinese cart with an indigo canopy. The driver must have been resting up there, but I didn't pay that any mind as I started into the bookstore. And then it happened. The driver snapped his whip and yelled to the horse, "Suo! Suo!" "Suo" is the word that Chinese use to make a horse back up. Even before the driver's words had ended, the wagon started creaking backward. And—could I have been any more shocked at what happened at that very moment?—with my eyes on the bookstore in front of me, I, also, started backing up a step at a time! There is no way I can describe here what I felt then: Terror? Horror? I tried without success to move forward—even a single step if I could—but under the influence of some terrifying, irresistible power, I could only move backward. Then, fortunately—for me, at least—the driver gave a long "Suooo!" When the cart came to a stop, I was finally able to stop moving backward. But this was not the only amazing thing that happened. With a sigh of relief, I half-consciously turned toward the cart. At that moment the horse—the dapple-gray horse that was pulling the cart—came out with an indescribable whinny. Indescribable? No, it was not indescribable. When I heard that shrill whinny, I knew without a doubt that the horse was laughing. And it was not alone: I felt something like a whinny rising in my own throat. I knew I could *not* allow this sound to emerge from my throat. I slapped my hands over my ears and ran away as fast as I could.

But destiny was still preparing its final blow for Hanzaburō. One noontime near the end of March, he noticed that his legs were suddenly beginning to dance and leap. Why, at this time, should his horse legs have suddenly started acting up? To find the answer to that question, we would have to examine Hanzaburō's diary. Unfortunately, however, the diary ends on the day before Hanzaburō suffered the final blow. We can, however, make an informed guess based upon events immediately preceding and following the day in question. Having examined the leading Chinese source books in the field (*Annals of Horse Governance*; *Horse Records*; *Yuan and Heng's Collection of Cures for Cows, Horses, and Camels*; and *Bo Le's Manual for Judging the Quality of Horses*),[3] I believe I know exactly what caused his horse legs to become excited when they did.

That day, there was a terrible Yellow Dust, the notorious storm that blows into Beijing from Mongolia every year at springtime. According to the *Shuntian Times*, that day's Yellow Dust was the worst in well over a decade: "Walk five steps from the Zhengyang Gate, look up, and you can no longer see the gate's superstructure." In other words, it must have been an exceptionally severe storm. Hanzaburō's legs had originally been attached to a horse that died at the market in Desheng Menwai. The animal must have been a Mongolian Kulun horse that came through Zhangjiakou and Jinzhou on its way to Beijing. The conclusion seems almost inescapable, then, that Hanzaburō's horse legs began to dance and leap the moment they sensed the Mongolian air moving in. This was the season when horses beyond the Great Wall begin galloping around in all directions, frantic to mate. Hanzaburō's horse legs thus were incapable of remaining still, for which Hanzaburō surely merits our sympathy.

Whether or not the reader finds my interpretation persuasive, we know from his colleagues that, at work that day, Hanzaburō was continually leaping about as if in a dance. And that in a mere three-block stretch on his way back to his house, he trampled seven rickshaws to bits. Things were no better when he reached home. According to Tsuneko, Hanzaburō staggered in, panting like a dog. And when he finally managed to stretch out on the sofa, he ordered his dumbfounded wife to bring him a length of cord. Tsuneko of course imagined from his appearance that something terrible had happened to him. His color was bad, for one thing. And he kept moving his boot-shod legs as if he found something unbearably irritating. Even Tsuneko forgot her usual smile, and she begged him to tell her what he was planning to do with the cord, but he would only wipe the sweat from his brow in apparent agony and repeat over and over, "Do it. Hurry. Hurry. You have to do it *now*."

Tsuneko had no choice but to bring her husband a bunch of the cords she used for tying packages. Boots and all, he started winding a cord around his legs. It was then that the fear began to germinate in her heart that Hanzaburō might be going mad. She stared at her husband and, with a quavering voice, urged him to call Dr. Yamai. He ignored her entreaties and went on winding the cord.

"What the hell does that quack know? That bandit! That swindler! Forget about him. Just come over here and hold me down."

They locked their arms around each other on the sofa. The Yellow Dust that blanketed Beijing seemed to be growing ever more intense. Now even the setting sun could do no more than lend a lightless muddy redness to the air beyond the window. Hanzaburō's legs were never still throughout this time, of course. Bound as they were, they continued to move as if pumping invisible pedals. Tsuneko tried to soothe him and encourage him as best she could:

"Hanzaburō, Hanzaburō, why are you shaking like this?"

"It's nothing. It's nothing."

"But look how you're sweating. —Let's go home to Japan this summer, Hanzaburō. Please, we've been away so long."

"Good. We'll do that. We'll go back to live in Japan."

Five minutes, ten minutes, twenty minutes: time moved over the couple in slow, painful steps. Tsuneko later told a woman reporter for the *Shuntian Times* that she felt all the while like a prisoner in chains. After thirty minutes, however, the chains were ready to snap—not Tsuneko's chains but the human chains that bound Hanzaburō to the household. Fanned, perhaps, by the flowing wind, the window with its muddy red view began to rattle. At that moment Hanzaburō released some kind of enormous cry and flew three feet into the air. Tsuneko says that she saw his bonds snap in that instant. Hanzaburō then— now, this is no longer Tsuneko's account. The last thing she saw was her husband flying up into the air, after which she fainted on the couch. Their Chinese houseboy, however, told the same reporter what happened next. Hanzaburō leaped to the entryway as if something were pursuing him. For a brief moment, he stood outside the door, but then, with a great shudder, he let out a long, eerie cry like the whinnying of a horse as he plunged straight into the Yellow Dust that enveloped the street.

What became of Hanzaburō after that? Even now, no one

knows for sure. The journalist from the *Shuntian Times* reported that sometime around eight o'clock that evening, in the smoky moonlight of the Yellow Dust, a man without a hat was seen galloping along the railroad tracks below Mt. Badaling, famous for its view of the Great Wall. This article, however, may not be entirely reliable. For in fact another journalist for the same newspaper reported that sometime around eight o'clock that evening, in the rain drenching the Yellow Dust, a man without a hat was seen galloping past the rows of stone men and animals on the Sacred Way to the thirteen Ming Tombs. This leads us to the inescapable conclusion that we have no idea where Hanzaburō went or what he did after he ran away from his company house on XX Lane.

Needless to say, Hanzaburō's disappearance caused as great a sensation as his resurrection had. Tsuneko, the company manager, Hanzaburō's colleagues, Dr. Yamai, and the editor-in-chief of the *Shuntian Times* all ascribed his disappearance to sudden insanity. No doubt this was simpler than blaming it on horse legs. For such is the Way of the World: to reject the difficult and go with the easy. One representative of this Way, Editor-in-Chief Mudaguchi of the *Shuntian Times*, brandished his lofty pen in the following editorial:

> Yesterday at 5:15 p.m. Mitsubishi employee Oshino Hanzaburō appears to have gone suddenly insane and, ignoring his wife Tsuneko's attempts to hold him back, ran away from home alone. According to Dr. Yamai, director of the Universalist Hospital, Mr. Oshino has been exhibiting somewhat abnormal psychological symptoms ever since he suffered a cerebral hemorrhage last summer and remained unconscious for three days. Judging also from a diary discovered by Mrs. Oshino, Mr. Oshino was continually experiencing strange obsessions. What we would like to ask, however, is not "What is the name of Mr. Oshino's malady?" but rather "What is Mr. Oshino's responsibility to his wife?"
>
> Like an unblemished golden jar, our glorious National Essence stands upon a foundation of belief in the family. We need not ask, then, how grave the responsibilities of the head of any one family might be. Does the head of a family have the right to go

mad any time he feels like it? To this question we must offer a
resounding "No!" Imagine what would happen if the husbands
of the world suddenly acquired the right to go mad. All, without
exception, would leave their families behind for a happy life of
song on the road, or wandering over hill and dale, or being kept
well fed and clothed in an insane asylum. Then our 2,000-year-
old belief in the family—our very pride in the eyes of the world—
could not fail to collapse. As the ancient records[4] have taught us,
"Hate the crime, not the criminal." We are not, of course, urging
that Mr. Oshino be treated harshly. We must, however, loudly
beat the drum[5] to condemn his rash crime of having gone mad.
No, let this not be limited to Mr. Oshino's crime alone. We must
also condemn the utter misfeasance of successive administrations
for having neglected our urgent need for a law prohibiting
insanity.

Mrs. Oshino tells us that she intends to go on living in the
company house on XX Lane for at least one year in the hopes
that Mr. Oshino will come home during that period. We express
our wholehearted sympathy to this faithful wife, and we sincerely
hope that the wise leaders of Mitsubishi will spare no expense in
seeing to it that Mrs. Oshino is afforded every opportunity to
accomplish her goal.

Six months later, however, Tsuneko, at least, had a new
encounter that made it impossible for her to go on contenting
herself with this grave misconception. It happened one October
twilight as Beijing's willows and pagoda trees were beginning
to drop their yellowing leaves. She was sitting on the sofa, sunk
in her memories of the past. Her lips no longer wore her eternal
smile. Her cheeks had lost their former plumpness. She went
on thinking of her vanished husband, the double bed he had
sold, those bedbugs of long ago . . . Just then, someone came
to the entryway and, after a moment of apparent hesitation,
rang the doorbell. She decided not to concern herself with this
but to let the houseboy take care of it. He made no appearance,
however: perhaps he had gone out. Soon the bell rang again.
Tsuneko at last moved away from the sofa and stepped quietly
to the entryway.

Stray withered leaves dotted the floor of the entryway, in the dim light of which stood a man without a hat. This lack was not his only distinguishing characteristic, however. He was wearing a torn and dust-smeared suit coat. Tsuneko felt something close to fear at the sight of this man.

"Yes? Can I help you?" she asked.

The man said nothing but stood there with head bowed, his long hair hanging down. Tsuneko peered through the darkness and again said with trepidation, "Can . . . can I help you?"

The man finally raised his head.

"Tsuneko . . ."

This one word was all he spoke. But it was enough to reveal his true form to her as clearly as if he had been bathed in moonlight. Tsuneko caught her breath and went on staring at him as if she had lost her voice. Not only had he let his hair grow long, but he was so emaciated he looked like a different person. The eyes that were focused on her now, however, were undeniably the ones that she had been longing to see.

"Hanzaburō! It's you!"

Tsuneko cried out and began to fly into his arms. No sooner had she taken the first step toward him, however, than she leaped back as if she had stepped on red-hot iron. Beneath the cuffs of his torn trousers, her husband revealed two hairy horse legs. Even in the dim light she could see their chestnut color.

"Hanzaburō!"

Tsuneko felt an indescribable revulsion toward the horse legs, but she also felt that if she missed her chance now, she might never see her husband again. He, meanwhile, went on staring at her with a sorrowful look in his eyes. Again she tried to fly to him. But again her revulsion overwhelmed her courage.

"Hanzaburō!"

The third time she cried out his name, Hanzaburō turned his back to her and started out of the entryway. Tsuneko whipped up her last ounce of courage and tried desperately to cling to him. But before she could take a single step in his direction, she heard the clip-clop of hooves. Utterly pale now, she stared at him moving away from her; she no longer had even the courage to call him back. Finally, she sank down among the entryway's fallen leaves in a swoon . . .

After this incident, Tsuneko came to believe in her husband's diary, but all the others—the company manager, Hanzaburō's colleagues, Dr. Yamai, and Editor-in-Chief Mudaguchi— refused to believe that Hanzaburō had developed horse legs. What they did believe was that Tsuneko had fallen prey to a hallucination when she thought she saw horse legs on Hanza- burō. While I was living in Beijing, I often met with Dr. Yamai and Mr. Mudaguchi in an attempt to break down their resist- ance, but derisive laughter was all I got in return. Thereafter— well, it appears that novelist Okada Saburō[6] recently heard the story from someone. He wrote to me to say he could not believe that Hanzaburō actually had horse legs. "If this happened at all," he said, "they probably gave him forelegs. If the legs were the quick, agile sort that are able to perform such stunts as Spanish trotting, they might also manage the feat of kicking, which is unusual for forelegs. Without a skilled trainer such as Major Yuasa, though, I doubt the horse itself would be able to do such kicking." To be sure, I have my own doubts regarding these matters, but does it not seem a bit premature to discount not only Hanzaburō's diary but Tsuneko's testimony as well on that basis alone? And in fact, my research has revealed the following article just a few columns down on the very same page of the very same issue of the *Shuntian Times* that had originally reported Hanzaburō's resurrection:

> Henry Barrett, president of the U.S.–China Temperance Society, died suddenly aboard a train on the Beijing–Hankou Line. His hand was clutching a medicine bottle, which gave rise to a sus- picion of suicide, but analysis of the bottle's contents determined the liquid to be alcoholic in nature.

(January 1925)

AKUTAGAWA'S OWN STORY

DAIDŌJI SHINSUKE: THE EARLY YEARS

—A Mental Landscape—

1. Honjo

Daidōji Shinsuke was born near the Ekōin Temple in the Honjo Ward[1] of Tokyo. As far as he can remember, Honjo contained not a single street—not a single house—of any beauty. His own house in particular was surrounded by drab shops—a confectionery, a cooper's workshop, a secondhand store. The street they faced on was a permanent muddy swamp that ended at "The Big Ditch" of Otakegura. The Ditch had weeds floating on its surface and it always gave off a terrific stench. Neighborhoods like this certainly made him melancholy, but other neighborhoods only made him feel worse. The fashionable "high city" residential areas in hilly Yamanote he found just as oppressive as those "low city" streets lined with pretty little shops from the Edo Period. No, rather than Hongō or Nihonbashi, it was dreary Honjo—the Ekōin, Halt-Pony Bridge, Yokoami, the open sewers, Hannoki Horse Ground, the Big Ditch—that he loved. Perhaps what he felt was closer to pity than to love. In any case, these are the only places that often enter his dreams even now, thirty years later.

Ever since he could remember, Shinsuke had felt love for the Honjo streets. Far from tree lined, they were always dusty, but it was those streets that taught young Shinsuke the beauty of nature. That was how he grew up: eating cheap sweets on the filthy streets of Honjo. The countryside—especially the expanse of rice paddies that opened to the east of Honjo—could never interest a boy who grew up that way. All it did was show him the ugliness of nature, not its beauty. The Honjo streets may have been wanting in nature, but blossoming roof-top grasses and spring clouds reflected in puddles displayed a sweet, sad kind of beauty. It was thanks to such beautiful things that he came to love nature. To be sure, the streets of Honjo were not the only things that gradually opened his eyes to natural beauty. Books, too, of course—Roka's *Nature and Man*, which he devoured again and again during his elementary school years, and a Japanese translation of Lubbock's *The Beauties of Nature*[2]—books enlightened him. Still, what most opened his eyes to nature were the neighborhoods of Honjo—their oddly shabby houses and trees and streets.

Later, he took short trips to other parts of Japan. The harshness of the mountainous Kiso region made him uneasy. The softness of the sheltered Inland Sea always bored him. He loved the shabbiness of Honjo far more than either of those. He especially loved nature that lived subtly, faintly amid the artificiality of human civilization. The Honjo of thirty years before still retained this kind of natural beauty everywhere—the willows along the open sewers, the broad courtyard of the Ekōin, the deciduous woods of Otakegura. He was unable to accompany his friends on school outings to such tourist destinations as Nikkō and Kamakura, but he did go walking with his father every morning through the surrounding neighborhoods of Honjo. This was undeniably a great source of joy to Shinsuke at the time, but it was a kind of joy he could never bring himself to boast of to his friends.

One morning, as the early glow was fading in the sky, he and his father walked to a frequent destination of theirs, the Hundred-Piling Bank of the Sumida River. There were always plenty of fishermen at this spot, but not on that particular morning. The only things moving were the sea lice crawling in the gaps of the bank's broad stone wall. He started to ask his father why there were no fishermen out this morning, but before he could open his mouth, he found the answer. A shaven-headed corpse lay bobbing on the still-glowing waves of the river where smelly water weeds and garbage clung to the irregularly-spaced pilings.

Shinsuke still vividly remembers the Hundred-Piling Bank from that morning. The Honjo of thirty years ago left numberless memorable landscapes in his impressionable heart, but at the same time that morning's Hundred-Piling Bank—that one landscape—also stood as the sum total of all the mental shadows cast by Honjo's many neighborhoods.

2. Cow's Milk

Shinsuke was a boy who had never sucked his mother's milk.[3] A frail woman, she never gave a drop of milk to her one-and-only child, and supporting a wet nurse was out of the question for his financially straitened family. Thus, from the moment of his birth, he was raised on cow's milk. This was a fate that the young Shinsuke could not help cursing. He despised the milk bottles that arrived in the kitchen every morning. And he envied his friends: they might know nothing else, but at least they knew their mother's milk. Around the time he entered grammar school, the breasts of a young aunt who was staying with them over New Year's or some such time became painfully swollen. She tried squeezing the milk into a brass bowl but could not produce any that way. She narrowed her eyes and said to him, half teasing, "How about you, little Shin? I wonder if you can suck it out for me?" Having been raised on cow's milk, though, he would not have known how to do it. Finally, his aunt got a child from next door—the cooper's little girl—to suck out her hardened breasts. The breasts were two swollen hemispheres stitched with blue veins. Shinsuke was such a shy little boy that he would never have been able to suck his aunt's breasts even if he had known how. Still, he hated the girl from next door. And he hated the aunt for having the girl from next door suck her breasts. This little incident left him with an oppressive sense of jealousy—though perhaps it was also the beginning of his *vita sexualis.*[4]

Shinsuke was ashamed both of the bottled cow's milk and of the fact that he had never tasted his mother's milk. This was his secret—the lifelong secret that he could never tell another soul and that carried with it a certain superstition. He was a weirdly skinny little boy with a huge head. Not only was he also shy, but his heart would start pounding at the slightest provocation—say, at the sight of a sharpened butcher's knife.

In this he differed utterly from his father, a man who prided himself on his courage and had undergone enemy gunfire in the battle of Fushimi-Toba.[5] Shinsuke firmly believed—though from what age and by what reasoning, he could not be sure—that it was the cow's milk that had made him so unlike his father. He believed just as firmly that the cow's milk was responsible for his frail constitution. If he was right about this, then the minute he displayed the slightest weakness, he was sure, his friends would discover his secret. So he took on any challenge that his friends might throw his way. And there were plenty of challenges. One was for him to jump over the Big Ditch without a pole. Another was to climb the big gingko tree in the Ekōin temple grounds without a ladder. And yet another was to have an all-out brawl with one of the friends. When he faced the Big Ditch, he felt his knees trembling, but he clamped his eyes shut and jumped with all his might, straight over the water weeds floating on the ditch's surface. The same sort of fear and hesitation attacked him when he climbed the Ekōin's gingko and when he had his fight with the friend, but he conquered his emotions each time. No matter its superstitious origin, this was Spartan training for him, training that left a permanent scar on his right knee—and possibly on his character as well. Shinsuke still remembers his father's withering tone: "You can be pretty damned stubborn for such a sissy."

Fortunately, though, his superstition gradually disappeared. Moreover, in Western history he discovered something that almost seemed to *dis*prove his superstition—namely, a passage stating that Romulus, the founder of Rome, had been suckled by a wolf. After that, he stopped minding that he had never known his mother's milk. Suddenly it became a point of pride for him that he had grown up on cow's milk. Shinsuke recalls going with his old uncle, the spring he entered middle school, to visit a dairy farm that the uncle owned[6] at the time. He recalls with special clarity feeding hay to a white cow that ambled right up to him when he leaned over the fence, the chest of his school uniform just barely coming to the top rail. Looking up at him, the cow quietly pressed its nose into the fistful of hay. There was something nearly human in the cow's eyes, he felt. Was it his imagination? It could well have been. In his memory, though, he leans over a fence beneath branches filled with apricot blossoms as a big white cow looks up at him— and into him—with real fondness.

3. Poverty

Shinsuke came from a poor family. To be sure, theirs was not the poverty of the lower classes who lived boxed together in the long, partitioned tenement houses. Rather, it was the poverty of the lower middle class, who must continually agonize over keeping up appearances. His father, a retired official, had to support a household of five, including the maid, on an annual pension of ¥500[7] plus a little interest from money in the bank. This meant endless scrimping and saving. They lived in a house that had five rooms (including the entryway), a small garden, and a rather impressive gate. They rarely made new kimono for anyone, however, and in the evening his father had to make do with a low-grade saké they could never serve to guests. His mother kept her patched obi hidden beneath a short jacket. And Shinsuke—Shinsuke still remembers the stink of varnish from the used desk they bought him. Actually, with its green baize surface and shiny silver-colored drawer pulls, the desk had a nice, neat look to it at first glance, but the cloth was worn thin, and the drawers never opened smoothly. This piece of furniture was not so much a desk as a symbol of the entire household, a symbol of the constant struggle to keep up appearances.

Shinsuke hated this poverty. Indeed, the unquenchable hatred he felt then continues to reverberate deep in his heart even now. He could never buy books. He could never go to summer school. He could never wear a new overcoat. His friends got all those things. He envied them—sometimes to the point of jealousy. But he would never admit to himself that he harbored such envy and jealousy because he was contemptuous of their abilities. His contempt, however, did nothing to change his hatred for his own family's poverty. He hated their old tatami mats, their dim oil lamps, their paper-covered sliding doors with peeling pictures of ivy—everything that made their house so shabby. Still worse, merely because of this shabbiness, he hated the very parents who gave him birth. He especially hated his father, who was bald and shorter than Shinsuke himself. His father would often attend school-sponsor meetings,[8] and Shinsuke felt shame at the sight of this father of his there in his friends' presence. At the same time, he was ashamed of his despicable nature for being ashamed of his own flesh-and-blood. He kept a "Diary without Self-Deceit" in imitation of the writer Kunikida Doppo;[9] on its lined pages he recorded passages like this:

> I am unable to love my father and mother. No, this is not true. I do love them, but I am unable to love their outward appearance. A gentleman should be ashamed to judge people by their appearance. How much more so should he be ashamed to find fault with that of his own parents. Still, I am unable to love the outward appearance of my father and mother. . . .

What he hated even more than the shabbiness, though, was the petty deceits to which the poverty gave rise. His mother once gave some relatives a piece of sponge cake packed in a box from the elegant Fūgetsu bakery. The cake itself, however, she had actually bought at the local confectioner's. And his father—how earnestly had his father taught him "Hard work, frugality, and martial prowess" as the central tenets of the Way of the Warrior.[10] According to his father, buying a Chinese character dictionary in addition to the old classic references was enough to make one guilty of "luxurious over-indulgence in high culture"! When it came to deceit, though, Shinsuke was not much better than his parents. He supplemented his fifty-sen-per-month allowance any way he could in order to buy the books and magazines he hungered for above all things. He used every possible excuse to steal his parents' money—by "losing" change on the way home from an errand, by saying that he had to buy a notebook or to pay dues to the students' association. When these failed to bring in enough, he would try charming his parents out of his next month's allowance, or cozying up to his old mother, who was particularly lenient with him. He disliked his own lies as much as his parents', but still he continued to lie—boldly and cunningly. He did this primarily out of need, but also for the pathological pleasure it gave him—something like the pleasure of killing a god. In this one point he came close to being a juvenile delinquent. The last page of his "Diary without Self-Deceit" contained these few lines:

Doppo said he was in love with love. I am trying to hate hatred. I am trying to hate my hatred for poverty, for falsehood, for everything.

These were Shinsuke's innermost feelings. He had indeed come to hate his own hatred for poverty. The double ring of hatred continued to pain this young man not yet twenty years old. Not that happiness was entirely lacking. He always made the third or fourth highest grade in examinations. And a beautiful young boy in one of the lower grades, all unbidden, expressed love for him. But for Shinsuke these were chance rays of sunlight shining through an overcast sky. Hatred oppressed him more than any other emotion, and before he knew it this hatred had left permanent scars on his heart. Even after he escaped from poverty, he could not stop hating it. And at the same time, he could not stop hating extravagance just as much. This hatred for extravagance was a brand burned into the skin by lower-middle-class poverty—and perhaps by that alone. To this day, Shinsuke feels this hatred inside himself, this petty-bourgeois moralistic fear of having to struggle against poverty.

The autumn he graduated from the university, Shinsuke visited the home of a friend still attending the Faculty of Law. They sat conversing on the tatami floor of the friend's good-sized room, the paper doors and walls of which were showing their age. From behind his friend, an old man of perhaps sixty poked his head in. Intuitively, Shinsuke sensed in the old man's alcoholic face a retired official.

"My father." The friend introduced the old man to him with this simple phrase.

Shinsuke offered a proper formal greeting, which the old man almost arrogantly ignored. Before he left the room, however, he told Shinsuke, "Make yourself comfortable. We have chairs out there . . ." Now Shinsuke noticed the two armchairs set on the darkened wood of the glassed-in corridor that ran past the room—long-legged chairs with fading red seat cushions from a half-century earlier. In these two pieces of furniture, Shinsuke sensed the entire lower middle class. He sensed, too, that his friend was just as ashamed of his father as Shinsuke was of his own. This is yet another minor incident that remains in Shinsuke's memory with painful clarity. Ideas might well come to cast new and varied shadows on his mind in the future, but he was, first and foremost, the son of a retired official, bred not of lower-class poverty but of lower-middle-class poverty and its need to trade in falsehood.

4. School

School, too, left Shinsuke with nothing but gloomy memories. Aside from two or three university lectures he attended without taking notes, none of the classes in any of his schools interested him in the least. Moving from one school to the next, however—from middle school to higher school,[11] from higher school to university—was the only thing that could save him from a life of poverty. Shinsuke did not realize this while he was still in middle school, of course—at least, not clearly. But from the time he graduated from middle school, the threat of poverty began to weigh on his heart like an overcast sky. In higher school and university, he thought frequently about quitting, but the threat of poverty would always put a quick stop to such plans by showing him the gloomy future he would face. He hated school, of course. He especially hated middle school with all its restrictions. How cruel the gatekeeper's bugle sounded to him! How melancholy was the color of the thick poplars on the school grounds! There Shinsuke studied only useless minutiae—the dates of Western history, chemical equations for which they did no experiments, the populations of the cities of Europe and America. With a little effort, this could be relatively painless work, but he could not forget the fact that it was all useless minutiae. In *The House of the Dead*, Dostoevsky says that a prisoner forced to do such useless work as pouring water from bucket number 1 into bucket number 2 and back again would eventually commit suicide.[12] In the rat-gray schoolhouse, amid the rustling of the tall poplars, Shinsuke felt the mental anguish that such a prisoner would experience. But there was more.

Yes, there was more: it was in middle school that he hated teachers most of all. As individuals, his teachers were surely not bad people. But their "educational responsibility"—and in particular their right to punish students—turned them into tyrants. They did not hesitate to use any means at their disposal to infect students' minds with their own prejudices. And in fact one of them, the English teacher they nicknamed "Dharma,"[13] often beat Shinsuke for being what he called a "smart aleck." What made Shinsuke a "smart aleck" was nothing worse than that he was reading such writers as Doppo and Katai.[14] Another of the teachers, the one with an artificial left eye who taught Japanese and classical Chinese, was not pleased with Shinsuke's lack of interest in martial arts and athletics. "What are you, a girl?" he would often taunt Shinsuke. Infuriated by this, Shinsuke once shot back at him, "And you, Sir? Are you a man?" for which he was of course severely punished. The number of humiliations he endured was endless, as he could see by re-reading his already-yellowing "Diary without Self-Deceit." He always had to counter such humiliations to protect himself, determined as he was to preserve his great self-esteem. Had he not done so, he would have ended up despising himself as did all juvenile delinquents. He naturally turned to his "Diary without Self-Deceit" to equip himself for his mental fitness program:

> Many are the criticisms that have been leveled at me, but they fall into three groups:
>
> 1. Bookish. A "bookish" person is one who prizes the power of the mind over the power of the flesh.
>
> 2. Frivolous. A "frivolous" person is one who prizes the beautiful over the useful.

3. Arrogant. An "arrogant" person is one who refuses to compromise his beliefs in deference to others.

Not all of his teachers tormented him, however. One invited him to family teas. Another lent him English novels. Shinsuke still remembers the joy with which he read the English translation of Turgenev's *A Hunter's Diary*,[15] when he discovered it among those borrowed books at the end of his fourth year of middle school. The teachers' "educational responsibility," however, always prevented him from interacting warmly with them as fellow human beings. For in his efforts to win their good graces, there always lurked his base need to play up to the teachers' authority—or their homosexuality. He could never behave with complete freedom in their presence. Sometimes he would make a show of grabbing a cigarette, or hold forth on a play he had seen on a standing-room ticket. They of course chalked up such behavior to his insolence, which was reasonable enough: he was never a very likeable student. The old photos he keeps stashed away show a sickly boy with a head too big for his body and huge, shining eyes. This pale-faced boy took his greatest pleasure in tormenting kindly teachers by constantly hurling venomous questions at them.

Shinsuke always received high grades in examinations, but his grade for deportment never rose above a 6. In the Arabic numeral "6" itself, he seemed to feel the sneers of the entire teachers' room. And the teachers actually were mocking him for his deportment grade. That 6 kept his class standing from going above third place. He hated this kind of revenge, and he hated the teachers for taking their revenge. Even now—no, no longer: Shinsuke has let go of his hatred. Middle school was a nightmare for him, but it was not necessarily a misfortune. At least it enabled him to develop a personality that could endure loneliness. Otherwise, the course of his life would have been far more painful than it is today. In fulfillment of his long-standing dream, he became the author of several books. But what he got in return was a desolate loneliness. And now that he has made peace with that loneliness—or, rather, now that he has learned that he has no choice but to make peace with that loneliness—

he can look back twenty years and see the schoolhouse where
he was so tormented standing before him in a rose-colored
twilight. Of course, the poplars still harbor the lonely sound of
the wind in their thick gloomy branches . . .

5. Books

Shinsuke's passion for books started when he was in elementary
school. What taught him this passion was the Teikoku Library
edition of *Outlaws of the Marsh*[16] that he found in his father's
bookcase. A grammar-school boy with an outsized head, he
read the novel over and over again in the dim glow of the lamp.
And even when the book wasn't open before him, he was
imagining scenes from it: the battle flag inscribed "We Act in
Heaven's Behalf"; the huge tiger of Jinyang Pass; the human
thigh meat hanging from the beam in the gardener Zhang
Qing's inn. Imagining? His imaginings were even realer than
reality to him. Any number of times, armed with his wooden
sword, he had done battle with characters from *Outlaws of the
Marsh*—with the fierce warrior beauty called Ten Feet of Steel,
and with the wild monk, Lu Zhishen. This passion continued
to rule him for thirty years. He still recalls many whole nights
he spent reading. He remembers reading with feverish energy
at his desk, in trains, in toilets—and sometimes even walking
down the street. He never picked up his wooden sword again
once he stopped reading *Outlaws of the Marsh*, but he had
gone on endlessly laughing and crying over books. Each was a
kind of transformation for him. He would become the characters in the books. Like India's Buddha, he traveled through
numberless past lives—Ivan Karamazov, Hamlet, Prince André,
Don Juan, Mephistopheles, Reineke Fuchs[17]—and his transformations were not always short-lived. One late autumn afternoon, for example, he visited his old uncle to pick up some
spending money. His uncle was from Hagi, the city in Chōshū
that had produced so many leaders in the overthrow of the
Tokugawa regime and the 1868 Restoration of imperial rule.
Standing before his uncle, he expounded on the great feats of
the Restoration and sang the praises of Chōshū's talented men,

everyone from Murata Seifū to Yamagata Aritomo.[18] As he was declaiming, though, this pale-faced higher-school student full of false emotion was not Daidōji Shinsuke but Julien Sorel, the hero of *The Red and the Black*.

Shinsuke thus quite naturally learned everything he knew from books—or at least there was nothing he knew that didn't owe something to books. He did not observe people on the street to learn about life but rather sought to learn about life in books in order to observe people on the streets. This might have been a roundabout way of doing it, but to him passersby on the street were nothing but passersby. In order to learn about them—their loves, their hatreds, their vanities—he had no choice but to read books, and in particular the novels and dramas of *fin-de-siècle* Europe. Only in their cold light did he discover the human comedy unfolding before him. Indeed, it was there as well that he discovered his own soul, which made no distinction between good and evil. Human life was not all he learned about from books. He discovered the beauty of nature in the neighborhoods of Honjo, but the eyes with which he observed nature owed some of their keenness to certain of his favorite books—most notably, books of haiku from the Genroku Period. Thanks to them, he discovered other natural beauties that Honjo could not teach him—"Shape of the mountain/Near the capital," "In turmeric fields/The wind of autumn," "Offshore in chilly rain/Sails running, sails reefed," "Into the darkness goes/A night heron's scream."[19] *From books to reality* was a constant truth for Shinsuke. He loved several women in the course of his life, but it was not they who taught him the beauties of woman—or at least none beyond those he had learned of from books. Sunlight shining through an ear, or the shadow of eyelashes falling on a cheek: these he learned from Gautier and Balzac and Tolstoy. Thanks to these writers, women could still communicate beauty to Shinsuke. Without them, he might have discovered only "the female," not "woman."

Because he was poor, though, Shinsuke could not afford to buy all the books he read. He managed to overcome this difficulty first of all through institutional libraries, secondly through commercial lending libraries, and thirdly by means of his own frugality, which went so far as to invite charges of stinginess. He still clearly remembers the lending library by the Big Ditch, the nice old lady who ran it, and the ornamental hairpins she made on the side. She called him "sonny boy" and believed in the perfect guilelessness of this new elementary-school student, but he very quickly figured out how to read her books on the sly while pretending to search for something. He still clearly remembers the clutter of used bookstores that lined Jinbōchō Avenue[20] twenty years ago and, above the shop roofs, Kudan-zaka hill shining in the sun. In those days, there were neither electric nor horse-drawn streetcars running down the avenue. As a twelve-year-old pupil clasping his lunch box or notebooks under his arms, he went up and down this avenue any number of times on his way to and from the Ōhashi Library—three-and-a-half miles roundtrip from the Ōhashi to the Imperial Library.[21] He still remembers his first impression of the Imperial Library: his fear of the high ceilings, his fear of the large windows, his fear of the numberless people who filled all the numberless chairs. Fortunately, his fears vanished after two or three visits to the place. He was soon familiar with the reading room, the iron stairway, the catalogue cases, the basement lunchroom. He moved on from there to the University Library and the Higher School Library, borrowing hundreds of volumes from them all, loving dozens of those volumes. And yet—

And yet, the books he loved most of all, the books he loved most as books irrespective of their contents, were the books he bought. In order to buy books, Shinsuke stayed away from cafés. Still, he never had enough money. And so he taught mathematics (!) to a middle-schooler relative of his three days a week. When even that failed to bring in the money he needed, he would, as a last resort, sell his own books. Never once did that earn him more than half what the book had cost him to buy, even when the book he sold was still new. Even worse, whenever he handed a used-book dealer a volume he had owned for some years, it felt like a tragedy to him.

One night there was a light dusting of snow on the ground as he made his way along Jinbōchō Avenue from one used

bookstore to the next. Before long, he came across a copy of
Zarathustra—and not just any copy. It was the very copy he
had sold them two months earlier, still smudged with the oil
from his hands. He stood out front re-reading passages from
this old *Zarathustra*, and the more he read, the more he missed
the book. After ten minutes of this, he finally asked the woman
who owned the shop, "How much is this?"

"One yen sixty sen, but for you I'll make it one yen fifty sen."

Shinsuke recalled that he had sold it to her for a mere seventy
sen, but he decided to buy it anyway after he had bargained her
down to one yen forty sen—exactly twice what he had sold
it for. The snowy nighttime streets were subtly quieter than
normal—the houses, the streetcars. All along the way, as he
trudged back to the university in Hongō, he felt the steel-colored
cover of *Zarathustra* against his chest. He also felt his mouth
working every now and then with derisive laughter, directed at
himself.

6. Friends

Shinsuke could not befriend anyone without evaluating the
person's intelligence. If all a young man had to recommend him
was his good behavior, the finest young gentleman in the world
was to Shinsuke a useless passerby—indeed, a clown deserving
only of his ridicule. This attitude was quite natural to Shinsuke,
with his grade in deportment a low 6. He made fun of such
people all along his way from one school to the next—middle
school to higher school, higher school to university. He angered
some of them, of course, but others were too nearly perfect as
gentlemen to perceive his ridicule. He always felt a certain
amusement when others found him obnoxious, but he could
not suppress his anger when his ridicule failed to have its
intended effect. One such unperceptive model gentleman, for
example, a student in the higher school's Faculty of Letters,
was a worshipper of Livingstone.[22] Shinsuke, who lived in the
same boarding house, once told him in the sincerest tone he
could manage that Byron had wept uncontrollably upon reading Livingstone's biography. Today, twenty years later, that

Livingstone worshipper is still singing the praises of the missionary-explorer in the official magazine of his Christian church, and his piece begins: "What does it tell us when even that satanic poet Byron himself shed tears upon reading the life of Livingstone?"

Shinsuke could not befriend anyone without evaluating the person's intelligence. Even a non-gentleman was a mere roadside bystander to him if the young man was not intellectually voracious. It was not kindness Shinsuke looked for in his friends. Nor did he mind if his friends were young men who lacked youthful hearts. If anything, he feared so-called "best friends." Friends of his had to have brains—strong, well-built brains. He loved the owner of such a brain far more than he did the handsomest boy. He also hated the owner of such a brain more than he did any gentleman. For him, the passion of friendship contained hatred in its love. Even today Shinsuke believes that there is no such thing as friendship apart from this passion—or at least that apart from this passion there is no friendship that does not stink of *Herr und Knecht.*[23] His friends in those days, especially, were in one sense irreconcilable mortal enemies to him: he engaged in endless combat with them, his brain his weapon. Everything was a battlefield: Whitman, free verse, creative evolution. He struck his friends down on these battlefields and there he was struck down by them. Surely it was the joy of carnage that propelled this mental combat, but just as surely the struggle revealed new ideas and new forms of beauty. Oh, how brightly a candle flame lighted their 3:00 a.m. war of words! How powerfully the works of Mushanokōji Saneatsu[24] ruled over that war of words! Shinsuke has vivid memories of the huge moths that crowded around the candle flame one September night. The moths were born from the deep darkness in a sudden brilliant flash, but no sooner did they touch the flame than they fluttered to their deaths as if they had never existed. Such a minor event may not be worth such latter-day wonderment, but whenever Shinsuke recalls it—this strangely beautiful death of moths in a flame—a bewildering loneliness fills his heart.

Shinsuke could not befriend anyone without evaluating the

person's intelligence. That was the only standard he applied. But
there was an exception to this standard: the class distinctions
between him and his friends. Shinsuke felt no strain with
middle-class young men who had an upbringing like his. But
toward the few upper-class (or upper-middle-class) young men
he knew, he felt a strangely impersonal hatred. Some of them
were lazy, others were cowardly, still others were slaves to
sensuality—but it was not necessarily for these qualities that
he hated them. No, it was for something vaguer—something
which a few of them hated in themselves, even if unconsciously,
and which caused them to yearn almost pathologically for their
diametrical opposites in society, the lower classes. Shinsuke
sympathized with them, but his sympathy finally led nowhere.
Before he managed to shake hands with them, this "something"
always stabbed his hand like a needle.

One windy, cold April afternoon, he was standing with one
of them—a higher-school student like himself, but the eldest
son of a baron—at the edge of a cliff on the island of Enoshima.
The rocky shore was just below them. They threw out a few
copper coins for boys on the shore to dive for. Whenever a coin
fell, the boys would plunge into the ocean. One girl diver,
however, simply watched the boys as she crouched smiling by
a fire at the base of the cliff.

"This time I'll make her dive in, too," Shinsuke's friend said,
wrapping a copper coin in the silver paper from his cigarette
pack. Then he leaned back and heaved the coin with all his
might. Sparkling like silver, the copper coin sailed far out
beyond the waves being stirred up by a high wind. This time
the girl diver was the first to jump into the sea. Shinsuke still
vividly remembers the cruel smile on his friend's lips. This boy
had a special talent for languages. He also had unusually sharp
canine teeth . . .

(9 December 1924: To be continued)[25]

THE WRITER'S CRAFT

"Could you write us a eulogy, Horikawa? The Headmaster needs something for Lieutenant Honda's funeral on Saturday."

Captain Fujita spoke to Yasukichi as they were leaving the mess hall.

Here at the Naval Engineering School, Horikawa Yasukichi taught the translation of English texts, but there were other jobs for him between classes. He had written some funeral orations, put together a textbook, touched up a lecture someone then gave in the presence of the Emperor, and translated articles from foreign newspapers. It was always Captain Fujita—a swarthy, high-strung, bony man perhaps forty years of age—who brought the new assignments.

Yasukichi was a step behind Captain Fujita in the gloomy hallway. "What! Lieutenant Honda is dead?" he exclaimed in surprise. The Captain turned to look at him; his own surprise seemed as great as Yasukichi's. Yasukichi had invented an excuse to skip work the day before and missed the notice on Honda's sudden death.

"It happened yesterday, in the morning. A stroke. Anyway, have it done by Friday morning, will you? That gives you two days."

"I suppose I can get it done all right . . ."

Fujita was quick to sense Yasukichi's hesitation. "You'll need some information for the eulogy. I'll send his file over."

"But what sort of man was he? I'd recognize him if I saw him on the street, but that's all."

"Well, let's see. He was a good brother . . . And he was always at the head of his class. Let your famous pen do the rest."

By now they were standing at the yellow door to Fujita's office. The Captain was Assistant Headmaster.

Yasukichi abandoned any hope of maintaining his artistic integrity in writing the eulogy. "I guess it's time for the old saws—'a man of innate brilliance,' 'affectionate to his brothers and sisters,' 'a swift and glorious end, like the shattering of a precious stone'—I'll make something up."

"Thanks, I'm sure you'll do fine."

Instead of stopping off at the lounge, Yasukichi went straight to the instructors' office, which was empty. November sunshine flooded his desk from the window on the right. He sat down and lit a cigarette.

So far he had written two eulogies. The first had been for young Lieutenant Shigeno, who died of appendicitis. Yasukichi had just started teaching then and barely knew the man by sight. But it was his debut in funeral oratory, and he had approached the task with some enthusiasm, turning elegant phrases in the lofty style of the Chinese masters. The second eulogy was for Lieutenant Kimura, who had accidentally drowned. Yasukichi had been commuting to the school with Lieutenant Kimura from the same seaside town, and so he was able to write an honest expression of grief. Lieutenant Honda, though, was just a face in the mess hall—and a vulture-like face at that. Yasukichi had lost all interest in the composition of eulogies, but now he had become Horikawa Yasukichi, Literary Mortician and Undertaker of the Spirit, with orders to bring the ceremonial lanterns and the artificial flowers at the right time on the right day of the right month. Cigarette dangling from his lips, Yasukichi began to sink into a state of melancholy.

"Excuse me, Sir. Mr. Horikawa?"

Yasukichi looked up, as if from a dream, to find Lieutenant Tanaka standing by his desk. The young lieutenant possessed an amiable face with a trim moustache and an opulent double chin.

"Lieutenant Honda's file, from Captain Fujita." He laid a bound sheaf of lined paper on Yasukichi's desk.

"Oh, yes." Yasukichi let his eyes drop to the lined paper. There, row after row of small square characters listed the dead man's assignments and their dates. This was no mere curriculum vitae; it was a symbol of all the lives spent in bureaucracies, both civil and military.

"And also, Sir, could I ask you to explain a word to me?— No, not seafaring lingo. Something I found in a novel." Tanaka held out a scrap of paper with a single foreign word scratched on it in blue pencil. "Masochism." Yasukichi's eyes went from the paper to the Lieutenant's boyish, rosy-cheeked face.

"This? 'Masochism'?"

"Yes. I can't seem to find it in a regular English–Japanese dictionary."

Sullenly, Yasukichi gave him the definition.

"Is *that* what it means!"

Lieutenant Tanaka's beaming smile never faded. In Yasukichi's present mood, nothing could be more irritating than this kind of self-satisfied grin. He was tempted to hurl every word from Krafft-Ebing into the Lieutenant's happy face.

"Now, this writer whose name the word comes from— Masoch,[1] you said?—are his novels any good?"

"No, they're all terrible."

"He must have been an interesting person, at least."

"Masoch? Masoch was an idiot. He tried to convince his government to take money out of defense and put it into keeping whores."

Newly apprised of the idiocy of Masoch, Tanaka at last gave Yasukichi his freedom. The business about whore support was far from certain, of course; Masoch probably believed in national defense as well. But Yasukichi knew there was no other way he could impress the cheerful lieutenant with the stupidity of abnormal sexuality.

Alone now, Yasukichi lit another cigarette and began roaming the office. True, he taught English, but that was not his real profession. Not to his mind, at least. His life's work, he felt, was the creation of literature. Even after coming to this job, he had continued to publish at least one short story every two months. The current issue of a certain literary monthly contained the first half of the piece he was writing now, a recasting of the Saint Christopher legend in the style of the old Japanese

Jesuit translations of Aesop.[2] They wanted the second half from him for the next issue, and today was the seventh of the month, which meant the manuscript was due in— No, this was no time to be turning out eulogies. Yasukichi wrote with such painstaking care that he could work day and night and still not finish the story on time. He felt his resentment toward the eulogy beginning to mount.

Just then the wall clock chimed for twelve-thirty, with much the same effect as the apple falling at Newton's feet: Yasukichi realized that his class was still thirty minutes away; if he could finish the eulogy in that time, there would be no "A sad occasion brings us together today" to intrude on his more anguished creative labors. It would not be easy to lament the passing of Lieutenant Honda, "a man of innate brilliance," "affectionate to his brothers and sisters," in just thirty minutes; but to shrink from the task would mean that twelve centuries of pride in the riches of the native tongue, from Kakinomoto no Hitomaro to Mushanokōji Saneatsu,[3] was sheer braggadocio. In an instant, Yasukichi was at his desk and writing.

*

The day of Lieutenant Honda's funeral brought flawless autumn weather. Yasukichi, dressed in frock coat and silk hat, joined a dozen other teachers and civilian officials near the end of the procession. Some moments later he glanced around to find several important men walking behind him—Admiral Sasaki, the Headmaster; Captain Fujita; and the chief civilian teacher, Mr. Awano. Embarrassed, he gestured humbly to Captain Fujita just in back of him.

"Pardon me, Captain. Please go ahead."

"No, that's all right," Captain Fujita said with an odd grin.

Awano, a man with a trim moustache, had been talking to Admiral Sasaki. "You know, Horikawa," he said to Yasukichi, "in Naval protocol, the higher the rank the farther back the position. You certainly wouldn't come behind Captain Fujita." Awano was smiling too, and Yasukichi thought for a moment that he might be joking. But, embarrassingly enough, there was the affable Lieutenant Tanaka far ahead in the procession. A few quick strides brought Yasukichi up alongside the young officer.

"Lovely day. Have you just joined us?" Tanaka spoke with such good cheer he seemed more a wedding guest than a mourner.

"No, I was back there." Yasukichi explained his change of place, which brought a hearty laugh from Tanaka that seemed to threaten the dignity of the cortege.

"Is this your first military funeral?"

"No, I was at Lieutenant Shigeno's and Lieutenant Kimura's."

"Where did you march then?"

"Way behind the Headmaster, of course."

"Oh, great—that made you an Admiral!"

The procession had entered a poor neighborhood not far from the temple. Yasukichi went on talking with the Lieutenant, but he took careful note of the people who lined the route. Experienced funeral-watchers from childhood, they had developed an uncommon talent for estimating the cost of a procession. The funeral for the father of the mathematics teacher Kiriyama had come this way on the day before summer vacation. Beneath the eaves of one house had stood an old man dressed for the hot weather. Arms bare, shading his eyes with a fan, he cried out, "Aha! Fifteen yen for this one!" Perhaps today, too— but unfortunately there was no roadside talent today. One sight would stay with Yasukichi, however: an Ōmoto priest with an albino child—his own, it seemed— perched on his shoulders. Yasukichi toyed with the idea of one day writing a story about the townsfolk here. He could call it "Funerals."[4]

But Lieutenant Tanaka would not stop wagging his tongue. "I see you have a story out this month—'Saint Christopher' or something. I saw a review in this morning's *Jiji*—or maybe it was the *Yomiuri*. I'll show it to you later. It's in my coat pocket."

"That won't be necessary, thanks."

"You don't write criticism, do you? That's one thing I'd like to try my hand at, maybe write something on Shakespeare's *Hamlet*. You know, the character of Hamlet is really . . ."

Epiphany for Yasukichi: it was no accident that the world
was full of critics.

The cortege finally entered the grounds of the temple, which
overlooked the sea. The calm surface of the water shone
through the pine trees at the back of the temple grounds. This
must have been a tranquil place ordinarily, but now it was
swarming with the squad of cadets who had formed the van-
guard of the procession. Yasukichi left his new patent-leather
shoes at the entrance to the priests' quarters and walked down
a long, sunny corridor to the mourners' section in an old chapel
with new floor mats.

The mourners were divided into two groups—the family in a
row on one side, and the guests facing them. The old gentleman
seated nearest the coffin at the head of the family row was
probably Lieutenant Honda's father. He had that same vulture-
like face, but his stark white hair made him look even more
ferocious than the son. The young man in university-student
uniform seated next to him was certainly Lieutenant Honda's
brother. The young lady in the third place was almost too
good-looking to be the Lieutenant's sister. Next to her— but
no one else in the family had distinguishing characteristics.

At the head of the guests' front row was Admiral Sasaki, and
next to him Captain Fujita. It was directly behind the Captain,
in the second row of guests, that Yasukichi lowered the seat of
his trousers to the mat—not in the formal position on his heels
like the Headmaster and the Captain, but cross-legged to keep
his legs from going numb.

The sutra chanting began immediately. Just as he liked the
old Shinnai style[5] of singing, Yasukichi enjoyed the chanting of
the different Buddhist sects. But the degeneracy of most Tokyo-
area temples was sadly evident in even this most basic discipline.
Long ago, it was said, the deities from Kimpusen, Kumano, and
Sumiyoshi came to hear the High Priest Dōmyō chanting the
sutra in the garden of the Hōrinji Temple.[6] But with the arrival
of American civilization, music of such ineffable beauty had
departed this polluted world forever. And now the bespectacled
chief priest—to say nothing of his four disciples—was reading

off the Daibabon as if it were something he had memorized from a government-approved textbook.

Soon the chanting ended and Admiral Sasaki approached the coffin. It rested in the entrance to this, the main chapel, facing the altar and covered in white figured satin. Before it stood a table decked with artificial lotus blossoms and flickering candles, among which lay cases holding Lieutenant Honda's medals and ribbons. After a bow toward the coffin, Admiral Sasaki opened the formally inscribed text of the eulogy. This, of course, was the literary gem that Yasukichi had composed three days earlier. It contained nothing of which he need feel ashamed. Such sensitivities had been scraped away from him long ago, like the surface of an old razor strop. And yet it was hardly comforting for him to be cast in the role of author of the eulogy in this comedy of a funeral—worse still to have that fact thrust in his face. The Headmaster cleared his throat, and Yasukichi's gaze dropped instantly to his knees.

The Headmaster began to read in subdued tones. Beneath a delicate patina of experience, his voice surged with a pathos beyond description. It was unthinkable that he could be reading another man's text. Yasukichi had to admire his acting ability. The hall was hushed, the mourners still. The Headmaster read on, the sorrow in his voice deepening—"a man of inborn brilliance, affectionate to his brothers and sisters"—when someone in the family group stifled a laugh. Once it started, it grew in volume. Yasukichi felt a rush of horror and strained to see past Captain Fujita's shoulder. But what he had taken for desecrating laughter, he discovered, was in fact the sound of weeping.

It was Lieutenant Honda's sister. Half hidden beneath the swirls of an old-fashioned hairdo, the lovely young girl pressed her face into a silk handkerchief. The brother, too, so stolid-looking a moment ago, was now sniffling and fighting back his tears. The father quietly blew his nose in one tissue after another. Yasukichi's first reaction to this scene was one of surprise. Then came the satisfaction of the playwright who has succeeded in wringing tears from his audience. But in the end he felt an emotion of far greater magnitude: a bitter self-reproach, a sense of wrongdoing for which there could be no penitence. All unknowing, he had tramped with muddy feet into the sacred recesses of the human heart. Yasukichi hung his head for the first time in the hour-long course of the funeral. . . . You, Lieutenant Honda's family, could not know that this English instructor even existed. But in Yasukichi's heart a Raskolnikov in clown's costume has been kneeling in the muddy roadway these eight long years, begging your forgiveness.

*

The sun was setting as Yasukichi stepped from the train and started down the back street that led to his lodging on the shore. Woven bamboo fences, a mark of this resort town, formed continuous walls down either side of the narrow lane. Moist sand clung to the soles of Yasukichi's shoes. A fog seemed to be closing in. Clumps of pine beyond the fences revealed patches of evening sky and released a light scent of resin into the air. Yasukichi hung his head and trudged toward the ocean, oblivious to the tranquil scene.

He had met Captain Fujita as they were leaving the temple. The captain congratulated him on the excellence of his eulogy. Particularly appropriate to the death of Lieutenant Honda, he said, was the phrase "a swift and glorious end, like the shattering of a precious stone." After the sight of the family in tears, this praise for his use of a military cliché was enough to reduce Yasukichi to despair. But there had been more. The ever-amiable Lieutenant Tanaka took the train with Yasukichi and showed him the *Yomiuri* review of his story by the then-fashionable critic N. After a thorough panning of the piece, N delivered the *coup de grâce* to Yasukichi himself: "The last thing we need in the literary world is the spare-time jottings of a Navy school teacher!"

The eulogy he wrote in less than half an hour evoked that amazing response, while the story he had spent endless evenings polishing by lamplight produced not a fraction of the effect he hoped for. Yasukichi retained the composure to laugh off N's critique, but his current situation was not something he could dismiss with a laugh. His eulogies worked, his stories failed miserably: it was funny for everyone but Yasukichi himself. When would Fate be kind enough to ring down the curtain on this sad comedy?

Yasukichi glanced up. Pine boughs stretched across the empty sky, and in them hung a copper-colored moon devoid of radiance. As he stood looking at the moon, Yasukichi felt the urge to urinate. The lane was hushed and empty, enclosed on either side by the bamboo fences. Aiming at the base of the right-hand fence, Yasukichi enjoyed a long, lonely pee.

He was still at it when the fence creaked and began to pull away from him. What he had thought to be a section of the fence was in fact a gate. And through it strode a man with a moustache. Unable to stop himself, Yasukichi turned aside as discreetly as he could.

"Oh, no," the man sighed, as if dismay itself had become a human voice. When he heard this, Yasukichi discovered that the sun was too far down for him to see his own stream.

(March 1924)

THE BABY'S SICKNESS

Natsume Sensei looked at the calligraphic scroll and muttered as if to himself, "It's a Kyokusō." He was right: the seal was Kyokusō's. I said to the Sensei, "Kyokusō was Ensō's grandson, wasn't he? What was the name of Ensō's son, I wonder?" He answered, "Musō,[1] probably."

Then I woke up. The light from the next room was shining into the mosquito net. My wife seemed to be changing the diaper of our seven-month-old baby boy, who was crying the whole time. I turned my back to them and tried to get more sleep.

I heard my wife say, "No, Taka,[2] I don't want you to get sick again."

"Is something wrong with him?" I asked.

"I think his stomach is a little funny."

This baby tended to get sick much more often than our older boy; I felt both worried and ready to ignore it as more of the same.

"Have Dr. S[3] look at him tomorrow," I said.

"I was thinking of calling the doctor now."

When the baby stopped crying, I went back to a sound sleep.

I still remembered my dream when I woke in the morning. I suspected that "Ensō" was Hirose Ensō, but Kyokusō and Musō were probably imaginary. Come to think of it, there was a storyteller named Nansō. I thought about these "-sō" names more than I did about the baby's sickness, but that started to change when my wife came home from Dr. S's.

"Another upset stomach, he says. He'll come to look at him later." She spoke almost angrily, cradling the baby in one arm.

"Fever?"

"Just a little. 37.6. But he didn't have *any* last night."

I went up to my study and set to work. As usual, I made little progress, not necessarily because of the baby's sickness. Soon a hot, steamy rain began to fall, rustling the trees in the garden. With my half-written story lying on the desk before me, I smoked one cigarette after another.

Dr. S came once before noon and once more in the evening. On his second visit he gave Takashi an enema. Takashi stared hard at the light bulb while this was being done to him. The liquid of the enema soon washed a thin blackish mucus out of him. I felt as if I were looking at his very illness.

"How's he going to do, Doctor?"

"Oh, it's nothing. Just don't stop icing his forehead. And don't hold him too much."

With that advice, the doctor left.

I continued working into the night and finally got to bed around one in the morning. Coming out of the toilet just before that, I heard a knocking sound in the pitch-dark kitchen.

"Who's there?"

"It's me." The voice belonged to my mother.

"What are you doing?"

"Cracking ice."

Embarrassed at my own stupidity, I said, "Why don't you turn the light on?"

"Don't worry. I can do it by touch."

I ignored this and switched the light on. She looked as if she had just crawled out of bed, her rumpled sleeping gown held closed by a slim sash. No wonder she had wanted the light off: this was no way to be seen, even at home. She was clumsily smashing ice with a hammer. The electric light glinted off the sharp water-washed angles of the smashed ice.

By morning, however, Takashi's fever had climbed to just over 39. Dr. S came before noon and gave him another enema. I helped him with the job, hoping to see less mucus this time. When he withdrew the nozzle, however, much more mucus came with it than the night before.

"So *much*!" my wife exclaimed to no one in particular. The

unseemly loudness of her voice made her seem like a schoolgirl again,[4] as if seven years had suddenly dropped off her age. I glanced at Dr. S.

"It's dysentery, isn't it, doctor?"

"No, it isn't dysentery. The children's variety never happens before the infant is weaned."

Dr. S was surprisingly calm.

After he left, I went back to work. I was writing a story for a special issue of the *Sunday Mainichi*, and the deadline was the next morning. I had little enthusiasm for the piece, but I forced myself to keep my pen moving. Takashi's crying was getting on my nerves, though, and no sooner would he stop than his elder brother Hiroshi would start wailing.

Nor was that the only thing that grated on my nerves. A young man I had never met before arrived in the afternoon to ask for a loan. "I'm a manual laborer, but Mr. C wrote me this letter of introduction to you, so I was hoping you could help me," he blurted out. I had no more than two or three yen in my purse at the time, so I handed him two books I could spare and told him to turn them into cash. The young man immediately opened the books and examined the publication data. "This one says 'Not for Sale.' Can you get money for 'Not for Sale' books?" I felt sorry for myself for having to put up with this, but I simply answered that he should be able to sell it. "Do you think so? All right, then, I guess I'll be going." Clearly dubious, the young man left without a word of thanks.

Dr. S came again that evening to do an enema. This time the volume of mucus had decreased significantly. "Oh, good, there's so much less," my mother said as she offered the doctor hot water to wash his hands. Her triumphant look almost suggested that she herself was responsible for the improvement. Not exactly relieved, I nevertheless felt something close to relief. This had to do not only with the amount of mucus but Takashi's color and behavior, which were both normal.

"The fever will probably go down tomorrow," Dr. S said to my mother as he washed his hands, looking pleased. "Fortunately, he doesn't seem to be needing to throw up, either."

When I awoke the next morning, my aunt was already awake

in the next room and folding up her mosquito net. I thought I heard her say something about Takashi over the clanking of the net's hardware. "What about Takashi?" I asked, my head still in a fog.

"He's much worse. I think we have to take him to the hospital."

I sat up in bed. This took me off guard after yesterday's improvement. "Doctor S?"

"He's here now. Hurry up. Get out of bed." She wore a strangely stiff expression as if hiding her emotions. I went immediately to wash my face. The weather outside looked bad, overcast as usual. Somebody had thrown two gold-banded lilies into the bucket in the bathing room. I felt as if their fragrance and their brown pollen were going to stick to my skin.

In the space of a single night, Takashi's eyes had become sunken. My wife said that when she went to pick him up this morning, his head dropped back and he vomited some kind of white stuff. He was yawning constantly as well, another bad sign. I felt a stab in the heart. At the same time, I felt a wave of revulsion. Dr. S was kneeling by the baby's pillow, mute, a cigarette dangling from his lips. He looked up at me and said, "I have to talk to you."

I showed him upstairs to my study. We sat on the matted floor, the unlighted hibachi between us. "I don't think it's bad enough to kill him," he began, "but his whole digestive tract has shut down." The only thing to do was starve him for a few days. "Probably the most convenient thing would be to put him in the hospital."

I suspected that Takashi was in much greater danger than Dr. S was saying, that it was probably too late to do anything for him, even in the hospital, but this was no time to start confronting him with such doubts. I asked him to have the baby admitted. "Let's make it U—— Hospital, then," he said, "it's so close by." The doctor refused a cup of tea and went off to telephone the hospital. I called my wife to come upstairs. We decided to have my aunt go to the hospital with them.

This was my day to receive visitors. I had four starting first thing in the morning. I was conscious of my wife and aunt

hurriedly preparing for the hospital as I carried on polite conversation with my first visitor. I suddenly became aware of
something that felt like a grain of sand on the tip of my tongue.
I had recently had a tooth filled and I wondered if some of the
cement had broken off. Picking it out, I saw that it was a piece
of the actual tooth. This gave me a superstitious twinge, but I
went on smoking and trading remarks with my guest about a
samisen that was up for sale. It was said to have belonged to
the painter Hōitsu.[5]

Next came the young laborer who had called on me the day
before. Standing in the entryway, he announced that he had
been unable to get more than ¥1.20 for the books I gave him
and started pressing me for another four or five yen. I refused,
but he showed no sign of leaving. I finally lost my temper and
shouted at him, "I don't have time to stand here listening to
this nonsense. Get out!"

"All right, but give me streetcar fare at least. Just fifty sen."

When he saw that this wasn't going to work either, he
slammed the door and retreated through the gate. I promised
myself never to respond to any such requests for money in the
future.

Before long, my four visitors had become five. The fifth was
a young scholar of French literature. As he entered my study, I
excused myself and went downstairs to see what the situation
was. My aunt was ready to leave, pacing up and down the
veranda holding Takashi, whose thick wrap made him look
chubby. I pressed my lips against his pale forehead, which was
quite hot. His eyelids were twitching as well.

Instead of commenting on this, I asked in a near-whisper,
"Did you call the rickshaws?"

"Pardon me? The rickshaws are already here," she said with
unusual formality as if speaking to a stranger.

At that point my wife came out. She had changed her clothes
and was carrying a down comforter and a basket. She knelt
before me with her hands on the floor mats. "We will be going
now," she announced with strange seriousness.

I suggested she change Takashi into his new hat—a summer
hat I had bought him a few days earlier.

"I did that," she said, peeking into the mirror on the clothes chest and pulling her kimono straight at the neck. I didn't stay to see them off but went back upstairs.

With the new visitor, I talked about George Sand among other things. The canopies of the two rickshaws were visible through the young green leaves of the garden trees. Then suddenly they passed before my eyes, swaying above the fence. "The early nineteenth-century writers—Balzac, Sand—are far superior to the writers of the late nineteenth-century, don't you think?" I remember with absolute clarity the passion with which the young man said this.

The stream of visitors continued into the afternoon. The sun was going down when I finally found the time to go to the hospital. The overcast skies had begun dropping rain. While I was changing into a better kimono, I ordered the maid to put out my rain clogs. Just then the Osaka editor N showed up to collect my manuscript. He wore mud-smeared boots, and his overcoat glittered with rain drops. I received him in the entryway, where I explained to him how the situation had prevented me from writing anything.

He expressed his sympathy and concluded, "I guess I'll have to give up on this one." I felt as if I had coerced his sympathy. I felt, too, that I had exploited my son's critical condition as an excuse.

N had barely left the front door when my aunt arrived from the hospital. Takashi had thrown up his milk twice, she said. Fortunately, his brain did not seem to have been affected by the illness. She went on to talk about what a nice person the nurse was, that tonight my wife's mother would be staying at the hospital with the baby, and so forth. "As soon as we got Taka there, they gave us a bunch of flowers, supposedly from some Sunday school pupils. I don't know, it was creepy, like for a funeral." This reminded me of my broken tooth of that morning, but I said nothing.

It was dark by the time I left the house, and a misty rain was falling. As I walked out through the gate, I realized I was wearing fair-weather clogs, not the rain clogs I had asked the maid to put out for me. To make matters worse, the left one's thong was loose in front. I couldn't help feeling that if the thong snapped my son's life would end, but I was too annoyed to go back and change clogs. Angry at the maid, I walked along with great care to avoid overturning the loose clog.

I got to the hospital after nine. Soaking in water in a wash basin outside Takashi's door were the flowers my aunt had mentioned—five or six lilies and pinks. Inside, the room itself was almost too dark to see faces: someone had put a piece of cloth over the light bulb. Still in their kimono, my wife and her mother were lying on a futon with Takashi between them. He was sound asleep, pillowed on my mother-in-law's arm. When she saw me come in, my wife sat up on her heels and, with a bow, whispered, "Thank you for coming." Her mother said the same thing to me. They seemed almost cheerful, which took me by surprise. I felt somewhat relieved and knelt down by their pillows. My wife said she was suffering doubly: since she wasn't allowed to give Takashi her milk, she had to listen to him cry for it; and her breasts were so full they hurt. "A rubber nipple doesn't help, either. I finally had to let him suck my tongue."

"Now he's drinking *my* milk," my mother-in-law said with a laugh, showing me her withered breasts. "He sucks so *hard*— look how red I am."

I found myself laughing with her. "But really, he's doing much better than I expected. I figured he'd be done for by now."

"Taka? Taka's just fine. We're cleaning him out, that's all. His fever will go down tomorrow for sure."

"Thanks to the Sainted Founder's awesome powers, no doubt," my wife teased her mother, a believer in the Lotus Sutra.[6] Her mother seemed not to hear her, though, as she pursed her lips and blew hard at Takashi's head, probably hoping to bring his fever down that way.

＊   ＊   ＊   ＊   ＊   ＊   ＊

Takashi finally eluded death. When he was doing a little better, I thought about writing a sketch of the events surrounding his stay in the hospital, but I decided against it because of a superstitious feeling that if I let my guard down and wrote such a piece, he might have a relapse. Now, though, he is sleeping in the garden hammock. Having been asked to write a story, I thought I would have a go at this. The reader might wish I had done otherwise.

(July 1923)

DEATH REGISTER

My mother was a madwoman. I never did feel close to her, as
a son should feel toward his mother. Hair held in place by a
comb, she would sit alone all day puffing on a long, skinny pipe
in the house of my birth family in Tokyo's Shiba Ward.[1] She
had a tiny face on a tiny body, and that face of hers, for some
reason, was always ashen and lifeless. Once, reading *The Story
of the Western Wing*,[2] I came upon the phrase "smell of earth,
taste of mud," and thought immediately of my mother—of her
emaciated face in profile.

And so I never had the experience of a mother's care. I do
seem to recall that one time, when my adoptive mother made a
point of taking me upstairs to see her, she suddenly conked me
on the head with her pipe. In general, though, she was a quiet
lunatic. I or my elder sister would sometimes press her to paint
a picture for us, and she would do it on a sheet of paper folded
in four. And not just with black ink, either. She would apply
my sister's watercolors to blossoming plants or the costumes of
children on an outing. The people in her pictures, though,
always had fox faces.

My mother died in the autumn of my eleventh year, not so
much from illness, I think, as from simply wasting away. I have
a fairly clear memory of the events surrounding her death.

A telegram must have arrived to alert us. Late on a windless
night, I climbed into a rickshaw with my adoptive mother and
sped across the city from Honjo to Shiba. Otherwise in my life
I have never used a scarf, but I do recall that on that particular
night I had a thin silk handkerchief wrapped around my neck.

I also recall that it had some kind of Chinese landscape motif, and that it smelled strongly of Iris Bouquet.[3]

My mother lay on a futon in the eight-mat parlor directly beneath her upstairs room. I knelt beside her, wailing, with my four-year-older sister. I felt especially miserable when I heard someone behind me say, "The end is near." My mother had been lying there as good as dead, but suddenly she opened her eyes and spoke. Sad as everyone felt, we couldn't help giggling.

I stayed up by my mother through the following night as well, but that night, for some reason, my tears simply wouldn't flow. Ashamed to be so unfeeling while right next to me my sister wept almost constantly, I struggled to pretend. Yet I also believed that as long as I was unable to cry, my mother would not die.

On the evening of the third day, though, she did die, with very little suffering. A few times before it happened, she would seem to regain consciousness, look us all in the face, and release an endless stream of tears, but as usual she said not a thing.

Even after her body had been placed in the coffin, I couldn't keep from breaking down time and again. The old woman we called our "Ōji Auntie," a distant relative, would say, "I'm so impressed with you!" My only thought was that here was a person who let herself be impressed by very strange things.

The day of my mother's funeral, my sister climbed into a rickshaw holding the memorial tablet,[4] and I followed her inside, holding the censer. I dozed off now and then, waking with a start each time the censer was about to drop from my hand. Still, we seemed never to reach Yanaka. Always I would wake to find the long funeral procession still winding its way through the streets of Tokyo in the autumn sunlight.

The anniversary of my mother's death is 28 November. The priest gave her the posthumous name of Kimyōin Myōjō Nisshin Daishi.[5] I can remember neither the anniversary of my birth father's death two decades later nor his posthumous name. Memorizing such things had probably been a matter of pride for me at the age of eleven.

2

I have just the one elder sister. Not very healthy, she is nevertheless the mother of two children. She is not, of course, one of
those I want to include in this "Death Register." Rather, it is
the sister who died suddenly just before I was born. Among us
three siblings, she was said to be the smartest.

She was certainly the first—which is why they named her
"Hatsuko" (First Daughter). Even now a small framed portrait
of "Little Hatsu"[6] adorns the Buddhist altar in my house. There
is nothing at all sickly-looking about her. Her cheeks, with their
little dimples, are as round as ripe apricots.

Little Hatsu was by far the one who received the greatest
outpouring of love from my parents. They made a point of
sending her all the way from Shiba Shinsenza to attend the
kindergarten of a Mrs. Summers—I think it was—in Tsukiji.[7]
On weekends, though, she would stay with my mother's family,
the Akutagawas, in Honjo. On these outings of hers, Little
Hatsu would probably wear Western dresses, which still, in the
Meiji twenties, would have seemed very modish. When I was
in elementary school, I remember, I used to get remnants of her
clothes to put on my rubber doll. Without exception, all the
cloth patches were imported calico scattered with tiny printed
flowers or musical instruments.

One Sunday afternoon in early spring, when Little Hatsu was
strolling through the garden (wearing a Western dress, as I
imagine her), she called out to our aunt Fuki in the parlor,
"Auntie, what's the name of this tree?"

"Which one?"

"This one, with the buds."

In the garden of my mother's family, a single low *boke*[8] trailed
its branches over the old well. Little Hatsu, in pigtails, was probably looking up at its thorny branches with big round eyes.

"It has the same name as you," my aunt said, but before she
could explain her joke, Hatsu made up one of her own:

"Then it must be a 'dummy' tree."

My aunt always tells this story whenever the conversation
turns to Little Hatsu. Indeed, it's the only story left to tell about

her. Probably not too many days later, Little Hatsu was in her coffin. I don't remember the posthumous name engraved on her tiny memorial tablet. I do have a strangely clear memory of her death date, though: 5 April.

For some unknown reason, I feel close to this sister I never knew. If "Little Hatsu" were still living, she would be over forty now. And maybe, at that age, she would look like my mother as I recall her upstairs in the Shiba house, blankly puffing away on her pipe. I often feel as if there is a fortyish woman somewhere—a phantom not exactly my mother nor this dead sister—watching over my life. Could this be the effect of nerves wracked by coffee and tobacco? Or might it be the work of some supernatural power giving occasional glimpses of itself to the real world?

3

Because my mother lost her mind, I was adopted into the family of her elder brother shortly after I was born, and so my real father was another parent for whom I had little feeling. He owned a dairy and seems to have been a small-scale success. That father was the person who taught me all about the newly imported fruits and drinks of the day: *banana, ice cream, pineapple, rum*—and probably much more. I remember once drinking rum in the shade of an oak tree outside the pasture, which was then located in Shinjuku.[9] Rum was an amber-colored drink with little alcohol.

When I was very young, my father would try to entice me back from my adoptive family by plying me with these rare treats. I remember how he once openly tempted me into running away while feeding me ice cream in the Uoei restaurant in Ōmori.[10] At times like this he could be a smooth talker and exude real charm. Unfortunately for him, though, his enticements never worked. This was because I loved my adoptive family too much—and especially my mother's elder sister, Aunt Fuki.

My father had a short temper and was always fighting with people. When I was in the third year of middle school, I beat him at sumo wrestling by tripping him backwards using a special judo move of mine. He got up and came right after me saying "One more go." I threw him easily again. He came charging at me for a third time, again saying "One more go," but now I could see he was angry. My other aunt (Aunt Fuyu, my mother's younger sister—by then my father's second wife) was watching all this, and she winked at me a few times behind my father's back. After grappling with him for a little while, I purposely fell over backwards. I'm sure if I hadn't lost to him, I would have ended up another victim of my father's temper.

When I was twenty-eight and still teaching, I received a telegram saying "Father hospitalized," and I rushed from Kamakura to Tokyo. He was in the Tokyo Hospital with influenza. I spent the next three days there with my Aunts Fuyu and Fuki, sleeping in a corner of the room. I was beginning to feel bored when a call came for me from an Irish reporter friend[11] inviting me out for a meal at a Tsukiji tea house. Using his upcoming departure for America as an excuse, I left for Tsukiji even though my father was on the verge of death.

We had a delightful Japanese dinner in the company of four or five geisha. I think the meal ended around ten o'clock. Leaving the reporter, I was headed down the steep, narrow stairway when, from behind, I heard a soft feminine voice calling me "Ah-san" in that playful geisha way. I stopped in mid-descent and turned to look up toward the top of the stairs. There, one of the geisha was looking down, her eyes fixed on mine. Wordlessly, I continued down the stairs and stepped into the cab waiting at the front door. The car moved off immediately, but instead of my father what came to mind was the fresh face of that geisha in her Western hairstyle—and in particular her eyes.

Back at the hospital, I found my father eagerly awaiting my return. He sent everyone else outside the two-panel folding screen by the bed, and, gripping and caressing my hand, he began to talk about long-ago matters that I had never known—things from the time when he married my mother. They were inconsequential things—how he and she had gone to shop for a storage chest, or how they had eaten home-delivered sushi—but before I knew it my eyelids were growing hot inside, and down my father's wasted cheeks, too, tears were flowing.

My father died the next morning without a great deal of suffering. His mind seemed to grow confused before he died, and he would say things like "Here comes a warship! Look at all the flags it has flying! Three cheers, everybody!" I don't remember his funeral at all. What I do remember is that when we transported his body from the hospital to his home, a great big spring moon was shining down on the hearse.

4

In mid-March of this year, when it was still cold enough for us to carry pocket warmers, my wife and I visited the cemetery for the first time in a long while—a very long while. Still, however, there was no change at all in either the small grave itself (of course) nor in the red pine stretching its branches above it.

The bones of all three people I have included in this "Death Register" lie buried in the same corner of the cemetery in Yanaka—indeed, beneath the same gravestone. I recalled the time my mother's coffin was gently lowered into the grave. They must have done the same with Little Hatsu. In my father's case, though, I remember the gold teeth mixed in with the tiny white shards of bone at the crematorium.

I don't much like visiting the cemetery, and I would prefer to forget about my parents and sister if I could. On that particular day, though, perhaps because I was physically debilitated, I found myself staring at the blackened gravestone in the early spring afternoon sunlight and wondering which of the three had been the most fortunate.

A shimmering of heat—
Outside the grave
Alone I dwell.

Never before had I sensed these feelings of Jōsō's[12] pressing in upon me with the force they truly had for me that day.

(September 1926)

THE LIFE OF A
STUPID MAN

To my friend, Kume Masao:[1]

I leave it to you to decide when and where to publish this manuscript—or whether to publish it at all.

You know most of the people who appear here, but if you do publish this, I don't want you adding an index identifying them.[2]

I am living now in the unhappiest happiness imaginable. Yet, strangely, I have no regrets. I just feel sorry for anyone unfortunate enough to have had a bad husband, a bad son, a bad father like me. So goodbye, then. I have not tried—*consciously*, at least—to vindicate myself here.

Finally, I entrust this manuscript to you because I believe you probably know me better than anyone else. I may wear the skin of an urbane sophisticate, but in this manuscript I invite you to strip it off and laugh at my stupidity.

Akutagawa Ryūnosuke

20 June 1927

1. The Era

He was upstairs in a bookstore. Twenty years old at the time, he had climbed a ladder set against a bookcase and was searching for the newly-arrived Western books: Maupassant, Baudelaire, Strindberg, Ibsen, Shaw, Tolstoy . . .

The sun threatened to set before long, but he went on reading book spines with undiminished intensity. Lined up before him was not so much an array of books as the *fin de siècle* itself.

Nietzsche, Verlaine, the Goncourt brothers, Dostoevsky, Hauptmann, Flaubert . . .

He took stock of their names as he struggled with the impending gloom. The books began to sink into the somber shadows. Finally his stamina gave out and he made ready to climb down. At that very moment, directly overhead, a single bare light bulb came on. Standing on his perch on top of the ladder, he looked down at the clerks and customers moving among the books. They were strangely small—and shabby.

Life is not worth a single line of Baudelaire.

He stood on the ladder, watching them below . . .

2. Mother

All the lunatics had been dressed in the same gray clothing, which seemed to give the large room an even more depressing look. One of them sat at an organ, playing a hymn over and over with great intensity. Another was dancing—or, rather, leaping about—in the very center of the room.

He stood watching this spectacle with a doctor of notably healthy complexion. Ten years earlier, his mother had been in no way different from these lunatics. In no way. And in fact in their smell he caught a whiff of his own mother's smell.

"Shall we go, then?"

The doctor led him down a corridor to another room. In a corner there were several brains soaking in large jars of alcohol. On one of the brains he noticed something faintly white, almost like a dollop of egg white. As he stood there chatting with the doctor, he thought again of his mother.

"The man who had this brain here was an engineer for the XX lighting company. He always thought of himself as a big shiny black dynamo."

To avoid the doctor's eyes, he kept looking out the window. There was nothing out there but a brick wall topped with embedded broken bottles. It did, though, have thin growths of moss in dull white patches.

3. The House

He was living in the upstairs room of a house in the suburbs.[3] The second story tilted oddly because the ground was unstable.

In this room, his aunt would often quarrel with him, though not without occasional interventions from his adoptive parents. Still, he loved this aunt more than anyone. She never married, and by the time he was twenty, she was an old woman close to sixty.

He often wondered, in that suburban second story, if people who loved each other had to cause each other pain. Even as the thought crossed his mind, he was aware of the floor's eerie tilt.

4. Tokyo

A thick layer of cloud hung above the Sumida River. From the window of the little steamer, he watched the Mukōjima bank drawing closer. To his eyes, the blossoming cherry trees there looked as dreary as rags in a row. But almost before he knew it, in those trees—those cherry trees that had lined the bank of Mukōjima since the Edo Period[4]—he was beginning to discover himself.

5. Ego

He and an elder colleague[5] sat at a café table puffing on cigarettes. He said very little, but he paid close attention to his companion's every word.

"I spent half the day riding around in an automobile."

"Was there something you needed to do?"

Cheek resting on his hand, the elder colleague replied with complete abandon, "No, I just felt like riding around."

The words released him into a world of which he knew nothing[6]—a world of "ego" close to the gods. He felt a kind of pain but, at the same time, a kind of joy.

The café was extremely small. Beneath a framed picture of the god Pan, however, a rubber tree in a red pot thrust its thick leaves out and down.

6. Illness

In a steady ocean breeze, he spread out the large English dictionary and let his fingertip find words for him.

Talaria: A winged sandal.

Tale: A story.

Talipot: A coconut palm native to the East Indies. Trunk
from 50 to 100 feet in height, leaves used for umbrellas, fans,
hats, etc. Blooms once in 70 years . . .

His imagination painted a vivid picture of this bloom. He
then experienced an unfamiliar scratchy feeling in his throat,
and before he knew it he had dropped a glob of phlegm[7] on the
dictionary. Phlegm? But it was not phlegm. He thought of the
shortness of life and once again imagined the coconut blossom—the blossom of the coconut palm soaring on high far
across the ocean.

7. Picture

It happened for him suddenly—quite suddenly. He was standing outside a bookstore, looking at a Van Gogh volume, when
he suddenly understood what a "picture" was. True, the Van
Gogh was just a book of reproductions, but even in the photo-
graphs of those paintings, he sensed the vivid presence of nature.

This passion for pictures gave him a whole new way of
looking at the world. He began to pay constant attention to the
curve of a branch or the swell of a woman's cheek.

One rainy autumn evening, he was walking beneath an iron
railroad bridge in the suburbs. Below the bank on the far side
of the bridge stood a horse cart. As he passed it, he sensed that
someone had come this way before. Someone? There was no
need for him to wonder who that "someone" might have been.
In his twenty-three-year-old heart, a Dutchman with a cut ear
and a long pipe in his mouth was fixing his gaze on this dreary
landscape.

8. Sparks: Flowers of Fire

Soaked by the rain, he trod along the asphalt. It was a heavy downpour. In the enveloping spray, he caught the smell of his rubberized coat.

Just then he saw the overhead trolley line giving off purple sparks and was strangely moved. His jacket pocket concealed the manuscript of the piece he was planning to publish in their little magazine. Walking through the rain, he looked back and up once again at the trolley line.

The cable was still sending sharp sparks into the air. He could think of nothing in life that he especially desired, but those purple sparks—those wildly-blooming flowers of fire—he would trade his life for the chance to hold them in his hands.

9. Cadavers

A tag on a wire dangled from the big toe of each cadaver. The tags were inscribed with names, ages, and such. His friend bent over one corpse, peeling back the skin of its face with a deftly wielded scalpel. An expanse of beautiful yellow fat lay beneath the skin.

He studied the cadaver. He needed to do this to finish writing a story—a piece set against a Heian Period background[8]—but he hated the stink of the corpses, which was like the smell of rotting apricots. Meanwhile, with wrinkled brow, his friend went on working his scalpel.

"You know, we're running out of cadavers these days," his friend said.

His reply was ready: "If *I* needed a corpse, I'd kill someone without the slightest malice." Of course the reply stayed where it was—inside his heart.

10. The Master[9]

He was reading the Master's book beneath a great oak tree. Not a leaf stirred on the oak in the autumn sunlight. Far off in the sky, a scale with glass pans hung in perfect balance. He imagined such a vision as he read the Master's book . . .

11. Dawn

Night gradually gave way to dawn. He found himself on a street corner surveying a vast market. The swarming people and vehicles in the market were increasingly bathed in rose light.

He lit a cigarette and ambled into the market. Just then a lean black dog started barking at him, but he was not afraid. Indeed, he even loved this dog.

In the very center of the marketplace, a sycamore spread its branches in all directions. He stood at the foot of the tree and looked up through the branches at the sky. A single star shone directly above him.

It was his twenty-fifth year—the third month after he first met the Master.[10]

12. Naval Port

Gloom filled the interior of the miniature submarine. Crouching down amid all the machinery, he peered into a small scope. What he saw there was a view of the bright naval port.

"You should be able to see the *Kongō*,[11] too," the naval officer explained to him.

As he was looking at the small warship through the square eyepiece, the thought of parsley popped into his mind for no reason—faintly aromatic parsley on top of a thirty-yen serving of beefsteak.

13. The Master's Death[12]

In the wind after the rain, he walked down the platform of the new station. The sky was still dark. Across from the platform three or four railway laborers were swinging picks and singing loudly. The wind tore at the men's song and at his own emotions.

He left his cigarette unlit and felt a pain close to joy. "Master near death," read the telegram he had thrust into his coat pocket.

Just then the 6:00 a.m. Tokyo-bound train began to snake its way toward the station, rounding a pine-covered hill in the distance and trailing a wisp of smoke.

14. Marriage

The day after he married her, he delivered a scolding to his wife: "No sooner do you arrive here than you start wasting our money." But the scolding was less from him than from his aunt, who had ordered him to deliver it.[13] His wife apologized to him, of course, and to the aunt as well—with the potted jonquils she had bought for him in the room.

15. He and She

They led a peaceful life, surrounded by the garden's broad green *bashō* leaves.[14]

It helped that their house was located in a town by the shore a full hour's train ride from Tokyo.

16. Pillow

Pillowing his head on his rose-scented skepticism, he read a book by Anatole France. That even such a pillow might hold a god half-horse, he remained unaware.

17. Butterfly[15]

A butterfly fluttered its wings in a wind thick with the smell of seaweed. His dry lips felt the touch of the butterfly for the briefest instant, yet the wisp of wing dust still shone on his lips years later.

18. Moon

He happened to pass her on the stairway of a certain hotel. Her face seemed to be bathed in moonglow even now, in daylight. As he watched her walk on (they had never met), he felt a loneliness he had not known before.

19. Man-Made Wings

He moved on from Anatole France to the eighteenth-century philosophers, though not to Rousseau. Perhaps this was because one side of him—the side easily moved by passion—was too close to Rousseau. Instead, he approached the author of *Candide*, who was closer to another side of him—the cool and richly intellectual side.

At twenty-nine, life no longer held any brightness for him, but Voltaire supplied him with man-made wings.

Spreading these man-made wings, he soared with ease into the sky. The higher he flew, the farther below him sank the joys and sorrows of a life bathed in the light of intellect. Dropping ironies and smiles upon the shabby towns below, he climbed through the open sky, straight for the sun—as if he had forgotten about that ancient Greek who plunged to his death in the ocean when his man-made wings were singed by the sun.

20. Shackles

He and his wife came to live with his adoptive parents when he went to work for a newspaper.[16] He saw his contract, written on a single sheet of yellow paper, as a great source of strength.

Later, however, he came to realize that the contract saddled *him* with all the obligations and the company with none.

21. Crazy Girl

Two rickshaws sped down a deserted country road beneath overcast skies. From the sea breeze it was clear that the road was headed toward the ocean. Puzzled that he felt not the slightest excitement about this rendezvous, he sat in the second rickshaw thinking about what had drawn him here. It was certainly not love. And if it was not love, then . . . but to avoid the conclusion, he had to tell himself, *At least we are in this as equals.*

The person riding in the front rickshaw was a crazy girl. And she was not alone in her madness: her younger sister had killed herself out of jealousy.

There's nothing I can do about this anymore.

He now felt a kind of loathing for this crazy girl—this woman who was all powerful animal instinct.

The two rickshaws soon passed a cemetery where the smell of the shore was strong. Several blackened, pagoda-shaped gravestones stood within the fence, which was woven of brushwood and decorated with oyster shells. He caught a glimpse of the ocean gleaming beyond the gravestones and suddenly—inexplicably—he felt contempt for the woman's husband for having failed to capture her heart.[17]

22. A Painter

It was just a magazine illustration, but the ink drawing of a rooster showed a remarkable individuality. He asked a friend to tell him about the painter.[18]

A week later, the painter himself came to pay him a visit. This was one of the most remarkable events in his entire life. He discovered in this painter a poetry of which no one else was aware. In addition, he discovered in himself a soul of which he himself had been unaware.

One chilly autumn evening, he was reminded of the painter

by a stalk of corn: the way it stood there armed in its rough coat of leaves, exposing its delicate roots atop the mounded earth like so many nerves, it was also a portrait of his own most vulnerable self. The discovery only served to increase his melancholy.

It's too late now. But when the time comes . . .

23. The Woman

From where he stood, the plaza was beginning to darken. He walked into the open space feeling slightly feverish. The electric lights in the windows of several large office buildings flashed against the clear, faintly silvery sky.

He halted at the curb and decided to wait for the woman there. Five minutes later she came walking toward him looking somewhat haggard. "I'm exhausted," she said with a smile when she caught sight of him. They walked through the fading light of the plaza side-by-side. This was their first time together. He felt ready to abandon anything and everything to be with her.

In the automobile she stared at him and asked, "You're not going to regret this?"

"Not at all," he answered with conviction.

She pressed her hand on his and said, "I know *I* won't have any regrets."

Again, as she said this, her face seemed to be bathed in moonlight.

24. The Birth

He stood by the sliding screen, looking down at the midwife in her white surgical gown washing the baby. Whenever soap got in its eyes, the baby would wrinkle up its sad little face and let out a loud wail. It looked like a baby rat, and its odor stirred him to these irrepressible thoughts—

Why did this one have to be born—to come into the world like all the others, this world so full of suffering? Why did this one have to bear the destiny of having a father like me?

This was the first son his wife bore him.

25. Strindberg

He stood in the doorway, watching some grimy Chinese men
playing Mahjongg in the moonlight where figs bloomed. Back in
his room, he started reading *The Confessions of a Fool* beneath
a squat lamp. He had barely read two pages when he caught
himself with a sour smile. So—the lies that Strindberg wrote
to his lover, the Countess, were hardly different from his own.

26. Antiquity

He was nearly overwhelmed by peeling Buddhas, heavenly
beings, horses and lotus blossoms. Looking up at them, he
forgot everything—even his good fortune at having escaped the
clutches of the crazy girl.

27. Spartan Discipline

He was walking down a back street with a friend when a
hooded rickshaw came charging in their direction. He was
surprised to recognize the passenger as the woman he had
been with the night before. Her face seemed to be bathed in
moonglow even now, in the daylight. With his friend present,
they could not exchange even ordinary greetings.

"Pretty woman," his friend said.

Eyes on the spring hills at the end of the street, he answered
without the slightest hesitation:

"Yes, very."

28. Murder

The country road stank of cow manure in the sun. Mopping
his sweat, he struggled up the steep hill. The ripened wheat on
either side of the road gave off a pleasant scent.

"Kill him, kill him . . ."

Before he knew it, he was muttering this aloud to himself
over and over. Kill whom? It was obvious to him. He recalled
the cringing fellow with close-cropped hair.

Just then, the domed roof of a Catholic church appeared beyond the yellow wheat.

29. Form

It was a cast-iron saké bottle. With its finely incised lines, it had managed at some point to teach him the beauty of "form."

30. Rain

In the big bed he talked with her about many things. Beyond the bedroom window it was raining. The blossoms of the crinum tree had begun to rot in the rain, it seemed. Her face, as always, looked as if it were in moonlight, yet talking with her was not entirely free of boredom. He lay on his stomach, had himself a quiet smoke, and realized he had now been with her for seven years.

Do I still love this woman? he asked himself. He was in the habit of observing himself so closely that the answer came as a surprise to him: *I do.*

31. The Great Earthquake[19]

The odor was something close to overripe apricots. Catching a hint of it as he walked through the charred ruins, he found himself thinking such thoughts as these: *The smell of corpses rotting in the sun is not as bad as I would have expected.* When he stood before a pond where bodies were piled upon bodies, however, he discovered that the old Chinese expression, "burning the nose," was no mere sensory exaggeration of grief and horror. What especially moved him was the corpse of a child of twelve or thirteen. He felt something like envy as he looked at it, recalling such expressions as "Those whom the gods love die young."[20] Both his sister and his half-brother had lost their houses to fire. His sister's husband, though, was on a suspended sentence for perjury.[21]

Too bad we didn't all die.

Standing in the charred ruins, he could hardly keep from feeling this way.

32. Fight

He had a quarrel with his half-brother that ended in a physical brawl. True, he was a constant source of pressure for this younger brother, who in turn cost him a good deal of freedom. Relatives were always telling the young man, "be like your brother," but for him, this was like being bound hand and foot. Locked in each other's grip, they fell near the edge of the veranda. He still remembers the one crape myrtle bush in the garden by the veranda—its load of brilliant red blossoms beneath a sky about to drop its rainy burden.

33. Hero

From the window of Voltaire's house, he found himself looking up toward a high mountain. There was nothing to be seen on the glacier-topped mountain, not even a vulture. There was, however, a short Russian man[22] doggedly climbing the trail.

After night fell, beneath the bright lamp in Voltaire's house, he wrote this didactic poem (still picturing that Russian man climbing the mountain).

You who more than anyone obeyed the Ten Commandments
Are you who more than anyone broke the Ten Commandments.

You who more than anyone loved the masses
Are you who more than anyone despised the masses.

You who more than anyone burned with ideals
Are you who more than anyone knew reality.

You are what our Eastern world has bred—
An electric locomotive that smells of flowering grasses.

34. Color

At thirty he found himself loving a piece of vacant land. It contained only some moss and scattered bits of brick and tile. To his eyes, however, it was exactly like a Cezanne landscape.

He suddenly recalled his passions of seven or eight years earlier. And when he did so, he realized that seven or eight years earlier he had known nothing about color.

35. Comic Puppet

He wanted to live life so intensely that he could die at any moment without regrets. But still, out of deference to his adoptive parents and his aunt, he kept himself in check. This created both light and dark sides to his life. Seeing a comic puppet in a Western tailor's shop made him wonder how close he himself was to such a figure. His self beyond consciousness, however—his "second self"—had long since put such feelings into a story.[23]

36. Tedium

He was walking through a field of plume grass with a university student. "You fellows still have a strong will to live, I suppose?"

"Yes, of course, but you, too . . ."

"Not any more," he said. He was telling the truth. At some point he had lost interest in life. "I *do* have the will to create, though."

"But surely the will to create is a form of the will to live . . . ?"

To this he did not reply. Above the field's red plumes rose the sharp outline of an active volcano. He viewed the peak with something close to envy, though he had no idea why this was so. . . .

37. "Woman of Hokuriku"[24]

He met a woman he could grapple with intellectually. He barely extricated himself from the crisis by writing a number of lyric poems, some under the title "Woman of Hokuriku." These conveyed a sense of heartbreak as when one knocks away a brilliant coating of snow frozen onto a tree trunk.

> Hat of sedge dancing in the wind:
> How could it fail to drop into the road?
> What need I fear for my name?
> For your name alone do I fear.

38. Punishment[25]

They were on the balcony of a hotel surrounded by trees in bud. He was drawing pictures to amuse a little boy—the only son of the crazy girl, with whom he had broken off relations seven years earlier.

The crazy girl lit a cigarette and watched them play. With an oppressive feeling, he went on drawing trains and airplanes. Fortunately, the boy was not his, but it still pained him greatly when the child called him "uncle."

After the boy wandered off, the crazy girl, still smoking her cigarette, said suggestively:

"Don't you think he looks like you?"

"Not at all. Besides—"

"But you do know about 'prenatal influence,' I'm sure."

He looked away from her in silence, but in his heart he wanted to strangle her.

39. Mirrors

He was in the corner of a café, chatting with a friend. The friend was eating a baked apple and talking about the recent cold weather when he himself began to sense a certain contradiction in the conversation.

"Hey, wait a minute—you're still a bachelor, right?"

"Not exactly: I'm getting married next month."

That silenced him. The mirrors set in the café walls reflected him in endless numbers. Coldly. Menacingly.

40. Dialogue

Why do you attack the present social system?
Because I see the evils that capitalism has engendered.
*Evils? I thought you recognized no difference between good
and evil. How do you make a living, then?*
He engaged thus in dialogue with an angel—an angel in an
impeccable top hat.

41. Illness

He suffered an onslaught of insomnia. His physical strength
began to fade as well. The doctors gave him various diag-
noses—gastric hyperacidity, gastric atony, dry pleurisy, neuras-
thenia, chronic conjunctivitis, brain fatigue . . .
But he knew well enough what was wrong with him: he was
ashamed of himself and afraid of *them*—afraid of the society
he so despised.
One afternoon when snow clouds hung over the city, he was
in the corner of a café, smoking a cigar and listening to music
from the gramophone on the other side of the room. He found
the music permeating his emotions in a strange new way. When
it ended, he walked over to the gramophone to read the label
on the record.
"Magic Flute—Mozart."
All at once it became clear to him: Mozart too had broken
the Ten Commandments and suffered. Probably not the way
he had, but . . .
He bowed his head and returned to his table in silence.

42. The Laughter of the Gods

At thirty-five, he was walking through a pinewood with the
spring sun beating down on it. He was recalling, too, the words
he had written a few years earlier: "It is unfortunate for the
gods that, unlike us, they cannot commit suicide."

43. Night

Night closed in again. The rough sea sent up spray in the fading light. Beneath these skies, he married his wife anew. This brought them joy, but there was suffering as well. With them, their three sons watched the lightning over the open sea. His wife, holding one of the boys in her arms, seemed to be fighting back tears.

"See the boat over there?" he asked her.

"Yes . . ."

"That boat with the mast cracked in two . . ."

44. Death

Taking advantage of his sleeping alone, he tried to hang himself with a sash tied over the window lattice. When he slipped his head into the sash, however, he suddenly became afraid of death. Not that he feared the suffering he would have to experience at the moment of dying. He decided to try it again, using his pocket watch to see how long it would take. This time, everything began to cloud over after a short interval of pain. He was sure that once he got past that, he would enter death. Checking the hands of his watch, he discovered that the pain lasted one minute and twenty-some seconds. It was pitch dark outside the lattices, but the wild clucking of chickens echoed in the darkness.

45. Divan[26]

Divan was giving him new inner power. This was an "Oriental Goethe" he had not known before. He saw the author standing with quiet confidence on the Other Shore, far beyond good and evil, and he felt an envy close to despair. In his eyes, the poet Goethe was even greater than the poet Christ. For in the heart of the poet Goethe, there bloomed not only the roses of the Acropolis and Golgotha but the rose of Arabia as well. If only he had the least ability to follow in this poet's footsteps!

Once he had finished reading *Divan* and recovered somewhat

from its terrifying emotional impact, he could only despise himself for having been born such a eunuch in life!

46. Lies

He felt the suicide of his sister's husband as a terrible blow. Now he was responsible for his sister's family as well. To him at least, his future looked as gloomy as the end of the day. He felt something like a sneer for his own spiritual bankruptcy (he was aware of all of his faults and weak points, every single one of them), but he went on reading one book after another. Even Rousseau's *Confessions*, though, was full of the most heroic lies. And when it came to Tōson's *New Life*,[27] he felt he had never met such a cunning hypocrite as that novel's protagonist. The one who truly moved him, though, was François Villon. He found in that poet's many works the "beautiful male."

Sometimes in his dreams the image would come to him of Villon waiting to be hanged. Like Villon, he had several times nearly fallen to the ultimate depths of life, but neither his situation nor his physical energy would permit him to keep this up. He grew gradually weaker, like the tree Swift saw[28] so long ago, withering from the top down.

47. Playing with Fire

She had a radiant face, like the morning sun on a thin sheet of ice. He was fond of her,[29] but he did not love her, nor had he ever laid a finger on her.

"I've heard you want to die," she said.

"Yes—or rather, it's not so much that I want to die as that I'm tired of living."

This dialogue led to a vow to die together.

"It would be a Platonic suicide, I suppose," she said.

"A Platonic double suicide."

He was amazed at his own sangfroid.

48. Death

He did not die with her, but he took a certain satisfaction in his never having touched her. She often spoke with him as though their dialogue had never happened. She did once give him a bottle of cyanide with the remark, "As long as we have this, it will give us both strength."

And it did indeed give him strength. Sitting in a rattan chair, observing the new growth of a *shii* tree,[30] he often thought of the peace that death would give him.

49. Stuffed Swan

With the last of his strength, he tried to write his autobiography, but it did not come together as easily as he had hoped. This was because of his remaining pride and skepticism, and a calculation of what was in his own best interest. He couldn't help despising these qualities in himself; but neither could he help feeling that "Everyone is the same under the skin." He tended to think that Goethe's title "Poetry and Truth"[31] could serve for anyone's autobiography, but he knew that not everyone is moved by literature. His own works were unlikely to appeal to people who were not like him and had not lived a life like his—this was another feeling that worked upon him. And so he decided to write his own brief "Poetry and Truth."

Once he had finished writing "The Life of a Stupid Man," he happened to see a stuffed swan in a secondhand shop. It stood with its head held high, but its wings were yellowed and moth-eaten. As he thought about his life, he felt both tears and mockery welling up inside him. All that lay before him was madness or suicide. He walked down the darkening street alone, determined now to wait for the destiny that would come to annihilate him.

50. Captive

One of his friends went mad.[32] He had always felt close to this man because he understood far more deeply than anyone else the loneliness that lurked beneath his jaunty mask. He visited him a few times after the madness struck.

"You and I are both possessed by a demon," the friend whispered, "the demon of the *fin de siècle*."

Two or three days later, he heard, the man ate roses on the way to a hot-spring resort. When the friend was hospitalized, he recalled once sending him a terra cotta piece. It was a bust of the author of *The Inspector General*, one of the friend's favorite writers. Thinking how Gogol, too, had gone mad, he could not help feeling that there was a force governing all of them.

Just as he reached the point of utter exhaustion, he happened to read Raymond Radiguet's dying words, "God's soldiers are coming to get me,"[33] and sensed once again the laughter of the gods. He tried to fight against his own superstitions and sentimentalism, but he was physically incapable of putting up any kind of struggle. The "demon of the *fin de siècle*" was preying on him without a doubt. He envied medieval men's ability to find strength in God. But for him, believing in God— in God's love—was an impossibility, though even Cocteau had done it!

51. Defeat

The hand with the pen began to tremble, and before long he was even drooling. The only time his head ever cleared was after a sleep induced by eight-tenths of a gram of Veronal, and even then it never lasted more than thirty minutes or an hour. He barely made it through each day in the gloom, leaning as it were upon a chipped and narrow sword.

(June 1927: posthumous manuscript)

SPINNING GEARS

1. Raincoats

I was on my way to Tokyo for the wedding reception of an acquaintance. Satchel in hand, I urged the taxi driver on toward a station on the Tōkaidō Line[1] from my home in a coastal resort town. Thick pinewoods lined both sides of the road. We weren't likely to make the Tokyo-bound train. The other passenger in the cab owned a barbershop. He was plump as a *natsume*[2] and wore a short beard. Concerned about the time, I still managed to respond to his occasional remark.

"Strange, the things that happen. I hear they've been seeing a ghost on Mr. X's property—even in the daytime."

"Even in the daytime, eh?" My response was halfhearted. I stared across to where the western sun struck a pine-covered hill.

"Not on good days, though. Mostly when it rains."

"Maybe the ghost comes to get wet."

"That's funny . . . but I *have* heard it wears a raincoat."

Sounding its horn, the taxi pulled up beside the station. I took leave of the barber and went inside. The Tokyo train had in fact pulled out two or three minutes earlier. One person—a man in a raincoat—sat on the waiting-room bench, blankly staring outside. I recalled the ghost story I had just heard, but gave the thought only a contorted little smile. I decided to wait for the next train in the café across from the station.

Actually, "café" was too grand a name for this place. I sat at a corner table and ordered a cup of cocoa. The table was covered in white oilcloth with a rough grid of narrow blue lines, but the slick coating was worn away in spots, revealing the dingy canvas beneath. I took a sip of the cocoa, which had a fishy, glue-like smell, and looked around the deserted room. On the grimy walls were slips of paper announcing the dishes available: *Oyako-donburi*,[3] Pork Cutlet, Omelet with Local Eggs.

These paper slips seemed so typical of the countryside near the Tōkaidō Line, where modern electric-powered locomotives pulled trains through fields of barley and cabbage.

It was close to sunset by the time I boarded the next Tokyo train. I always rode second class, but this time I decided to go third class.

The train was fairly crowded. I was surrounded by a group of elementary-school girls[4] on their way back from a swim at Ōiso or some such place. I observed them as I lit a cigarette. They all seemed to be in a merry mood, and most of them jabbered on without a break.

"Mr. Cameraman, what does 'love scene' mean? It's English, isn't it?"

Sitting across from me, the "Mr. Cameraman" in question, who had apparently accompanied the school outing, did his best to avoid a straight answer, but a girl of fourteen or so kept plying him with questions. It suddenly occurred to me that her nasal whine might be due to an infection,[5] and I couldn't help smiling. Then the girl next to me, who must have been twelve or thirteen, went to sit on the lap of the young lady-teacher, hooking her arm around the woman's neck and stroking her cheek. Between remarks to her friends, she would say things like, "You're so pretty, teacher! You have such pretty eyes."

As a group they seemed to me more like women than school-girls—if you ignored the fact that some were unwrapping cara-mels or munching on unpeeled apples. But then the one I took to be the oldest girl must have stepped on someone's foot as she passed my seat. "Oh, do forgive me!" she said. Oddly, her very maturity made her seem more like a schoolgirl than the rest. I couldn't help sneering at myself, cigarette in my lips, for my own contradictory impression.

Eventually the train, in which the lights had come on at some point, pulled into a suburban station. I stepped down to the cold, windy platform, crossed a footbridge, and waited for the connecting train. At that point I ran into T, who worked for a large company. While waiting, we talked about things such as the faltering economy. He, of course, knew a lot more about such matters than I did, but one of his powerful-looking fingers bore a turquoise ring that had nothing to do with hard economic times.

"That's quite a ring," I said.

"This? Oh, a friend of mine made me buy it from him when he went over to Harbin on business. He's having a tough time, too. He can't deal with the cooperatives[6] anymore."

The train we boarded was, fortunately, not as crowded as the first one. T and I sat next to each other and kept on talking. He had just returned to Tokyo from an assignment in Paris this past spring, and so Paris tended to dominate our conversation. We talked about Mme. Caillaux's shooting[7] of the owner of *Le Figaro*, about crab cuisine, about an Imperial Prince who was traveling abroad . . .

"France is having surprisingly little trouble with the economy. The French really hate to pay taxes, though, so their cabinets are always falling."

"But the franc's gone through the floor."

"That's if you believe what you read in the papers. Over there, the papers'll tell you Japan has nothing but earthquakes and floods."

Just then, a man in a raincoat sat down across from us. This gave me an eerie feeling, and I wanted to tell T about the ghost story I had heard, but before I could do so, he tipped the handle of his cane to the left and, still facing forward, quietly said to me, "See that woman over there? The one with the gray woolen shawl."

"With the Western hairdo?"

"Uh-huh, and the cloth bundle. She was in Karuizawa[8] this summer. Always wearing chic Western clothing."

She certainly would have looked very shabby to anyone who saw her at the moment, however. I stole a few glances at her while talking with T. There was a hint of insanity between her brows. And protruding from her cloth bundle was a sea sponge with leopard-like spots.

"I heard she was always dancing with some young American in Karuizawa. She's one of those *modern* whatchamacallems."[9]

When I said goodbye to T, I realized that the man in the raincoat had disappeared at some point. Bag in hand, I walked from the station to a hotel. Tall buildings lined both sides of the street. As I walked along, I thought about this morning's pinewoods. I also realized that something strange had entered my field of vision—a set of translucent spinning gears. I had had this experience several times before, and it was always the same: the number of gears would gradually increase until half my field of vision was blocked. This would last only a few moments, and then the gears would vanish, to be replaced by a headache. My eye doctor had often ordered me to cut down on smoking to rid myself of this optical illusion (if that's what it was), but actually I had begun seeing the gears before I turned twenty, well before I started smoking. "Here it comes again," I told myself, and covered my right eye to test the sight of the left one. The left eye was fine, but behind the lid of the right several gears were spinning. I hurried down the street as the buildings on the right side gradually disappeared.

By the time I entered the hotel, the gears were gone, but the headache was still there. As I was checking my overcoat and hat at the desk, I decided to reserve a room; then I telephoned a magazine publisher to talk about money.

The wedding banquet had apparently long since started. I found a seat at a far corner of the table and began moving my knife and fork. There were more than fifty people seated at the U-shaped table, and all of them, from the bride and groom at the center on down, were naturally in high spirits. I, however, grew increasingly depressed beneath the bright lights. To escape this feeling, I tried chatting with my neighbor, an old gentleman with a white beard like a lion's mane. He was actually a famous scholar of Chinese whose name I knew. Our conversation soon turned to the classics.

"The *kirin* is, finally, a kind of unicorn," I said. "And the *hōō*[10] corresponds to the Western phoenix."

He seemed interested in my remarks, but the longer I sustained the mechanical process of making conversation, the more

I began to feel a sick, destructive urge coming on. I declared that the legendary sage emperors Yao and Shun were "of course" fictional creations, and that the author of the *Spring and Autumn Annals* was actually a person of the much later Han period.[11] At this, the China scholar made an open show of his displeasure. He turned away and, with a tiger-like growl, cut me off in mid-sentence.

"If you start saying Yao and Shun never existed, you make a liar out of Confucius, and that sage would never tell a lie."

I shut up then, of course, and began to slice the meat on my plate. I noticed a tiny maggot silently squirming on the edge of the meat. The maggot called to mind the English word "Worm." This was probably another word like *"kirin"* or *"hōō"* designating a legendary creature.[12] I laid down my knife and fork and watched my champagne glass being filled.

When, at last, the banquet ended, I walked down a deserted corridor to shut myself up in the room I had booked. The corridor struck me as more like that of a prison than a hotel, but fortunately my headache had subsided.

They had brought my suitcase to the room, and my hat and coat as well. Hanging on the wall, the coat looked to me like my own standing figure. I hurriedly threw it into a corner wardrobe. Then I went to the mirror and stared at my reflection. My face in the mirror revealed the bones beneath the skin. Into the memory contained in this skull of mine leaped a vivid image of the maggot.

I opened the door, stepped out, and wandered down the hall. In a corner where the corridor joined the lobby stood a tall lamp, its green shade brilliantly reflected against a glass door. The sight gave me a peaceful sensation. I sat in a nearby chair and mused on many things, but I was unable to remain seated there for as long as five minutes: there was another raincoat, this one dangling over the back of the sofa next to me where someone had tossed it.

And this is supposed to be the coldest time of the year!

Thinking this, I headed back down the hallway. At the bell-boy station in a corner of the corridor, there was not a bellboy to be seen, though I could hear their voices. In response to some

remark, one said in English, "All right." All right? I struggled
to grasp the meaning of the exchange. "All right"? "All right"?
What could possibly be all right?

My room, of course, was silent, but the thought of going
through the door I found unsettling. After a moment's hesitation, I steeled myself and went in. I sat at the desk, taking care
not to look in the mirror. The seat was an armchair done in a
green Moroccan leather like a lizard skin. I opened my bag,
took out a sheaf of manuscript paper, and tried to work on a
story I had been writing. But even after I had dipped it in ink,
my pen would not move. And when at last it did, it just kept
writing the same words over and over: "All right . . . All right
. . . All right, Sir . . . All right . . ."

Suddenly the phone by the bed rang. Startled, I stood up and
put the receiver to my ear.

"Who is it?" I asked.

"It's me. *Me* . . ." It was my elder sister's daughter.

"What is it? Is something wrong?"

"Yes, something terrible," she said. "So I . . . It's so terrible,
I called your house, and Auntie told me to . . ."

"Is it really so terrible?"

"Yes, really—please come right away. Right away!"

She cut the connection. I set the receiver down and pressed
the button to summon a bellboy. My hand moved reflexively,
but I was fully aware that it was trembling. No one came in
response to the bell. More out of anguish than annoyance, I
pressed the button again and again, understanding at last what
Fate was trying to tell me with the words "All right."

That afternoon, in a nearby Tokyo suburb, my sister's husband had been killed by a train. Despite the season, he had
been wearing a raincoat.

I am in that same hotel room now, writing the same story.
No one goes down the hall in the middle of the night, but
sometimes I hear the sound of wings outside my door. Perhaps
someone is keeping birds nearby.

2. Vengeance

I woke in the hotel room at eight o'clock this morning but, strangely enough, when I tried to get out of bed I found only one slipper on the floor. This was a phenomenon that had been causing me both fear and anxiety over the past year or more— a phenomenon that reminded me, too, of the prince in the Greek myth who wore only one sandal.[13] I rang for a bellboy and had him search for the other slipper. He explored the small room with a puzzled expression.

"Here it is," he said, "in the bathroom."

"How could it have gotten over there?"

"I wonder. A rat, maybe?"

When he left, I had a cup of coffee without milk and set about finishing my story. Framed in volcanic stone,[14] the room's square window looked out on a snowy garden. Whenever I set down my pen, I let my eyes wander over the snow. Spread out beneath a budding daphne, the snow was soiled by the smoky air of the city; the view pained my heart. Before I knew it, my pen had stopped moving, and I was puffing away on my cigarette and thinking about all kinds of things—my wife, my children, and especially my sister's husband.

Before he killed himself, my sister's husband had been under suspicion of arson. And little wonder: he had insured his house for twice its worth before it burned down. He had also been serving a suspended sentence for perjury.[15] What disturbed me even more than his suicide, however, was the fact that on my visits to Tokyo I would invariably see something burning. Once it was a farmer burning his hillside field that I saw from the train; another time it was the Tokiwabashi district fire that I saw from the taxi (I had my wife and the baby with me then). So I had a strong premonition of fire well before his house went up in flames.

"Our house might burn down this year," I said to my wife.

"Oh, please, don't say such things," she protested. "It's bad luck. . . . Still, if we ever did have a fire, it would be awful. We have so little insurance."

So far, my house had been spared, but . . . I forced myself to stop daydreaming and tried to get my pen moving again, but I couldn't write so much as a line. I ended up leaving the desk and stretched out on the bed to read Tolstoy's "Polikushka." The protagonist of the story was a complicated jumble of vanity, pathology, and lust for fame. A few small revisions to the tragicomedy of his life, though, and you could end up with a caricature of my own life. Sensing the sneer of Fate in his particular tragicomedy gave me an increasingly weird feeling. Before an hour passed, I sprang from the bed and, with all my might, hurled the book into the curtained corner of the room. "Die, damn you!"[16]

Instantly a large rat scurried from beneath the curtains, cutting diagonally across the floor to the bathroom. I bounded over to the bathroom door and flung it open to search for the rat, but there was no sign of it, even behind the white tub. Suddenly overcome by that eerie feeling, I hurriedly switched from slippers to shoes and walked down the deserted corridor.

Again today, the corridor was as depressing as a prison. Hanging my head, I climbed and descended one stairway after another until I found myself in the hotel kitchen. The brightness of the place took me by surprise. Several of the rice cauldrons lining one wall had flames moving beneath them. I felt the mocking stares of the white-hatted chefs as I passed through the room, and I sensed the inferno that I had fallen into. I could not suppress the prayer that rose to my lips: "Oh, Lord, I beg thy punishment. Withhold thy wrath from me, for I may soon perish."[17]

I left the hotel and hurried toward my sister's house along streets reflecting blue sky in pools of snowmelt. All the branches and leaves of the park trees along the street had a blackish look, and each tree had a front and a back the way we human beings do. This, too, gave me a sensation closer to fear than annoyance. I recalled the souls in Dante's Inferno who had been turned into trees, and I decided instead to walk on the other side, across the streetcar line, where only buildings edged the street.

Even there, however, I could not manage to walk a full block without interference.

"I know it's very impolite of me to approach you on the

street like this, but . . ." He was a young man in his early
twenties wearing a uniform with gold buttons. I stared at him
in silence and noticed a mole on the left side of his nose. He
had removed his hat and he spoke nervously.

"You are Mr. A, are you not?"

"I am."

"I thought so."

"Is there something I can do for you?"

"Oh, no, I just wanted to meet you, Sensei. I'm a devoted
reader of your works, and . . ."

I was already walking on before he could finish; I gave him a
quick tip of my hat and left him behind. "Sensei," "A-Sensei":
such titles of respect were the worst thing that anyone could
use for me these days. I believed that I had committed every sin
known to man, but they went on calling me "Sensei" whenever
they had the chance, as if I were some sort of guru. I couldn't
help but feel in this the presence of something mocking me.
"The presence of something"? But my materialism could only
reject such mysticism. Just a few months earlier, I had written
in a small coterie magazine: "I have no conscience at all—least
of all an artistic conscience. All I have is nerves."[18]

My sister had taken refuge with three of her children in a
back-alley shed. Covered in brown paper, the place was almost
colder inside than out. We warmed our hands over a hibachi as
we talked. My sister's stocky husband had always instinctively
despised me for being far skinnier than most people. He also
publicly criticized my work as immoral. I always coolly dismissed his views, and never once had an honest conversation
with him. As I spoke about him with my sister, however, I
gradually began to realize that, like me, he had fallen into his
own particular hell. She tried to tell me something about how
he had once actually seen a ghost in a railway sleeper car, but
I lit a cigarette and worked to keep the conversation focused
on money.

"There's not much I can do in my situation," she said. "I
think I'll just sell everything."

"You'll probably have to," I said. "You should be able to get something for the typewriter."

"And there are a few pictures, you know."

"Which reminds me: are you going to sell the portrait of N (her husband)? But maybe not. It's not exactly . . ."

I looked at the unframed crayon portrait on the wall of the shed and realized this was no time for flippancy. The man had thrown himself under a train, which had apparently turned his face into a mass of flesh, with only the moustache intact. As if this in itself weren't unnerving enough, his portrait had been rendered flawlessly except for the moustache area, which seemed oddly indistinct. I wondered if the direction of the light could be causing this, and looked at the picture from different angles.

"What are you doing?"

"Nothing . . . It's just that the area around the mouth . . ."

My sister glanced back. "Yes, strange, isn't it, the way just the moustache looks so pale?" She said this without seeming to notice the connection I was making.

What I had seen was no optical illusion. And if that was the case—

I decided to leave before my sister would have to start making me lunch.

"You don't have to run off so soon," she said.

"I'll be back tomorrow maybe. I've got to go to Aoyama today."

"You mean . . . *that* place? Are you all right?"

"Still taking tons of medicine, of course. The sleeping pills alone are bad enough: Veronal, Neuronal, Trional, Numal . . ."[19]

Thirty minutes later I walked into a building and took the elevator to the third floor. I tried pushing open the glass door of a restaurant, but it wouldn't budge. A lacquered plaque hung there: "Closed Today." With mounting annoyance, I looked at a pile of fruit—apples, bananas—on a table on the other side of the door, then decided to go out to the street again. On my way out, I brushed shoulders with one of two businessmen

engaged in a lively conversation as they entered the building.
". . . really tantalizing . . ." one of them happened to be saying
at the moment of contact.

I stood outside waiting for a taxi, but not many came that
way. The only cabs that did come by were, without exception,
yellow. (For some reason, the yellow taxis I took were always
having accidents.) Before too long, I found a lucky green one
and decided to take it to the mental hospital near the cemetery
in Aoyama.

"Really tantalizing . . . Tantalus . . . Inferno . . ."

I myself had been Tantalus when looking through the glass
door at the fruit. I stared at the driver's back, cursing the two
occasions when Dante's Inferno had appeared before my eyes.
I began to feel that anything and everything was a lie. Politics,
business, art, science: all seemed just a mottled layer of enamel
covering over this life in all its horror. I felt more and more as if I
were suffocating. I opened the taxi window as wide as possible,
but the constriction around my heart would not give way.

At last the green cab reached the main intersection at Jingū-
mae. We should have been able to turn down a side street
leading to the mental hospital, but today, for some reason, I
couldn't find it. I had the taxi go back and forth along the
streetcar line, but finally gave up and got out.

I did finally manage to find the right street, but after dodging
its muddy patches for a while, I lost my way and ended up at
the Aoyama Funeral Hall. I had never even passed the front
gate of this building in the ten long years since the memorial
service there for Natsume Sōseki Sensei. I had not been happy
back then, either, but at least I had been at peace. Peering in at
the graveled courtyard and recalling the delicate *bashō* plants
at the Sōseki Retreat,[20] I could not help feeling that a stage of
my life had come to an end. But I also felt the presence of the
force that had drawn me to this burial place ten years later.

After emerging from the mental hospital gate, I took a cab
back to the hotel. When I stepped out at the entrance, however,
a man in a raincoat was arguing with a bellboy. With a bellboy?
No, this was no bellboy but a cab dispatcher in a green uniform.
Going into the hotel now came to seem like an ominous pros-

pect. I turned on my heel and went back down the street I had just come up.

The sun was beginning to set as I reached the Ginza. The shops lining both sides of the street and the dizzying flow of people only made me more depressed. I was especially bothered by the way people were casually strolling along as if they had never known the existence of sin. I walked on northward, through a mix of the day's fading brightness and the light of electric lamps. What soon caught my eye was a bookstore piled high with magazines and such. I walked in and let my eyes wander upward over several shelves of books. I picked out a volume of Greek myths to browse through. The yellow-covered book was apparently meant for children. The line I chanced to read, however, practically knocked me over:

"Even the greatest of gods, Zeus himself, was no match for those gods of vengeance, the Furies."

I left the bookstore and plunged into the crowd. As I walked along I felt the relentless gaze of the Furies on my rounded back (when had that started to happen?).

3. Night

I found a copy of Strindberg's *Legends*[21] on the second floor of Maruzen Books, and skimmed through it a few pages at a time. It described an experience that was not much different from my own. Not only that: it had a yellow cover. I put *Legends* back on the shelf and pulled down another thick volume almost at random, but it too had something for me: one of its illustrations showed rows of gears with human eyes and noses. (The book was a German editor's compilation of pictures by mental patients.) In the midst of my depression I felt a spirit of defiance rising and I started opening book after book with the desperation of a compulsive gambler. Every single one of them, however, concealed some kind of needle to stab me, whether in the text or an illustration. Every single one? I picked up *Madame Bovary*, which I had read any number of times, only to sense that I myself was the bourgeois Monsieur Bovary.

Evening was drawing near, and I seemed to be the only

customer in Maruzen's second-floor Western book department. I wandered among the bookcases under the electric lights, coming to a halt before a case labeled "Religion." There I looked through a volume with a green cover. The Table of Contents listed one chapter as "The Four Fearsome Enemies— Doubt, Fear, Arrogance, Sensual Desire." When I saw this, I felt still more defiant: these so-called "enemies" were, at least to my mind, simply different names for sensitivity and intellect. I found it increasingly intolerable, however, that the traditional spirit should make me as unhappy as the modern spirit was now doing. The book in my hand brought to mind a pen name I had used long before: Juryō Yoshi—The Young Man of Shou Ling. This was from the Chinese story by Han Fei of the youth who left rural Shou Ling to study the elegant walking style of people in the city of Handan but who ended up crawling home because he had forgotten how to walk in the Shou Ling manner before mastering the Handan style.[22] Anyone who saw me now would find me a perfect "Young Man of Shou Ling." To think that I had used this pen name long before I ever fell into my present hell! I turned my back on this big bookcase and, in an attempt to sweep away my daydreams, I strode into the poster display room directly opposite. This was no better, however. The first thing I saw in there was a poster of a St. George figure running his sword through a winged dragon—the caption written with the same "dragon" character I use in my name. To make matters worse, the grimacing face half-revealed beneath the knight's helmet looked like an enemy of mine. This reminded me in turn of another Chinese story by Han Fei on the art of slaughtering dragons.[23] Rather than going on through the exhibition room, I went out down the broad stairway.

Night had fallen in Nihonbashi, and as I walked down the dark street I thought about the expression "slaughtering dragons." This was the inscription on an inkstone[24] I owned. The stone was given to me by a young businessman who had since failed at his every venture until going bankrupt at the end of last year. I looked up at the sky and began to think how small the earth is—and, consequently, how small I am—among the light of numberless stars. But the sky, which had been so clear all day, had clouded over at some point. All of a sudden, I felt something was determined to get me, and I decided to seek refuge in the café across the streetcar tracks.

"Refuge" was exactly what this place was. The café's rose-colored walls gave me a feeling close to peace, and sitting at the innermost table I finally succeeded in attaining a sense of ease. Fortunately there were few other customers. I sipped a cup of cocoa and, as usual, lit a cigarette. The smoke rose in faint blue streams against the pink walls. The gentle harmony of the colors was another source of pleasure for me. Soon, however, I noticed a portrait of Napoleon on the wall to my left, and I began to feel uneasy again. While still a student, Napoleon had written on the last page of his geography book: "St. Helena. Small island." This may have been what we call a coincidence, but the thought must certainly have aroused terror in him in his last days.

Staring at Napoleon, I thought about my own works. The first thing that came to mind was an aphorism in my *Words of a Dwarf*: "Life is more hellish than hell itself."[25] Next I thought about the fate of the painter Yoshihide, the hero of my story "Hell Screen." Then— But to escape these memories, I began to survey the interior of the café. Not five minutes had gone by since I sought refuge here, but in that short time the café had undergone a dramatic change in appearance. What made me most uncomfortable was the total *lack* of harmony between the fake mahogany furniture and the pink walls. Afraid that I would once again sink into an agony invisible to others, I threw a silver coin on the table and started out of the café.

"That will be twenty sen, Sir."

The coin I had tossed out was copper, not silver.

Feeling humiliated, I walked alone along the sidewalk, when thoughts sprang to mind of my home in a pinewood far away. This was not the home of my adoptive parents in a Tokyo suburb but the country house I was renting for my family, where I was the central figure. I had been living in a house like that a good ten years earlier as well. But then I had been rash enough to return to living with my parents, which instantly changed me into a slave, a tyrant, a powerless egotist. . . .

It was ten o'clock by the time I got back to the hotel. After all the walking I had done, I no longer had the strength to make it to my room and instead sat down before the lobby fireplace, where thick logs were burning. I started to think about a long piece I was planning. It would string together in chronological order some thirty short stories with commoner heroes of every period from Suiko to Meiji. Watching the fire's sparks leap up, I thought suddenly of a bronze figure outside the imperial palace. It wore a samurai's armor and helmet and sat high astride a horse, the very embodiment of loyalty.[26] Yet the man's enemies were—

"Lies! All lies!"

Again I slipped from the distant past to the immediate present. Just then, fortunately, there happened along an older school friend, now a sculptor. He was wearing his usual velvet jacket and a stiff, short goatee that curved to a point. I stood and grasped his outstretched hand. (This Western-style hand-shaking was his custom, not mine. He had lived much of his life in places like Paris and Berlin.) His skin had a strangely reptilian clamminess to it.

"Are you staying here?" he asked.

"Well, yes . . ."

"To work?"

"I *have* been getting some work done."

He looked me right in the eye. There was something nearly detective-like in his expression. I took the offensive: "How about coming to my room for a chat?" (This kind of switch from my usual weakness to a sudden aggressiveness was one of my worst traits.)

He smiled and asked, "Where's your room?"

Walking shoulder-to-shoulder like close friends, we made our way among the quietly conversing foreigners to my room. There he sat with his back to the mirror and started talking about all sorts of things—which is to say, mostly women. True, I was in hell for my sins, but that very fact made such talk about human vices all the more depressing to me. Suddenly I was the puritan heaping abuse on these women.

"Just look at those lips of S-ko's," I said. "They've been kissed by so many men that—"

I clamped my mouth shut and studied the reflection of his back in the mirror. He had some kind of yellow medicinal patch pasted under one ear.

"Kissed by so many men . . . ?"

"I'd say so."

He smiled and nodded. I felt as if he were keeping a vigilant eye on me in order to learn my secrets. Still, our conversation remained focused on women. Instead of hating him for this, I could not help but feel ashamed and increasingly depressed because of my own weak-willed nature.

Once he was gone, I sprawled on the bed reading *A Dark Night's Passing.*[27] Everything about the protagonist's spiritual struggle was painfully familiar to me. Compared with him, I felt like such an idiot that it brought tears to my eyes—which, in turn, lent me a degree of peace. That did not last long. Again my right eye began to see translucent gears, and again, as the gears went on spinning, they gradually increased in number. Dreading the onset of a headache, I laid the book by my pillow and took eight-tenths of a gram of Veronal, determined to knock myself out.

In my dream, however, I was looking at a swimming pool. There, a number of boys and girls were swimming and dipping below the surface. I turned my back on the pool and started walking toward the pinewood across the way. Just then someone called me from behind: "Papa!" I looked around to see my wife standing by the pool, and in that moment I felt an intense regret.

"Papa, what about your towel?"

"I don't need a towel. Take care of the kids."

I started walking again, but the place had changed into a railway platform. The station must have been somewhere in the country: the platform had a long hedge. A college student named H and an old woman were standing there. As soon as they spotted me, they started walking in my direction, both talking to me at the same time.

"It was a huge fire!"

"I just barely got out."

I seemed to recognize the old woman, and I felt pleasantly excited to be talking with her. At that point a train glided up to the platform, raising clouds of smoke. I got on alone and walked down the aisle between rows of sleeper berths, over each of which hung a white curtain. In one berth lay a nearly-mummified naked woman facing toward me. It was my Fury again, my goddess of vengeance—the crazy girl.[28]

I woke and jumped out of bed. Electric lights made the room as bright as ever, but somewhere I could hear the sound of wings and the scratching of rats. I opened my door and hurried down the corridor to the fireplace. I sat down in front of it and watched the fading flames. A bellboy dressed in white approached with fresh firewood.

"What time is it?" I asked.

"I believe it's 3:30, Sir."

Over in a corner of the lobby sat a woman—probably an American—reading a book. Even at this distance, I could see that her dress was green. Feeling a kind of salvation, I determined that I would sit and wait for the night to end, just as a sick old man waits quietly for death after long years of intense suffering.

4. More?

I finally finished writing the story in this hotel room and planned to send it to a certain magazine. Of course I would not be paid enough for it to cover the bill for a week's stay here, but I felt the satisfaction of having brought a piece of work to completion, and now I would go out to a Ginza bookstore to find a tonic for my weary soul.

Paper scraps lay scattered on the asphalt in the winter sun. Perhaps because of the angle of the light, each scrap looked exactly like a rose petal. I felt that some kind of good will was being directed toward me as I entered the bookstore. The place was neater and cleaner than usual, though I was somewhat bothered by the way a young girl in glasses was talking with one of the employees. Bringing to mind the paper rose petals on the street, however, I decided to buy *Conversations with Anatole France* and *The Collected Letters of Prosper Mérimée.*[29]

With the two books under my arm, I entered a café and decided to wait for my coffee at the innermost table. Sitting opposite me were a couple who appeared to be mother and son. Though younger than I, the son looked almost exactly like me. The two were chatting like lovers, their faces pressed close together. Watching them, I realized that the son, at least, was conscious how much erotic pleasure he was giving his mother. This was a classic case of a kind of attractive force that I knew well. It was a classic case, too, of a kind of will that turns this world of ours into a hell. And yet—

The arrival of my coffee saved me from descending again into the anguish I feared, and started me reading Mérimée. The writer filled his letters with the same kind of pithy aphorisms that lent spark to his novels. Soon these aphorisms helped to steel my nerves. (Being easily influenced by such things was another of my weaknesses.) Draining my cup, I left the café feeling I could handle anything that might come my way.

I walked along looking into display windows. One framer's shop had a portrait of Beethoven hanging there, a typical image of the genius with hair sticking out in all directions. I couldn't help but feel amused by it.

Shortly afterward I bumped into a higher-school friend of mine, now a professor of applied chemistry. He was hugging a big briefcase and one eye was bloody-red.

"What happened to you?"

"This? Oh, it's just pinkeye."

It suddenly occurred to me that this kind of pinkeye had been happening to me over the past fifteen years or so whenever I felt that attractive force, but I said nothing about it to him. He clapped me on the shoulder and started talking about our mutual friends. The conversation was still going when he led me into a café.

"It's been years since I last saw you," he said. "Must've been at the dedication ceremony for the Shu Shunsui stone."[30]

"You're right, the Shu Shun . . ."

I could not seem to pronounce the name "Shu Shunsui" properly. I found this disconcerting: it was Japanese, after all, not some foreign language. My friend, however, seemed unaware of my difficulty and went on talking—about the novelist K, about the bulldog he had bought, about the poison gas lewisite.

"You haven't been writing much lately, have you? I did read 'Death Register,' though. Is it autobiographical?"

"It is," I said.

"That was kind of a sick piece. Feeling better these days?"

"Same as always, taking pills constantly."

"I've been having trouble sleeping lately myself."

"'Myself'? Why 'myself'?"

"Well, *you're* supposed to be the big insomniac, aren't you? Better be careful: insomnia can be dangerous."

Something like a smile formed around his blood-gorged left eye. Before I could answer, I sensed that I would be unable to pronounce the word "insomnia."[31]

"Nothing new for the son of a madwoman," I said instead.

Before ten minutes had gone by, I was out walking down the street again. Now and then the paper scraps on the asphalt could almost be said to look like human faces. I saw a woman with bobbed hair coming in my direction. She looked beautiful at a distance, but close up I could see she had tiny wrinkles and an ugly face. In addition to which, she was obviously pregnant. I found myself averting my gaze and turning into a broad side street. After a few minutes of walking, I felt my hemorrhoids beginning to hurt. A sitz bath was the only way to remedy this kind of pain. *Sitz baths: Beethoven himself used to take them . . .*

All at once the smell of the sulfur used in sitz baths assaulted my nose. There was, of course, no sulfur to be seen on the street. Recalling the paper rose petals again, I struggled to keep my gait steady.

An hour later I was shut up in my room and seated at the desk, starting a new story. My pen sailed over the manuscript paper with a speed that I myself found amazing, but it came to a sudden stop after two or three hours as if pinned down by some invisible being. I gave up trying to write, left the desk and started wandering around the room. These were the times when my megalomania was at its most extreme. In my savage joy, I felt as if I had no parents, no wife, no children, just the life that flowed forth from my pen.

Five minutes later, however, I had to take the phone. Despite my repeated attempts to answer, the phone conveyed nothing more to me than some kind of indistinct foreign word pronounced over and over. I seemed to be hearing "more" or "mole." I finally abandoned the phone and walked around the room again, but the word stuck to me with a strange tenacity.

"Mole . . ." I didn't like the idea of the animal referred to by this English word, but a few seconds later I recast "mole" as the French word "*la mort*." "Death": with that came a new rush of anxiety. Death seemed to be bearing down on me just as it had borne down on my sister's husband. And yet I sensed the presence of something comical within my own anxiety. Before I knew it, I was smiling. Where had this come from? Not even I knew the answer to that. I went to look in the mirror for the first time in quite a while, and stood face-to-face with my own reflection. It, too, was smiling, of course. As I stared at my image, I thought about my second self. Fortunately, I had never seen my second self—what the Germans call a Doppelgänger. The wife of my friend K, however, who had become an American film actor,[32] had spotted my second self in the lobby of the Imperial Theatre. I recalled my confusion when she suddenly said to me, "Sorry I didn't have a chance to speak with you the other night." And then there was the time a certain one-legged translator, now dead, saw my second self in a Ginza tobacco shop. Maybe death was coming for my second self rather than for me. And even if it did come for me—

I turned my back on the mirror and returned to the desk by the window.

The square window, framed in volcanic stone, looked out on the withered lawn and a pond. Gazing at this garden scene, I thought about the notebooks and the unfinished play I had burned in that faraway pinewood.[33] Then I took up my pen and returned to work on the new story.

5. Red Lights

Now the light of the sun became a source of agony for me. A mole indeed, I lowered the blinds and kept electric lights burning as I forged on with my story. Whenever the work tired me, I would open Taine's *History of English Literature* and peruse the lives of the poets. Every one of them was unhappy. Even the giants of the Elizabethan age—Ben Jonson, the greatest scholar of his day, had succumbed to such a case of nervous exhaustion that he saw the armies of Rome and Carthage launching a battle on his big toe.[34] I couldn't suppress my wicked glee at their misfortune.

One night when there was a strong east wind blowing (for me, a lucky sign), I cut through the basement and out to the street, in search of a certain old man.[35] He lived alone in the attic of a Bible publishing house, where he worked as a handyman and devoted himself to prayers and reading. Beneath the crucifix on his wall we warmed our hands over his hibachi and talked of many things. Why had my mother gone mad? Why had my father's business failed? And why had I been punished? Only he knew the answers to these mysteries, and with a strangely solemn smile he kept me company until all hours of the night. Sometimes, too, he would paint short verbal caricatures of human life. I had to respect this attic-dwelling hermit, but as we spoke I discovered that he, too, was moved by the force of attraction.

"That gardener's daughter I mentioned—she's a pretty thing, and such a sweet girl! She's awfully nice to me."

"How old is she?"

"Just turned eighteen this year."

His feeling for the girl may have been fatherly love as far as he was concerned, but I couldn't help noticing the passion in his eyes. And on the yellowing skin of the apple he offered me there appeared the figure of a unicorn. (I often found mythical animals in the grain of wood or the cracks of a coffee cup.) The unicorn was the same thing as the *kirin*, that was certain. I recalled the time a hostile critic called me "the *kirin* child of the 1910s"[36] and felt that even this attic with its crucifix was no safe haven for me.

"How have you been lately?" he asked.

"Same as always, a bundle of nerves."

"Drugs are not going to help you, you know. Wouldn't you like to become a believer?"

"If only I could . . ."

"It's not hard. All you have to do is believe in God, believe in Christ as the son of God, and believe in the miracles that Christ performed."

"I *can* believe in the devil."

"Then why not God? If you believe in the shadow, you have to believe in the light as well, don't you think?"

"There's such a thing as darkness without light, you know."

"Darkness without light?"

I could only fall silent. Like me, he too was walking through darkness, but he believed that if there is darkness there must be light. His logic and mine differed on this one point alone. Yet surely for me it would always be an unbridgeable gulf.

"But there must be light. Miracles prove it. Even now miracles occur every once in a while."

"Yes, the devil's miracles perhaps . . ."

"What is all this talk about the devil?"

I felt tempted to tell him what I had experienced over the past year or so, but I was afraid it might go from him to my wife and children and I would end up like my mother in an insane asylum.

"What have you got over there?" I asked.

This sturdy old man turned to look at his aging bookcase with a playful Pan-like expression.

"The complete works of Dostoevsky. Have you read *Crime and Punishment*?"

I had of course become familiar with four or five Dostoevsky novels some ten years earlier. But I found myself moved by the title *Crime and Punishment* which he had just happened (?) to

mention, and so I asked him to lend it to me as I was leaving
for my hotel. Again the electric-lit streets full of people were a
burden to me, and I would have felt it especially unbearable
had I chanced to meet any acquaintances. I slunk along like a
thief, choosing only the darkest streets.

Soon I began to notice that I had a pain in my stomach. I
knew the only thing to stop it was a glass of whiskey. I found
a bar and started in through the door until I saw what a
cramped, smoke-filled place it was. A small crowd of young
men—probably artists—stood there drinking. They were gathered around a woman, her hair arranged in coils over her ears,[37]
who was playing passionately on the mandolin. This was too
much for me, and I backed out. It was then that I noticed my
shadow rocking from side to side, and I realized that the light
shining on me was a sickening red. I came to a halt on the
street, but my shadow continued its side-to-side movement.
With apprehension, I turned to discover at last the colored glass
lantern hanging from the eaves of the bar, swaying slowly in
powerful gusts of wind.

The next place I tried was a basement restaurant. I walked up
to the bar and ordered a glass of whiskey.

"Whiskey? All we have is Black and White, Sir."

I poured my whiskey into soda water and began sipping it in
silence. Next to me were two men in their late twenties or early
thirties, newspaper reporters, it seemed. They were conversing
in low voices—in French. I kept my back toward them but
could feel them looking me over from head to toe. I actually
felt their gazes on my flesh, like electrical impulses. They knew
my name, that was clear, and they seemed to be talking about
me.

"Bien . . . très mauvais . . . pourquoi?"

"Pourquoi? . . . le diable est mort!"

"Oui, oui . . . d'enfer[38] . . ."

I threw a silver coin on the bar (my last one) and fled from
this underground chamber. Swept by the night wind, the street
helped steady my nerves now that my stomachache had subsided somewhat. Thinking of Raskolnikov, I felt the desire to

confess everything I had done, but that would give rise to a
tragedy for others besides me—besides even my immediate
family. And it was far from certain whether the desire itself was
even genuine. If only my nerves could be as steady as those of
ordinary people! But for that to happen I would have to go
somewhere—to Madrid, to Rio, to Samarkand . . .

Soon I was disturbed by a small white signboard hanging from
the eaves of a shop. It was emblazoned with a trade mark: an
automobile tire with wings. This made me think of an ancient
Greek who relied on man-made wings. He flew high into the
sky until his wings were burned by the sun,[39] and he plunged
into the ocean and drowned. To Madrid, to Rio, to Samarkand:
I had to scoff at my own reverie. But neither could I help
thinking of Orestes pursued by the Furies.

I walked down a dark street along a canal. Soon I was
reminded of my adoptive parents' home in the suburbs. The
two of them were surely waiting there each day for my return.
My children probably were, too. But I dreaded the power that
would naturally bind me if I went home to them. Upon the
choppy waters of the canal a barge was moored at the embankment, a dim glow seeping from within. Even in a place like this,
no doubt, families were living, men and women hating each
other in order to love each other . . . But, calling forth my own
combative spirit once again, and feeling the whiskey, I went
back to my hotel room.

I sat at the desk again, reading more *Mérimée* letters, and
again I found them giving me the strength to go on living. When
I learned, however, that the author had become a Protestant[40]
at the end of his life, I felt as if I were seeing the face behind
the mask for the first time. He, too, was one of us: those who
walk through the darkness. Through the darkness? Now *A
Dark Night's Passing* began to frighten me. To forget my melancholy, I started to read *Conversations with Anatole France*, but
this modern Pan, too, was another man who bore a cross . . .

An hour had gone by when a bellboy poked his head in to
deliver a packet of letters. One was from a Leipzig publisher
asking me to write an essay on the theme of "The Modern

Japanese Woman." Why *me* of all people on a subject like that?
The letter, in English, carried a handwritten P.S.: "We would
be most pleased if your portrait of the Japanese woman were
done like a Japanese ink painting, entirely in black and white."
This reminded me of the Black and White whiskey I had drunk
earlier, and I ripped the letter to shreds. I opened another
envelope at random and ran my eyes over the yellow letter
paper that emerged from it. This one was from a young man I
had never met. The words "your story, 'Hell Screen'" could
hardly fail to disturb me. The third letter I opened was from
my nephew. At last I could turn to family matters with a
momentary sense of relief. But even this letter delivered a blow
at the end:

"I will be sending you a second-edition copy of *Red Lights*."[41]

Red lights! I fled from the room, convinced that I was being
mocked. The corridor was empty. Leaning one hand against
the wall, I made my way to the lobby. There I took a seat and
decided that I would at least give myself the pleasure of a
smoke. The cigarette pack for some inexplicable reason carried
the brand name "Airship." (I had been smoking nothing but
"Star" since settling into this hotel.) Once again man-made
wings presented themselves to my eyes. I called over a bellboy
and ordered two packs of Star. If what he said was true, Star
was the one brand they had sold out of.

"We *do* have Airship, though, Sir."

I shook my head and surveyed the broad lobby. Across from
me four or five foreigners were chatting around a table. One of
them—a woman in a red dress—seemed to be glancing at me
from time to time while speaking to her companions in low
tones.

"Mrs. Townshead . . ." Some invisible something whispered
to me. I had of course never heard of anyone named "Mrs.
Townshead." Even supposing it *was* the name of the woman
over there—

I stood up and, fearing I might suddenly go mad, decided to
return to my room.

Once there, I considered telephoning a mental hospital, but
I knew that, for me, to enter such a place would be tantamount

to dying. After much indecision, I started reading *Crime and Punishment* to dispel my fear. The page to which I opened by chance, however, turned out to be from *The Brothers Karamazov*. Had I picked up the wrong book? I looked at the cover. *Crime and Punishment*—the book was *Crime and Punishment*, that was certain. The bindery had accidentally included pages from the wrong book. That I had, in turn, accidentally opened the book to those misbound pages: I sensed the agency of the finger of destiny and felt compelled to read that passage. Before I had read a single page, however, my entire body began to tremble. It was the scene in which the devil torments Ivan. Ivan, and Strindberg, and Maupassant—and, here in this room: me . . .

Sleep was the only thing that could save me. But all my narcotics were gone. I could hardly stand the thought of being kept awake in torment, but I generated enough desperate courage to have coffee brought to the room and started writing with frantic intensity. Two pages, five pages, seven pages, ten pages: the manuscript went on growing before my eyes. I was filling the world of this story with supernatural beasts, one of which was becoming my own self-portrait.[42] Fatigue, however, began to cloud my brain. I finally left the desk and lay down on the bed. I slept for what must have been forty or fifty minutes. But when I became aware of someone whispering these words in my ear, I came suddenly awake and stood up:

"Le diable est mort."

Beyond the window and its volcanic stone frame, the night was beginning to give way to a chilly-looking morning. I stood against the door and surveyed the empty room. Clouded in patches by the outside air, the glass of the window on the other side of the room seemed to display a tiny landscape: a yellow-tinged pinewood, and beyond it, the sea. I approached the window with some trepidation, only to discover that the elements that made up the landscape were simply the garden's withered grass and pond. The illusion had had its effect on me, though, for it called forth an emotion close to homesickness.

Stuffing my books and the manuscript into the bag on the desk, I made a decision: as soon as it turned nine o'clock, I would call a certain magazine publisher and, one way or another, arrange for some money. Then I would go home.

6. Airplane

I urged the taxi on from a station on the Tōkaidō Line to my home in a coastal resort town. In spite of the cold, for some reason, the driver had nothing but an old raincoat thrown over his shoulders. I found the coincidence unsettling and tried not to look at him, keeping my eyes trained instead out the window. I saw a funeral procession passing beyond some low pines— probably on the old highway. It seemed to include none of the usual white paper lanterns or dragon lamps, but artificial lotuses of gold and silver waved gently before and after the pole-borne coffin . . .

Home at last, I spent the next three days in relative peace, thanks to my wife and child and to the power of narcotics. My second-floor study gave me a glimpse of the sea beyond the pinewoods. I spent only the mornings at my desk, listening to pigeons as I wrote. Aside from the pigeons and crows, we also had sparrows landing now and then on the veranda. This was another source of pleasure for me. Pen in hand, I would think of the phrase from the Chinese classics whenever I heard the birds: "The Sparrow of Joy[43] enters the hall."

One cloudy warmish afternoon I went to a variety store to buy some ink. The only kind on the shelf was sepia, the one color I have always been uncomfortable with. I gave up and left the store for a solitary stroll down the nearly empty street. A foreigner came swaggering in my direction, a man around forty who appeared to be near-sighted. This was the neighborhood Swede who suffered from persecution delusion and whose name was actually Strindberg. I had a physical reaction to him as he passed by.

This street was no more than three blocks long, but in the time it took me to cover that distance, the same dog passed by me four separate times.[44] Half its face was black. As I turned into a side street I recalled the Black and White whiskey, and it occurred to me that "Strindberg" had just been wearing a black and white necktie. I could not believe this had been a coincidence, and if it was *not* a coincidence—

I came to a momentary stop on the street, feeling as if my mind were still walking on alone. Next to the road, behind a wire fence, lay a glass bowl that someone had tossed away. It had a slight rainbow-like shimmer, and around its bottom was embossed a design that seemed to be of wings. Just then several sparrows flew down toward it from the branches of a pine tree. No sooner had they reached the bowl than they soared again upward as if making their escape together . . .

I went to the house of my wife's family and sat in a cane chair on the veranda by the garden. In a wire mesh enclosure in a corner of the garden, several white leghorns were quietly moving around. At my feet lay a black dog. Even as I struggled to solve unanswerable riddles, I went on chatting calmly (outwardly, at least) with my wife's mother and younger brother.

"Quiet here, isn't it?"

"Certainly quieter than Tokyo!"

"You mean, disturbing things happen even in a place like this?"

"We *are* in the real world here, after all."

My mother-in-law said this with a smile, but she was right: even this place of refuge from the heat was part of the real world. I knew all too well what sins and tragedies had occurred here in the space of one short year. The doctor bent on murdering his patients by slow poisoning, the old woman who set fire to the home of her adopted son and his wife, the lawyer who tried to snatch his younger sister's assets: for me, seeing the homes of such people was always like seeing hell in human life itself.

"You have a crazy person living in the neighborhood, don't you?"

"Oh, you mean little H? He's not crazy. He just turned out to be an idiot," she said.

"I'm sure he's got 'schizophrenia.' The sight of him always gives me an eerie feeling. The other day—I don't know—I saw him bowing to the Horsehead Kannon."[45]

"Gives you an eerie feeling? Come on, you've got to be tougher than that."

"He's tougher than I am," my wife's younger brother[46] interjected in his usually hesitant manner, sitting up in his futon in the room opened to the veranda. He wore several days' growth of beard.

"Even tough guys have tender spots," I said.

"Oh dear, that's too bad," my mother-in-law said. I had to smile at this, which brought a smile from my brother-in-law as well. He gazed off at the pinewoods far beyond the fence and spoke in dreamy tones. (Still recovering from an illness, this young man often looked to me like pure spirit free of flesh.)

To me he said, "You can be strangely detached from all things human one minute and the next thing I know you have these incredibly intense human desires, and . . ."

"Well sure, I can be good and the next thing you know I'm bad."

"No, it's not so much good and bad as that you've got these opposites in you that are . . ."

"You mean, like a grownup with a child inside?"

"No, not that, either. I don't know, I can't put it very well, but . . . maybe it's like the two poles of electricity. Sort of like having the two opposites in one."

What startled us both at this point was the violent roar of an airplane. I looked up to see a plane all but touching the pine trees above us as it soared upward. It was an unusual model, its single set of wings painted yellow. The chickens and the family dog, also startled by the sound, scattered in all directions. The dog howled as it crawled under the veranda with its tail between its legs.

"That plane might crash," I said.

"No, it'll be fine. By the way, have you ever heard of airplane disease?"

Instead of speaking, I answered with a shake of my head as I lit a cigarette.

"I've heard that people who fly airplanes are always breathing the air up high, so after a while they can't stand breathing the air down here . . ."

After leaving my mother-in-law's house, I walked through the utterly still pinewoods, feeling ever more depressed. Why had that airplane flown directly over me instead of someone else? Why did the hotel have only Airship cigarettes? Struggling with painful questions like these, I chose a deserted road to walk down.

Beyond the low sand dunes, the sea was a cloudy stretch of gray. A swing set without swings jutted upward on a dune. It looked like a gallows to me. There were even a few crows perched on the topmost pole. They all looked at me but gave no sign of flying off. Far from it: the middle crow lifted its big beak heavenward and cawed exactly four times.

Following a sandy bank with withered grass, I turned down a path where there were many summer homes. Among more tall pines on the right side there should have been the white presence of a two-story wood-frame Western-style house. (A good friend of mine liked to call it "The House Where Spring-time Lives.") Instead there was only a bathtub perched on a concrete slab. *Fire*, I thought at once, and I tried not to look as I walked by. Just then I saw a man on a bicycle coming straight at me. He wore a dark brown cap, and he was hunched over the handlebars, his eyes fixed strangely straight ahead. For a moment I thought I recognized the face of my sister's dead husband, and I turned into a side path before he could reach me. But in the very center of this new path lay the rotting corpse of a mole, belly upward.

Something was out to get me. The thought increased my anxiety with every step I took. Then, one at a time, translucent gears began to block my field of vision. Afraid that my final moments were nearing, I yet managed to walk on with head erect. The number of gears increased, and they began to spin ever faster. At the same time the interwoven branches of the pines on the right began to look as if I were seeing them through finely cut glass. I felt my heartbeat rising and kept trying to make myself stand still at the side of the road, but someone seemed to be pushing me from behind: stopping was out of the question . . .

Thirty minutes later I was on my back on the floor in my upstairs room, eyes shut tight, struggling with the pain of a violent headache. Behind my closed eyelids I began to see a single wing with silver feathers overlapping like fish scales. The image was projected on my retinas with perfect clarity. I opened my eyes, and shut them again once I had confirmed that no such image existed on the ceiling. Again the silver wing shone in the darkness. I remembered that the radiator cap of the taxi I had just taken had had wings on it.

Just then someone clattered up the stairs and clattered right down again. When I realized the "someone" was my wife, the shock of it roused me from the floor and I immediately went down and stuck my head into the gloomy family room at the bottom of the stairs. My wife had flung herself face down on the matted floor, trying to catch her breath, shoulders heaving.

"What's wrong?"

"Nothing, I'm fine," she said. With a great effort she raised her face from the mat and forced herself to smile as she went on to explain, "It wasn't any one thing. I just had this feeling that you were going to die, Papa, and—"

This was the most terrifying experience of my life.

—I don't have the strength to keep writing this. To go on living with this feeling is painful beyond description. Isn't there someone kind enough to strangle me in my sleep?

(1927: Posthumous manuscript)

Notes

ARSJ Sekiguchi Yasuyoshi, *Akutagawa Ryūnosuke to sono jidai* (Tokyo: Chikuma shobō, 1999)

CARZ Yoshida Seiichi et al. (eds.), *Akutagawa Ryūnosuke zenshū*, 8 vols. (Tokyo: Chikuma shobō, 1964–5)

IARZ Kōno Toshirō et al. (eds.), *Akutagawa Ryūnosuke zenshū*, 24 vols. (Tokyo: Iwanami shoten, 1995–8)

NKBT Yoshida Seiichi et al. (eds.), *Akutagawa Ryūnosuke shū*, in *Nihon kindai bungaku taikei*, 60 vols. (Tokyo: Kadokawa shoten, 1968–74), vol. 38 (1970)

RASHŌMON
(Rashōmon)

"Mon" means "gate." The Rashōmon (originally, Rajōmon: outer castle gate) was the great southern main entrance to Kyoto during the golden age of the imperial court, the Heian Period. Massive pillars supported a cavernous chamber topped by a sloping tile roof, with stone steps leading into and out of its towering archway. In its heyday, all its wooden surfaces wore a coat of vermilion lacquer. The broad Suzaku Avenue running north from the Rashōmon led straight to the gate of the Imperial Palace, where lived the tiny, aesthetically refined fraction of the populace depicted in the country's greatest literary monument, Murasaki Shikibu's *The Tale of Genji*.

Based on a twelfth-century tale, Akutagawa's retold story is set at the decaying end of the era, when power had largely shifted from the courtiers to the warlords who would dominate the coming centuries, and much of the city—and the gate itself—lay in ruins. Despite its title, Kurosawa Akira's celebrated film, *Rashōmon* (1950), owes little to this tale—perhaps the scruffy servant, whose cynical view of human nature the film ultimately rejects, and the setting beneath the gate where Kurosawa's characters wait out the rain and tell the famous story reflecting multiple angles on truth (see "In a Bamboo Grove").

1. *To borrow a phrase from a writer of old*: Akutagawa's narrator uses an expression found in the twelfth-century *Konjaku monogatari* (*Tales of Times Now Past*) for the sensation of the hair standing on end. For an English translation, see Translator's Note, note 2.

IN A BAMBOO GROVE
(Yabu no naka)

Kurosawa's *Rashōmon* is based primarily on this story, set in the late Heian Period. Akutagawa's "Rashōmon" contributed little more to the film than the frame (see that story's headnote). While this story is based on a twelfth-century tale (for an English translation, see Translator's Note, note 2), the place names are real, and most relate to the steep hills that line the ancient capital Kyoto's eastern flank. Yamashina, now an eastern ward of the city, was a village lying just beyond the hills. Situated in the foothills on the city side, Toribe Temple was connected with a burial ground toward the south. Lying just to the north in those foothills, Kiyomizu Temple is still a major site of popular worship. Awataguchi was a familiar northeasterly point of entry from the hills. Wakasa Province would have been several days' journey on foot to the northeast of Kyoto. The "Magistrate" (*Kebiishi*, literally "Examiner of Misdeeds," also translated "Police Commissioner") to whom the characters speak was a Kyoto city official who exercised both police and judicial authority. In the original tale, the highwayman has no name; Akutagawa seems to have borrowed "Tajōmaru" from another story about a "famous bandit" in the same collection.

1. *the first watch*: 8:00 p.m.
2. *Binzuru*: The Japanese version of the Sanskrit name Pindola-bharadvaja, who was one of the Buddha's more important disciples and a focus of popular worship.
3. *bodhisattva of a woman*: In Mahayana Buddhism, an enlightened being who compassionately defers entry into Nirvana in order to help others attain enlightenment. By extension, a perfectly beautiful woman.
4. *burial mound*: Prehistoric Japanese aristocrats were often buried

in mounded graves containing jewels, weapons, and other valuables.
5. *Kanzeon*: Also known as Kannon. See also "The Nose," note 1.

THE NOSE
(Hana)

"Naigu," an honorary title for a priest privileged to perform rites within the Imperial Palace, is pronounced "nigh-goo." While his name, Zenchi, derives from an abstract Zen Buddhist concept of enlightenment, he is a practitioner of a simpler, more widely practiced kind of Buddhism, in which the believer is transported to a more concretely-conceived western paradise, or Pure Land, after death. His fictional temple is located in Ike-no-o, a village now part of the city of Uji, south of Kyoto.

1. *Kannon Sutra*: Actually a chapter of the Lotus Sutra (*Myōhō-renge-kyō*; Sanskrit: *Saddharma Pundarika Sutra*; English: *Sutra on the Lotus of the Wonderful Law* or *Scripture of the Lotus Blossom of the Fine Dharma*), which is the premier scripture of Japanese Mahayana Buddhism. Chapter 25 details the miraculous power of the bodhisattva of compassion, Kannon (Sanskrit: Avalokitesvara), to respond to all cries for help from the world's faithful. Akutagawa's choice of scriptures in this story is not entirely consistent with any one Buddhist sect.
2. *Mokuren . . . Shu Han emperor*: Mokuren and Sharihotsu: two of Shakyamuni Buddha's sixteen disciples; Sanskrit: Maudgalyayana and Sariputra. Ryūju and Memyō: Sanskrit: Nagarjuna and Asvaghosa. Liu Bei (162–223) was the first emperor of the Shu Han dynasty (221–64) in southwestern China.
3. *Fugen*: Sanskrit: Samantabhadra. Often depicted riding a white elephant to the Buddha's right, Fugen symbolizes, among other things, the Buddha's concentration of mind. The trunk of the elephant might also have attracted the Naigu's attention.

DRAGON: THE OLD POTTER'S TALE
(Ryū)

Borrowed from China, the dragon, often deified, is one of the oldest East Asian symbols of awesome power and good fortune. Akutagawa's given name, Ryūnosuke, or "dragon-son," was meant to confer on him some of the imaginary creature's auspicious nature. While this story is based on a fictional thirteenth-century tale (for an English translation, see Translator's Note, note 3), it is set in the very real city of Nara, which was Japan's capital from 710 to 784 and is still a major religious center for both Buddhism and Shintō, Japan's indigenous, nature-loving faith. Sarusawa Pond is a good-sized pond (some 340 meters in circumference) situated just across the road from the Great South Gate of the massive Kōfukuji Temple, where the priestly protagonist E'in lives. (The Kasuga Shrine, one of the most important Shintō establishments, is a short walk to the east.) The name E'in is a two-syllable word: "e" as in "yes" followed smoothly (without a glottal stop) by "een" as in "seen." The name of E'in's "brother monk," Emon, has the same short "e" followed by "mon." According to the lunar calendar in use in pre-modern times, the third day of the third month could occur anywhere from the end of March to late April. The "distant" places mentioned in the text would all have been within a fifty-mile radius, the aunt's village of Sakurai about twenty miles.

1.   *Amida*: Adherents of Pure Land Buddhism repeatedly call upon the name of Amida (Sanskrit: Amitabha), the Buddha of Infinite Light, in hopes of being reborn in his paradise.

2.   *great annual Kyoto processions . . . out of season*: As the imperial capital at the time, and having broad avenues, Kyoto had far grander seasonal processions than Nara. The Hollyhock Festival (Aoi Matsuri) was (and is) one of the grandest of all, occurring in the fourth lunar month (now 15 May) with elaborately decorated oxcarts and viewing stands and hundreds of participants marching between the imperial palace and two major Shintō shrines to pray for good crops and relief from storms.

THE SPIDER THREAD
(Kumo no ito)

1.   *Lord Buddha Shakyamuni*: The Japanese often refer to the so-called "historical Buddha," Siddhartha Gautama (*c.* 563–*c.* 483 BC) by his designation as "Sage of the Shakya Clan" ("Shakyamuni"). The image here of "Lord Shakyamuni" (Japanese, "Shaka-sama") as a supernatural being in Paradise derives from the elaborate Buddhist canon that took shape after his death. For sources of this story, see Translator's Note. See also note 2 to "O-Gin."

2.   *the River of Three Crossings and the Mountain of Needles . . .*

peep-box: "Topographical" features of the Japanese Buddhist Hell. The Stygian river, crossed by the soul on the seventh day after death, had routes of graduated difficulty depending on the individual's accumulated sinfulness. The *peep-box* (*nozoki-megane* or *nozoki-karakuri*) enabled the paying customer to view a series of still pictures (often including images of heaven and hell) through openings in the side of a box. The devices had their heyday in the late eighteenth century. See Timon Screech, *The Lens within the Heart: The Western Scientific Gaze and Popular Imagery in Later Edo Japan* (Honolulu: University of Hawaii Press, 2002).

HELL SCREEN
(Jigokuhen)

"Yoshihide" has four evenly-stressed syllables, pronounced: Yo-shee-hee-deh. "Monkeyhide" also has four syllables. For the source of this tale (and an English translation), see Translator's Note (and note 5).

1. *China's First Emperor . . . Sui emperor Yang*: China's self-proclaimed "First Emperor" (259–210 BC; reigned 247–210). His construction of the Great Wall, which began *c.* 228 BC and was completed a few years after his death, cost the lives of many of his subjects. Yang, the second and last emperor of the Sui Dynasty (569–618; reigned 604–618), was another ruler whose ambitious public works cost many lives and much treasure.

2. *Nijō-Ōmiya in the Capital*: Several eleventh- or twelfth-century stories marked this intersection outside the southeastern corner of the Imperial Palace grounds as a place where one might encounter a procession of goblins. See, for example, Helen Craig McCullough, *Ōkagami: The Great Mirror* (Princeton University Press, 1980), p. 136.

3. *the minister had recreated . . . spirit vanish*: For the translation of a Nō play on the legend of Minamoto no Tōru (822–895), his lavish garden, and his ghost, see Kenneth Yasuda, *Masterworks of the Nō Theatre* (Bloomington: Indiana University Press, 1989), pp. 460–84.

4. *human sacrifice . . . a pillar*: This echoes an ancient legend which also inspired a fifteenth-century Nō play, *Nagara*, in which the spirit of the sacrificial victim returns to seek vengeance for his unjust death.

5. *Kawanari or Kanaoka*: Both artists, Kose no Kanaoka (*fl. c.* 895)

and Kudara no Kawanari (782–853) were noted for the uncanny realism of their works, none of which survives. A horse that Kanaoka painted on the Imperial Palace wall was said to escape at night and tear up nearby fields. See Yoshiko K. Dykstra, *The Konjaku Tales*, 3 vols. (Osaka: Intercultural Research Institute, Kansai Gaidai University, 1998–2003), 2:282–4, for a story about Kawanari.

6. *Five Levels of Rebirth . . . Ryūgaiji temple gate*: In Buddhism, the five graduated realms to which the dead proceed depending on their virtue in past lives: heaven, human, animal, hungry ghost, hell. Ryūgaiji is a temple near Nara (see "Dragon: The Potter's Tale").

7. *Monju*: Sanskrit: Manjusri, bodhisattva of wisdom.

8. *a fox spirit*: Japan is particularly rich in folklore about foxes as spiritual creatures with both threatening and nurturing aspects. See Karen A. Smyers, *The Fox and the Jewel: Shared and Private Meanings in Contemporary Japanese Inari Worship* (Honolulu: University of Hawaii Press, 1998).

9. *the Five Virtues*: The five Confucian virtues: benevolence, justice, courtesy, wisdom, and fidelity.

DR. OGATA RYŌSAI: MEMORANDUM
(Ogata Ryōsai oboegaki)

Portuguese Jesuits arrived in Japan in 1549, and edicts forbidding the practice of Christianity were issued as early as 1587. The story is set in 1620 (the year of the Monkey), when the Tokugawa government was still observing adherents for signs of subversive activity, and foreign missionaries were not yet being jailed and executed. After the martyrdom of fifty-one Christians in 1622, the government would move against the foreign religion with increasing severity, all but obliterating it in 1638 with the suppression of the Christian-inspired Shimabara Rebellion (see headnote to "O-Gin"). One favored technique for ascertaining an apostate's sincerity was to have the person tread upon a holy image such as a picture of the virgin or a cross. The place is a remote village in the Province of Iyo at the western end of the island of Shikoku, far from such active Christian (Kirishitan) centers as Shimabara and Nagasaki on the island of Kyushu. Dr. Ogata Ryōsai is a practitioner of traditional Chinese medicine, in which the taking of the pulse was (and is) a major diagnostic tool.

1. *Bateren*: From the Portuguese "Padre."
2. *Deus Come Thus*: *Deusu-Nyorai*, an amalgam of Japanized Latin and an honorific suffix for the Buddha. The combined term was used by Portuguese missionaries to give the foreign word "Deus" a familiar religious cachet. The Buddha is sometimes referred to as one who has "come thus" from the world of truth to save all sentient beings in the world of illusion.
3. *the people of our village*: *Murakata* normally means the three peasant-class officials of a village (headman, assistant headman, and peasants' representative), but here and in the crowd scene below, Akutagawa seems to be using it to refer to villagers in general.
4. *the hour of the hare*: 6:00 a.m.
5. *pillow to the south*: In Buddhism, the dead before cremation are laid out with the head pointing north; the living try to avoid this inauspicious position.
6. *cold damage disorder*: *Shōkan*, the equivalent in Chinese medicine of typhoid fever.
7. *the hour of the dragon*: I.e. close to 9:00 a.m.
8. *the red-hairs*: "Red-hair" (*kōmōjin*) originally meant Dutchman as opposed to a Portuguese, but came to designate all foreigners in Japan during the Edo Period.
9. *iruman . . . kohisan*: Both from the Portuguese: *irmão*, a missionary next in rank to a Bateren, and *confissão*, confession.

O-GIN
(O-Gin)

The historical periods mentioned in the opening line, Genna (1615–24) and Kan'ei (1624–44), came near the beginning of the relatively peaceful Tokugawa Period, during which Christianity was suppressed as a destabilizing force (see headnote to "Dr. Ogata Ryōsai"). The Catholic Church officially recognized 3,125 martyrdoms in Japan between 1597 and 1660 (Edwin O. Reischauer and John K. Fairbank, *East Asia: The Great Tradition* (Boston: Houghton Mifflin, 1958), p. 597), but the smashing of the Shimabara Rebellion of 1637–8 marked the virtual end of the "teachings of the Heavenly Lord" in Japan. The events in "O-Gin" take place shortly before the rebellion and are set some fifteen miles to the west of Shimabara, in Urakami, a district just north of the city of Nagasaki, where the secret practice was especially strong. (In modern times, after Urakami was absorbed by the city and Christianity ceased to be an outlaw religion, an impressive cathedral was built there, only to be destroyed, along with hundreds of Japanese Catholics, by the atomic bomb. The community has survived in the area, however, and the cathedral was rebuilt in 1959.)

Akutagawa takes most of his doctrinal language from *Dochirina-Kirishitan*, a book of Christian dialogues published in Nagasaki in 1600 for the propagation of the faith. Having learned their Catholicism from Portuguese missionaries, the secret Christians of the Tokugawa Period frequently used religious terms that were accurate neither as Portuguese (or Latin or Hebrew) nor as Japanese, and this is reflected in the translation. "Amen," for example, appears as "Ammei," and "Inferno" as "Inherno." The "g" of "O-Gin" is hard, as in "gingham."

1. *San Jo-an Batista . . . Miguel–Yahei*: St. John the Baptist. Believers often took Christian names which they linked with their Japanese personal names.
2. *Jean Crasset . . . Amida*: Jean Crasset (1618–92) wrote the two-volume *Histoire de l'église du Japon* in 1689. Akutagawa paraphrases the opening passage of the Japanese translation of Volume 1, an edition commissioned by the Japanese government in 1878 (an English translation appeared in 1705–7). Shakyamuni lived about a thousand years before Japan received Buddhism from China (see "The Spider Thread," note 1). He never preached outside the Indian subcontinent, and the worship of Amida (Sanskrit: Amitabha), which was such a widespread hindrance to the spread of Christianity in Japan, was a much later elaboration of Buddhist doctrine.

LOYALTY
(Chūgi)

This story is based on an actual event that occurred in 1747 (the fourth year of the Enkyō Period), about a century and a half into the long rule of the Tokugawa family. From the time of family founder Tokugawa Ieyasu (1542–1616), the Tokugawa Shōgun was the *de facto* ruler of Japan. He received his title from the Emperor, who was little more than a ceremonial figurehead. The Tokugawas ruled from their huge castle (called simply "the Castle") in the new capital, Edo (modern Tokyo), while the Emperor remained in Kyoto.

Under the Tokugawa system of "centralized feudalism," a feudal lord's importance was indicated by the amount of rice produced in his domain, as measured in a unit called the *koku* (180.30 liters/4.96

bushels). A "Great Lord" (*daimyō*) had lands that produced at least 10,000 *koku*, while the most important of those had over 1,000,000 and the Tokugawa Shōgun himself had some 7,000,000. The House of Itakura had an income of 30,000 *koku*, but Itakura Shuri (1725–47), the central character of "Loyalty," was head of a minor Itakura branch family earning only 7,000 *koku*. As one of approximately 5,000 "bannermen" (*hatamoto*) of the Tokugawa, Shuri was permitted to come into the presence of the Shōgun on certain formal occasions. Although he is certainly a "lord and master" to those who serve him, his status is much lower than those normally associated with the title "lord."

Readers might at first find daunting the large number of names in "Loyalty," but to follow the action one need keep track of only four characters plus another who enters near the end of the story:

Shuri: The central character, 22-year-old head of his branch of the Itakura family; he is best known for the events recounted in this story.

Rin'emon: The "House Elder" assigned by the Itakura main family to watch over Shuri.

Sado-no-kami: Head of a more important branch of the Itakura family and currently serving as a "Junior Councilor" to the Shōgun.

Usaemon: Shuri's old tutor and second "House Elder" called to replace Rin'emon.

Etchū-no-kami (Munenori, Hosokawa Etchū): A "Great Lord" of the immensely wealthy Hosokawa family.

The names of other characters can be enjoyed—or at least tolerated—as a sort of background music. One of the best stylistic features of fiction about the samurai—in the original—is their wonderfully resonant names. The following information is provided for those who desire to know more about samurai names, but it is not necessary in order to follow the story.

Like Mori Ōgai, that other great modern writer who created stirring fictional narratives about actual Tokugawa Period samurai, Akutagawa lards his prose with more of these evocative names than are necessary to the plot. At one point, for example, he gives the names of the lowly foot patrolmen who rush to the scene of the crime. For a Japanese reader, these names give the text a special sense of being anchored in reality: each such name is a string of Chinese characters that suggest imposing architectural structures—castle gates, guard houses—and the armed men who actually populated them. The formality of the style reflects the formality of this privileged stratum of society when samurai were more bureaucrats than warriors, engaged more in documentation than swordplay.

A warrior usually has three names: a family name, a rank designation of some kind, and finally a personal name, each ringing with pride and tradition—and with the constraints on the individual that such tradition imposes. The full name of Shuri, for example, is Itakura Shuri Katsukane. This tells us that he is of the noble Itakura lineage; that he has been granted a modest title by the imperial court naming him a palace repairs officer (which of course he was not: "Shuri" was strictly ceremonial); and that he has a personal name, Katsukane, which echoes those of the many other Itakura men with *katsu* ("victory") in their names, including the deified clan progenitor, Itakura Shirōzaemon Katsushige (1545–1624).

Another important character, Itakura Sado-no-kami Katsukiyo, has a far more impressive "middle name" than Shuri's. It tells us that the imperial court has made him titular "Governor of Sado" in keeping with an income that is more than four times larger than his cousin Shuri's.

Likewise, Etchū-no-kami is the titular "Governor of Etchū," and his income was nearly twenty times the size of Sado-no-kami's. Etchū-no-kami is sometimes called by that title and sometimes by his personal name, Munenori; at one point he also uses his surname when he identifies himself as Hosokawa Etchū. Use of the rank name, when there is one, tends to be more respectful (one thinks of the lords in Macbeth referring to each other by their domain names), the personal name more intimate. The choice was often a matter of personal preference.

1. *Maejima Rin'emon . . . Itakura Shikibu*: No dates are available for the character identified as Maejima Rin'emon in Akutagawa's immediate source but as Noguchi Bun'emon in earlier source material. See Takahashi Keiichi, "Itakura Shuri no ninjō," in *Kokugo to kokubungaku* 73:5 (May 1996), pp. 73–84. At the age of nine, Itakura Shikibu Katsutsugu (1735–65) became the sixth-generation head of the Itakura family and fourth-generation lord of Fukushima Castle. Decisions in his name as a minor at the time of the story were actually made by a senior retainer.

2. *Ōkubo Hikoza*: (Or Tadataka, or Hikozaemon) (1560–1639) served the first three Tokugawa Shōguns with legendary dedication.

3. *Hotta–Inaba clash*: Even drawing a sword inside the Castle precincts could be punished with death. The killing of Hotta by Inaba in the Castle had occurred in 1684. Still closer to hand and even more sensational had been the events behind the famous tale of *The 47 Loyal Retainers*, which started in 1701 when a slighted lord drew his sword in the Castle and wounded his opponent. He was forced to commit *seppuku* (*hara-kiri*) and his domain was confiscated. See Donald Keene, *Chūshingura* (New York: Columbia University Press, 1971).

4. *Mencius*: The Chinese philosopher Mencius (372–289 BC) was not a believer in unswerving loyalty but taught, rather, that a ruler should be replaced if he failed to heed proper advice.

5. *Military Governor*: The *Shoshidai* kept an eye on the doings of the Imperial Household and the aristocratic families of Kyoto for the Shōgun to help ensure that they would remain politically harmless. He also wielded more general police and judicial powers. Matazaemon (1586–1656) held the post for more than thirty years. Mondo Shigemasa (1588–1638).

6. *the nineteenth year of Keichō*: 1614–15. The Tokugawa forces failed to take the Castle then and concluded a peace treaty, but they attacked again, successfully, the following summer.

7. *siege of Amakusa*: 1637–8. Amakusa was a Christian stronghold crushed as part of the Shimabara Rebellion (see headnote to "O-Gin").

8. *Junior Councilor*: Three to five Junior Councilors (*wakadoshi-yori*) served on a monthly rotating basis below the Senior Councilors (*rōjū*) and overseeing "bannermen" such as Shuri. Itakura Katsukiyo (1706–80).

9. *Usaemon*: No dates are available for this character, who is identified as Katō Usaemon in both Akutagawa's immediate source and earlier source material. See Takahashi, "Itakura Shuri no ninjō."

10. *His Sequestered Lordship of the Western Enclosure*: The grandiloquent title (*Nishimaru no ōgosho-sama*) for the retired (but still powerful) eighth Tokugawa Shōgun, Yoshimune (1684–1751; ruled 1716–45).

11. *the fifth hour of the morning … Munenori*: 8 a.m. One of Akutagawa's sources had the personal name of Shuri's victim wrong: it should be Munetaka (1716–1747), who had a huge domain of 540,000 *koku*.

12. *the General's Star*: In Chinese astrology, a reddish star in the Andromeda galaxy thought to be shaped like a general in battle gear.

13. *Kyōgen*: Short comic plays performed between the more somber works of the Nō theatre.

14. *Tashiro Yūetsu*: A Buddhist attendant dressed like a priest and took a priestly personal name ("Yūetsu") but did not actually take the tonsure and retained his "worldly" surname ("Tashiro"). Many of the great lords kept such low-ranking samurai on stipend as advisors in the tea ceremony and other aesthetic and religious matters. The Akutagawas were of such a lineage.

15. *cutting his hair*: Perhaps as a sign of religious atonement, as in taking the tonsure.

16. *Mizuno Hayato-no-shō*: This incident occurred in 1725. The victim recovered from his severe wounds. The attacker and his family were punished by confiscation of their considerable holdings (70,000 *koku*), but the family was allowed to keep its name. Altogether, there were seven such armed attacks in Edo Castle during the Tokugawas' two and a half centuries of rule.

THE STORY OF A HEAD THAT FELL OFF
(Kubi ga ochita hanashi)

The Sino-Japanese War (1894–5), fought over control of Korea, was Japan's first foreign war in modern times. Japan succeeded in capturing the valuable Liaodong Peninsula from China but was soon forced to give it back by the "Triple Intervention" of Russia, Germany and France, which laid the groundwork for the Russo-Japanese War (1904–5). The central character of this story, He Xiao-er (Kashōji in Japanese), is a Chinese soldier caught in the first struggle for Liaodong. The translation omits most mentions of the surname to avoid confusion with the English pronoun.

1. *Empress Dowager*: Cixi (1835–1908), the powerful "Last Empress" of China.

2. *Strange Tales of Liaozhai*: The collection of supernatural tales is *Liao zhai zhi yi* by Pu Songling (1640–1715), which has been partially rendered into English as *Strange Tales from a Chinese Studio*, tr. John Minford (London: Penguin Books, 2006), and *Strange Tales of Liaozhai*. Story 72, "A Final Joke" (in Minford's edition), tells how a certain man named Jia literally laughed his head off many years after receiving a near-fatal wound. It gave Akutagawa the idea for this story (IARZ 3:394).

GREEN ONIONS
(Negi)

1. *Takehisa Yumeji's illustrations*: Painter, poet, and graphic designer Takehisa Yumeji (1884–1934) was one of the most sought-after illustrators of fictional works of his day, specializing in tall, slim beauties projecting a dreamy, elegiac mood.

2. *Miss Mary Pickford*: "Green Onions" appeared in 1920, four years before Tanizaki Jun'ichirō's novel *Chijin no ai* (translated by Anthony Chambers as *Naomi* (New York: Alfred A. Knopf, 1985)), with its waitress-heroine who resembles the screen star Mary Pickford (1892–1979).

3. *naniwa-bushi, eat mitsu-mame*: The *naniwa-bushi* style of chanting with stringed accompaniment was oral literature for the semi-literate, recounting rousing tales based on old-fashioned plots that pitted duty against personal desire; *mitsu-mame* is an equally plebeian and old-fashioned dessert of sweet beans and agar-agar cubes in thick syrup, rather like Western canned mixed fruit.

4. *The Cuckoo ... in the Valley*: All but the last could be ranked as sentimental or melodramatic works appealing to popular taste, though in O-Kimi's eyes their Western and modern elements would certainly place them above the pre-modern plebeian preferences of O-Matsu: Tokutomi Roka (1868–1927), *Hototogisu* (1900), tr. Sakae Shioya and E. F. Edgett, as *Nami-ko: A Realistic Novel* (Tokyo: Yurakusha, 1905)—see also note 7 and "Daidōji Shinsuke: The Early Years"; Shimazaki Tōson, *Tōson shishū* (1904) and see "The Life of a Stupid Man," Section 46 (and note 27); Akita Ujaku (1883–1962) et al., *Matsui Sumako no isshō* (1919), biography of the life and loves of a notoriously "liberated" actress; Okamoto Kidō (1872–1939), *Shin-Asagao nikki* (1912), a modern version of an 1832 puppet play; Prosper Mérimée, "Carmen" (1845), the story upon which the Bizet opera was based; *Takai yama kara tanizoko mireba* (possibly just an echo of a line from a popular song of 1870) has not been identified (IARZ 5:340).

5. *Kaburagi Kiyokata*: Major figure (1878–1927) in the self-consciously nativist modern Nihonga (literally, "Japan picture") movement, which distinguished itself from Western oil painting by use of watercolors on paper and silk. Kaburagi was noted for his portraits of traditional beauties, of which *Genroku Woman* was representative. The Genroku Period (1688–1704), saw a

flowering of arts produced for an audience of commoners—
woodblock prints, Kabuki drama, the puppet theater, etc.

6. *Kitamura Shikai*: Modern pioneer (1871–1927) in marble sculp-
ture. His *Eve* (1915) is owned by the Tokyo National Museum
of Modern Art. Akutagawa wrote to a friend in 1915 that he
found one of Kitamura's works (not *Eve*) just as "stupid" and
"unbearable" as most of the other sculptures in an art show he
had attended (IARZ 5:340).

7. *tragedy based on The Cuckoo*: A heart-rending melodrama about
a handsome young couple forced apart by the groom Takeo's
mother upon her discovery that the beautiful heroine Namiko
has tuberculosis, *The Cuckoo* was a blockbuster as a book, as a
play in the modernized Kabuki-style theater (i.e. Shinpa, which,
unlike Kabuki, uses actresses in female parts), and as a movie.
Several film versions were made between 1909 and 1958, but
this story is probably referring to the 1918 version—in which a
male actor played the heroine.

8. *two mirrors . . . slipcovers*: A beauty parlor customer would sit
at a typical Japanese low cabinet to which was attached a tall
mirror that was normally kept covered when not in use. Ancient
feelings about mirrors as objects of special power still survive in
Japan, though in greatly diluted form.

9. *6-yen . . . 70 sen it cost for a measure of rice*: A sen is a hundredth
of a yen. Waitresses were paid around 10 yen per month at the
time of the story (a college graduate could expect a starting salary
of 65 yen or more; Akutagawa was paid 100 yen monthly by the
Naval Engineering School in 1917). What with 6 yen of her base
pay being consumed by rent, a 3-measure monthly rice supply
costing her over 2 yen, and a daily dip in the public bath costing
5 sen, O-Kimi would have had to depend on tips to make ends
meet. See Iwasaki Jirō, *Bukka no sesō 100-nen* (Tokyo: Yomiuri
Shinbunsha, 1982), pp. 286–301.

10. *the Hundred Poets card game . . . the martial music of Satsuma*:
Tanaka's talents include the memorization of 100 short poems
needed to excel in a traditional popular New Year's card game
that calls for snatching up the appropriate card as quickly as
possible when the first few lines of a poem are read aloud. He
can also accompany himself on a 4- or 5-string lute known as a
"biwa" while singing stirring tales of war and heroism, an especially manly art that originated in the Satsuma domain in the
sixteenth century.

11. *Douglas Fairbanks . . . Mori Ritsuko*: Douglas Fairbanks (1883–

1939), a Hollywood film star, and Mori Ritsuko (1890–1961), a popular stage actress of the day.

12. *Puvis de Chavannes' St. Geneviève: Watch of St. Geneviève*, the last painting by Puvis de Chavannes (1824–98) is considered one of his most stirring, another of the art works evoking *sentimental-isme* in this story.

13. *"The Wanderer's Lament"*: "Sasurai," a song made popular at the time by its use in a Tokyo performance of Tolstoy's *The Living Corpse* (1911) in Japanese translation.

HORSE LEGS
(Uma no ashi)

1. *the recently overthrown Qing dynasty*: The Republican (First) Revolution began in October 1911 and brought down the Qing dynasty (1644–1912).

2. *Shuntian Times*: The *Shuntian shibao* (in Japanese: *Junten jihō*), founded in 1901 by Japanese entrepreneur Nakajima Masao, was a Chinese-language newspaper for Beijing, the surrounding area of which was known as Shuntian during the Qing era. For some reason, the editor "quoted" below has a Japanese "name," Mudaguchi, which means "idle chatter."

3. *Annals of Horse Governance . . . Quality of Horses*: All are genuine Chinese reference works: *Ma zheng ji, Ma ji, Yuan Heng liao niu ma tuo ji, Bo Le xiang ma jing*.

4. *ancient records*: From the chapter on punishment in *Kongcongzi* (*The Kong Family Masters' Anthology*), a fictitious Confucian text compiled in the third century AD.

5. *loudly beat the drum*: Echoing Chapter 11, Verse 16 of the Confucian *Analects* (*c.* 450 BC).

6. *Okada Saburō*: Novelist (1890–1954), went to France in 1921 and began publishing French *contes* that contrasted sharply with the autobiographical fiction that dominated much of Japanese publishing. In 1920, Akutagawa found some of his work at least "promising" (IARZ 6:61). Major Yuasa has not been identified.

DAIDŌJI SHINSUKE: THE EARLY YEARS
(Daidōji Shinsuke no hansei/—Aru seishinteki fūkeiga—)

1. *Ekōin Temple . . . Honjo Ward*: Founded in 1657, the Ekōin Temple remains an important center of neighborhood life. Akutagawa grew up in this strongly traditional neighborhood of

Honjo Ward on the flat, low-lying east bank of the Sumida River after he was adopted, though he was born in Kyōbashi Ward in another, west bank, part of Tokyo's "low city." See Edward Seidensticker, *Low City, High City* (New York: Alfred A. Knopf, 1983), pp. 4–5, 8–9, 214–20.

2. *Roka's Nature and Man . . . Beauties of Nature*: Tokutomi Roka (1868–1927), *Shizen to jinsei* (1900), tr. Arthur Lloyd et al., as *Nature and Man* (Tokyo, 1913)—see also "Green Onions"; Sir John Lubbock (1834–1913), *The Beauties of Nature and the Wonders of the World We Live In* (1893).

3. *mother's milk*: Akutagawa conflates his birth parents and adoptive parents in this story. See the notes below, plus the other stories in this section, and the Chronology for factual accounts of his life.

4. *vita sexualis*: For an English translation of the controversial novel to which this refers indirectly, see Mori Ōgai, *Vita Sexualis* (1909), tr. by Kazuji Ninomiya and Sanford Goldstein (Tokyo: Tuttle, 1972).

5. *battle of Fushimi-Toba*: Akutagawa's birth father fought with the rebel Satsuma troops against the army of the Tokugawa government on 3 January 1868 in the Kyoto suburbs of Fushimi and Toba, the single greatest clash leading to the downfall of the regime.

6. *dairy farm that the uncle owned*: Actually Akutagawa's birth father, who would have been about fifty-five at the time.

7. *father ... ¥500*: The uncle who adopted Akutagawa retired in 1898 as an assistant department head in the Tokyo government's internal affairs division with an annual stipend of ¥720, rather better than Shinsuke's father (IARZ 24:57). Compared with the average middle-class annual income of ¥600, Shinsuke's father's was on the low side: they were not poor, but not comfortable.

8. *school-sponsor meetings*: *Hoshōnin kaigi*, precursor of modern parent-teacher groups.

9. *Kunikida Doppo*: As a pioneer of the modern Japanese short story, Kunikida Doppo (1871–1908) was Akutagawa's single most important predecessor. The highly wrought diary that covered Doppo's mid-twenties, *Azamukazaru no ki* (*Diary without Deceit*) was one of the most successful and influential pieces of introspective writing of its day. If Akutagawa himself kept a diary like Shinsuke's, it has not survived, but the passages "quoted" here read much like Doppo's; indeed, this story's per-

vasive self-conscious use of parallel prose owes much to him. See also notes 14 and 15.

10. *Way of the Warrior*: Low-ranking samurai like the Buddhist attendants in the story "Loyalty," the Akutagawas had for generations served as tea masters to the Tokugawa Shōgun. On the Way of the Warrior (*bushidō*), see *Hagakure: The Book of the Samurai*, tr. William Scott Wilson (Tokyo: Kodansha International, 1992).

11. *middle school to higher school*: In Akutagawa's day, four years of compulsory elementary school were followed by three of upper-level elementary school, five of middle school, and three of higher school. He attended middle school from age 13 to 18 and higher school from 18 to 21.

12. *suicide*: A hypothetical situation briefly described in *Notes from the House of the Dead* (1860–61), Part I, Chapter 2.

13. *"Dharma"*: Good-luck dolls representing the Zen patriarch Bodhidharma tend to be round and have enormous eyes.

14. *Katai*: Doppo and Tayama Katai (1871–1930) were associated with the "Naturalist School" of fiction that flourished in Japan in the first decade of the twentieth century.

15. *A Hunter's Diary*: Turgenev's *A Sportsman's Notebook* (1847–51) had deeply influenced modern Japanese lyricism since its partial translation into Japanese (as *Ryōjin nikki* (*A Hunter's Diary*)) in 1888. Doppo was among those who wrote affectingly about the work. Akutagawa (or at least Shinsuke) would have read the 1906 Constance Garnett translation, *A Sportsman's Sketches*, in 1909 when he was seventeen.

16. *Outlaws of the Marsh*: Translated into English variously as *Water Margin*, *The Men of the Marshes*, *Outlaws of the Marsh*, *The Marshes of Mt. Liang*, and *All Men are Brothers*, the multi-volume vernacular Chinese adventure novel of the fourteenth century known in China as *Shuihu zhuan* by Shi Nai-an was translated into Japanese in the early nineteenth century and since then has been widely known and loved in Japan as *Suikoden*. Akutagawa read it in the edited translation by the Edo novelist Takizawa Bakin (1767–1848) which was included in a popular uniform library called *Teikoku bunko*. *Battle flag . . . Zhang Qing's inn*: from Chapters 76, 23, and 27 respectively; *done battle with characters*: from Chapters 48 and 4 passim respectively.

17. *Reineke Fuchs*: Goethe's 1792 version of *Reynard the Fox*, first translated into Japanese in 1884.

18. *Murata Seifū to Yamagata Aritomo*: Murata Seifū (1783–1855) was a pioneer advocate of the kind of strong military policy that Yamagata Aritomo (1838–1922) helped realize as one of the central Restoration leaders.

19. *Genroku Period . . . night heron's scream*: The greatest haiku poet, Matsuo Bashō (1644–1694), flourished during the Genroku Period (see "Green Onions," note 5). All four images are from haiku by Bashō and his disciples: "Matsutake, oh!/Shape of the mountain/Near the capital" (*Matsutake ya/Miyako ni chikaki/Yama no nari*) by Hirose Izen (d. 1711); "Here the morning dew!/In turmeric fields/The wind of autumn" (*Asa-tsuyu ya/Ukon-batake no/Aki no kaze*) by Nozawa Bonchō (d. 1714); "How busy they are—/Offshore in chilly rain/Sails running, sails reefed" (*Isogashiya/oki no shigure no/maho-kataho*) by Mukai Kyorai (1651–1704); and "A lightning flash!/Into the darkness goes/A night heron's scream" (*Inazumaya/Yami no kata yuku/Goi no koe*) by Bashō.

20. *used bookstores that lined Jinbōchō Avenue*: On Jinbōchō, see "Green Onions," p. 120.

21. *Ōhashi to the Imperial Library*: The Ōhashi Library was a private institution founded in 1901 by the publisher and politician Ōhashi Shintarō (1863–1944). The Imperial Library was the fourth incarnation of a public library founded in 1872 in Ueno Park by the national government, and, generally known as the Ueno Library, it is now part of the National Diet Library.

22. *Livingstone*: David Livingstone (1813–73), Scottish doctor, missionary, and explorer, and author of *Missionary Travels and Researches in South Africa* (1857).

23. *Herr und Knecht*: Master and servant (German).

24. *Mushanokōji Saneatsu*: (1885–1976), novelist much admired by young readers of Akutagawa's day for his philosophical musings. See also "The Writer's Craft" (and note 3).

25. *To be continued*: Akutagawa appended a note indicating his intention to expand the story to three or four times its present length. He never did write the longer version, but the other stories in this section have been arranged to continue the narrative of a life resembling Akutagawa's.

THE WRITER'S CRAFT
(Bunshō)

1. *Krafft-Ebing* ... *Masoch*: Baron Richard von Krafft-Ebing (1840–1902), German neuropsychologist, author of *Psychopathia Sexualis* (1886). Leopold von Sacher-Masoch (1836–95), Austrian novelist.

2. *in the style of the old Japanese Jesuit translations of Aesop*: Akutagawa's "Kirishitohoro-shōnin den" ("The Life of Saint Christopher") (March 1919), a stylistic tour-de-force which has not been translated into English, employs archaic language modeled on the sixteenth-century Japanese Jesuit translation of *Aesop's Fables*.

3. *Hitomaro* ... *Saneatsu*: Kakinomoto no Hitomaro (late seventh century) and Mushanokōji Saneatsu (1885–1976) mark either end of Japanese literary history as seen at the time of the story. Akutagawa undoubtedly chose Mushanokōji, a master of pseudo-profundities, for his sonorous aristocratic name (see also "Daidōji Shinsuke: The Early Years," note 24).

4. *"Funerals"*: Akutagawa never wrote such a story. Ōmoto-kyō, a religion of spirit possession with Shintō roots, was founded in 1892 and suppressed by the Japanese government in 1921 (and again in the 1935–45 wartime period). His predecessor at the Naval Engineering School inadvertently created the position for Akutagawa in 1916 by resigning to enter the controversial sect.

5. *Shinnai style*: A school of plaintive narrative singing with samisen accompaniment that originated in the eighteenth century.

6. *Dōmyō* ... *Hōrinji Temple*: Dōmyō (?–1020) was said to be such a marvelous chanter of the Lotus Sutra that deities once came from some of the holiest sites in Japan to hear him chanting at the Hōrinji Temple in Kyoto. For a translation of a twelfth-century story about the event, see Dykstra, *The Konjaku Tales*, 1:156–9.

THE BABY'S SICKNESS
(Kodomo no byōki)

1. *Natsume Sensei* ... *Musō*: Natsume Sensei—"Master Natsume" —is the novelist Natsume Sōseki, Akutagawa's late literary "master." See Chronology and "Spinning Gears." In this brief dream sequence, Akutagawa deliberately jumbles references to two nineteenth-century Confucian scholars, brothers Hirose

Kyokusō (1807–1863) and Hirose Ensō (1782–1856), and the fourteenth-century Zen priest Musō Soseki (1275–1351), whose name means "Dream Window." The storyteller Tanabe Nansō (1775–1846) will be added to the mix a few paragraphs later.

2. *Taka*: "Taka" is Akutagawa Takashi, who was seven months old at the time of the story (1923). Since he had already lived in two calendar years, the original text calls him "two years old" following the traditional method of counting ages. His elder brother Hiroshi was three years old.

3. *Dr. S*: Dr. Shimojima Isaoshi, Akutagawa's own physician—and close friend—since the family moved to Tabata. The baby's temperature below (37.6°C) is 99.7°F.

4. *like a schoolgirl again*: Tsukamoto Fumi was a fifteen-year-old schoolgirl when Akutagawa, eight years her senior, first began to consider the possibility of marrying her.

5. *Hōitsu*: Sakurai Hōitsu (1761–1828), a figure associated with late-Edo frivolity.

6. *Sainted Founder . . . Lotus Sutra*: The founder of the Nichiren sect, the central scripture of which is the Lotus Sutra, was Nichiren (1222–82). On the Lotus Sutra, see "The Nose," note 1.

DEATH REGISTER
(Tenkibo)

1. *Shiba Ward*: A west-bank "low city" ward near Akutagawa's birthplace. See also "Daidōji Shinsuke: The Early Years," note 1. His "Ōji Auntie" (p. 181) is from Ōji Ward at the north end of Tokyo. Yanaka (p. 181) is a west-bank low-city neighborhood with many temples and cemeteries.

2. *Story of the Western Wing*: Xixiang ji (Seisōki or Seishōki in Japanese), by Wang Shifu (c. 1250–1300). Akutagawa slightly misquotes the source but with little change in impact. See Wang Shifu, *The Story of the Western Wing*, tr. Stephen H. West and Wilt L. Idema (Berkeley: University of California Press, 1995), p. 242.

3. *Iris Bouquet*: Ayame Kōsui seems to have been the brand name of a perfume.

4. *memorial tablet*: A plain wooden slat, usually 4 or 5 feet long, 4 inches wide and perhaps ⅜" thick, inscribed vertically in black India-ink characters with the posthumous Buddhist name of the deceased (see next note) and erected at the cemetery during the interment ceremony. After the first forty-nine days of mourning,

a smaller tablet, perhaps 8 inches high and 3 inches wide and usually finished in glossy black lacquer with the posthumous name inscribed in gold characters, is installed in the family altar at home, where prayers are offered up to the departed spirit. On the "tiny memorial tablet" (p. 183) for Little Hatsu: as her younger brother, Akutagawa would have seen only the small tablet in the shrine at home.

5. *Kimyōin Myōjō Nisshin Daishi*: The lengthy "preceptive appellation" (*kaimyō*) was an entirely typical agglomeration of Sino-Japanese labels indicating that she was a faithful adult female lay member of the Nichiren sect: Kimyōin (Taking (faithful) refuge in the hall (of Buddha))/Myōjō (Wondrous Vehicle (of the Buddhist Law))/Nisshin (Sun-Advance: a name in the style of sect founder Nichiren (Sun-Lotus))/Daishi (Elder (Lay) Sister). On the Nichiren sect, see "The Baby's Sickness," note 6.

6. *Little Hatsu*: Niihara Hatsu (1885–91).

7. *a Mrs. Summers ... Tsukiji*: Ellen Summers (1843–1907), the wife of English literature instructor James Summers, ran a school in her home *c.* 1884–1908. Among her pupils was the writer Tanizaki Jun'ichirō (see "The Life of a Stupid Man," note 5). Perhaps a fifteen-minute rickshaw trip northeast of Shiba, Tsukiji was a treaty-designated foreign residential area in the early Meiji period, until such segregated housing was abrogated by new treaties signed in 1899.

8. *boke*: The name of the tree, known as a Japanese quince (*Pyrus japonica*) in English, is a homonym for "dimwit." Before the aunt can joke with her that both she and the tree are "*boke*," Hatsu cleverly makes up her own remarkably similar word play using "*baka*" (dummy).

9. *Shinjuku*: Then a western suburb, but now one of the most intensively developed commercial, municipal government, and entertainment districts in Tokyo, Shinjuku could not have supported a pasture much after the death of Akutagawa's father (in 1919), and certainly not after the earthquake of 1923 triggered its transformation.

10. *Uoei restaurant in Ōmori*: Local records indicate that the restaurant was in business from approximately 1895 to the mid-Taishō period. Ōmori was a southern ward of Tokyo.

11. *Irish reporter friend*: Thomas Jones (1890?–1923) came to Japan in 1915 as an English teacher and became a correspondent in the Reuters Tokyo office. Called "my brother's best friend" by Jones's sister Mabel, Akutagawa wrote movingly of this some-

what naïve admirer of Japan when both were idealistic 25-year-olds and then again when they were closer to 30 and more jaded. Jones was killed by smallpox after being reassigned to Shanghai in 1919 ("Kare/Dai ni" (1926) and IARZ 14:289).

12. *Jōsō's*: Naitō Jōsō (1662–1704), one of Bashō's "ten wise disciples," wrote this haiku (*Kagerō ya/Tsuka yori soto ni/Sumu bakari*) on the occasion of a visit to Bashō's grave that gave rise to thoughts about his own declining health. Jōsō must have sensed that the entire difference between himself and the dead occupant of the grave was as insubstantial as a shimmering wave of heat.

THE LIFE OF A STUPID MAN
(Aru ahō no isshō)

1. *Kume Masao*: The writer (1891–1952) had been one of Akutagawa's closest friends and literary collaborators since their days together in higher school and university.

2. *I don't want you adding an index identifying them*: Scholars of Japanese literature have, of course, done their best to subvert this dying wish of Akutagawa's, as I shall.

3. *house in the suburbs*: Akutagawa was eighteen years old in 1910 when he, his adoptive parents, and Aunt Fuki moved into a house owned by his biological father near the latter's pastureland.

4. *Mukōjima . . . since the Edo Period*: Before the Meiji Restoration and the renaming of the city of Edo as Tokyo in 1868, Edo had been the capital of the Tokugawa Shōguns. The eastern bank of the Sumida River, known as Mukōjima, was one of Edo's prime spots for viewing cherry blossoms.

5. *elder colleague*: The writer Tanizaki Jun'ichirō (1886–1965), best known in the West for such novels as *The Key* (1956) and *The Makioka Sisters* (1943–8), attended Tokyo Imperial University from 1908 until he was expelled in 1911 following his widely heralded debut on the literary scene. In 1914 Akutagawa and some friends revived the short-lived literary magazine (see Section 8) that Tanizaki had used to attract critical attention to his own work.

6. *a world of which he knew nothing*: Automobiles were still in development and far beyond the reach of ordinary people during Akutagawa's lifetime. Having left home, Tanizaki was a far more free-spirited individual than Akutagawa, especially after the successful launching of his writing career in 1910, some three or

four years before the presumed setting of this episode, and Akutagawa is inordinately impressed at his elder's ability to fritter away
several hours in such a luxurious way.

7. *phlegm*: In May 1915 Akutagawa seems to have been coughing
up phlegm, perhaps mixed with blood, and feared he might have
tuberculosis, but tests proved otherwise.

8. *a piece set against a Heian Period background*: This probably
refers to "Rashōmon" (see its headnote).

9. *The Master*: Natsume Sōseki: see "The Writer's Craft," "The
Baby's Sickness," and "Spinning Gears."

10. *he first met the Master*: Akutagawa was probably first honored
by an invitation to attend a "Thursday Evening" literary gathering in Sōseki's home on 18 November 1915 with his friend and
fellow Sōseki "disciple" Kume (see ARSJ, p. 163).

11. *the Kongō*: The name of an actual cruiser in the Japanese navy.
Akutagawa was treated to a cruise on it in 1917.

12. *The Master's Death*: When Sōseki died on 9 December 1916,
Akutagawa was in Kamakura, and finally got back to Tokyo on
the 11th and manned the reception table at the Aoyama Funeral
Hall service (see IARZ 24:94–5; ARSJ, pp. 224–5).

13. *his aunt, who had ordered him to deliver it*: Akutagawa married
Tsukamoto Fumi on 2 February 1918, and Aunt Fuki lived
with them at first and took the traditional role of overbearing
mother-in-law. She returned to Tokyo in mid-April, which
undoubtedly accounts for the serenity of Section 15.

14. *bashō leaves*: Akutagawa wrote to a friend that their house was
"a little too big for us" but that "the surroundings, with a lotus
pond and bashō plants, are rather elegant" (NKBT 38:248
n. 5). On the poetic *bashō* plant, see "Spinning Gears" (and
note 20).

15. *Butterfly*: Besides his wife, four women of interest appear in this
story: (1) the woman in this section, who is thought to be the
same as the "crazy girl" in Sections 21, 26 and 38, with an
indirect reference via her husband in 28; (2) the unidentified
woman whose face seems to be bathed in moonlight in sections
18, 23, 27, and 30; (3) the "Woman of Hokuriku" in Section
37; and (4) the "Platonic suicide" woman in Sections 47 and 48.

16. *went to work for a newspaper*: Akutagawa offered to join the
Tokyo branch of the *Osaka Mainichi Shinbun* newspaper in
March 1919 and moved to Tokyo the following month; in return
for writing "several" stories a year for the paper, this contract
gave him a regular income of 130 yen per month but no manu-

script fees. He had been an "associate" of the paper since 1918, an arrangement that left him free to publish stories in any magazines he liked but prohibited him from writing for any other newspaper (see NKBT 38:250 nn. 5, 6).

17. *Crazy Girl . . . failed to capture her heart*: In a last letter to his artist friend Oana Ryūichi (see next note), Akutagawa mentioned his affair with the poet Hide Shigeko (1890–1973; early pen name Tomone Shigeko), when he was twenty-nine, as one source of the suffering that was impelling him to suicide: it was not a matter of conscience, he said, but regret at what his involvement with such a headstrong, lustful woman had done to his life. He had spotted her at a literary gathering in June 1919 and pursued her aggressively, only to be repelled by her greater aggressiveness. (At the time, Fumi was pregnant with their first child: see Section 24.) The "crazy girl" (he calls her a "girl" despite her being two years his senior and married, with a five-year-old son) also appears in Sections 26 and 38, and in "Spinning Gears" as "my Fury . . . my goddess of vengeance" (p. 222). Her husband (thought also to be the man in Section 28) was an electrical engineer who had studied modern theatrical lighting abroad before they married in 1912. She would have a second son with him in January 1921 and tell Akutagawa the child was his. See IARZ 23:84–5; Kikuchi Hiroshi et al. (eds.), *Akutagawa Ryūnosuke jiten* (Meiji shoin, 1985), p. 419; ARSJ, pp. 344–50; Sekiguchi Yasuyoshi (ed.), *Akutagawa Ryūnosuke shin-jiten* (Kanrin shobō, 2003), pp. 397, 505–6.

18. *the painter*: Thus, in 1919, began Akutagawa's close friendship with the Western painter Oana Ryūichi (1894–1966), who did the cover art for most of Akutagawa's books after 1921. Akutagawa dedicated "The Baby's Sickness" to him.

19. *The Great Earthquake*: The writer Kawabata Yasunari (1899–1972) has recorded his impressions of his trek with Akutagawa and another friend through the devastation of the Great Kantō Earthquake. The pond was located in the Yoshiwara pleasure district.

20. *"Those whom the gods love die young"*: In Greek mythology, after the brothers Trophonius and Agamedes had built the temple of Apollo at Delphi, they were rewarded by the gods with death as the fulfillment of their greatest wish (Micha F. Lindemans, *Encyclopedia Mythica* (online)).

21. *His sister's husband . . . perjury*: Akutagawa's brother-in-law, lawyer Nishikawa Yutaka (1885–1927), the second husband of

his sister Hisa, had been disbarred and jailed in 1923 for inciting a client to commit perjury. He was under suspicion of arson when he killed himself in January 1927 after his over-insured house burned down (hence the reference to Akutagawa's sister having lost her house to fire). Hisa had two children with each husband and remarried the first husband, a veterinarian, after the second's death. Akutagawa never got along well with her or with his half-brother, Tokuji, "but his position as first son gave him a lifelong responsibility for their welfare" (Howard S. Hibbett, "Akutagawa Ryūnosuke," in Jay Rubin (ed.), *Modern Japanese Writers* (New York: Scribners, 2001), p. 20). All three appear in "Spinning Gears."

22. *a short Russian man*: This is thought to be an image of Lenin.

23. *a story*: This has been thought to refer to "Noroma ningyō" ("Noroma puppets"), an early story (1916) in which a nearly defunct form of traditional Japanese comic puppetry provokes the narrator to thoughts of universality vs. cultural determination in the arts. If there is any hint of self-reproach in the story regarding his inability to be fully liberated, it is very subtle. Other scholars have noted thematic ties with "Loyalty" (see IARZ 16:338, n. 57.2).

24. *"Woman of Hokuriku"*: Akutagawa stated that he had no affairs after the age of thirty and that writing lyric poetry helped him avoid the complications of an affair when he did feel love for a married woman one last time. "Woman of Hokuriku" ("Koshi-bito") was a series of twenty-five poems in the archaic *sedōka* form (5-7-7, 5-7-7 syllables), though the piece he quotes is one of three archaic four-line "Love Letter Poems" (*sōmon*) (7-5, 7-5, 7-5, 7-5) that were also prompted by the near affair. Akutagawa no doubt chose the old forms because the fear of compromised reputations was a theme in Japanese love poetry from the earliest times. Katayama Hiroko (1878–1957), wife of a prominent bureaucrat, wrote poetry and achieved fame as a translator of Irish literature under the name Matsumura Mineko. She was not actually from Hokuriku, but Akutagawa's close call with her occurred in the resort town of Karuizawa (see "Spinning Gears," note 8), near the old route to Hokuriku, in the summer of 1924 (CARZ 6:207, 214; 8:117; NKBT 38:258, nn. 3–7).

25. *Punishment*: Here, "*fukushū*" (normally "vengeance") is thought to mean the punishment that later events can wreak for earlier actions (NKBT 38:258, n. 8).

26. *Divan*: Goethe's *West-östlicher Divan* (*West-Eastern Divan*

(1819)), a volume of poetry inspired in part by his reading of the Persian poet Hafiz in German translation.

27. *Tōson's New Life*: Shimazaki Tōson (1872–1943) has often been criticized for exploiting his family to create his autobiographical novels. In *Shinsei* (*New Life* (1918–19)), he exposed his affair with a niece.

28. *the tree Swift saw*: While barely fifty, Jonathan Swift (1667–1745) is reported to have pointed to a withered tree and predicted, with unsettling accuracy, "I shall be like that tree. I shall die from the top." See Robert Wyse Jackson, *Jonathan Swift: Dean and Pastor* (London: Society for Promoting Christian Knowledge, 1939), p. 94.

29. *fond of her*: Hiramatsu Masuko, a close friend of Fumi, had been ill in her youth, and never married.

30. *a shii tree*: *Shii* can designate either *Castanopsis cuspidata* or *Castanopsis sieboldi*. The "Japanese chinquapin" is related to the Giant Evergreen-chinkapin of the northwestern United States.

31. *"Poetry and Truth"*: *Dichtung und Wahrheit* is the subtitle of Goethe's autobiography *Aus meinem Leben* (1811–33).

32. *One of his friends went mad*: Akutagawa's good friend, the novelist Uno Kōji, was suffering from mental illness and was treated (first with a rest cure at a hot-spring resort, later with actual hospitalization) by Saitō Mokichi, who also treated Akutagawa (see "Spinning Gears," note 19). The rose-eating episode was simply one example of Uno's odd behavior at the time (ARSJ, pp. 605–10).

33. *"God's soldiers are coming to get me"*: Given as, "Listen to something terrible. In three days I am going to be shot by God's soldiers," in "Foreword" by Jean Cocteau, in Raymond Radiguet, *Count d'Orgel's Ball* (1924), tr. Annapaola Cancogni (Hygiene, Colorado: Eridanos Press, 1989), p. xii.

SPINNING GEARS
(Haguruma)

1. *Tōkaidō Line*: The 320-mile-long Tōkaidō (Eastern Sea Road) has been the main route between Kyoto and Tokyo since the seventeenth century, traveled at first on foot and horseback (nowadays on the Shinkansen "Bullet" train). In late April 1926, Akutagawa, suffering from a host of ills including insomnia and nervous exhaustion, left his two older sons at home and took his wife Fumi and infant son Yasushi for the first of several lengthy

stays through the end of that year in Kugenuma, off the Tōkaidō main rail-line, to which he would connect by car for the thirty-mile trip to Tokyo (see ARSJ, p. 350). For further autobiographical details, see the Chronology.

2. *natsume*: This round fruit comes from a jujube or Chinese date tree. The word also echoes the name of Natsume Sōseki, whose presence as Akutagawa's erstwhile literary "Master" (Sensei) can be felt on many levels in this reconsideration of the role of the writer and the man-made wings that bring him too close to the sun. See also note 20.

3. *Oyako-donburi*: Literally, "parent-child bowl," a bowl of rice topped with a moist concoction of chicken cooked in eggs.

4. *elementary-school girls*: Under the revised school system of 1907, six years of compulsory elementary education could be followed by another four years of "higher elementary school." The girls mentioned here would be of middle-school age today.

5. *infection*: Literally he senses she has empyema (*chikunōshō*) in her nose. The term was used loosely, with none of its dire clinical overtones, to describe a nasal voice when there were no obvious cold symptoms.

6. *cooperatives*: Farmers' cooperative societies were an increasingly important feature of the Chinese economy at the time, and the friend's overseas venture may have been doomed by a failure to obtain credit with such organizations.

7. *Mme. Caillaux's shooting*: In 1914, Henriette, the wife of the French Minister of Finance, Joseph Caillaux, killed the newspaper's owner for attacks on her husband's reputation. Joseph resigned to participate in her successful defense.

8. *Karuizawa*: A fashionable summer resort with a large foreign contingent.

9. *modern whatchamacallems*: He is trying to recall "*modan gāru*" (modern girl), Japan's equivalent of "flapper."

10. *kirin . . . hōō*: Japanese pronunciations of the Chinese mythical beasts *qilin* (or *kylin*) and *fenghuang*. The *kirin*, which is said to appear on auspicious occasions such as prior to the birth of a sage, is a composite of several animals but is overall deerlike and does indeed have a single horn like a unicorn's. (The word has been borrowed to mean "giraffe" in modern Japanese.) See also note 36. The equally auspicious *hōō* is often compared with the Western phoenix.

11. *Yao and Shun . . . Han period*: Yao and Shun were model emperors from the misty legendary era of Chinese history. Also

known as the *Chronicles of Lu*, the *Spring and Autumn Annals* is a simple chronology of the Chinese state of Lu, covering the years 722–481 BC. As with the other classics discussed by Confucius in the sixth century BC, its authorship is unknown, but it certainly predated the Han dynasty (206 BC–220 AD).

12. *"Worm" . . . a legendary creature*: Akutagawa is probably relating this to the Old English "wyrm," meaning "serpent," and also to a part of his own name meaning "dragon."

13. *one sandal*: Jason's single sandal marked him as an enemy of the wicked king Pelias and led to his being sent on the quest for the golden fleece.

14. *volcanic stone*: The stone referred to here is tufa, or Neocene quartz, a greenish-gray rock formed of heat-fused volcanic detritus, and this architectural detail leaves little doubt that "Spinning Gears" is set in Frank Lloyd Wright's fashionable, expensive Imperial Hotel, a Tokyo landmark. Wright's liberal use of the soft, easily-carved stone was a mark of his architecture in Japan. He found his supply in the town of Ōya-machi, where it was popularly called Ōya stone, but Akutagawa repeatedly refers to it by the more general term *gyōkaigan* (fused ash stone), perhaps recalling its volcanic (= hellish?) origin. Hiramatsu Masuko's father (see Sections 47 and 48 of "The Life of a Stupid Man" and note 29), a lawyer connected with the hotel, probably was able to make affordable arrangements for the famous author (see ARSJ, pp. 566–79).

15. *arson . . . perjury*: See "The Life of a Stupid Man," Section 31 (and note 21).

16. *Die, damn you*: "*Kutabatte shimae!*" This was the curse hurled at the young Hasegawa Tatsunosuke (1864–1909) when he told his father he wanted to be a novelist, and from which he created his pen name, Futabatei Shimei. Akutagawa is probably echoing Futabatei's well-known misgivings about the writing of fiction as a profession.

17. *"Oh, Lord . . . soon perish"*: This "prayer," which begs the deity of the Bible both for punishment and for a withholding of wrath, bears some resemblance to Psalm 38, in which David begs God to ease off on his anger, which is causing him a laundry list of physical and mental afflictions: "O Lord, rebuke me not in thy wrath: neither chasten me in thy hot displeasure. For thine arrows stick fast in me, and thy hand presseth me sore" (verses 1–2; King James Version).

18. *nerves*: Akutagawa wrote similar aphorisms several times. E.g.

in *Words of a Dwarf* (*Shuju no kotoba*), an aphoristic essay series, which was serialized in 1923: see also note 25 below (see IARZ 16:82).

19. *Aoyama ... Numal*: Akutagawa was obtaining drugs from the head of the Aoyama Hospital, Saitō Mokichi, who was shocked to hear that Akutagawa had killed himself, perhaps with the very drugs that he had given him ("Introduction," Mokichi Saitō, *Red Lights*, tr. and introduction by Seishi Shinoda and Sanford Goldstein (West Lafayette, IN: Purdue Research Foundation, 1989), p. 59). (See also note 41.) Veronal (a white crystalline British product known also as Diethylmalonyl urea, diethylbarbituric acid, and Barbital) was a brand-name barbiturate that Virginia Woolf had used in an early suicide attempt. Akutagawa succeeded in ending his life with it. The other drugs have not been identified.

20. *bashō plants at the Sōseki Retreat*: Sōseki Sanbō ("retreat") was the poetic name for Sōseki's study (and, more generally, his home), especially in connection with the Thursday gatherings. See also "The Life of a Stupid Man," notes 10 and 12. The large but fragile leaves of the *bashō* (banana or plantain) are a traditional symbol of evanescence, as employed in the pen name of Bashō; see also Section 13 of "The Life of a Stupid Man" (and note 14).

21. *Legends*: Akutagawa uses a Japanese translation of the title of August Strindberg's *Legender* (1898). Maruzen is the bookstore mentioned in Section 1 of "The Life of a Stupid Man." It remains the premier retailer of foreign books in Japan.

22. *Chinese story ... Handan style*: Akutagawa mistakenly attributes this anecdote by Zuangzi (or Chuang Tzu, fourth-century BC Daoist philosopher) to Han Fei (280?–233? BC). For an English translation, see Zuangzi, *The Complete Works of Chuang Tzu*, tr. Burton Watson (New York: Columbia University Press, 1968), p. 187.

23. *art of slaughtering dragons*: A metaphor for a useless skill. Again the anecdote comes from Zuangzi. For an English translation, see *The Complete Works of Chuang Tzu*, tr. Watson, p. 355.

24. *inkstone*: A flat, usually rectangular, carved stone slab used for grinding sticks of dried India ink with a few drops of water to make black ink for use in calligraphy, ink painting, etc.

25. *"Life is ... hell itself"*: The quotation appears in the section titled "Hell" ("Jigoku") (IARZ 13:52 and CARZ 5:80).

26. *Suiko ... embodiment of loyalty*: Suiko was an empress who

reigned from 592 to 628. Akutagawa never wrote this piece. The (bronze) statue of Kusunoki Masashige (1294–1336) was of a general known for his absolute loyalty to the emperor. Though considered a rebel by many of his contemporaries, Masashige was honored after 1868 in support of the modern myth of imperial divinity.

27. *A Dark Night's Passing: An'ya kōro* (1921; 1922–37) by Shiga Naoya (1883–1971), tr. by Edwin McClellan (Kodansha International, 1976). The anguished hero was still far from attaining his final calm when Akutagawa read the parts of the novel available in his day.

28. *crazy girl*: See "The Life of a Stupid Man," Sections 21, 26 and 38 (and notes 15 and 17).

29. *Anatole France . . . Prosper Mérimée*: Akutagawa gives the titles in Japanese. He is known to have owned Nicolas Ségur's *Conversations avec Anatole France* (1925) and Paul Gsell's *Propos recueillis d'Anatole France* (1921). Several editions of Mérimée's letters would have been available to Akutagawa: see also note 40.

30. *Shu Shunsui stone*: Zhu Shun-Shui (1600–1682) was a late-Ming Chinese Confucianist whose politics led him to seek asylum in Japan in 1659, where he won official patronage and flourished as the scholar Shu Shunsui. Akutagawa obviously feels this Japanese pronunciation of his name to be a fully naturalized part of the language. A stone memorial was erected on the campus of the First Higher School, Akutagawa's alma mater, on 2 June 1912.

31. *"insomnia"*: More precisely, the narrator feels he will not be able to pronounce the syllable "shō" in the word for insomnia, *"fuminshō."* The fact that he is having trouble with words containing "sh" (or, in the translation, with four-syllable words) seems less significant than that he is obsessively perceiving this as a psychological problem. Hence his subsequent remark.

32. *The wife . . . American film actor*: Kamiyama Sōjin (1884–1954; actual name Mita Tadashi) and his wife, the actress Yamakawa Uraji (1884–1947), were the primary founders in 1912 of the Modern Theater Society (Kindaigeki kyōkai), which performed such major productions as *Hedda Gabler* in 1912, with Uraji in the title role, and Mori Ōgai's translations of *Faust* and *Macbeth* at the Imperial Theatre in 1913. The Society survived until 1919, when the couple left for America. With her superior English, Uraji became Sōjin's agent. He acted in many Western-made films, mainly as an "Oriental villain," and in a number of Japan-

ese films. He played the Mongol Prince opposite Douglas Fair-banks in *The Thief of Bagdad* (1924) and the blind lute-playing priest in Kurosawa's *Seven Samurai* (1954). See Nihon Kindai Bungakkan (ed.), *Nihon kindai bungaku daijiten*, 6 vols. (Tokyo: Kōdansha, 1977–8), 4:53–4.

33.   *the unfinished play . . . burned in that faraway pinewood*: Akuta-gawa wrote only a handful of armchair dramas. In a letter of 24 May 1926, written while he was living among the pines at the Kugenuma shore, Akutagawa mentions an attempt to write a play. Since no such work has survived, it may well have been consigned to flames. (See IARZ 15:311, 20:234.)

34.   *his big toe*: Hippolyte Taine (1828–93) described Ben Jonson as "often morose, and prone to strange splenetic imaginations. He told Drummond that for a whole night he imagined 'that he saw the Carthaginians and Romans fighting on his great toe,'" commenting in a footnote that "There is a similar hallucination to be met with in the life of Lord Castlereagh, who afterwards committed suicide," in *History of English Literature* (1863), Book II, Chapter Third, Section I.

35.   *a certain old man*: Muroga Fumitake (1869–1949) had been employed as a milk deliveryman in the Niiharas' dairy, after which he became a door-to-door peddler, and later worked for the American Bible Society on the Ginza. In a letter of 5 March 1926, Akutagawa thanks him for a Bible and says he has been reading the Sermon on the Mount with a new sense of its meaning (IARZ 20:227).

36.   *kirin child of the 1910s*: A child prodigy, a "whiz kid" of the sort that Akutagawa would have been in the mid-1910s when he made his spectacular debut. The "1910s" given here assumes that the "910s" in the original text is either a misprint or a deliberate abbreviation. See also note 10.

37.   *coils over her ears*: This look was one of the Western hair styles popular in the early 1920s.

38.   *Bien . . . d'enfer*: Good . . . very bad . . . why? / Why? . . . the devil's dead! / Yes, yes . . . from Hell . . .

39.   *burned by the sun*: Akutagawa says Icarus' wings were "burned" rather than melted.

40.   *author had become a Protestant*: A lifelong skeptic to the point of being rabidly anticlerical, Prosper Mérimée (1803–70) was nonetheless upset enough by the lack of ceremony at Stendhal's funeral to declare himself an adherent of "the Augsburg con-fession" and have himself buried in a Protestant cemetery. His

funeral was cut short when an atheist admirer caused an uproar in response to anti-Catholic remarks by the Protestant minister (A. W. Raitt, *Prosper Mérimée* (New York: Scribner's, 1979), pp. 19, 23, 354, 359). Akutagawa may have been familiar with Sainte-Beuve's comment that "Mérimée does not believe that God exists, but he is not altogether sure that the Devil does not" (ibid., p. 24).

41. *Red Lights*: (*Shakkō*) Saitō Mokichi's first poetry collection was published in 1913 (translated into English in 1989). Notable here for themes of madness, death of the mother, and the color red. See also note 19.

42. *my own self-portrait*: Akutagawa finished "Kappa" on 11 February 1927.

43. *Sparrow of Joy*: The magpie, a sign of good luck when it enters the home.

44. *four separate times*: The number four in Japanese can be a homonym for "death."

45. *Horsehead Kannon*: Usually a gentle, androgynous Buddhist god(dess) of mercy, Kannon (or Kanzeon; Sanskrit: Avalokitesvara). In this variation, wearing a crown containing the image of a horse's head (or with a full horse's head), Batō Kannon (Sanskrit: Hayagrīva) is a fierce deity designed to defeat all evil spirits and passions; in early modern times, it was often worshiped as a protector of horses.

46. *my wife's younger brother*: Akutagawa's in-laws had brought their tubercular son to Kugenuma for extended rest therapy; hence the Akutagawas' stay there in an attempt to soothe Akutagawa's own mental and physical ills.